The Empty Hearth

Also by Kitty Neale

A Cuckoo in Candle Lane
Outcast Child

The Empty Hearth

Kitty Neale

ORION

First published in Great Britain in 2006 by Orion,
an imprint of the Orion Publishing Group Ltd.

Copyright © Kitty Neale 2006

The moral right of Kitty Neale to be identified as the
author of this work has been asserted in accordance with
the Copyright, Designs and Patents Act of 1988.

A CIP catalogue record for this book
is available from the British Library.

ISBN 0 75285 740 1 (hardback),
0 75287 315 6 (trade paperback)

Typeset at The Spartan Press Ltd,
Lymington, Hants

Printed in Great Britain by
Clays Ltd, St Ives plc

All the characters in this book are fictitious,
and any resemblance to actual persons living or dead
is purely coincidental.

The Orion Publishing Group Ltd
Orion House
5 Upper Saint Martin's Lane
London, WC2H 9EA

www.orionbooks.co.uk

This book is dedicated to my wonderful grandson, Andrew Blofeld. He has always brought such joy into my life, and I am so proud of the wonderful young man he has become. As he travels life's highways, I pray that his journey will be a safe one – of happiness, discovery and spiritual growth.
This one is for you, my darling, with all my love.

Acknowledgements

Writing has brought special friends, and in my first novel, *A Cuckoo in Candle Lane*, I thanked Jean Vivian for her help and support. My thanks will always remain with her, but I would also like to mention Chris Mulcaster, a lovely lady who patiently reads my first drafts, and one who is a joy to call my friend.

Author's Note

Many places and street names mentioned in the book are real. However, others and some of the topography, along with all of the characters, are just figments of my imagination.

Chapter One

Battersea, South London, 1954

'God, the girl's as plain as a pikestaff! He shouldn't bring her here, she's enough to frighten the horses.'

'Shush, she'll hear you.'

Millie Pratchett *had* heard, and glancing quickly at her brother John, she was relieved that he'd missed the remarks made by the stableman, knowing that if he had, he would have jumped to her defence.

The comment had cut her to the quick, and as she walked along beside her brother Millie wondered yet again why she was so different from the rest of her family. 'John, why am I ugly?'

Her brother's head shot round. 'Ugly!' he exclaimed as his neck seemed to stretch out of his collar. 'You're not ugly,' and looking down he studied her features. 'You've got nice, big brown eyes, and anyway,' he added, with a shrug of his shoulders, 'lots of girls are plain at your age. Wait and see, when you get older you'll change. You've heard that song haven't you, the one about the ugly duckling that turns into a beautiful swan? That'll be you, Millie. One day you'll turn into a beautiful swan too.'

Oh John, she thought, lowering her pain-filled eyes from his. Her brother was trying to be kind, he always tried to be kind, yet his words still had the power to hurt her. Plain, he said – and was that any different from ugly?

Change? No, she wouldn't change; at nearly fifteen her features were set. When looking in her mirror she saw a long, thin face, framed by straight, mousy-coloured hair. Her nose was long and thin too, as was her mouth. John said she had nice eyes, but to her they were like those of a cow, and slightly bulbous. Millie sighed deeply, wishing that she took after their mother. Eileen Pratchett had beautiful blonde hair, deep blue eyes that always looked soft and dreamy, and skin like porcelain.

'Samson's pleased to see us,' John said, hearing the horse snickering a welcome as they approached the stable. He patted his thick neck, saying affectionately, 'Look who's come to see you, lad.'

Millie reached into her coat pocket to find a piece of apple, and holding it out on the palm of her hand she said softly, 'Here, boy.'

Samson tossed his huge head up and down in a nodding motion of excitement, and then lowering his mouth to Millie's hand he snuffled the apple before gently taking it.

'I wish I could come out on the cart with you, John.'

'Don't be daft, it ain't a girl's job.'

Millie hid a smile. It was lucky their mother wasn't around to hear him saying 'ain't'. Though they lived in a working-class area of London, their mother was determined that her children should speak *correctly* as she called it. It had caused them no end of problems growing up in Battersea, and they'd suffered much name-calling. John had fought many fights in their defence, but it had made him tough, and nowadays nobody would dare to deride him.

Her brother now began to croon softly to Samson as he groomed him, instructing her to give the carthorse another piece of apple. 'Hurry up, Millie. It's the only way to keep him still.'

She quickly held out her hand, and as the horse munched on the core he quietened again. Samson was gentle in nature, except when it came to grooming, and they'd soon found that this little treat was the only way to placate him.

When their tasks were completed, John said, 'Come on, I'm flippin' freezing and we'd best be off. Mum won't be happy if we're late for dinner.'

Millie gave Samson another affectionate pat before they left, and approaching the gate she looked the other way as they passed the two men again, relieved when this time they made no derogatory comments.

Once outside the depot she hooked an arm through John's,

slowing his stride. She was determined to bring up the subject again – a subject he always skirted. 'John, you said that one day you'd explain to me why Dad acts the way he does.'

'Oh, not this again. For Christ's sake, Millie, it ain't so bad, and anyway I don't think you're old enough to understand yet.'

'Of course I am. For goodness' sake, I leave school at Easter.'

'I don't know why you have to harp on about it. All right, we have to be careful, 'cos if we're not it's Mum that has to put up with his moods. But Dad's never laid a hand on us and you've seen the way Billy Benson belts his kids. How would you fancy *him* as a father?'

'I wouldn't, he's a brute, but I still don't understand. She's our mother, for God's sake, and why shouldn't she cuddle us?'

'We're too big for all that now, so why don't you just forget it?'

'I can't, John. Have you forgotten what it was like when you were a little boy? Dad would fly into a temper if you so much as sat on Mum's lap.'

'Of course I haven't forgotten, but we've survived, ain't we?'

'Stop saying *ain't* or Mum will have your guts for garters. Anyway, I know we've survived, but I still need to understand why she can't even give us a hug.'

Her brother's breath came out in a long sigh. 'It's a bit hard to explain.'

Millie tugged on John's arm, and as he drew to a halt she said, 'Please try.'

'All right. If it's the only way I'm going to get any peace, I'll do my best.' And scratching his chin as though to gather his thoughts, he then said, 'Dad loves Mum – loves her to the point of obsession. He behaves the way he does because he's jealous when she shows us any affection.'

'Jealous!' she cried in amazement. 'How can he be jealous of his own children?'

'I don't know. His love is warped in some way, but don't ask me to explain why, because I can't.'

'He must be barmy! How can you say he loves her when she's not allowed to touch her own children? God, when I think of the tantrums she's had to put up with.'

'Don't exaggerate. All right, when Dad's in a mood he can be murder, but all we have to do is keep away from Mum when he's around.'

'Oh, and that's supposed to make it all right, is it?' Millie snapped, bristling with indignation. 'I can't believe you're defending him!'

'I'm not defending him.'

'It sounds as if you are to me. As soon as you started working with Dad you changed your tune, and now you two are as thick as thieves!' Anger increased her pace, and as they turned into Harmond Street, John grabbed her arm.

'Calm down, Millie. Dad isn't so bad, and when we're out on the round he's like a different person. In fact, we often have a good laugh.'

'Well, all I can say is you're lucky, because I've never seen that side of him. Laugh! When was the last time he laughed when I'm around?'

'Look, that's enough now. Mum will know something's wrong if you go indoors with that expression on your face.'

Millie glared at her brother, but as they reached number ten she fought to gain her composure. John was right, and the last thing she wanted was to upset her mother. She watched now as her brother put the key in the lock, and bracing herself, followed him indoors.

Eileen Pratchett heard the kitchen door open and despite having her back to them, she knew it was the children. Embarrassed, she tried to pull herself out of her husband's embrace, but Alfie Pratchett held on, staring at Millie and John over his wife's shoulder with a look of triumph in his eyes.

'Come on, Alfie, let me go,' she gently admonished.

'Why do you pull away from me just 'cos the kids 'ave come in?' he snapped, his face suffusing with colour. 'I was only giving you a cuddle, for Gawd's sake. Anybody would think I had you on the floor, the way you're carrying on.'

'Shush, dear,' Eileen said, her own face flushing, and recognising the signs of an imminent tantrum she tried to defuse the situation. 'Of course you can cuddle me. It's just that I need to go to the lavvie,' she whispered.

Alfie released her abruptly, and giving him a quick conciliatory smile she hurried from the room.

On reaching the tiny upstairs bathroom Eileen closed the door, her stomach jumping with nerves. God, if the kids had come in five minutes later they might have seen more than just a cuddle. Held in Alfie's arms she could feel his passion mounting as yet again he wanted to assert his dominance over her. And that's what it was – dominance, not love. How much longer could she go on? How much longer could she live on her nerves like this? They'd been married for over sixteen years and Alfie's passion never waned. If anything it seemed to grow, strangling the life out of her year after year.

It was at times like this when she doubted her faith, doubted her religion, one that forbade both contraceptives and divorce.

She washed her hands and then splashed cold water onto her face. Somehow she had to break the news to her husband, but dreaded his reaction. Alfie would go mad, she knew that, but when all was said and done it wasn't her fault. If he'd just leave her alone this wouldn't have happened. And the children, what would *they* say?

After scrubbing her face roughly with a towel, Eileen took a deep breath. Should she tell them now and get it over with, or wait until she and Alfie were in bed? Staring at herself in the mirror as if expecting the face reflected back to answer her question, she bit hard on her bottom lip. *Later, I'll wait till later*, she finally decided. At least then, if Alfie made a fuss, the children wouldn't have to see it.

Stiffening her shoulders, Eileen made her way back to the kitchen, opening the door tentatively. Alfie was sitting in a fireside chair reading the newspaper, whilst Millicent was perched at the table looking at him warily. The room was strangely silent, the atmosphere heavy, and there was no sign of John. Poor Millie, she was always a bundle of nerves when her father was around, and it was hardly surprising. After all these years Alfie still seethed with resentment, and sometimes there was hate in his eyes when he looked at his daughter. Fortunately he was never violent; in fact, he hardly acknowledged the girl's existence, and though Eileen did her best to compensate, it was impossible when Alfie was around.

Catching her daughter's eye now, she mouthed the question, and with a slight inflection of her head Millie indicated that John was upstairs.

'Dinner's nearly ready so would you lay the table, please.'

'Yes, all right, Mum.'

As Eileen drained the vegetables her thoughts were still distracted and her tummy fluttered as she glanced across at her husband. She hadn't expected to fall pregnant again, not after what she'd gone through the last time, and the doctor had said it would be unlikely. So why now? Why, after all these years?

The hot steam rising from the saucepan scorched her face, forcing her to concentrate on the task in hand, and after placing the plates on the table she crossed to the bottom of the stairs. 'John, come on! Dinner's ready.'

As her son came clattering down she smiled at him fondly. He was the light of her life, and though almost a replica of Alfie in looks, being tall with jet-black hair and green eyes, his nature was the exact opposite. He was a sensitive and caring lad – unlike his father.

'That looks tasty,' he grinned, pulling out a chair and licking his lips at the sight of lamb chops, potatoes and vegetables.

Eileen shook her head frantically. What was John thinking of, daring to sit down before his father! Was he looking for trouble? 'Alfie, dinner's ready,' she said urgently, trying to avert what could be a disaster.

It was one of her husband's rules, one that he expected to be obeyed without question. He would sit down first, followed by both her and the children, and woe betide them if this routine wasn't kept to. It was something his own father had insisted on, and until both his parents had died, Alfie had deferred to them. Eileen grimaced as she thought about old Percy Pratchett, a taciturn man who had ruled his family with a rod of iron. After his death Alfie had taken up not only the old man's coal-round, but his persona too, becoming almost a replica in his demands for obedience.

As her husband took his seat Eileen nodded gently to her children, indicating they could now sit down. With her hands clenched in her lap she gave a silent prayer of thanks for the food, knowing that it was something she couldn't do out loud.

Why had she done it? Eileen agonised, and it was the same question that plagued her, year after year. In the beginning she'd thought herself in love with Alfie and still played the scene over and over in her mind. She remembered saying no, remembered fighting Alfie's hands, but had little strength against him. Alfie had overwhelmed her, held her down, yet even now she wondered if she could have tried harder to resist.

'Would you pass the gravy, Mum.'

'Sorry, John, what did you say?'

'You were miles away. I asked for the gravy.'

Eileen gave him the jug, watching as he poured the rich dark liquid over his lamb chops. He then looked across the table and as their eyes met she felt a surge of love. 'How was work today, Son?'

'Fine, and are you all right?'

'Yes, dear.'

'Ain't you gonna ask how *my* day went?' Alfie asked sarcastically. 'Or are you only interested in yer son?'

'Of course I'm not, and I was just about to ask you the same question.' She saw the sneer on her husband's face, wondering why he felt such rivalry. John was his son too, but Alfie saw him as competition – competition for her attention.

Her mind drifted once again to the past, remembering when she'd fallen pregnant. Her father had nearly had a fit; and she'd been thrown out of the house without ceremony. With no one else to turn to she'd been forced to go to Alfie, and though his parents had also shown disapproval, they'd taken her in.

After her parents' spacious house it had felt strange to be living in a tiny terrace, and she hated the lack of privacy. Mrs Pratchett had a room that she called her best, unusually situated at the back of the house, which she kept in pristine condition. It was hardly ever used, and so the whole family sat in the kitchen, Alfie's parents in the only comfortable chairs set around the fire. She and Alfie had to sit at the kitchen table on hard wooden seats, and every evening Mr Pratchett demanded silence whilst he listened to the wireless. It had seemed a strange and alien household in those days, but in her ignorance she had thought it would be different when she and Alfie had their own home.

'Are there any more spuds? Eileen . . . I'm talking to you!'

With a start she looked at her husband. 'Sorry, what did you say?'

'Christ, woman, I might as well talk to myself. I said I want more potatoes.'

'I'll get you some,' she said, scuttling from her chair, unable to miss the concern on her daughter's face. Oh Millie, I wasn't always like this, she thought, hating this show of meekness, but years of marriage to Alfie had drained all the fight out of her.

There were a few more potatoes in the pan and as Eileen spooned them onto Alfie's plate she remembered her earlier courage. Of course, in the beginning she'd had no idea of what she was letting herself in for, and bravely refused to get married in a register office. Alfie, like his parents, wasn't a Catholic, and no amount of persuasion from the priest all those years ago had convinced him to turn. He had finally agreed to allow their children to be brought up as Catholics, enabling him to marry her in St Margaret's, but it was a promise he failed to keep. Shortly after their marriage he'd forbidden the priest to enter their house, and returning to her chair Eileen remembered her shame and humiliation when Father McEwan had been unceremoniously turned away from their door.

Yet now Eileen wondered why she kept up her faith, a faith that held her tied to this man. So many times she'd asked herself this question, and the answer was always the same. Without her beliefs, life would seem empty, meaningless, and many times when in despair, the Church was her only comfort.

Now she was living in a house identical to the Pratchetts', and lifting her fork she picked at her food, listening to Alfie and John talking, the subject the coal-round as usual.

Why on earth had her son chosen to follow in his father's footsteps, instead of continuing with his education? John was an intelligent boy and could have gone on to college, but instead he'd left school at fifteen, becoming a coalman like his father. She had tried to talk to him about it, tried to persuade him to stay on at school, but he wouldn't hear of it. 'The Pratchetts have always been coalmen!' he'd protested, his voice ringing with pride. A pride she was at a loss to understand.

The evening passed and reluctantly Eileen got ready for bed. It was freezing in their spartan bedroom and she shivered not just from the cold, but with fear. She had to tell Alfie she was pregnant, but cringed at the prospect.

Now, hoping that both Millie and John were asleep, she sucked in a deep breath before speaking. 'I . . . I've got something to tell you, dear. Now promise me you'll stay calm.'

In some ways it was the worst thing she could have said, because he paused in the act of shrugging off his braces, turning to look at her with his brow furrowed. 'Oh yeah? That sounds ominous. Spit it out then.'

'I . . . I haven't had a show for two months.'

'What! No, you can't be, not after all this time!'

'I am, Alfie.'

'Christ, woman, how could you? No, I ain't standing for it.'

'What do you expect me to do?' she pleaded, and showing a bit of spirit added, 'It takes two, you know, so don't lay all the blame on me.'

The look her husband gave her was venomous. 'I've been careful, Eileen. I'm always careful,' and with narrowed eyes he spat, 'Is it mine?'

'Of course it is! How can you say that? I've never been unfaithful and you know it, which is more than I can say about you,' she said on an aside, wondering at her second show of bravery.

'Shut up! I'm sick of you throwing that in my face.'

'But I haven't mentioned it for years!'

'Next you'll be making digs about there always being a constant reminder,' and before Eileen had time to refute that comment, he added, 'Anyway, like I said, I don't want any more kids so you'll 'ave to get rid of it.'

'No, it goes against my beliefs.'

'Your beliefs mean nothing to me – they're a load of old tosh. I'm warning you, woman, don't try to defy me. You'll do as I say and get rid of it.'

'It's impossible, and even if I went against the teachings of the Church, the doctor would never agree to it. That only leaves a back-street abortionist, and surely you don't expect me to go to one of those?'

'I don't see why not. Others 'ave done it, so why not you? But then you've always thought yourself a cut above the rest of us, 'aven't you. Too good for Battersea, too good for this street, and too good to be married to a lowly coalman.'

'You know that isn't true.'

'Yes, it is. Yer father was an accountant, yer mother a school-teacher, and you grew up in that big house in Streatham. Yet who took you in when you got pregnant, eh? Who married you? Me – yes, me! Huh, and yer posh parents didn't leave you a penny when they died, did they? No, the bastards left everything they owned to the Church.'

Eileen closed her eyes in despair. Why did Alfie have to keep harping on about it? Yes, her parents had disowned her, but she had let them down badly. They were strictly religious and she hadn't been surprised at the decision to cut her out of their will. 'Alfie, I'm not going into all that again now, and as for marrying me, it was your baby I was carrying,' she said, this argument a familiar one.

'Huh, so you told me.'

'But you've only got to look at John to see that he's your son. You're like two peas in a pod.'

Alfie sat on the side of the bed, his shoulders stiff. 'All right, all right, so he's mine, but to get back to the subject in hand, I don't want another kid and that's an end to it. You can 'ave a word with Granny Baxter at number seventeen, she'll get rid of it for you.'

'No, I can't! I can't!'

'You'll do as I bloody well say!' he yelled, spittle flying out of his mouth.

'I won't have an abortion!'

'I said you will!'

Determined to protect the tiny life growing within her, Eileen stood her ground, amazed at her own courage. The argument raged, but then suddenly there was a moment of silence, whilst Alfie, his eyes dark with anger, glared at her. Then, like a chameleon, his demeanour suddenly changed. He licked his lips lasciviously, a slow smile spreading across his features.

Oh, God help me, Eileen thought, her legs beginning to tremble, any further protests dying on her lips as her husband stood up and began walking slowly towards her. He wouldn't hit her, she knew that – but there were worse forms of punishment. 'No, Alfie, please don't.'

Chapter Two

John, seeing the mood his father was in, watched him warily. He'd heard shouting coming from his parents' bedroom the night before, but had been unable to hear what the row was about and now, as they left the house to go to the coal depot, he decided that it might be prudent to keep his mouth shut.

As they turned onto Lavender Hill his teeth chattered. It was early on this January morning, the busy main road was quiet, and as they stepped over the tramlines it began to drizzle with rain. He hated rainy days, hated the smell of wet coal and damp sacks. However, the walk was brisk, and by the time they reached the yard he'd warmed up, greeting the other coalmen as they entered the gates.

'See to Samson, and get his nosebag ready for later,' his father ordered brusquely.

'All right, Dad,' John answered quietly, making his way to the stable. As usual the horse whinnied a welcome and he stroked his neck affectionately, smiling as he said, 'Hello, boy.'

In no time John had completed his tasks, glad that the sky had cleared. He gave Samson another pat before heading for the scales, joining the gang of men who were shovelling coal into hundredweight sacks in preparation for their rounds.

All the men had broad shoulders with slightly bowed legs, a legacy of years of lifting, and in a very short space of time all were covered in coal-dust, the whites of their eyes gleaming in the early-morning light. John still looked in amazement at how easily they lifted the sacks, and though their backs bent they made it look easy as they heaved their load, first onto the raised centre, and then onto the shelves on each side of the carts.

'Come on, get a move on!' his father snapped. 'We've got a big round today and I want to get away early.'

Stooping low, John held his breath as a sack was placed on his shoulders. He'd been working with his father for a year now, and though his muscles were developing, each sack felt as though it weighed far more than a hundredweight.

However, with his father's help the job was completed, and now Samson just had to be given some water before being led into the staves. He was a lovely horse, mostly chestnut brown, but with a white blaze on his face, and John hated the load he had to pull when they first left the yard. Both he and his father would walk the first part of the round to lessen the weight, but with a hill to start the round today, Samson had an extra burden.

They were ready now, and as his father said, 'Come on, let's be off,' John led the horse out of the gates.

Wendy Hall stood at the upstairs window of the flat above the ironmonger's, and with a good view along Lavender Hill she watched the coal-wagon as it passed, her eyes fixed on John Pratchett. God, he was gorgeous, but despite trying she'd been unable to catch his attention. Why didn't he notice her? They had gone to the same school, but in those days it wasn't surprising that she hadn't caught his eye. Boys showed little interest in girls and at break times they were segregated into different playgrounds. She had looked through the dividing gate on many occasions, and watched John playing football with a crowd of his friends, all totally engrossed in the game.

Nowadays though, thanks to her petite but shapely looks, she was used to attention from blokes. Only five feet in height with honey-blonde hair – home-permed with a Toni kit – and baby-blue eyes, Wendy knew she was referred to as 'cute'. Yet John Pratchett hadn't given her so much as a glance.

The wagon now went out of sight and with a pout she bent over to fasten the last suspender to her stocking-top. Then, smoothing her straight, calf-length black skirt she looked in the mirror. Her white blouse with its Peter Pan collar just needed re-tucking, and after adding a black-patent belt she was happy with her appearance. With a swift final glance at her stocking seams, she grabbed her three-quarter-length swagger coat from the wardrobe before hurrying downstairs, asking as she entered the kitchen, 'Do I look all right, Mum?'

Bertha Hill's eyes roamed over her daughter. 'Yeah, you look a treat.'

'It'll be my first time on a proper switchboard today.'

'You're a lucky girl. Once you've finished training you'll be able to work anywhere. All the jobs I've seen advertised for telephonists ask for GPO-trained staff.'

'Yes, I know, but I just hope I can keep up this posh accent. I didn't have to worry when I was a packer, but now . . .'

'You passed the interview so you must be doing all right. Mind you, it didn't half take a long time to hear you'd got the job.'

'I know, but they check your background really thoroughly and I had to sign the Official Secrets Act too.'

'Sit down and eat yer breakfast 'cos I don't want you going out on an empty stomach. Here, hold on – check yer background indeed! We may not 'ave much, my girl, but we've nothing to be ashamed of.'

Wendy smiled at the indignant look on her mum's face. The two of them were close, similar in build, and both the same height. Mind you, small as her mother was, she wasn't someone you messed with, and if she lost her temper, God help you.

'I know that, Mum, but the Civil Service do background checks on all their employees.'

Bertha rubbed her knees, a grimace on her face, and seeing this Wendy frowned. She hated the fact that her mother had to get up at five o'clock every morning to do office cleaning. It was the outside steps and staircases that played havoc with her mother's knees, and years of toil were wearing her down, making her look prematurely old.

'You've got a right gob on, Wendy. What's up, love?'

'I was just thinking that you look tired.'

'Stop worrying, I'm fine.'

'If you say so,' Wendy said, used to being fobbed off whenever her mother's health came into question. She glanced at the clock and quickly drained her cup. 'I'd best be off or I'll be late for my first shift. I'll see you at about six this evening.'

'Yeah, all right, and I'll make a nice meat pie for our tea.'

'Great! I'll see ya later,' Wendy called, hurrying down the narrow flight of stairs. Once outside, she walked briskly along Lavender Hill, heading for Clapham Junction railway station. Steam trains hissed and clanked over rails, the huge intersection busy as Wendy joined the throng of people on the platform. She was surrounded by men in smart three-piece suits, some in overcoats and bowler hats, and most clutching briefcases with newspapers tucked under their arms. Others wore trenchcoats and trilby hats – equally smart, but reminding Wendy of the spy stories she loved to read.

The women were dressed smartly too, wearing a variety of hats, and perhaps heading for the many offices in Victoria. Wendy loved to fantasise about the other passengers, making up stories in her head about their lives. Of course they were all rubbish she thought, a small smile on her face, but it helped to pass the journey.

A train hooted as it came in, appearing like a wild beast with huge pistons fighting and heaving to slow down the metal wheels. Smoke billowed from the funnel and, as though proud of its achievement, when the engine drew to a halt it let out what sounded like a huge sigh. Steam belched out, engulfing both the engine and the passengers daft enough to stand at the far end of the platform.

There was a surge in the crowd towards the carriages, and hoping to get a seat Wendy quickly stepped forward. The man in front of her opened the door, politely indicating with a wave of his arm that she should get on first. She smiled prettily at him, raising her foot to step into the carriage, but at that moment her shoe came off, falling between the platform and the train.

She hopped on one foot, staring at the man with horror, her blue eyes wide. 'My shoe! I've lost my shoe!'

'Oh dear, I think you'll have to wait until the train pulls out and then ask one of the guards to retrieve it for you.'

'Yes, yes, of course,' Wendy said, her face red with humiliation as she watched the man climbing aboard the train, followed by other passengers who were smiling with amusement. As the carriage door closed firmly Wendy looked wildly about her. Oh

God, this was awful, she was going to be late! On her first shift she was going to be late, and what sort of impression was that?

Bertha quickly cleared the breakfast things, and then deciding to check on Annie Oliphant she crossed to her neighbour's door. Annie's flat was identical to hers, except that it was above the grocer's, with a shared staircase and landing interconnecting them. They had been neighbours for twenty years and as Annie had aged, Bertha had taken to keeping an eye on her. With hardly two pennies to rub together, she worried that the old lady had enough to eat, and with few visitors, she seemed a lonely soul.

'Annie, it's me,' she called through the letterbox, peering through the small gap to see the woman shuffling towards the door.

'Hello, my dear, come on in. I'd offer you a cup of tea but I've no milk.'

'Put the kettle on and I'll be back in a tick,' Bertha said, dashing back to her own flat and filling a jug. 'Here, that should be enough to get you through today and I'll fetch you a nice bit of meat pie for yer dinner.'

'You're so good to me and I don't know how I'd manage without you.'

'Have you eaten this morning?'

'Yes, I had a slice of toast, but I must admit a nice hot cup of tea would be nice.'

'It's your birthday next week, ain't it?' Bertha asked as she bustled around her neighbour's kitchen, appalled as usual by how bare her cupboards were. She had given Annie some sugar yesterday, but other than a small knob of bread and a couple of tins of soup, there was little else to be seen.

'Yes, and I'll be eighty years old. Not bad, eh?'

'Blimey, and you don't look a day over twenty-one.'

'Get away, twenty-one indeed! Mind you, I don't look too bad for my age.'

'You look smashing,' she said, and meant it. Though Annie was painfully thin, she had a wonderful complexion, only marred by tiny wrinkles. Her white hair, which she refused to have cut, was pulled back into the familiar bun, a style that never changed. She was a reclusive, secretive woman and despite the many years they'd been neighbours, Bertha knew little about her past. Yet she'd become fond of Annie and wondered again why she was so hard up.

'You're quiet this morning,' Annie said, breaking Bertha out of her reveries.

'I was just thinking about your birthday and how, as it's gonna be yer eightieth, I reckon we should make it a bit special. How about I make you a nice cake and you come over to my place for a birthday tea?'

'That sounds lovely, but can't we have it here?'

'Now listen, when was the last time you left your flat? I'm only asking you to cross the landing. It's only a few steps and I'll be with you.'

There was silence for a few moments, until at last with a small smile Annie said, 'All right, I'll come over.'

'Good!' And using this opportunity to probe, Bertha added, 'Is there anyone you'd like to invite?'

'Like who?'

Bertha's lips tightened. For as long as she could remember she had been trying to find out if Annie had any family, but the woman always remained evasive. 'Surely you've got some relatives.'

'None that I'd want at my birthday tea, and talking of tea, how about pouring us both a cup?'

She handed Annie her drink, knowing by the tone of her neighbour's voice that the subject was closed. As she sipped her own tea Bertha wondered who she could invite to make the birthday party a bit more special. There was Mr Goodwood who ran the ironmonger's. He was a widower and might agree to come, but it would be no good asking the grocer and his wife, a stuck-up couple who kept themselves to themselves. Her friends Harriet and Maud would come, and maybe a couple of old biddies from the Labour Club. Mind, with only one man it could be a bit awkward, she now decided, dropping Mr Goodwood from her mental list.

'Penny for your thoughts, Bertha.'

'They ain't worth a farthing, love, but I'd best be off now. I need to get some meat for the pie and then it's a trip to the market for some spuds. Is there anything I can get you while I'm out?'

'A bit of margarine, if it isn't too much trouble.'

'How about some nice butter instead?'

'No, butter is far too expensive,' and on saying this the old lady pulled out a tattered purse from her apron pocket, carefully counting out a few pennies. 'Is that enough for a quarter of salted?'

'Yeah, of course it is,' Bertha said, deciding that she would add any extra if necessary. 'Right, I'll see ya when I get back.'

As Bertha made her way to the shops she looked anxiously into her purse. Supplementing Annie's food was putting a strain on her finances, yet she couldn't let her neighbour go hungry. She closed her eyes momentarily, thinking how awful it must be to end up alone and penniless. 'God, please don't let that happen to me,' she prayed, then berated herself. No, Wendy would always see her all right. Children could be such a comfort, and with a wonderful daughter like hers there was no chance of having a lonely old age. What a shame that Annie had never married.

Wendy had finally managed to retrieve her shoe, profusely thanking the guard who had jumped down onto the track to get it.

When she got off the next train to Victoria she almost ran all the way to Green Street, arriving at the Exchange gasping and out of breath. Her heels echoed on the tiled floor as she approached the Head Supervisor, heart sinking when she saw the tight expression on the woman's face.

'Lateness is something we can't tolerate, Miss Hall. The night-shift telephonists are waiting to be relieved, and if someone arrives late it means a board remains uncovered. Losing your shoe under a train sounds rather far-fetched to me, and this incident of lateness will go on your record.'

'Yes, miss,' Wendy whispered, yet inwardly seething. The woman had virtually accused her of lying, and instead of flaring up as usual, here she was fighting to act as though she wouldn't say boo to a goose. In reality she took after her mother, and if it weren't for the GPO training she'd tell this nasty cow to shove the bloody job up her arse. One year, just one year, the magic number ran through her mind, but could she really stick it out for that long?

'In future, see that you arrive on time. Now I'll hand you over to Miss Leggart who will supervise your training.'

'Right, Miss Hall, follow me please,' Miss Leggart said, her face sour as she led Wendy into a huge room.

Wide-eyed, she saw long banks of switchboards lining three of the walls, and a dissonance of voices immediately assailed her ears. So many women, their backs towards her, busily plugging cords into the mass of lights on their switchboards.

'Sit there, please,' the supervisor ordered.

Wendy stared at the switchboard nervously, aware that the supervisor had taken a seat a little behind her. Miss Leggart then leaned forward to plug her own headset into a jack, indicating that Wendy should do the same.

Right, this is it, she thought, placing the wide band over the top of her head and angling the horn-shaped mouthpiece into what she hoped was the correct position. It had seemed easy when she sat at a mock board during training, but this was the real thing, and told to begin she picked up a cord, plugging it into one of the lights. 'Number, please.'

For the first hour Wendy was so engrossed as she answered call after call that she hardly noticed the supervisor, who was monitoring every word. 'I'm sorry, the number is engaged. Please try later,' she said for the umpteenth time, plugging into yet another light. This call was from a telephone box and her eyes widened as a barrage of filthy words assailed her ears. With her hand held over her mouth in horror, she turned in panic to the supervisor.

'Leave this one to me,' Miss Leggart said.

Wendy then listened in amazement as this prim-looking woman spoke into her mouthpiece. 'Yes, I'm sure you'd like to see my knickers. What's that? Oh, you have a big one! Well now, why don't you put it into the slot, then press Button B and we can all have a look.'

Fighting to control her laughter, Wendy's eyes filled with tears of mirth, and as the supervisor unplugged the call she said, 'Don't upset yourself, my dear. I'm afraid those types of calls are a hazard of the job. Of course, the best advice is to cut the caller off immediately, but sometimes I can't resist a bit of repartee and I did that to show you that these pathetic men are usually harmless.'

It was too much – the supervisor thought she was crying! With a howl of uncontrollable laughter, Wendy ripped off her headset. 'Oh dear, can I go to the toilet?'

'Yes, but please calm yourself. We can't have this sort of disruption as it distracts the other telephonists. Oh, and don't use *that word*. In future, if you need a break from your position, hold up your hand to attract a supervisor's attention and ask for an *Urgent*.'

'A . . . an urgent?' Wendy spluttered. My God, this was ridiculous! One minute she was dealing with a filthy phone call, the next minute the supervisor had become prim again as though 'toilet' was a dirty word.

'Now off you go, but don't dally and come straight back to your board. I think you can manage without me now, but if you have any problems, you only have to raise your arm and one of us will come to your assistance.'

'Yes, miss,' Wendy said, and catching the eye of the girl at the next board she had to lower her head quickly. The young girl was fighting laughter too, and Wendy liked the look of her. Perhaps when she returned they could exchange a few words.

'Hello, my name's Wendy,' she said, slipping back onto her seat.

'Mine's Laura, but don't let the supervisors see you talking to me. You'll have to learn, as we all have, to speak from the side of your mouth.'

'What! Can't we chat between calls?'

'Not on the day-shift as we're far too busy. See that clock up there? Well, woe betide us if the time to answer calls goes above six seconds.'

'But . . .'

'Shush, there's a supervisor coming round. Look, come to the canteen at lunchtime and I'll put you in the picture.' Laura then hastily picked up a cord, and plugging into a light she said briskly, 'Number, please.'

For another hour Wendy worked diligently, with only one

short stop for a tea break. When lunchtime came around her head was aching and she was more than anxious to leave her board, handing over to her replacement with relief.

'Come on,' Laura said, leading her upstairs to the canteen.

Wendy saw a large room that seemed segregated. Men sat at tables along one end, women at the other, and even the supervisors seemed to have their own table.

'Why are we separated from the men?' she asked.

'I don't know, but I think it has something to do with tradition. See that dark-haired chap on the end table?' At Wendy's nod Laura continued, 'He's my fiancé, but I don't sit with him at lunchtimes.'

'That seems daft, if you ask me. When are you getting married?'

'In three months, and I'll be leaving then.'

'Doesn't your fiancé want you to work?'

'Oh, he doesn't mind, but if I leave I receive the dowry.'

'Dowry!'

'Yes, you receive a gift of money called a dowry when you leave to get married. Surely you knew that?'

'To be honest, there was so much stuff to read through that I just skimmed it. I don't intend to stay long enough to qualify for a dowry. I just want the training.'

'You should rethink that. It's a good job and there are opportunities for promotion.'

'No, it isn't for me, and I'm already finding it a bit archaic. I mean, fancy having to ask for an *Urgent* when we want to leave our board?'

'I know, daft isn't it, but there was a time when you had to leave the GPO if you got married. A lot of the supervisors are spinsters who put their careers first and yes, some of them do seem to act like puritan old maids. Yet once you get to know them they aren't like that at all – they're really nice. Now come on, let's get our lunch and I'll introduce you to some of the other girls.'

In Battersea at the same time, John and his father were returning to the yard for a load of the hated, dusty, grade-six coal. It was for

delivery to Penny Street School and twenty sacks would have to be carried into the boiler-room. Running his fingers around his collar, feeling the sting of coal-dust that lodged in every nook and cranny of his clothes, John grimaced at the thought.

They drove through the gates, and after tethering the horse, Alfie Pratchett went across the yard to talk to one of the other men. At the same time the door to the office suddenly flew open and Jack Jenkins's latest secretary marched briskly off. Yet another one doing a runner, John noted as the coal merchant appeared, watching ruefully as the girl left the yard.

The boss then turned his head and seeing John, strode over with an exasperated look on his craggy face. 'I don't know what's the matter with young women nowadays. I only swore once, and that wasn't at her, yet it must have offended her delicate ears.'

John grinned. Despite the man's reputation, he liked him. As long as you did your job and didn't take liberties, Jenkins was fair. Mind you, if he caught anyone on the fiddle they were out, and John prayed that his father was wily enough not to get caught. 'So, you've lost another secretary, and how many does that make this month?' he joked.

'You cheeky young bugger,' the man said, yet with a smile on his face. 'I'll have you know that this one lasted nearly nine weeks, and that's a record for me. Oh well, I suppose I had better get on to the Labour Exchange and ask them to send me a replacement.'

The loading finally completed, John and his father left the depot, and it was almost two o'clock when they entered the schoolyard. The caretaker saw their arrival, and as he walked towards the cart John heard his father hiss, 'Here comes Ferret Face, but I think I've found a way to scupper him at last.'

John groaned inwardly. The fact that his father hadn't been able to pull a fiddle on this particular caretaker was something he seemed determined to overcome. The man watched them like a hawk, and insisted that each empty sack be laid in a pile in the yard so that he could count them before they left.

'Have you brought me grade-six coal?' the caretaker now asked.

'Yeah, it's what you ordered,' Alfie replied.

'Let's 'ave a look at it then. I don't want any more of that rubbish you fobbed me off with last time. Nutty slack is supposed to be all right for boilers, but that last delivery was less than useless.'

John jumped down from the cart and heaved a sack onto the ground, holding it open for the caretaker to inspect.

With a grunt the man nodded his head. 'Yeah, it looks all right.'

When he left to unlock the boiler-room door, John turned to his father. 'How are you gonna pull a fiddle on him?'

With a wink Alfie replied enigmatically, 'Just you watch. I've got him this time.'

They carried in sack after sack, and when emptied, laid them on the ground in the yard. The pile gradually began to grow and by the time John had carried in seven hundredweight, his back felt as though it were breaking. Sweat ran down his face, making rivulets in the coal-dust, and as he reached for another sack his father whispered, 'John, take that one, and make it look heavy.'

He shot him a puzzled glance, but did as he was told, pretending to be bent double as he carried it across to the boiler-room.

Once inside, Alfie Pratchett tipped his own sack onto the heap, the coal-dust rising like a cloud and making them cough. He then turned to grab John's, emptying it swiftly before saying, 'Look, it's only three-quarters full and the rest is two empty sacks. Now I'll go outside and engage the caretaker in conversation while you add these to the pile. Just make sure he doesn't clock what you're doing.'

John couldn't help smiling. It looked like his dad had got one over on the caretaker at last, and now they'd be able to make a little bit of cash on the side. When he'd first joined his father on the round it had been a shock to discover the various tricks he got up to, but gradually he'd come to accept them. Alfie Pratchett didn't pull a fast one on any of the working-class households they delivered to, but thought nothing of fiddling businesses or the large houses that ordered vast amounts of coal. It seemed to be something some of the coalmen got up to, and John's guilt was assuaged when he thought about their poor wages of just seven quid a week. They worked like dogs, many suffering with back problems later in life, just as his grandad had, and the few extra bob they managed to fiddle added a little extra to their wages.

The unloading finished, they exchanged a conspiratorial glance before climbing back onto the cart, both trying to mask their smiles. The caretaker hadn't noticed their ruse and when he counted twenty sacks he gave a small nod before signing the delivery note.

Now there was just the rest of the round to do, and with two extra sacks of coal to sell, it wouldn't seem so hard.

Chapter Three

For Wendy the rest of the day seemed to fly by, and at five-thirty she left the Exchange, glad that her first day was over without too many mishaps. Her eyes ached from filling out the call cards, and as she hurried to the station she hoped it wouldn't be a long wait for the train home.

She was lucky and in no time she was walking along Lavender Hill, her eyes peeled in the hope of seeing John Pratchett. There he was, she suddenly realised, walking beside his father on the opposite side of the road. God, even covered in coal-dust he looked handsome. For a moment she was tempted to cross to their side, but as the thought entered her head they turned into Harmond Street. Wendy's mouth drooped with disappointment – yet again John had failed to notice her.

As soon as Wendy walked into the kitchen, Bertha asked eagerly, 'How did it go today?'

'Honestly, Mum, you wouldn't believe me if I told you. It's just like being back at school. We're not even allowed to say we want to go to the toilet – instead we have to ask for an *Urgent*.'

'Blimey, that's a new one on me for having a pee.'

'To be honest I don't know if I'm gonna be able to stick it.'

'You can do it for a year, and it'll be worth it,' Bertha gently admonished as she placed two steaming plates on the table.

'Yes, perhaps, and at least the other telephonists seem really nice. Now what have you been up to today?'

Her mother's eyes suddenly saddened. 'I didn't do much. It's the anniversary of yer dad's death today and it always seems to hit me, even after all this time.'

'Oh, I'm sorry, I forgot all about it.'

'Never mind, love, you've had enough to think about with yer new job.' Bertha then pushed her plate to one side, and rising from her chair she crossed to the mantelpiece, where she took down her husband's photograph. With one finger she gently stroked his beloved features and with a sigh said, 'I still can't believe he didn't make it home. It was 1944 before he copped it, and I told the silly sod to dodge the bloody bullets. Ten years ago today, and sometimes it still feels like yesterday. Huh, they said the First World War was the one to end all wars, but they got that well and truly wrong. Let's hope the Second World War really will be the last.'

'You're forgetting the Korean War, Mum, but at least an armistice was signed last year. Now come on, sit down and finish your dinner before it gets cold.'

'Yeah, all right, and I'm sorry for sounding maudlin. Are you going out tonight?'

'The Chris Barber Jazz Band is playing at Battersea Town Hall and I was going with Lucy, but I don't want to leave you.'

'No, you go, I'll be fine.'

'Listen, come with us. You know you like a bit of jazz.'

'Nah, it wouldn't seem right somehow.'

'Right, then I'll stay in. I can see Chris Barber next time round.'

'Are you sure, love?'

'Yes, of course. Lucy will understand, and as another girl was joining us she won't be on her own. Now, what about some fruit cocktail with lashings of evaporated milk for pudding?'

'You're a good kid, and I don't know what I'd do without you.'

'Mum, you won't ever have to do without me. Now go and put the wireless on and I'll do the pudding, along with a cup of Camp coffee.'

John puffed out his cheeks with exhaustion, but at last their rounds were completed and they were nearly home.

In Harmond Street, boys were playing marbles, skimming them along the gutter and he smiled, remembering his own liking for the game. There were a few girls playing too, skipping ropes humming. Innocent days, he thought, wondering as his limbs ached why he'd been in such a hurry to leave school.

He pulled off his cap, slapping the leather neck-flap against a wall, and then ran a hand over his forehead, feeling the familiar coal-grit stinging his skin. As they turned into the alley that led to the back of the house he thought of his mother and suppressed a smile. The fact that they didn't come in through the front door was the only thing his mother had any control over, and his father deferred to this demand. She was an absolute stickler when it came to cleanliness, and woe betide them if they got a speck of coal-dust on her immaculately clean floors.

He followed his father into the outhouse where, after stripping off their clothes, they gave them a brisk thump to remove some of the debris. Then it was a good slosh down under a shower his father had rigged up, and a change of clothes before they dared to enter the house.

As they stepped into the kitchen the house seemed strangely quiet and John's brow creased. He could hear the kettle hissing gently on the gas stove, and the smell of stew made his nostrils twitch with appreciation, but there was no sign of his mother, or Millie.

He shot his father a puzzled glance, but before either spoke there was a clatter of feet coming down the stairs and his sister appeared, looked white-faced and anxious. 'Thank goodness you're home. Mum's not well and I didn't know what to do. She's insisting on getting up now and won't let me call the doctor.'

'What's wrong with her, girl?' Alfie Pratchett snapped.

'I . . . I don't know, Dad. She just sort of fainted, and then when she came round I persuaded her to lie down.'

John made to go upstairs but his father put a detaining hand on his arm. 'It's nothing to worry about. Stay down here and I'll go up to see her.'

Before John had time to protest his father pushed past him and he was left gazing at his back as he stomped up the stairs. Turning quickly to Millie, he asked, 'What do you mean, she fainted? What caused it?'

'I don't know. She looked fine when I came home from school, but then all of a sudden she passed out.'

Just then, their father reappeared, and behind him was their mother. John studied her face, thinking that she looked pale and tired. 'Are you all right, Mum?'

'Yes. Don't fuss, my dear, I'm fine.'

'But why did you faint?'

Eileen Pratchett's face flushed and she turned hurriedly away from her son's gaze. 'I think I must have overdone it, that's all. I gave the bedrooms a good clean today and after turning the mattresses I felt worn out.'

John's eyes narrowed as he watched his mother bustling around preparing their evening meal. She always worked like a beaver in the house, polishing everything until it sparkled, but she had never fainted before so why should today be any different? As she lifted the lid of a saucepan, the delicious aroma of stew filled the room and made his mouth salivate, yet even with this distraction he carried on watching her carefully. There was something wrong, and if she fainted again he would insist that she went to see Dr King.

His father was showing no sign of concern as he flopped onto a chair, and a thought struck John. Before going upstairs he seemed to know in advance that the fainting fit was nothing to worry about – yet how?

Later that evening, Millie glanced at her mother as the sound of raised voices penetrated the thin walls. Billy Benson was at it again and Millie cringed, hoping that her best friend Pat wasn't on the receiving end of his temper.

She saw her father lean forward to turn up the volume on the wireless, and watching his movements Millie frowned. John was right: her dad might ignore her, but at least she never received the beatings that Pat suffered on a regular basis. Why was Billie Benson so violent? Were all men the same? No, she thought, all men couldn't be as horrible as Billy Benson. There was Cyril Blake, for instance, who lived on the other side of them in number eight. He was a lovely man and his wife Stella was nice too, and though she suffered dreadfully with rheumatoid arthritis she always appeared cheerful and kind.

Millie heard a scream and jerked in her chair. Oh Pat – poor Pat!

'It's time you were in bed, Millie.'

Another scream, something crashing. 'But Mum, can't we stop Mr Benson, he's—'

'You heard your mother. Clear off up to bed!'

She scrambled to her feet, instantly obeying her father, her thoughts churning as she ran upstairs. Why didn't they do something? Why was Mr Benson allowed to get away with it? Millie undressed quickly, shivering in the cold room and finding the lino freezing underfoot as she scampered across the room to turn off the light. Hurrying back she dived into bed, and burrowed under the blankets, her feet fishing around for the hot-water bottle.

Then, just as she pulled the eiderdown up so high that only her nose was visible, the noise from next door ceased abruptly. She screwed her eyes tightly shut, offering up a silent prayer that her friend was all right, and not only Pat, her little sisters too.

At eight-thirty the next morning Millie ran to answer the knock on the door, relieved to see Pat on the step. 'I heard the racket last night,' she whispered. 'Are you all right?'

'Yeah,' Pat said, her voice dismissive as she avoided her friend's eyes. 'Are you ready to go?'

'I'll just get my satchel.' Millie dashed into the kitchen and took it off a chair. 'Bye, Mum, I'm off. *Mum*, did you hear me? I'm going to school now.'

'What? Oh sorry, I was miles away. Have you got your dinner-money?'

'Yes, but are you sure you're all right?' Millie gazed worriedly at her mother, wondering if she was ill again.

'I'm fine, now off you go,' and with both hands flat on the table, Eileen pushed herself up.

She looks tired, Millie thought. Her mother's movements were like those of an old woman. 'Perhaps I should stay home today.'

'No, I've told you, I'm fine,' Eileen said again, beginning to bustle around as usual as she cleared the table.

Relieved to see her mother acting normally, Millie gave her a quick kiss and then hurriedly left the house to walk to school with Pat.

As they ambled along, Millie tried to pump her friend about

last night's row, but as usual Pat evaded her questions. They'd been friends since their last year in junior school, Millie befriending Pat when she'd joined her class as a new girl. Shortly after that, Pat's mother died, and gradually as they progressed from junior to secondary school, Millie had seen her friend change. She acquired a hard exterior and showed little emotion, alienating herself from most people. Gradually their other friends dropped away, but Millie knew it was just a veneer that hid Pat's vulnerability, and they remained steadfast best mates.

The antithesis of each other in looks, Millie thought her friend beautiful. Pat had fine facial features with a full mouth and lovely auburn hair, but it was her eyes that were the most striking – cat-shaped and an arresting amber colour. She had two younger sisters whom she protected fiercely from their father's temper, bearing the brunt of his beatings when she jumped to their defence. They were strange little girls who clung to each other and seemed withdrawn, living in their own little world.

'Millie, what are you gonna do when we leave school at Easter?'

'I don't know, but I don't want to work in a factory. What about you?'

'I don't care, but it's got to be a job that pays good money. I wish now I'd tried harder and hadn't failed my eleven-plus.'

'Me too, although we won't earn much at first whatever we do.'

'I've got to earn good money – I've just got to!'

'Why?' Millie asked, seeing her friend's face set in hard lines.

'I wanna leave home.'

It didn't surprise her to hear Pat say that, and who could blame her? 'Tate and Lyle's pay isn't bad – perhaps you could try there?'

'No, it won't be enough. I need to pay the rent on a flat.'

'A flat! Why do you need a flat?'

' 'Cos I ain't leaving me sisters with *him*.'

'But how will you be able to work, *and* look after your sisters?'

'I dunno, Millie, but I can't leave them. If I'm not there he'll start on them . . . I just know he will.'

'Hello, girls – off to school, are you?' Dora Saunders asked, preventing Millie from questioning her friend any further.

'Yes, Mrs Saunders,' the two girls answered simultaneously, smiling at the woman leaning against the stanchion on her doorstep.

Dora Saunders was a lovely old lady, short and tubby, who bore the brunt of many jokes. She had a love of long words and this had earned her the nickname of 'Dictionary Dora'. Unfortunately, the words were often mispronounced or out of context, and many times she had people in the street doubled up with laughter.

'Mind you pay attention to your teacher,' she now said, wagging her finger to emphasise her advice. 'Education is important and you need to be convergent in all your subjects.'

Putting a hand over their mouths to hide their splutters the girls just nodded, hurrying past Dora before bursting into laughter. 'Convergent,' Pat gasped, wiping her wet eyes. 'I haven't heard that word before and as usual she's probably got it mixed up. We'll have to look it up at lunchtime.'

'I know,' Millie giggled. 'But Dora's lovely, isn't she?'

'Yeah, she's a good sort.'

Both girls grimaced as they arrived at school. The grey stone Victorian building looked forbidding, the playground wet after the earlier rain as they hurried through the gates. 'Not much longer now, Millie. We'll be leaving in March.'

'Yes, and I can't wait – but come on, let's hurry. If we're late for register we're bound to get detention.'

At lunchtime, thinking themselves too grown up for the playground, both girls ate their food hastily and then made for the school library.

They wanted to look up Dora's word, and finding it in the dictionary they grinned at each other. *Convergent – of lines – coming together to a point.*

'Somehow I don't think she meant that,' Millie commented as she read the meaning. 'But look, the next entry is *conversant*, and that means to be well-acquainted with either a person or a subject. Dora wasn't far off getting it right this time. What she was trying to say was that we should strive to know all our subjects.'

'Yeah, it's been easier to sort out than usual. Do you remember when she was complaining that me dad had called out *explicates* to her?'

'Crumbs yes, it took us ages to work out that she meant expletives.' The girls laughed at the memory, neither of them aware as yet that Dora was playing a part in their education, and their eventual love of words.

Millie flicked through a few more pages of the dictionary and then stood up to scan the books on the shelves, her mind distracted as she thought back to her conversation with Pat that morning. It seemed impossible that her friend would be able to take her sisters with her when she left home. Billy Benson would never allow it, and come to think of it, surely Pat couldn't legally leave until she was sixteen?

Thinking about Pat's father, she shuddered. Billy Benson may once have been good looking, but now his face was bloated by heavy drinking. Yet it wasn't his appearance that made Millie cringe; there was just something about him – something that always made her skin crawl.

Chapter Four

As soon as her daughter had left the house, Eileen Pratchett sat down again. Last night Alfie had again ordered her to see Granny Baxter about an abortion, and though she had begged and pleaded he refused to listen. Finally, unable to stand any more of his special kind of torment, she had given in, as she always did.

She now clutched her arms around her tummy as though to protect the tiny life within, and raised her eyes in silent prayer. The church — she needed to go to church! If she kneeled in supplication before Mary, perhaps the Blessed Mother would show her the way.

Rising quickly, Eileen put on her coat, and ignoring her usual chores, she hurried down the street to St Margaret's. Early Mass was over and the church silent as she genuflected in front of the statue, tears filling her eyes at the sight of the Baby Jesus in the Holy Mother's arms.

Once again she touched her stomach. Surely Mary could save her baby! Surely She could show her how to save this precious life? Eileen turned now to enter a pew, and kneeling with her head bent in prayer she begged for help, clutching her rosary as she repeated the same supplication over and over again.

Silence, she was aware only of silence, and after about thirty minutes she rose stiffly, once again gazing at the statue. Was it her imagination, or were there tears in the Holy Mother's eyes? Eileen blinked and the vision disappeared. Had she really seen tears? Was the Blessed Mary trying to tell her something? Confused, she shook her head, and turning swiftly to go, she passed by a young priest, one whom she hadn't seen in St Margaret's before.

'Can I help you, my child?' he asked.

'No, Father, no one can help me,' she choked.

'Would you like me to hear your Confession?'

'No, no, thank you,' Eileen said hastily, and with a forced smile she added, 'I must go now, Father.'

Walking quickly she left the church, her heart beating hard against her ribs. How could she go to Confession? She couldn't tell a priest what she was being forced to do. To abort a baby was a sin, a terrible sin, and there was no penance that could bring forgiveness if she destroyed this tiny life.

Rain began to fall again, and with no umbrella or scarf Eileen was soon drenched. She hurried home, unaware of the water that ran in rivulets down her face, mingling with her tears. Alone, she had never felt so alone, and didn't know where to turn. If only she had the strength to fight Alfie, but after years of the same abuse when he wanted his own way, Eileen knew she was powerless. Just one of those looks, an expression on his face that turned her legs to jelly, and she would agree to anything.

Oh God, but not this, she couldn't agree to this, and when Alfie came home he would ask her if she'd been to see Granny Baxter. What could she tell him?

Stella Blake was looking out of her window, but with heavy rain teeming down, large droplets dancing on the pavement, there was little to see. She sighed with boredom. Cyril wouldn't be home from work for hours yet and there was little to fill her day. Housework was almost impossible and she felt a surge of guilt that her husband had to tackle most of it, despite doing a long shift in the brewery.

Stella stretched out her legs, grimacing with pain, then grasping her stick she pushed herself to her feet, determined to at least flick a duster around the room. It was then that she saw Eileen Pratchett hurrying past. In that fleeting moment she saw that her neighbour's hair was soaked and hanging in rats-tails around her face, but it was her expression that worried Stella. The woman looked absolutely distraught!

The Pratchetts were a strange family, and Stella was at a loss to understand why someone as beautiful and refined as Eileen had ended up marrying Alfie. Yes, the man might be quite good-looking, but she wouldn't like him for a husband. Her Cyril might not have anything in looks to shout about, but he'd never lifted a finger to her, and in all the years they'd been married there had hardly been a cross word between them. Unlike the Pratchetts she thought grimly. The walls were thin and there had been many times when she'd heard Alfie's voice raised in anger. Mind you, she didn't know if he hit Eileen, but seeing how downtrodden the woman was, she suspected he might.

Eileen Pratchett had never really fitted into Harmond Street and had found it difficult to make friends, but gradually over the years Stella had broken through her reserve. They hadn't been terribly close at first, only seeing each other for the odd cup of tea, but as Stella's arthritis had worsened the woman had turned into a godsend. Eileen went shopping for her, and though most of their washing went to the laundry, Eileen insisted on doing the delicates, saying that the laundry would ruin them.

Stella now frowned worriedly: was that the sound of crying she could hear? Moving painfully, she crossed to the dividing wall and placing her ear against it, was convinced that she could hear Eileen sobbing. She lifted her stick and rapped on the wall, something that would be sure to bring her neighbour round. It was a signal they'd devised earlier in the year when she'd fallen over – lying on the floor for many hours until Cyril came home from work. Nowadays Eileen popped in every day to see if she was all right, and the signal had been put in place for emergencies.

Finding that the exertion had already exhausted her, Stella flopped onto a chair, and in only minutes the back door flew open.

'What is it? Are you all right?' Eileen panted as she stood on the threshold, her eyes wild with concern and her hair still hanging straggly and wet onto her shoulders.

'I'm fine. It's you I'm worried about.'

'God, Stella, you frightened the life out of me. I thought you had fallen over again!' Her eyes now flashing with anger, Eileen snapped, 'What on earth possessed you to bang on the wall like that?'

'I heard you crying and I was worried,' Stella said, her tone conciliatory.

Eileen advanced across the room and dropped onto the

opposite chair, her hands held out towards the fire. 'Don't ever do that to me again,' she said, yet as the words left her mouth her eyes filled with tears, and with a sob she covered her face with both hands.

'What's wrong, love? Why are you so upset?'

There was no reply and Eileen seemed unable to speak. Deciding it might be best to let her cry out her emotions, Stella sat quietly.

Minutes passed, but finally Eileen raised her head, a look of utter devastation on her face. 'I . . . I'm pregnant,' she blurted out.

'Christ, is that all? I thought someone had died, but here you are telling me you're having a baby. It's wonderful news and I can't understand why you're so unhappy.'

'Alfie doesn't want it.'

'Well, he'll just have to put up with it, won't he. Come on now, buck up. You ain't the first woman to fall pregnant late in life, and you won't be the last.'

'You don't understand, Stella. It isn't that simple.'

'Understand what? You're having a baby and you wait and see, Alfie will come round to the idea eventually. Or is there something else you ain't telling me?'

Eileen gazed across the short distance between them, her eyes pools of misery and for a moment Stella thought her friend might confide in her, but with a small shake of her head, she said, 'Nothing, it's nothing. Look, if you're all right, I must go now.'

'I'm fine, but if you're going down to the shops later, could you get me a few bits?'

'Yes, of course,' she croaked. 'I . . . I'll see you later.'

Stella sighed as the door closed behind her neighbour. How could anyone be unhappy about being pregnant? Eileen had looked absolutely devastated, but surely once Alfie got used to the idea he'd be pleased. After all, a baby was a gift, a gift she had always yearned for. She and Cyril had tried and tried without success to have a family and it had taken them twenty years to become reconciled to the fact that there'd be no children.

Nowadays, with the pain of her arthritis, sex was just a

memory. Poor Cyril, she thought, it was a wonder that he hadn't gone off and got himself another woman. She chuckled then, knowing it was something her husband would never do. Only a few days ago when she'd apologised he had said with a grin, 'Don't worry, love. Me old todger's given up the ghost now anyway!'

Millie and Pat hurried home from school, heads down against the driving rain that hadn't eased as the day progressed. There was little conversation between them in the inclement weather and as they parted outside her front door, Millie called, 'I'll see you in the morning.'

Without waiting to hear her friend's reply she dashed indoors, anxious to get into the warm, and out of her wet things.

This was one of her favourite times of the day, when for a short while she had her mum all to herself. When they were alone, Eileen would frequently wrap an arm around her, giving quick affectionate hugs, and they would chatter and laugh together as they prepared the evening meal. The time was shortlived, however, because as soon as her father and brother came home she would see a rapid change in her mother's demeanour. She became silent and withdrawn, scurrying around like a frightened little mouse to attend to her husband's needs. Millie hated it, hated seeing her fear.

As a child she hadn't understood and if she hurt herself whilst playing, she would run to her mother for a cuddle, only to see her father rear up in anger. He would shout at her, telling her to clear off out of it. It had been the same for John, and on numerous occasions she had seen him break down in tears when their mother rebuffed him. In the end, her brother had been the one she would run to, and they became close, fiercely protective of each other.

Of course, when their father was out, Eileen would try to make it up to them, showering them both with love and affection. By school age they'd learned not to demand any attention when their father was around, both now protective of their mother.

'Hello, Mum,' Millie cried, now bursting into the kitchen. 'It's coming down in stair-rods out there.'

Instead of her usual cheerful greeting, Eileen was sitting gazing into the fire, and as she turned, Millie noticed that her eyes were dull and shadowed. 'You're home early, dear,' she said.

'Only by a few minutes. It's four-fifteen.'

'What! Oh, I didn't realise it was that late and I must get the dinner on! Millie, will you peel some potatoes – quickly.'

Millie flung off her wet coat and rushed to do her mother's bidding, surprised that she hadn't even started to prepare the evening meal. Usually her mum was a stickler for routine: washing on Monday, ironing on Tuesday, turning the bedrooms out on Wednesday, with every day having a designated task. A memory surfaced then, and her eyes widened. When her mother fainted she'd told John it was because she'd turned out the bedrooms. That couldn't be right! Yesterday had been washing day!

She glanced around and seeing that her mother was busily chopping onions she quickly dried her hands, saying as she rushed to the outhouse, 'I need to go to the toilet – I won't be long.'

Once there Millie opened the back door, and then, without going outside, she slammed it shut, hoping it would fool her mother. She then lifted the lid of the box where their dirty linen was stowed. It was almost full, and as the musty smell assailed her nostrils her thoughts were racing. Why hadn't she noticed that the washing hadn't been done? On winter Mondays the kitchen was usually full of damp washing, strewn across racks suspended from the ceiling and draped around the fireguard.

If her mother hadn't done the laundry, something must be very wrong – but what?

Millie opened the back door then slammed it again, and hurrying back into the kitchen she gazed at her mother worriedly. 'Mum, are you feeling all right?'

'Yes, I told you this morning, I'm fine, and for goodness sake finish those potatoes. Cut them into small pieces so they'll cook quickly for mash, and hurry up, your father and John will be home soon.'

'You haven't done the washing.'

Millie saw her mother blanch, and gulping deeply she blustered, 'I . . . I forgot to get the washing powder. I . . . I'll do it tomorrow.'

'But . . .'

'That's enough, my girl. It isn't your place to question me. Now do as I say and get on with those potatoes.'

Surprised at the angry tone in her mother's voice Millie plunged her hands into the sink, unanswered questions still churning. Forgot to get the washing powder? That wasn't true, she'd seen the packet of Oxydol on the shelf. Why was her mother telling lies? Despite her denial, she must have been too ill to do the laundry. It was hard work, as not only did her mother boil all the linen and towels in the copper, she also hung over the sink in the outhouse, scrubbing their clothes on the washboard until every trace of dirt was removed. Then it all had to be rinsed, with a blue bag in the final soak, then put through the mangle. The task took up most of the day.

Yet as Millie finished peeling the potatoes and turned to look at her mother again, she saw no trace of illness. Her cheeks were pink and though Millie could still detect an expression of sadness on her face, her mum looked a picture of health.

'Well, what did Granny Baxter say?' Alfie asked as soon as they were alone that evening.

Eileen knew he'd been itching to ask, his impatience obvious until both Millie and John had gone to bed. Oh, why hadn't she had the sense to wait until she was too far gone before telling him? He would never have noticed if she'd been a bit careful, and then it would have been too late for an abortion. That's it, she thought, sitting upright in her chair. If she could just stall him for a few weeks she'd be able to save her baby. Quietly she said, 'The woman said she'd do it.'

'When are yer getting it done?'

'Soon,' she answered, hoping he wouldn't see the lie reflected on her face.

'Soon! What do you mean, soon? When exactly?'

Eileen felt her face suffuse with colour and lowered her head, her mind floundering. 'She . . . she said I could have it done in a few weeks.'

'Oh yeah, she said that, did she?' Alfie suddenly reared to his feet, and advancing towards her chair he leaned over until their faces were almost touching. 'You're a bloody liar, woman! Do you think I don't know you after all these years? A few weeks my arse. You didn't go to see her, did you?' he spat.

'I . . . I did,' she cried, fear compounding her lie.

'Don't take me for a mug, Eileen,' and abruptly he marched towards the door, his words ominous before he slammed it behind him. 'I'll go to see Granny Baxter myself – and *I'll* make sure that she gets rid of it as soon as possible.'

'Mum, are you all right?'

Millie had crept into the kitchen and Eileen surreptitiously wiped the tears from her cheeks before turning to look at her daughter. 'Go back to bed.'

'Did he hit you?'

'No, of course not. Your father doesn't hit me. Now do as I say and go to bed before he comes back in.'

'Where has he gone?'

'Out,' she said shortly.

'But . . .'

'*Bed!*' Eileen shouted, her nerves at fever pitch. If Alfie came back and found Millie up, there would be another row and she just couldn't take any more. Without another word her daughter scampered from the room, and biting her lip worriedly, Eileen sat gazing into the fire.

It was only a few minutes later when the street door opened, and as Alfie spoke, the breath caught in her throat.

'I got a right ear-bashing for knocking on Granny Baxter's door at this time of night,' he snapped, 'and it didn't take long to find out that you 'aven't been to see her. I should knock your bloody block off for lying to me. Well, it's all sorted now, so there's no getting out of it. She's gonna do it tomorrow and you're to go along there at midday.'

'No, Alfie! No!'

'You'll do as I bloody well say! The arrangements are made and I've already paid her.'

Eileen closed her eyes at the finality in Alfie's tone. There was no way out now – no way to keep her baby. Sobbing, she held a hand over her mouth, unaware that her daughter was still on the staircase, cowering against the wall as she listened to the conversation.

Chapter Five

Eileen hardly slept – she lay close to the edge of the bed as far away from her husband as possible, her mind full of hate; hate for him and what he was forcing her to do. With a shudder she wondered what method Granny Baxter used to end the life of a child. She had once heard someone talking about a back-street abortionist, alluding to the use of a knitting needle, and at the thought she turned icy cold with fear.

Unable to stand the image of Granny Baxter's methods she turned her mind to John, and behind closed lids tears welled in her eyes. Her son, her handsome son – so like her husband in looks, but entirely different in character. John had a softness that was lacking in Alfie and she was sure he wouldn't have her husband's perversions. No, one day he would make some lucky girl a wonderful husband.

As she turned restlessly, Eileen realised how little happiness there had been in her life: John had been her only compensation. Yet eventually her son would leave home and then what would she have to look forward to? Nothing, she thought in despair.

Millie drifted into her mind – Millie the child who despite everything, she had grown to love. Oh, not in the same way she loved her son – that would be impossible – but she was proud of the young woman her daughter was turning into. *Please, Lord*, she prayed, *when the girl is old enough – please let her find a man who will be good to her.*

Dawn was casting a wintry glow on the rooftops before Eileen finally drifted off to sleep, only to be awoken an hour later by the sound of the alarm clock reverberating in the bleak room. She crawled out of bed, shivering as she made her way downstairs to light the fire, but finding as she put the kettle on to boil that she felt strangely remote and calm.

After lying awake for hour after hour with her mind churning in desperation, she had finally come to a decision. She knew now what she had to do – knew that there was no other choice. Alfie had seen to that.

'How are you feeling, Mum?' John asked as he ate his breakfast.

'I'm fine, dear.'

'Are you sure you're not feeling faint again? You look as if you're in a dream.'

'I've told you, I'm fine.'

'For Gawd's sake, boy, shut up and stop fussing like an old woman,' Alfie grumbled. 'You heard yer mother so get that grub down you and let's go!'

Eileen glanced at the clock, wishing them both away. She had things to do before midday when Granny Baxter was expecting her – important things that had to be sorted out.

At last, she thought when they both rose to their feet, and after handing them their sandwiches she began to clear the plates. As they left the house, John following his father, he suddenly turned, and with a frown asked, 'Mum, are you *sure* there's nothing wrong?'

Eileen quickly bowed her head. She couldn't look at him, couldn't bear to see the worry on his beloved face, knowing it would be her undoing. 'I'm all right, honestly. Now off you go. Goodbye, darling, and John – I . . . I love you, son.'

'Come on, boy, get a bloody move on, will yer!'

Eileen was glad of the distraction; relieved too that Alfie hadn't heard her words. Yet what did it matter if he had? Nothing mattered any more.

'Bye, Mum, I'd better go,' John called, hurriedly closing the door behind him.

Now there was only Millie, Eileen thought, but it was far too early to get the girl up.

The sound of the clock ticking filled the silence as she stood looking disconsolately around the room. Then, throwing herself onto a fireside chair, she prayed for strength, her supplications ending abruptly as she realised that God wouldn't be listening. How could He? She was going to commit the greatest sin of all, a sin that could never be forgiven.

At seven-thirty Eileen called Millie, and knowing how perceptive her daughter could be, she fought to put on a front. They sat opposite each other at the kitchen table, Millie eating her Shredded Wheat and Eileen sipping a cup of tea.

'Mum, I heard what Dad said last night, but I don't understand. Who is he making you see today? He said he'd paid her, but what for?'

Eileen's face blanched and to cover her distress she said harshly, 'What do you mean, you heard your dad? How did you manage to do that?'

'I . . . I was on the stairs.'

'I'm surprised at you, Millie. What we were talking about was none of your business and you had no right to eavesdrop on our conversation. Now eat your breakfast and get yourself off to school.'

'Please don't be cross with me, Mum. I was worried about you and that's why I listened in. I . . . I thought Dad was going to hit you.'

When she saw the unhappiness on her daughter's face Eileen's resolve began to weaken, but then Millie spoke again.

'Why do you put up with it, Mum?'

'Your father doesn't hit me, and I've told you that umpteen times before.'

'Maybe not, but you're scared of him . . . I know you are.'

Oh God, Eileen thought with a surge of guilt. Her daughter was an innocent young girl, and despite trying to hide her fear it was obvious now that she'd been unsuccessful. Would it taint Millie? Would it turn her off marriage and a family? *Dear God, don't let that happen*, she prayed. After all, not every marriage was like hers.

She reached across the table to squeeze her daughter's hand. 'Listen, darling, I can't talk to you about your father as it wouldn't be right.' She smiled gently, adding, 'You're a good girl, and I love you very much. I want you to remember that.'

Millie frowned and Eileen realised that she'd put her foot in it. Telling her children that she loved them was something she rarely did. When Alfie wasn't around she tried to show them affection, but having been brought up without demonstrations of love from her own parents, she found it hard. She'd been an only child, born when her mother was in her late thirties, and as she grew up she'd felt in the way. Her parents were always wrapped up in each other and had little time for the quiet, introverted child they seemed surprised to find in their midst. She had rarely been cuddled, and then when she'd married Alfie, he only showed affection when he wanted sex.

Now, seeing that Millie was still staring at her strangely, she rapidly changed her tone, saying brusquely, 'Come on, get yourself off to school or you'll be late.'

Thankfully at that moment there was a knock on the door and Millie rose quickly. 'That'll be Pat. I'll see you later, Mum.'

After swallowing the last dregs of her tea, Eileen went upstairs. In her bedroom she pulled a chair across the room, balancing precariously on it as she groped for a small wooden box hidden on top of the wardrobe. Holding it clutched tightly in her hand she hurried back downstairs, and taking a notepad from the dresser drawer she sat at the table to compose a letter.

Hate for her husband surged through her again as she wrote the words. He had sworn her to secrecy, forbade her to tell Millie, but the girl had a right to know and there was nothing to stop her now. The letter finished, Eileen opened the box and placed it inside, her eyes ranging over the rest of the contents. There wasn't much, just enough for Millie to know the truth, but in the meantime she would have to trust the precious contents to Stella Blake's care.

Entering Stella's house through the back door, Eileen passed the sitting room and walked into the kitchen, calling, 'It's only me.'

'Hello, love, you're early and you look a bit down in the mouth. Here, I know what'll cheer you up. You know how much my Cyril loves silly little ditties, and he heard a new one at work yesterday.' To the tune of a lively jig, Stella now began to sing, '*Oh, the black cat piddled in the white cat's eye, and the white cat said*

"Cor blimey". Then the black cat said, "It's your own darn fault, you shouldn't have stood behind me".'

Whilst Stella chuckled, Eileen forced a smile before saying, 'I've come to ask if you'll do me a favour and look after this box for me.'

'Why, what's in it?'

'It's something for Millie, something I want her to have if anything happens to me.'

'But why give it to me?'

'Because I know you'll keep it safe.'

Stella gazed at the box, her eyes puzzled. 'What's going on, Eileen, are you planning something? Yer not gonna do a runner, are you?'

'No, of course not,' Eileen told her, searching for words. 'The contents of that box are important, and . . . and I don't want Alfie to find it, that's all. It frightens the life out of me having it in the house and I know I can trust you with it.'

'Oh, is it valuable then?'

'Yes,' Eileen lied, relieved that her friend had given her the perfect excuse. 'It's jewellery, you see, jewellery that belonged to my mother, and if Alfie found it he would probably want to sell it.'

'Christ, love, I'm not sure about having valuables in the house. It's too much of a responsibility.'

'Please, Stella, I promise it won't be for long – just until I can sort something else out.'

'All right, if it's only for a few days I'll keep it for you. Pop into the sitting room and put it in the sideboard. That'll be the safest place.'

'Thanks,' Eileen said, closing her eyes momentarily with relief. She'd been in Stella's best room to dust and polish the furniture, but like hers, the room was hardly used. Eileen loved to bring a shine to the lovely mahogany dining-room table, finding it a pleasure after her own Utility furniture. Alfie refused to buy anything new, saying the stuff they had now was good enough and would last for years. She hated its ugliness, its plain lines, and longed for a room as nice as Stella's. With a small shake of her head she berated herself for being foolish. What did furniture matter now?

Eileen opened the lower cupboard of the sideboard, pushing the box well to the rear and then went back to Stella, hurriedly saying goodbye before returning to her own house.

That was it, everything had been done, and now she just had one more letter to write. Taking the notepad, Eileen sat at the table again, her brow furrowed as she licked the end of her pencil . . .

Dear Alfie,

I have thought long and hard about this, and I have come to realise that there is no other way. If I let Granny Baxter kill our baby, then I am committing an act of murder, an act that I know can never be forgiven. It would destroy my life, and destroy everything that I believe in and hold dear. I know that I couldn't live with the guilt, and that for the rest of my life it would torture me to know that I have been condemned to Purgatory. At least this way, though I still know I can never be forgiven, my torture will end quickly. Please tell the children that I'm sorry, and that I love them. Eileen

Eileen read the note through again, and somehow the words sealed her decision. It was badly written, but it would have to do. She stuffed it into an envelope and rising to her feet, propped it on the mantelpiece, before making her way to the outhouse where she opened the laundry bin.

With armfuls of dirty sheets she made her way back to the kitchen, stuffing them tightly into the gaps under the doors.

Eileen's mind felt strangely calm and detached as she made these preparations. The children would not suffer; in fact, they'd be better off without her. What sort of mother had she been anyway? Weak and useless, her fear of Alfie keeping her from showing them the affection they deserved.

Both Millie and John had seen her unhappiness from a young age, and they were still seeing it now. Well, it had to stop – and it *would* stop, here and now. Yes, she was doing the right thing – the right thing for all of them.

Never again would Alfie be able to tie her to the bed when he wanted his own way. Never again would he be able to stuff a rag in her mouth to drown out her cries while he abused her body, driving into her again and again as she lay helpless beneath him. She hated it, hated the feeling of helplessness. Alfie loved it; she knew that – knew that he got a perverse pleasure from having control over her. He would continue the assault all night if necessary, becoming more violent, pinching and biting her body until, unable to stand it any longer, she would give in.

Yes, he always won. But not this time, she thought, stiffening with determination. He wouldn't win this time.

Eileen sighed deeply as she fed shillings into the gas meter, her tormented thoughts still at last. As though in a dream she moved slowly towards the cooker and turned on the gas tap. Then, opening the door, she pulled out the single rack before shoving a cushion onto the base of the oven.

There was no one else in her thoughts now, only herself and the wish to end it all – to end the agony of her existence. Kneeling down, she looked into the dark cavern of the oven, and then leaning forward she placed her head inside, arms out to her side as though in supplication.

Chapter Six

Millie jerked as a piece of chalk hit her on the shoulder and Mr Lampard's voice boomed across the classroom.

'You are here to learn, Millie Pratchett, not to gaze out of the window. Now what was I just talking about?'

'Er . . . verbs, sir?' she stammered, her heart sinking at the expression on the English teacher's face.

The frown caused his dark, bushy brows to meet in the centre, the look in his eyes ferocious. 'Verbs! No, I wasn't talking about verbs; I was talking about the writer Edgar Allen Poe.'

Millie's stomach churned. Mr Lampard was one of her favourite teachers and she usually loved his classes. This morning she'd been unable to concentrate, her thoughts constantly flying to her mother's strange behaviour, and there had been such sadness in her eyes. It was unusual for her to express words of love, and this convinced Millie that there really was something wrong, despite her protestations. Then there was the conversation she'd overheard, her father's words twisting and turning in her mind. Who was her mother going to see at midday? And why had her father given this person money?

Mr Lampard spoke again and wondering what her punishment would be, Millie looked at the teacher with apprehension. She crossed her fingers, hoping that she wouldn't get detention.

'Edgar Allen Poe wrote *The Pit and the Pendulum*, Miss Pratchett. Now, let's see if you're listening. What did he write?'

'*The Pit and the Pendulum*, sir.'

'Ah, so I have your attention at last. You will write "Edgar Allen Poe wrote *The Pit and the Pendulum*" one hundred times and present it to me tomorrow morning.'

'Yes sir,' Millie whispered, relieved that she had got off so lightly. He was an old softy really, despite the scary look on his craggy face, and though the boys felt the rough end of his hand if they weren't paying attention, the girls seemed to get off more lightly. He'd only thrown a piece of chalk at her, but if she'd been a boy she might have been on the receiving end of the wooden block he used as a blackboard duster.

The lesson came to an end, and as Millie walked with Pat across the playground to the dining hall, she pulled out her rota for the afternoon. In the carefully drawn boxes, she had written Needle-work for the first afternoon period, but then her eyes widened. Oh God, the last period was netball and she'd forgotten her gym kit! Miss Ford was a teacher she feared and one who would accept no excuses. In fact, only last week when one of the girls had forgotten her kit, she'd been forced to play netball in her vest and navy-blue knickers. The court was on Clapham Common, in full view of passers-by, and Millie dreaded suffering the same humiliation. Grabbing her friend's arm she said urgently, 'Pat, I'll have to miss lunch and run home. I've forgotten my gym kit.'

'I'll come with you, but we'd better get a move on.'

'It's all right, I'll go on my own. There's no need for you to miss lunch.'

'It's no loss, Millie. I ain't keen on school grub anyway, especially the lumpy mash. Not forgetting tapioca pudding – ugh, it reminds me of frogspawn. We can grab a bag of chips instead 'cos I went shopping for Dora after school yesterday and she gave me a tanner.'

At the thought of hot chips smothered in salt and vinegar, Millie's mouth watered. 'Right, come on then, let's get a move on.'

Both girls ran out of the school gates, and by the time they reached Millie's house they were out of breath and gasping.

Millie unlocked the street door, and as she stepped into the small hall her nose wrinkled. What was that sickly smell?

'Mum!' she called, trying to enter the kitchen but finding that the door refused to open.

'God, it stinks of gas in here!' Pat cried from behind her.

'Mum!' Millie shouted again, pushing her shoulder against the door and managing to move it a few inches. The stench became stronger, making them both cough, and as Millie continued shoving with all her might she felt her stomach heave.

'There must be a leak! We've got to get out of here!' Pat yelled, grabbing Millie's arm.

'No, no! My mum must be in there and I can't leave her!' Millie choked, finding speech difficult as the gas caused the breath to catch in her throat. With all the strength she could muster she pushed at the door again, finding that it opened just enough for her to squeeze through, and as she forced her way into the gap Pat was still pulling on her arm.

'No, Millie, you can't go in there! We need help and . . .' Pat's voice died as she lost her grip on her friend, and almost immediately she heard a terrible scream. She peered into the kitchen, her eyes streaming, horrified to see Millie struggling to drag her mother across the room.

'Pat, help me!'

Turning sideways, Pat managed to squeeze her body through the gap and ran to her friend's side, but as she reached down to grab Mrs Pratchett, Millie suddenly staggered.

Pat floundered, her heart thumping with fear, but finding the smell of gas overpowering, she turned on her heels. Desperately yanking the rag out from under the door she opened it fully, shouting as she ran into the street, 'Help! Somebody help! Oh please, help me!'

Doors opened, and a couple walking towards her broke into a run. 'Gas,' she choked, pointing wildly towards Millie's door, relieved to see the man rushing into the house.

Within seconds there was the sound of a window shattering as a wooden chair came flying outside to land in the street amongst a shower of broken glass. Then almost immediately the man came staggering out of the door, Millie in his arms. He laid her down and instantly she seemed surrounded by people, obscuring Pat's view. She saw the man dashing inside the house again and then Stella Blake appeared at her side, struggling on two walking sticks.

'Patricia, what on earth's going on?'

'Gas, the place is full of gas!' she sobbed, turning from Mrs

Blake and pushing her way through the neighbours. *Oh please, don't let Millie be dead!* her mind screamed.

At last she could see her friend, and the breath left Pat's body in a huge gasp of relief. Millie was sitting up now, vomiting onto the pavement as she reached her.

'My mum, I must help my mum!' she cried, wiping her mouth with the back of her hand and trying to rise to her feet.

'It's all right, love, that bloke's just gone in to get her,' Dora Saunders said as she bent down to pat Millie kindly on the back.

All eyes then turned as the man came outside again, his face grim as he held Eileen Pratchett, her head lolling in his arms. It was obvious she was dead, but before anyone could stop her Millie scrambled up, howling as she ran to the man's side. He stood helplessly holding Eileen Pratchett, but taken by a fit of coughing he had to double over, placing her as gently as he could onto the pavement.

'Mum, Mum! Wake up!' Millie wailed, shaking her mother's shoulders.

'You can't leave her on the pavement like that,' Stella Blake said, her distress obvious. 'Please, will you pick her up again and carry her into my house.'

The man gulped in air and then ran a hand over his face. 'All right, missus, but somebody had better ring the police.'

'The police!' Stella exclaimed.

'They'll 'ave to be called . . . you see, it wasn't an accident.' With a sad nod at Eileen Pratchett's body, he added, 'From what I saw, she done it deliberately.'

The next twenty minutes were a nightmare for Millie. Dazed, she sat in Stella Blake's sitting room, unable to accept that her mother was dead and her eyes avoiding the body lying on the sofa.

'Come on, darlin', why don't you go and wait in Dora's house.'

'No, I'm not leaving her! Oh, when is the doctor going to come?'

Stella's eyes were full of sympathy and she cast a meaningful look towards Dora Saunders.

'Listen, ducks,' Dora said, moving across the room to stand at Millie's side. 'When the doctor gets here he'll want to examine yer mum in private. It really would be best if you came home with me.'

'No!' Millie shook her head stubbornly. She knew that after a frantic conversation earlier, someone had been dispatched to find her father, and she had no intention of leaving her mother until either he, or the doctor arrived. They would sort it out. They would make her mother better, and nodding her head in affirmation she withdrew into herself again, refusing to acknowledge the truth.

There was a commotion outside in the street, the sound of horses' hooves, and then Stella's door flew open, crashing back against the wall.

'Eileen! Eileen!' Alfie Pratchett screamed as he rushed into the room, dragging his wife into his arms. His howls became like those of a wild animal as he rocked her back and forth, whilst the others in the room stood watching helplessly.

It was Millie who suddenly came to life and ran to his side. 'Mum isn't dead, is she? Dad, tell me she isn't dead!'

The look on her father's face was terrible to see. His lips drew back revealing his teeth, and with a ferocious growl his arm shot out, shoving Millie with such force that she staggered across the room before toppling backwards onto the floor. 'Get away!' he yelled. 'Get away from me!'

Stella and Dora were frozen in shock, but John had come into the room behind his father and was now galvanised into action. Rushing to Millie's side he helped her up, and as their eyes met, Millie broke.

'No, no, she isn't dead – Mum can't be dead,' she sobbed, collapsing against her brother. She was aware then of being led outside, saw neighbours standing around in groups, their faces avid with interest as they saw her, and then she found herself in Dora's house.

'Sit her by the fire, she's in shock,' Dora ordered.

Millie hunched in the chair, her eyes on the flickering flames, and only dimly aware of the conversation around her.

'I don't know why that bloke had to smash yer window like

that, but don't worry, Mrs Hardcastle is going to sweep up the glass.'

'Sod the window!' John snapped. 'Oh sorry, Mrs Saunders, I shouldn't have said that. Anyway, the sash was broken so he couldn't have opened it.'

'There's no need to apologise, lad. You're upset and it ain't surprising. I can't believe this has happened, I really can't. Why would yer mother do such a thing?'

'Wha . . . what do you mean?' John asked, his bewilderment obvious.

'Well, you know, the gas and that.'

'But . . . but it was a leak, wasn't it?'

Millie looked up then to see Dora shaking her head sadly. 'No, love, from what I heard she did it deliberately. I'm so sorry, and you 'ave my commemorations.'

Millie laughed then, hysterical laughter that caused both John and Doris to stare at her in shock. 'Commemorations! Oh dear, commemorations! She said the wrong word again. Commiserations – that's what Dora means, John.' Her laughter grew, rising in volume, and only cutting off abruptly when she felt the sting of her brother's hand across her face.

'Stop it, Millie! Stop it!' John cried, his voice high with shock.

The tears came then, pouring down her cheeks and flooding her face, her distress so great that she felt she was drowning . . .

In Stella's, Alfie staggered to his feet, and with his face lined in anguish he threw one last glance at his wife's body before stumbling out of the street door and into his own house. The smell of gas still hung in the air, and as he entered the kitchen he immediately saw the envelope propped on the mantelpiece. Alfie ripped it open, his eyes quickly scanning the contents.

Moments later, all hell seemed to break loose as officialdom arrived. Ambulance and police cars raced down the street, bells pealing, the cacophony of sound echoing in Harmond Street as they pulled to a screech outside the house. With another quick look around the room Alfie closed his eyes against the sight of the open oven door, then he ran upstairs, and opening his wardrobe, he shoved the note into the inside pocket of his suit.

As if in synchronisation with the other emergency services, the doctor's black Morris Minor pulled up, and making his way outside again Alfie indicated Stella's house, leading him inside.

The room was strangely silent as they entered, and his eyes bruised with pain, Alfie watched the doctor as he bent over his wife. He noticed his shake of the head, saw him beckon to the ambulance crew, and then watched helplessly as Eileen was carried out on a stretcher.

The words in the suicide note seemed to be burning a hole in his brain, but there was no way he was going to let anyone else see it. Rather than have an abortion, Eileen had killed herself and he was still reeling with shock. It didn't make sense, none of it made sense, and what would people think if they knew? They would blame him and that wasn't fair, not when all she had to do was to get rid of the bloody baby. The doctor spoke, and startled at this intrusion of sound, Alfie stared at the man.

'Do you want to go with your wife, Mr Pratchett?'

'Go with her! But she's dead, ain't she?'

'Yes, I'm afraid she is.'

At the finality of the doctor's words Alfie felt his legs buckle, and almost falling onto a chair he gave way to his grief.

Wendy Hall's eyes were wide as she watched the commotion outside the Pratchetts' house. She had finished her early shift at the Exchange, and on her way home had seen the crowds in Harmond Street, hurrying to join them as she wondered what had happened. Now, standing amongst a throng of women who were obviously neighbours, she listened to their conversation.

'That bloke who carried her out said it was deliberate,' one put in, her voice high with excitement.

'Yeah, I heard him, Jessie, and I wonder why she did it?'

'Well, if you ask me she was a strange one, and a bit stuck-up too. Still, it's awful to think she topped herself, and like you I'd love to know why.'

'We'll find out at the inquest.'

'How are we gonna do that?'

'There's always an inquest in cases like this, and it's open to the public. I expect the local press will be there too. Gawd, her poor kids! Did you see the state Millie Pratchett was in?'

'Yeah, the poor girl looked terrible and it ain't surprising. Young John was in a dreadful state too, and what about Alfie Pratchett, did you see his face?'

Wendy turned away, sickened by the relish in the women's voices. Poor John had just lost his mother, and her heart ached for him. She moved to one side, watching the activities for a while before retracing her footsteps to Lavender Hill, not surprised to see her mother leaning out of the window.

Her mum was a worrier, and as an only child Wendy had sometimes felt stifled and over-protected. Yet she loved her mother dearly, and not wanting to cause her further anxiety she quickened her pace.

'Where the devil 'ave you been?' Bertha shouted, causing other heads besides Wendy's to look up at the window.

'I'll tell you in a minute,' she called, hurrying in the door sandwiched between the ironmonger's and grocer's. When she reached the landing her mother was there, standing with her hands on hips.

'Well, come on, tell me where you've been.'

'I saw something going on in Harmond Street.'

'Oh yes, and what was that?'

'Let me get inside first.'

Her mother tutted impatiently, saying as they reached the kitchen, 'What was so important that it made you late?'

'Mrs Pratchett committed suicide, and it was mayhem outside her house. There was an ambulance, the police, and crowds of nosy old biddies standing around.'

'No! Surely you don't mean the coalman's wife?'

'Yes, that's the one.'

'Christ, that's awful! I used to chat to her occasionally after Sunday Mass and she seemed such a quiet, gentle lady. Why on earth did she kill herself?'

'I don't know, but some of the neighbours were saying they'll find out at the inquest.'

'I've always thought they should hold them things in private, instead of letting anyone in, and I expect the bloody press will be sniffing around too. The poor Pratchetts will 'ave all their dirty linen washed in public and it ain't right. Did you see Alfie?'

'No, but I wish I'd seen John. I'd like to have offered my condolences.'

'John! Do you mean Alfie Pratchett's son?'

'Yes.'

'I hope you ain't got any ideas in that direction, my girl, 'cos I don't want you mixing with a bloody coalman. You need to set yer sights higher than that.'

'Mum, listen to yourself. Dad was a dustman before the war so what's wrong with a coalman?'

'Yes, yer dad was a binman, and we never had a pot to piss in half the time. I want something better for you, that's all, and you can fall in love just as easily with a rich man as a poor one.'

'But I thought you loved Dad!'

'Of course I did, but why struggle all yer life like me? Find yourself a bloke with prospects and forget John Pratchett. All right, don't look at me like that, I'm only telling you for yer own good. Now let's change the bloody subject. How did you like the early shift at the Exchange?'

'It was quieter than usual and nice to be able to chat to the girl next to me for a change – mind you, we still made sure a supervisor didn't spot us. I was given alarm calls to do so that was something different.'

'What are alarm calls? Was it people ringing for help?'

'No, of course not. They're wake-up calls that are booked in advance. Honestly, Mum, we have to say the same thing every time,' and affecting a haughty voice she said, 'Good morning, it is seven o'clock, and this is your morning alarm call.'

'Why don't they just use an alarm clock?'

'I don't know, but some of them sounded so dozy when they answered the telephone that I had a job not to shout, *"Wake up, you lazy bugger!"'*

Bertha roared out laughing, but then suddenly sobered. 'Alarm calls, who'd 'ave thought it? Gawd, how the other half live. Yer dad had to get up early, but he didn't even use a clock. He just seemed to wake up every morning on his own accord, almost like he had an internal alarm. Now, there's an example, my girl. I had to be up at the crack of dawn to get his breakfast and packed lunch. Coalmen earn poor wages too and you might end up doing early-morning cleaning like me. Christ, Wendy, have some sense! Do you really want that sort of life? Because if you don't forget John Pratchett, then that's what you're likely to get.'

Wendy lowered her head, her expression veiled. No matter what her mother said she was determined to get John's attention. He was the man for her, and she knew it . . . knew it by the fluttering in her stomach every time she saw him. At night she lay in bed, dreaming of walking down the aisle to see John waiting for her at the other end, his face alight with adoration. All right, so he was only a coalman, but what did that matter? And if she had to get up early, that was no hardship. She'd been up at five that morning for her early shift, hadn't she.

Chapter Seven

Stella Blake listened tiredly to Dora Saunders as she prattled on, sickened by the glee on her face. Over a month had passed since Eileen Pratchett's death, and it seemed that half the street had attended the inquest, Dora amongst them. Now the woman obviously couldn't wait to pass on the gossip, not just to her, but to the other half of the street that hadn't shown any inclination to go.

'Blimey, Stella, you could 'ave knocked me down with a feather when the pathologic said the post mortem revealed that Eileen was pregnant.'

'Pathologist,' Stella corrected tiredly. What was the matter with her? Why did she feel so strange? Her head was all muzzy. Tears suddenly filled her eyes. Yes, she had known that Eileen was pregnant, but had decided to keep that bit of information to herself. She thought the family had enough to deal with without adding gossip to their grief, but hadn't thought about an inquest. Now of course everyone knew, and she wondered how John and Millie were taking it.

'When Alfie Pratchett gave his evidence, he said he didn't know about the baby, and the poor man looked devastated,' Dora said, before prattling on again about the press being there and the likelihood of the story appearing in the local paper.

Didn't know! Of course Alfie knew, Stella thought, and according to Eileen he hadn't wanted the baby. None of this made sense. Why had he lied? There was a strange buzzing in her head, and dimly she heard Dora's shout.

'What is it, love! What's the matter!'

Stella tried to respond, but instead closed her eyes as blackness swamped her.

In number ten, after weeks of anguish whilst they waited for the inquest, John Pratchett faced his father across the kitchen table.

'You told the Coroner that you didn't know Mum was pregnant, but I don't believe you.'

'Why would I lie about a thing like that?'

'I dunno, Dad, but it doesn't make sense that Mum would take her own life just because she couldn't face having another child.'

'What other reason could there be?'

'Mum was a Catholic and would have seen suicide as a terrible sin. There's more to this than meets the eye and I think you should tell us the truth.'

'There's nothing to tell. Why don't you just shut up and leave me alone,' Alfie spat, his face red as he shoved on his jacket. 'I'm sick of being interrogated. Don't you think I've had enough of that from the bloody police? The Coroner was satisfied and gave his verdict, so that's an end to it. Now if you don't mind, I'm going down the pub.'

'Dad . . . Dad, wait! What about the funeral arrangements?'

Choosing to ignore his son, Alfie stormed out, and it was only then that Millie spoke. 'I don't believe him, John.'

'No, neither do I, and I keep thinking about that time when Mum fainted. Dad seemed to know what was wrong with her and it all makes sense now. I'm sure he knew she was pregnant, but why is he denying it?'

'I don't know, but he's never going to admit it, that's for sure. Oh John, how are we going to cope without her?'

'We'll cope, we have to. Somehow we've got to pick up the pieces and get on with our lives, but to be honest I'm gonna hate working with Dad now.'

'You could get another job.'

'Yeah, I might just do that. And what about you, Millie? What are you going to do when you leave school next month?'

'I'll find a job, I suppose, but I don't know what I want to do. Since Mum died I just seem to exist from day to day.'

'There's no rush. You could stay at home for a while, and God knows we need someone to sort this place out.'

Millie glanced around the room, a room that had once been immaculate but now looked as if a bomb had hit it. Mum would have hated this, she realised. Yes, maybe John was right, maybe it wouldn't hurt to stay at home to look after things for a while when she left school.

Only moments later, there was a frantic knocking on the front door and Millie hurried to open it, her eyes stretching when she saw Dora hopping about with anxiety.

'Quick, I need help! Something's the matter with Stella.'

'John, come quickly!' Millie called before rushing next door with Dora, and as they entered the room Stella stared at them dazedly.

'What's going on?' she slurred, spittle running from the corner of her mouth.

'Gawd, you gave me such a turn,' Dora said.

'I did?'

'Yeah, you seemed to sort of pass out. Are you all right?'

'I feel a bit muzzy-headed,' Stella admitted as John joined them.

'I reckon we should get the doctor to have a look at you, Mrs Blake,' he said, obviously concerned. 'What do you think, Mrs Saunders?'

'Yeah, I think you're right, lad. Millie, would you run down to Dr King and ask him to make a house call?'

'Yes, all right,' she agreed.

As John walked with her to the door, he whispered, 'You'd better tell the doctor it's urgent. I think Mrs Blake looks really rough, and did you notice that one side of her mouth looked a bit slack?'

'No, but I did think she looked a bit odd. I'll be as quick as I can.'

Millie was lucky. The doctor was at home and agreed to come straight away. After examining Stella he said she'd suffered a slight stroke, and without further ado he arranged for her to be admitted to hospital.

Dora then asked John to get a message to Cyril Blake, and

when Stella was carried outside, she accompanied her. Millie stood on the pavement, not surprised to see other neighbours on their steps, obviously alerted by the arrival of an ambulance.

'Look at those nosy buggers!' Dora said as she climbed inside the vehicle, then shouted, 'Ain't you lot got anything better to do?'

Millie found herself smiling for the first time since her mother's death. Dora Saunders was the biggest gossip on the street, and Jessie Hardcastle obviously thought the same. As the back doors of the ambulance closed, shutting Dora from view, Jessie shouted indignantly, 'Bloody cheek! You're the mouthpiece of the street, Dora Saunders, so who are you to talk?'

Other neighbours nodded and as the ambulance drove off, Jessie called, 'Here, Millie, what happened to Stella Blake?'

'She was taken ill.'

'What's wrong with her?'

'The doctor thinks she's had a stroke,' Millie called back, and before the women could ask any more questions, she hurried indoors – but not before she heard Jessie Hardcastle's comment.

'Christ, people are falling like pins in this street. Still, at least Stella didn't top herself.'

Alfie Pratchett staggered home drunk that night, unaware that his son undressed him and put him to bed. Luckily they didn't have to go to work the next morning and it was almost midday before he resurfaced.

'Where's Millie?' he asked as he stumbled into the kitchen. 'I need a cup of tea.'

'She's gone to get some shopping. I gave her some money, but I think you had better start tipping up the housekeeping to her.'

'But she's just a bit of a kid.'

'She leaves school soon and anyway, what choice have you got? Someone has to get the food in, and with us at work all day that only leaves Millie.'

'Yeah, I suppose so,' Alfie said distantly, his mind once again on his wife. What was he going to do without Eileen? he thought for the umpteenth time. Oh God, why had she gone and gassed herself?

'Dad, please tell me the truth. Why did Mum kill herself?'

Oh, not again, Alfie thought, and swallowing deeply he found his throat was rasping, 'I don't know! Christ, John, you just can't let it go, can you? You're like a dog gnawing at a bleedin' bone.' He glanced at the clock, amazed to see that it was after midday, but glad that the pub would be open for the lunchtime session. 'I'm having a slosh-down then I'm off to the pub. You're enough to drive a man to drink!'

'There's still Mum's funeral to arrange, and drowning your sorrows isn't the answer, Dad.'

'Maybe not, but it gets me away from you for a few hours!' Alfie growled as he made for the outhouse, and after a quick shower he left by the back door. Funeral, yes, there was the funeral, but he couldn't face it yet, and as he entered the King's Head he asked for a pint and a chaser. When the whisky arrived he lifted the glass quickly, downing it in one gulp and ordering another.

Wendy Hall couldn't believe her luck when she saw Millie Pratchett struggling along Lavender Hill, loaded down with bags of shopping. If she befriended the girl it might be a way to get John's attention, and with a smile she walked to her side.

'Hello, it's Millie Pratchett, isn't it?'

'Yes,' Millie said, her expression puzzled as their eyes met.

'My name's Wendy Hall and I used to be in your brother's class at school. I just wanted to offer my condolences. It must have been terrible for you to lose your mother.'

Wendy watched in horror as Millie's eyes filled with tears and she could have kicked herself. It was obvious that the girl's feelings were still raw, and now she hastily opened her clutch bag, thrusting a handkerchief towards Millie.

'Thanks,' she choked, and quickly wiped her eyes. 'I'm sorry, but sympathy always makes me break down.'

'It's all right, I understand,' Wendy said, rapidly changing the subject. 'Goodness, you have an awful lot of shopping there. I'm going your way, so please let me give you a hand.'

'It's all right, I can manage.'

'I'm sure you can, but why struggle when I can help you? Now come on, give me one of those bags.'

Millie seemed grateful as she relinquished her hold on the bag of vegetables, and even managed a watery smile. 'Thanks, it's kind of you.'

For a few minutes they walked along Lavender Hill in silence, and then Wendy plucked up the courage to ask, 'How is your brother?'

'He's coping – just about. Do you live far from Harmond Street?'

'No, I live here on Lavender Hill, just past your street and above the ironmonger's.'

'Oh, but that means I'm taking you out of your way.'

'It doesn't matter and anyway, I'm glad to help. Now tell me, have you left school yet?'

'I'll be leaving shortly,' Millie said as they turned the corner, and on reaching the front door she rattled the letterbox. 'Thank you so much for helping me.'

'It was no trouble,' Wendy said as the front door opened, and as John stepped to one side she followed Millie into the kitchen.

'John, this is Wendy Hall and she helped me to carry the shopping home. Wasn't that kind of her?'

'Yes, it was,' John said, scratching his head distractedly as he met Wendy's gaze.

'I don't suppose you remember me,' she said shyly, 'but we were in the same class at school.'

'Were we?' John said as he continued to study her.

Wendy was glad that she had put on her pale grey, woollen fitted suit, knowing that she looked her best. Underneath she wore a pink and white polka dot blouse, and her little half-hat had a pink feather curled perkily on the side. 'Yes, I used to sit behind you, but I don't think you even knew I existed.'

'Oh, I can't believe that,' John said, then with a small frown he added, 'Wait a minute – yes, I do remember you. Wendy Hall! You were a mousy little thing and a lot different to how you look now.' His hand then flew to his hair again, his expression showing chagrin. 'Christ, sorry, I shouldn't have said that.'

'That's all right, I know I wasn't much to look at.'

'Well, you've certainly blossomed since then,' John said.

'Thank you, kind sir. Now I really must be off.'

'Please stay and have a cup of tea or something,' he said hurriedly.

'If it isn't too much trouble, I'd love to,' Wendy said with what she hoped was a captivating smile.

'Millie, put the kettle on,' John urged.

'Yes, *sir*,' his sister said sarcastically.

'Sorry, love, I didn't mean to make it sound like an order.'

'That's all right,' Millie said, adding, 'aren't you going to offer Wendy a seat?'

As she sat at the kitchen table Wendy fought to control her trembling hands. She couldn't believe it; she was actually sitting opposite John Pratchett, and hoped she wasn't imagining the look of admiration in his eyes.

Chapter Eight

It was three days later and as the family finished their dinner, Alfie Pratchett said, 'The Co-op insurance money won't stretch to an expensive funeral.'

At last, John thought, relieved his father was clear-headed enough to make the arrangements. 'Why didn't you tell me you were sorting the funeral out when you went off early today?'

'I don't 'ave to account to you for my movements.'

John's lips tightened. His father's behaviour had been almost impossible since the inquest. Was it guilt, he wondered, sure his father was hiding something. When they were out on the round he seemed edgy, taciturn, but for now, swallowing his suspicions he asked, 'What have you arranged so far?'

'I picked up the Death Certificate, and then went down to the undertaker's to choose a . . . a coffin. I've ordered one car, and other than that, the undertaker handles it all.'

'What about the service?' Millie asked.

'The priest from St Margaret's is coming to talk to us and he'll be here shortly.'

'Blimey, Dad, couldn't you have told us earlier?' John said.

'I'm telling you now, ain't I.'

'And flowers?' Millie asked. 'What about flowers?'

'I'll leave that to you, but just order one wreath from all of us.'

'But . . .'

'You heard me, girl, now shut up and leave me in peace.'

Shortly afterwards, there was a knock on the door and Millie answered it to find a young priest standing on the step. 'Er . . . come in, Father,' she invited, standing to one side.

The atmosphere was strained as they discussed the service, with

Millie and John embarrassed by their father's behaviour. He made it plain that he had no interest in choosing the order of hymns, or the reading, and left the selection to them. It was a relief when the priest left, and soon after that their father rose to his feet. 'Right, that's done, now I'm off out.'

'Wait, we've still got things to sort out. What about laying on some food for afterwards?' John said.

'I don't see why we should. No, we'll just keep it a quiet family affair.'

'What, just the three of us? Dad, you can't mean that. What about the neighbours?'

Alfie Pratchett scowled. 'Sod the lot of them. They're just a load of bleedin' gossips.'

'They're not all like that, Dad.'

'Are you deaf? I've told you the insurance money won't run to feeding half the street.'

'Surely we could invite just a few and lay on some sandwiches or something.'

'Sod it, do what you like, but don't expect me to put any money towards it.'

As the door shut behind his father, John turned to Millie. 'How much will it cost to lay on a bit of grub?'

'If I just do paste sandwiches and perhaps a bit of ham and pickle, it shouldn't run to much.'

'Right, I'll drop you a few extra bob to cover it. Now I'm going to smarten myself up and then I'm off out too.'

'Oh, where are you going?'

'I've made a date with Wendy Hall and I'm taking her to the pictures.'

As John left the house he wondered if he had made the right decision. Yes, he was attracted to Wendy, but should he be going out on a date so soon after his mother's death? The thought worried him until he reached the cinema, but seeing Wendy already there waiting he couldn't help feeling gratified by the delight on her face as their eyes met.

'You came then?' she said.

'Did you expect me to stand you up?'

'I thought you might.'

'Now why would you think that? Come on, we'd better join the queue if we want a decent seat,' and taking her arm he moved forward. Blimey, she looked gorgeous, her blonde hair shining and blue eyes wide as she looked up at him. She was so tiny, like a little porcelain doll, and he felt a surge of protectiveness. In some ways her colouring reminded him of his mother, and at that thought his eyes darkened with sadness.

'Are you all right, John? You look a bit upset.'

'I'm fine, it's just that we were discussing the arrangements for my mother's funeral before I left home.'

'Oh, you should have said, and if there's anything I can do to help, please don't hesitate to ask. Look, I don't mind missing the film, and if you'd rather put off our date I'll understand.'

Wendy's face was soft with concern, and reaching out John took her hand. 'No, it's all right. The film might just take my mind off things for a while.'

'Well, if you're sure.'

'I'm sure,' he said, thinking that his mother would have approved of this girl. She was nice, really nice, and as the queue moved forward he still held her tiny hand in his.

As the months passed, Millie observed the growing fondness between her brother and Wendy. At first she was surprised to find herself jealous, but it soon became obvious that John's girlfriend was helping him to deal with his grief. She remembered too what a brick Wendy had been on the day of the funeral, even coming round to help with the sandwiches. Maybe he speaks to her, Millie thought, maybe he tells her how he really feels. There had been so many times when she had tried to talk to John about their mother's death, hoping that it would help to make sense of it all, but he would just shake his head and walk away.

She and Pat had left school at Easter, and as both were staying at home, they often popped into each other's houses during the day for a chat. Now, as Pat spoke, Millie was startled by her friend's words. They sounded intuitive, almost as if Pat had known what she'd been thinking about.

'I see yer brother's still going out with that girl.'

'Yes, and has been since February. It's nearly the end of April, so he's been going out with her for two months.'

'They look odd when you see them together. She's so tiny, and her head only reaches John's shoulder.'

'I know, but Wendy's nice and even though she's a bit bossy, I like her.'

'Oh, by the way,' Pat said, changing the subject. 'I bumped into Dora on the way in. She said Stella Blake's coming home today and that she's made a good recovery.'

'She was kept in hospital for a lot longer than I expected. I should have gone to see her, but what with the inquest and then the funeral . . .'

'She'd understand, Millie.'

'Yes, maybe, but my mother used to do quite a lot for Stella and I should offer to help as she did.'

'There's no need. Dora said she'll be keeping an eye on her from now on, and apparently Cyril Blake is gonna drop her a few bob each week.'

Millie sighed with relief. 'Thank goodness for that. I want to get a job, but with the housework and cooking to do I was worried about finding the time to help Stella.'

'I thought you was gonna stay at home.'

'Not permanently, and listening to Wendy talking about her work at the Exchange has made me realise that I want to get a job too. The house is up to scratch again now, and it would be nice to have a few bob of my own to spend.'

'You're lucky, I wish I could get a job.'

'Well, why don't you?'

' 'Cos I have to be here when me sisters come home from school.'

'What about part-time work?'

'I've thought about that, but there would still be the school holidays. Christ, Millie, I'll miss you if you get a job.'

'We can still see each other in the evenings, and at weekends.'

'I know, but when do I ever get the chance to go out in the evenings? Me dad's down the pub nearly every night, and anyway I can't leave the girls with him.'

'I'll still come round to see you once he's gone out, but surely it wouldn't hurt to leave your sisters once in a while?'

'No, I can't risk it. My dad's a brute and you've no idea what he's capable of.'

'My father's getting just as bad and most nights he's down the pub too. He comes home absolutely paralytic, and not only that, with what he's spending on beer we're finding money a bit tight. It's as much as I can do to get the housekeeping money out of him every week. John is having to tip up more than he used to, and with him courting, it isn't fair.'

'I never thought yer dad would turn to drink, Millie.'

'No, neither did I, and I must admit I'm nervous of him when he comes home drunk. The least little thing seems to spark him off.'

'Yeah, but at least you've got John to protect you. Anyway, I'd best be off 'cos the girls are due home soon. I'll see you later.'

Millie walked Pat to the door and then returning to the kitchen she looked around the now spotless room. It was too early to start preparing the dinner, and with nothing else to do it reinforced her desire to get a job. It had been all right staying at home for a while, but now she had just too much time to think.

'John, I want to get a job,' Millie said as she cleared the kitchen table after dinner on Friday evening.

'Yeah, right,' her brother said from behind his newspaper.

'John, are you listening to me?'

With a sigh he lowered the paper. 'Yes, but what's the hurry?'

'I need to get out of the house. Yes, I do the housework and cooking, but being at home gives me too much time to brood. Mind you, I don't really know what sort of job I want.'

'You could try some of the local factories, or what about working in a shop?'

'I suppose so, but I'd love to work in an office.'

'Well, you should have tried harder to pass your eleven-plus. Yeah, all right, don't look at me like that, I know I left school at fifteen too. What about trying for the GPO like Wendy?'

'No, thanks. After hearing what she puts up with I don't think it's for me.'

'Yeah, she does make you laugh with some of her stories,' John observed, smiling fondly. His eyes then widened. 'Here, I've just remembered. Mr Jenkins lost yet another secretary, so why don't you apply for the job?'

'But I can't even type.'

'He doesn't know that, and surely it can't be that hard to learn?'

'No, perhaps not. Do you really think I'd stand a chance?'

'You won't know unless you try, and anyway you've nothing to lose. If you don't get it, then look for something else.'

'All right, I will,' Millie decided. 'I'll ring to ask for an interview on Monday morning, but God knows what I'll wear. I haven't got any smart clothes.'

'As long as you're clean and tidy I don't suppose it will matter.'

Millie held back the retort that sprang to her lips. When was the last time she had any new clothes? She'd hoped for a couple of outfits when leaving school, but then, with all that had happened, clothes were the last thing on her mind. Dare she ask her father for some money to buy an outfit? She shook her head, quickly realising that he'd refuse. Sometimes she felt that he hated her, resented even having to feed her, so to ask for clothes would be hopeless. Oh well, she'd just have to wear her old skirt and blouse, and if she starched them before giving them a good press, they might be presentable. 'Are you going out with Wendy tonight?'

'Yeah, we're going to the pictures to see a musical, and you're coming with us.'

'Coming with you! But . . .'

'No arguments. Wendy said it's about time you got out of the house, and I agree with her. We've got to get on with our lives, love, and it's what Mum would have wanted.'

'It seems too soon, John.'

'Mum's been gone for over three months now, and moping around in here all the time isn't the answer. Anyway, Wendy wants you to come, and small as she is, she's a little firebrand when it comes to getting her own way.'

Perhaps John's right, Millie thought. Maybe it was time to get on with their lives, and at the thought of going to see a musical, her mood lightened.

On Sunday, Millie tackled the bedrooms, and finding her father's trousers flung across the bed she picked them up, giving them a good shake before going to hang them up. It was as she rifled inside the wardrobe for a hanger that she noticed her mother's clothes – clothes that hadn't been touched since she died. Millie flicked through them, tears filling her eyes at the memories they evoked, and then her brow creased. Almost at the far end of the rail she came across a blue wool suit, one that she couldn't remember her mother wearing. It was old-fashioned, a relic of the 1940s, but even so Millie recognised the quality. She fingered the material before raking further, finding another suit, this one dark green. It was of equally good quality, and as she stroked the material a thought entered her mind, one that made her draw in a deep gulp of air. They were smart, very smart, and perfect for working in an office. With a little bit of alteration they could be brought up to date, but could she wear them, and come to that, would her father allow it?

Taking the blue suit she went downstairs, deciding to see what John would say, and as she entered the kitchen she held it up in front of her. 'I haven't got anything to wear for the interview with Mr Jenkins. Do . . . do you think Dad would mind if I made use of this?'

Her brother's brows furrowed. 'I haven't seen that before. Where did you get it?'

'I found it in the wardrobe – it must have belonged to Mum.'

'Are you sure? I don't remember her wearing it.'

'It's very old-fashioned and must be years old.'

'I'm sorry, love. When you asked me what to wear for the interview, I should have realised that you'd want something smart. I wish I could offer to buy you something, but to be honest I just can't afford it.'

'I don't expect you to buy me clothes.'

'Listen, if I didn't recognise that suit as belonging to Mum, I doubt Dad will. Why don't you just take it, along with anything else you can find, and say nothing to him about it.'

'Are you sure?'

'Yes, and anyway I'm sure Mum would want you to have it.'

'All right, I will,' Millie said, and clutching the suit to her chest she ran back upstairs.

Chapter Nine

On Tuesday morning Millie awoke just after dawn. She hurried downstairs and, preparing breakfast, she found herself humming a tune from the film they'd seen the previous Friday night. With a start the sound died in her throat. How could she sing? It seemed obscene when their mother had been dead for such a short time.

Her mood darkened as she tackled both John's and her father's sandwiches, but then her brother appeared, his hair tousled and his braces round his hips.

'Dad not up?' he asked.

'No, and you'd better give him a shout.'

'He was as drunk as a skunk again last night and I've just about had enough. It's as much as he can do to complete our rounds now, and if the boss gets wind of it there could be trouble.'

'Don't forget – I've got an interview with Jack Jenkins today,' Millie reminded her brother.

'I haven't forgotten, but be warned, he's not the easiest man to work for.'

'I've only seen him a couple of times. When I used to help groom Samson on Sundays he was never in the yard, but you're confusing me, John. It was you who suggested that I apply for the job, and now it sounds as if you're trying to put me off.'

'I'm just warning you, although despite his reputation I've always found Jack Jenkins fair. Anyway, if you don't like working for him you can always leave, and believe me, he's used to that. Now, I'd best get the old man up or we'll be late.'

John then went back upstairs to wake their father and when he returned his face was tight with annoyance. 'He stinks like a polecat, and it took ages to rouse him. We've got a big load on today, but there's no chance of him pulling his weight. This can't go on, Millie.'

'I know, but what can we do?'

'I dunno, but I'm just about sick of it. When he first started drinking I knew it was because he couldn't face up to Mum's death, and I understood. But as the weeks pass he's getting worse and worse. At first the other coalmen rallied round to cover up for him, but I don't think they'll keep it up for much longer.'

'Perhaps you should try talking to him,' Millie suggested as she wrapped the sandwiches in greaseproof paper. Her father then appeared, putting an end to their conversation, and plonking his porridge in front of him she headed for the bathroom. The smell emanating from his body was disgusting, and no wonder John was fed up with working alongside him. Yet even as this thought crossed her mind, Millie berated herself. Dad was still grieving, they all were, and though she couldn't condone his behaviour, she understood it. He was drowning his sorrow with drink, and could she really blame him?

Millie was relieved when they both left, glad to have the house to herself whilst she prepared for the interview. She had altered the suits and thought they looked quite smart. Today she was wearing the dark green one.

Now, just before eleven o'clock, she hurried along Harmond Street, her stomach fluttering with nerves.

It was quiet when she entered the coal yard, as all the men were out on their rounds; with trepidation she approached the office, which was nothing more than a pre-fabricated one-storey building.

'Come in,' a voice growled when she knocked tentatively on the door.

As Millie stepped inside, her eyes widened at the sight that greeted her and she blinked rapidly. Jack Jenkins was sitting behind a desk, yelling into a telephone, his hand raking through his steel-grey hair in agitation. Millie had to cover her mouth to hide her smile when she saw that one side of his greasy hair was now standing on end, while the other remained plastered down. His face was red, his eyes wild as he continued to yell, and with his other hand flapping, he gestured that she should sit down.

Millie perched on the edge of a chair placed in front of the desk, pulling her skirt over her knees self-consciously. Was the skirt too short, she wondered now, realising that she hadn't thought about it rising up when she sat down. Feeling her face flood with colour, she kept her eyes lowered as she listened to the man ranting and raving.

'Now look here, the coal train was due two hours ago, and I've got deliveries to fill. What did you say? Oh, it left the pits and Gateshead on time? Well, it can't have disappeared into thin air so I suggest you find out just *when* I can expect it!' He then slammed the receiver down and with his face still livid with temper he barked, 'Well, what do you want?'

'I . . . I'm here for an interview.'

As if to calm himself, Jack Jenkins took in a great gulp of air, and this his eyes roamed over her before he said, 'Christ, with all that's going on in the yard I'd forgotten you were coming, and our first batch of lorries are arriving shortly.'

Millie stared at the man; her eyes still wide. She didn't understand what he was talking about – lorries, what lorries?

Before he could say anything further the telephone rang again, and heaving a sigh he grabbed the receiver. 'Yes, this is Jack Jenkins, what can I do for you? No, I'm *not* interested in buying more vehicles – I haven't had the first ones yet.' As he impatiently slammed the handset down again, his eyes returned to Millie. 'Right, remind me. What's your name?'

'Millie Pratchett.'

The telephone rang yet again, and looking as if he was about to explode with exasperation he picked it up. 'For God's sake not now, Lettie, I'm up to my eyes in it! No, I may not be home for dinner. What? Oh bloody hell, I forgot the Hethringtons are coming. You'll just have to cancel.' Millie watched his face suffuse with colour again, before he yelled, 'I don't care if you lose face, Lettie. My business is more important than your upstart friends,' and then with a terse goodbye he banged the receiver onto the cradle.

With another great gulp of air his vivid blue eyes alighted on Millie, and then he said, 'Right, you're Alfie Pratchett's daughter and you left school in March, is that right?'

'Er . . . er . . . yes.'

'I wouldn't usually consider a school-leaver, but it seems the Labour Exchange has given up on me and refused to send anyone else. Without a secretary I'm in a bit of a fix, so can you start work right away?'

'I . . . I suppose so.'

'Good girl. Right, you're only fifteen so the wages will be one pound fifteen shillings a week. Of course if you stick it, which I doubt, the pay will gradually go up. I haven't got time to explain the job to you now, so just answer the telephone and take messages.' And with his arm gesturing to another desk set against the wall he added, 'That one's yours, and there's a few bits and pieces that need typing. Do the best you can, but if you can't understand my handwriting they'll have to wait because I won't be in the office much today. Once the lorries have arrived – and the coal train, I hope – I've got to go to the bank. After that, I've arranged to see a couple of potential customers.'

Millie gawked at Jack Jenkins, hardly taking in his rush of words. Typing, yes of course there was typing, and she prayed to God she could master it. But what if she couldn't? The man reminded her of a great big grizzly bear, and if she failed she dreaded his reaction. She pinched her lower lip between her teeth, endeavouring to stop it trembling, and hoped that her fear didn't show.

'Christ, you look like a frightened rabbit, and I can't see you lasting long. No one ever does.'

'Wh . . . what?' Millie managed to stammer.

'Nobody can stick it out with me and you may as well know why from the start. I'm a bully and a brute – at least, that's what the last girl said. The one before that couldn't stand my so-called bad language, and her predecessor my wife got rid of. You see, she was far too pretty.' He ran his eyes over Millie again before commenting, 'Well, at least she won't be able to say that about you.' His hand flew to his hair again, and he had the grace to look apologetic. 'See what I mean? My mouth always runs away with me. I'm sorry though, I shouldn't have said that.'

Millie stared at this great hulk of a man and found that despite what he'd said, she liked him. 'It's all right, it doesn't matter. I know I'm no oil painting.'

The two gazed at each other, neither speaking, and in that moment Millie realised that she had no fear of this man. There was something about him, something that inspired trust, and to her surprise she felt the urge to walk into his arms, to be held and comforted by his bearlike bulk. If she could have chosen a father, she would have chosen someone like Jack Jenkins.

He spoke again, his voice softer now. 'Right then, you can hang your jacket up over there.'

After removing her coat, Millie sat apprehensively at the desk, and licking her lips nervously she eyed the typewriter. As she stared at the top row of lettered keys her brows creased with puzzlement. Q W E R T Y. Why weren't they in alphabetical order? Below, were two further rows of keys, equally jumbled, and her heart sank. How on earth was she going to type the letters lying on her desk? God, she didn't even know how to put paper into the machine!

'Is something wrong?'

Millie jumped as Mr Jenkins spoke, and trying to hide her confusion she said, 'Oh no, it's only that this typewriter is a little different from the one I used at school.'

'It's the latest model and I think there's a book of instructions somewhere in your desk.' He pushed back his chair, adding as he stood up, 'I'm sure you'll manage. Right now I've got to get these lorries sorted out, and as I said, after that I've got customers to deal with. I doubt you'll see me until late this afternoon, so keep a list of phone calls and take down any urgent messages.'

'Yes sir,' Millie said primly, relieved that she'd have a chance to study the typewriter. As soon as the door closed behind Jack Jenkins she began to rifle through her desk for the instructions, and on finding the booklet she read it avidly, hoping that it would give her a chance to master the machine.

Four hours later, and Millie had a bin full of discarded attempts at typing when Mr Jenkins returned to the office.

'What do you call this?' he asked, his face a picture as he

surveyed her latest effort. 'Why didn't you tell me that you can't type?'

'You didn't ask,' she replied, her eyes like saucers as she waited for him to explode.

Instead, to her surprise, he roared with mirth, an infectious sound that had her joining in. But then, with the frustration of spending hours trying to master the machine, her laughter turned hysterical as she was racked with uncontrollable sobs.

'Come on, just because you can't type it isn't the end of the world,' Jack said, looking at her worriedly as he handed her a huge white handkerchief.

Scrubbing at her face while he pulled up a chair and sat down beside her, Millie fought to bring herself under control. When she finally managed to stop crying, Jack said, 'It isn't just the typing that's making you cry, is it? I know you lost your mother recently and that must have been terrible for you.'

For some inexplicable reason his words set off an avalanche and Millie found herself gabbling, pouring out her grief, talking to this man about her feelings as she had never talked before. When she stopped there was an embarrassed silence and Millie couldn't look Jack Jenkins in the face. Whatever had come over her? Well, she'd ruined everything now, and rising quickly to her feet she hurried across the room to get her jacket.

'And where do you think you're going?'

'Home,' she croaked. 'I'm sorry for crying like that, and I should have told you that I hadn't learned any office skills at school.'

As she shrugged on her jacket she looked at him warily, surprised to see him smiling. Then, to her amazement he said, 'Well, girl, I didn't really give you a chance to tell me anything, did I? That must have been the shortest interview on record, but things were chaotic this morning and my priority was sorting out the lorries and the customers.'

Jack Jenkins now walked towards his desk, saying cheerfully, 'Listen, love, what jobs need doing in the office I'm sure you can soon learn, even typing. So put your coat back on the hanger and then put the kettle on. I like my tea hot, strong, and with three sugars.'

Chapter Ten

Bertha Hall handed Annie Oliphant a jar of Vick's Vapour Rub. 'Put that on yer chest tonight and it should ease it. Honestly, trust you to get a cold at this time of year.'

'It's my own fault for leaving my vest off. I know it's only the end of April, but the weather is lovely and mild. My mother used to say, "Ne'er cast a clout till May is out", and I should have remembered that.'

Bertha hid a smile. From what she'd seen of Annie's vests they had more holes in them than material, but she kept this thought to herself. It was rare that Annie made any mention of her family and seizing the moment she said, 'Well, if you ask me it sounds like yer mother was a sensible woman.'

'Yes, she was, and that's all I'm going to tell you so don't bother to cross-examine me.'

'Me! When 'ave I ever done that?'

'Often enough.'

'And a fat lot of good it's done me,' Bertha said, grinning widely. 'Anyway, Wendy's due home soon so I'd best be off. Now are you sure there's nothing else I can do for you before I go?'

'No, I'll be fine,' the old lady said, suddenly hit by a bout of coughing.

'You really should see the doctor, Annie.'

'There's nothing much a doctor can do for a cold and I just hope I don't pass it on to you. Now before you go, tell me, is Wendy still seeing that chap?'

'Yeah, and I ain't happy about it. Oh, don't get me wrong, he seems a decent enough chap, but I had hopes of her meeting a nice white-collar worker. My Wendy was always such a precocious child, and then when she asked you for help with her diction I was really chuffed. Somehow I had visions of her aiming higher and making something of her life.'

'If I didn't know you better I'd say you're a snob, Bertha Hall. All right, so he's a coalman, but from what you've told me she's happy – and surely that's what counts?'

'Yeah, I suppose so,' Bertha said, yet knowing her voice lacked enthusiasm. She forced a smile now, saying, 'Right, I'll be over first thing in the morning with a bottle of camphorated oil. Don't forget to put that Vick's on yer chest.'

As she made her way across the landing, Bertha's face was creased with anxiety. She was sure that Annie had more than just a cold, but no amount of nagging would persuade her to see the doctor. The cough had started ages ago – in fact, a couple of days after her eightieth birthday party – and guiltily, Bertha wondered if the room full of cigarette smoke had aggravated the old lady's chest. Her friends Harriet and Maud smoked like trains, and poor Annie had been stuck between them on the sofa. They'd also had one too many glasses of stout and by eleven o'clock had become rowdy, singing some of the old music-hall songs.

Yet Annie had seemed to enjoy herself, Bertha thought as she went into her own flat, and she'd thanked everyone profusely for making her birthday special.

She had barely closed the door behind her when Wendy came in, and startled, she said, 'Oh hello, love. You're early.'

'No, I'm not, Mum. It's nearly six o'clock.'

'Is it? Blimey, I've only just left Annie and didn't realise what the time was. I'd best get yer dinner on.'

'I'm not seeing John tonight so it doesn't matter if dinner's late.'

'Not seeing John? Huh, that makes a change.'

'Please, Mum, stop acting like this. Every time I mention his name you turn sniffy. Why can't you just accept that he's the man for me?'

'The man for you! Blimey, you sound as if you're thinking of marrying the bloke.'

'There's nothing I want more, and if he asked me I'd jump at the chance.'

'B . . . but you hardly know him.'

'Ever since I sat behind him at school, I've always known that he's the one I want.'

'Don't be silly! You were just a kid then, and even now you're far too young to think about marriage. You've hardly lived, girl, and should be seeing other blokes.'

'I've been out with a few, and it didn't work. No, John's the one I love, and whether you like it or not, you've got to accept it, Mum.'

When Millie arrived home from work she kicked off her shoes and immediately began to prepare dinner, thinking that with a job now she'd have to be more organised. In future the veg would have to be prepared the night before, but working full-time and running the house wasn't going to be easy. Still, she liked the job and found it absorbing, so somehow, no matter what, she'd manage.

Her mind turned over the events of the day as she peeled potatoes, and she smiled. Yes, Jack Jenkins swore. Yes, he had a filthy temper, but despite that she liked him, sensing a kind man under the rough exterior.

It was strange to be working in the coal depot, but she hadn't glimpsed John and her father. The office was like another world, insulated from the activities in the yard, and she wondered now why John and her father hadn't mentioned the lorries. The gradual change to motorised vehicles was sure to affect them, and what about the horses?

Only minutes later she heard them both in the outhouse so, quickly putting the potatoes on to boil, she hoped they wouldn't mind that dinner would be late. The kettle began to whistle then, and after filling the large, earthenware brown teapot, she took two mugs from the dresser.

They were just entering the kitchen as Millie poured out the tea, and sighing in unison, both sank onto the fireside chairs.

'What's for dinner, girl?'

'Liver casserole, but it won't be ready for a while.'

'Why?' her father snapped.

'I got the job in the office, and as Jack Jenkins wanted me to start straight away, I've only been home for about twenty minutes. By the way, did you see the new lorries?'

'Sod the lorries. What's this about a job?'

'It was my idea, Dad,' John said.

'Oh yeah? How come *I* wasn't told about it?'

'It only came up on Friday, and let's face it, when are you ever sober enough to discuss anything?'

'I ain't bleedin' drunk when we're working.'

'Maybe not, but you're still not fit to talk to.'

'Shut yer mouth! You're getting too big for your boots lately and I ain't standing for it. Now back to this job. Millie can pack it in 'cos she's needed at home.'

Annoyed that as usual, her father was talking as though she wasn't there, Millie bristled. 'No, Dad, I don't want to.'

'You'll do as I bloody well say!'

'But I can still work and run the house.'

'How come our dinner ain't ready then?'

'Because it's my first day and I haven't got anything organised. Please, Dad, don't make me leave. I . . . I need to get out of the house – surely you can understand that?'

'I said you're needed at home and that's an end to it.'

'Let her keep the job, Dad. If we all muck in a bit, everything will run smoothly.'

'Muck in! What do you mean, muck in? Housework and cooking are woman's work, and it's Millie's responsibility to take over from her mother.'

'Responsibility? You've got the cheek to talk about responsibility when you're running the coal-round into the ground! Hasn't it occurred to you that we need the money you throw over the bar? At least with Millie working there'll be a few extra bob coming in.'

'What I do with my wages is my business, and it wouldn't hurt you to tip up a bit more.'

'I am, but you've been too addled with drink to notice. I'll tell you something else, Dad. I'm sick of carrying you, and either you knock the drinking on the head or I'll find another job.'

'Carrying me! Since when 'ave you carried me? I'm twice the bloody man you are, and don't you forget it. This is my house, and who do you think you are to be making demands? If I want a drink I'll bloody 'ave one and if you don't like it, well, you can get out!'

'Don't push me or I might just do that,' John shouted back, and with a look of disgust on his face he left the room, his footsteps resounding on the stairs.

Millie stood frozen in front of the kitchen table, wondering what her father would do next. Would he turn on her now? She licked her dry lips, jumping with nerves when he suddenly reared up from the chair, red with anger as he shouted, 'Sod the bloody dinner! I'm going out!'

The street door slammed, rattling the glass in the windows, and only moments later John appeared again. Running to his side Millie cried, 'You won't leave home, will you?'

'No, I won't leave, but I meant what I said. Things have got to change or I'll find another job.'

'I suppose I'll have to give my notice in too.'

'No, don't do that. You leave Dad to me.'

'But he said . . .'

'Never mind what he said. You're entitled to work if you want to, and I'll talk to him tomorrow when we're out on the round.'

'All right, if you're sure,' Millie said, hoping that he could persuade their father to let her keep the job. 'Talking about the round, do you know what's going to happen now that Jack Jenkins is changing over to motorised vehicles?'

'We were put in the picture some time ago. Most of the men are happy with the change, although Dad and a couple of others baulked at the idea. The boss said they can carry on using the horses and carts.'

'But for how long?'

'As far as I know, it's for as long as we want, but eventually I suppose they'll be phased out.'

'In that case it might be a good idea if you learn to drive.'

'Yes, I suppose so, but there's no hurry. To be honest I can't imagine delivering coal from a lorry, and prefer going out with good old Samson.'

'It's gone quiet now, but things seem to be going from bad to worse next door, Cyril,' Stella Blake said to her husband.

'It's none of our business, Stel.'

'I know, but from what Dora tells me, Alfie Pratchett is turning into a drunk.' With a sigh, she added, 'Who'd 'ave thought it? He always seemed such a steady chap.'

'He lost his wife, and it's early days yet. You can't blame him for having a few pints.'

'He deserved to lose her!' Stella snapped.

'What's that supposed to mean?'

'Oh nothing, but from what Dora said he's taken to drinking with Billy Benson and rolling home drunk every night. It's those two kids I feel sorry for, and God knows how they're coping.'

'John's a good lad, and he's courting now. Millie will be all right too, so stop worrying.'

'But from what Dor—'

'Dora, Dora, Dora! I'm sick of hearing her bloody name. I pay her a few bob to see to your needs, not to fill your head with gossip.'

Stella flushed. 'But I like to hear what's going on in the street,' she said in a small voice.

'All right, don't get upset, love, but I'd rather Dora didn't worry you with tales about the Pratchetts.'

'You don't understand, Cyril. Eileen was my friend and I feel I should be keeping an eye on her children.'

'They aren't children any more, and anyway there's nothing we can do. Alfie Pratchett will pull himself together. Just give him time.'

Stella said nothing, but she knew her husband was wrong. It was guilt that had driven Alfie to drink and she doubted he'd stop. Something else niggled at her brain, something Eileen had asked her to do before she died, but try as she might she couldn't remember what it was.

She cursed her memory, cursed the stroke that had left her so woolly-minded, and prayed that one day she would remember.

Chapter Eleven

Millie sat at her desk, endeavouring to fiddle a sheet of paper around the roller of her typewriter. John had managed to talk her father round and she'd been working for Jack Jenkins for a month now, but the machine was still the bane of her life. Blast it, she thought as once again the sheet of paper pulled to one side.

Mr Jenkins spoke, his voice a bark. 'Surely you've worked out how to put the paper into that bloody machine by now?'

'Nearly,' she bantered back. 'Just give me another week to get the hang of it.'

'God, I must have been mad when I took you on. You can't type, your filing is atrocious, and you can only just cope with the telephone.'

'Yeah, but I make a great cup of tea.'

Jack grinned, showing his large teeth. 'You've got me there, Millie. Have you done that invoice for Harringtons?'

'Yes, it's on your desk and right under your nose.'

'Less of your lip, madam,' he said, rifling amongst the papers that were piled haphazardly across the wide top, grumbling when he couldn't find what he was looking for.

Millie tutted loudly as she stood up, and crossing to his desk she extracted a buff-coloured file, placing it in front of him. 'Here – and if you didn't make a mess every time I tidy this lot up you'd find things easily.' She pointed her finger, adding, 'I've told you before – the tray on the right contains invoices that are typed up and ready, and the tray in the centre contains things you need to look at. That just leaves the tray on the left for paperwork you've finished with and is awaiting filing.'

'And how do you expect me to remember all that?' he said with a hint of sarcasm.

'They *have* got labels on,' Millie told him primly.

'My God, you're a cheeky piece,' he said, his smile belying the harshness of his tone. 'I don't know why I put up with you.'

'Ditto, I don't know how *I* put up with *you*.'

And so the banter went on as Millie returned to her seat, a grin on her face. She loved her job, loved her boss, and if it weren't for her father's behaviour she could honestly say she was happy, happier than she had been for a long time. When John and Wendy went out they sometimes took her with them, and on other evenings she often sneaked round to Pat's when both their fathers were out. There was only one fly in the ointment, and that was her dread that Jack would find out about her father's drinking. Yes, he had a kind side, but he wouldn't tolerate a man who was still suffering from the effects of alcohol when he took a horse and cart out.

Nowadays it was John who ran the round, and as soon as they left the gates she knew that he took control of Samson. Her brother also did the bulk of the unloading, and looked exhausted when they arrived home each night. It couldn't go on much longer, Millie knew that, and she worried that John would carry out his continuing threat to find another job. If he did that, she doubted her father could manage without him, and what would happen to the round then?

Shaking off her worries and frowning in concentration, Millie began again the task of threading paper into the typewriter. That done, she commenced her slow two-fingered typing, glad that she had shown an interest in English at school because her boss's spelling was terrible. The telephone rang and she picked up the receiver. 'Jack Jenkins, Coal Merchants, how can I help you?'

'I wish to speak to my husband,' the refined voice said frostily.

Millie grimaced. She had only met Mrs Jenkins twice, the first time being a week after she'd started work in the office. It soon became obvious that she'd come to inspect her husband's latest secretary, and after looking Millie over from head to toe, no objections were offered to her employment. Lettie Jenkins was in her late forties and it hadn't taken Millie long to realise that she was a snob, of the worst type – the type that came from a poor background and had risen on the back of her husband's success.

'Well, is he there?'

The sharp voice snapped Millie back to attention. 'Yes, I'll just put you through,' and as she transferred the call, she said, 'Mr Jenkins, your wife is on line one.'

'Blimey, you sound competent at last,' Jack grinned as he picked up his receiver. 'Yes, what is it, Lettie? No, I haven't spoken to the builder yet. There's no hurry to get the extension built and surely it can wait? All right, calm down, I'll ring them today,' he promised, his voice betraying his impatience as he said goodbye and replaced the receiver. Turning to Millie he then said, 'Christ, that bloody woman will be the death of me. Put the kettle on, love, and make the tea good and strong.'

'Yes, Mr Jenkins.'

As Jack followed Millie's movements he mused aloud, 'What does Lettie want a bloody extension for, anyway? Surely two reception rooms and six bedrooms are enough for the pair of us? The woman's never satisfied. We started out with nothing. A two up, two down in Peckham, that's all we had. My father was a bus driver and Lettie's a postman – men who worked hard all their lives.' He shook his head ruefully before adding, 'But Lettie's ashamed of them, ashamed of her roots, and woe betide me if I mention our past to her posh friends.'

As Millie handed him his mug of tea the phone rang. Jack's musing ending as she went to answer it, and finding someone wanting a delivery, she transferred the call to her boss before returning to her desk.

The rest of the day passed without event and at five-thirty she tidied up before taking her coat from the hook. Jack Jenkins was out, so after a quick glance around the office she locked the door behind her. There was only one man left in the yard, the stableman, and Millie tensed. Every time she looked at him he reminded her of a ferret and she knew it was coming – his usual jibe.

'Hello, Olive Oyl, off to see Popeye, are you?'

She ignored him and averting her eyes hurried past, still hearing his laughter as she went through the gate. Why did he have to be so cruel? Yes, she knew she could be likened to Olive Oyl, but who was he to talk? Why was it that some men felt they could call out disparaging remarks despite the fact that many of them were nothing to look at either?

Millie sighed heavily, and pushing the man out of her mind she hurried home. She had a routine now, and one that seemed to be working. With the veg prepared every morning, dinner didn't take long to cook, and with it being Friday evening she would put the washing into soak ready to tackle it on Saturday morning. When that was done she would do housework, leaving upstairs for Sunday. She was managing, just, but ironing was the bane of her life. She hated it, hated the pile of shirts that never seemed to go down.

Her lack of decent clothes was becoming a problem too. It was near the end of May and the weather was warming up, making wool suits unsuitable. She had taken to removing her suit jacket when in the office, but with only two blouses she had to wash them frequently. They were becoming limp and faded, with only a liberal amount of starch making them just about presentable.

By the time her father and John arrived home, the haddock poached in milk was almost ready and she sighed with relief, glad that for once her father would have no cause for complaint. As they sat down Millie slid the fish onto their plates, and taking a seat opposite her brother she studied him worriedly. Lines of exhaustion were visible on his face, and when their eyes met she smiled at him sympathetically. 'Are you seeing Wendy tonight?'

'Yes, we're going dancing. We've tackled the waltz and quickstep, but now Wendy is determined that I learn how to tango.'

'That girl seems to have you wrapped round her little finger.'

'Why is that, Dad? Just because I'm learning to dance?'

'No, there ain't nothing wrong with that, but you're hardly in these days.'

'Oh, and when are *you* ever in to notice that? By the way, have you given Millie the housekeeping?'

'No. I'll give it to her when I'm good and ready.'

Millie bit her lip worriedly. He father hardly gave her any money now, and last week he hadn't given her any. She'd used all her wages to get the shopping in, her choices frugal, and worried that John was nearing the end of his tether, she hadn't told him. But what her brother stumped up didn't cover the rent, and now they were many weeks behind, with John's money only paying off some of the arrears.

Her brother now pulled out his wage-packet, and checking the contents he passed three pounds across the table. Yet even as she picked it up, Millie knew it wouldn't be enough.

'Come on, Dad, stump up,' John said.

'That's it! I've had enough! I've told you before that I don't take orders from you, and you're getting too bloody big for yer boots.' Thrusting his half-eaten plate of food to one side, Alfie rose to his feet and with a snarl grabbed his jacket, the street door slamming behind him.

Millie's heart sank. John had driven their father to the pub and she doubted now that any money would be forthcoming. How on earth was she going to manage? 'You shouldn't have said anything, John.'

'Shouldn't I? And why not? His wage-packet is thicker than mine, but it's me that does all the work. I'm fed up with it, Millie, and I'm definitely going to start looking around for another job. Yes, I know I've threatened it before, but this time I really mean it.' Thrusting back his chair he stood up, and without another word, stomped upstairs.

'Wait! What about the coal-round?' Millie cried, but no answer was forthcoming.

On Sunday morning the atmosphere was still strained and Millie was relieved when her father left to go for a lunchtime drink. She had finished cleaning both hers and John's rooms, and was now going to tackle her father's. The musty smell made her nose wrinkle as she entered, and crossing to the window she threw it open, letting in fresh air.

Clothes lay strewn across the floor, his bed a heap of jumbled sheets and blankets. With a sigh she decided to sort out the clothing first, most obviously destined for the wash-bin. Thrown in the corner she saw her father's suit jacket, and seeing the state it was in, Millie's lips tightened. It would need a good press before it was fit to wear again and grimly she added it to the pile of washing to take downstairs.

An hour later Millie was standing at the kitchen table ready to tackle the hated ironing, whilst John sat in a fireside chair reading the Sunday paper. Her father's jacket was on top of the pile, and before placing a wet piece of cloth over it to press out the creases, she checked the pockets. Her hands found something, and puzzled she pulled an envelope out of the inside pocket. Written on the front was just one word – *Alfie* – and she was sure it was her mother's writing. For a moment she hesitated, wondering if she dared to open it, but her curiosity was so great, she pulled out the sheet of paper.

After quickly reading it, the shock was like a knife to her heart.

'No! Oh no!' she cried.

'What's the matter?'

'It's, it's . . . Oh John, it's from Mum!' Millie sobbed. 'It's a note she left before she died.'

'What? Show me!'

After John had read the note there was a stunned silence, but then his eyes blazed with anger. 'He drove her to it! The bastard! My God, I'll never forgive him for this!'

Millie stared at her brother, her thoughts echoing his. Yes, their mother may have taken her own life, but now they knew it was their father who had caused it.

'I can't believe this, Millie. When Dad's drunk, he continuously whines with self-pity about how Mum left him. Yet all this time he's known that he was to blame. An abortion – he was forcing her to get rid of the baby, our brother or sister. Dear God, Mum must have been going out of her mind. Why didn't I see it? Why?'

'I knew something was wrong too, but I just thought she was ill,' Millie wept. 'I overheard a strange conversation the night before Mum died, but at the time it didn't make sense. Dad was telling her that she had to see someone the next day, and that he'd already paid the money.' Millie could barely say the words. 'Oh John, do you think he was talking about the abortion?'

'Could be, and you should have told me about it,' he said harshly.

'But I didn't know what he meant!' Millie choked, wracked with guilt.

'Look, don't cry,' John said gruffly. 'I'm sorry, how could you have known what he was trying to make her do? The bastard!' he spat again. 'That's it – that's the final straw!' Pacing the room, his face white with anger, John suddenly spun around. 'I've got to get out of here, Millie. I'm going round to Wendy's. If I see Dad at the moment, I'll kill him.'

'Take me with . . .' Millie cried, her sentence dying on her lips as her brother stormed out.

As John strode along Harmond Street his face was still pale with shock and his thoughts racing. He had to get out; had to get away from his father or he wouldn't be responsible for his actions. Yet without finding another job first, he wouldn't be able to afford the rent on a flat. His mind grappled with the problem and just before he reached Wendy's door, it came up with the answer. Yes, if only for the short term it could solve his problem, and not only that, it would give him the chance to save a few bob.

'John, I wasn't expecting you!' Wendy exclaimed as she opened the door to his knock.

'I know, but can you come out for a walk? We . . . we need to talk.'

'Oh, is something wrong?'

'You could say that.'

'All right, hang on, I'll just tell my mother.'

John watched Wendy as she tripped lightly back upstairs, admiring her trim little figure. God, he would miss her – and would she wait for him? In such a short time she had come to mean so much to him, but if he was out of the picture there were sure to be other blokes sniffing around. Yet he was too young to contemplate settling down, wasn't he? He saw her come running back downstairs, her lovely blonde curls bouncing, and in that moment he came to a decision.

'Right, I'm ready,' she said, closing the street door firmly behind her.

John tucked her arm in his and they walked a little way along Lavender Hill before turning into Elspeth Road, heading for

Clapham Common. The sky was blue with just a few puffs of high, wispy clouds, and as they reached the common John steered Wendy towards the nearest bench, his hand running through his hair in agitation as they sat down.

'What is it, love?' she asked apprehensively.

John told her briefly what had happened, watching her pretty blue eyes stretch with disbelief, and then said, 'So you can see why I want to get away.'

'Yes, of course. I suppose you could find somewhere else to live.'

'Until I find another job I can't afford the rent, but I think I've come up with a solution.'

'Oh good.'

'You may not think so when I've told you what it is. You see, I've decided to join the Merchant Navy.'

'Oh John! You'll be away for ages!' Wendy cried, her expression aghast.

'I'll only make one trip, and I'll save every penny I earn,' he promised earnestly. 'Will you wait for me, and when I come back, can . . . can we get engaged?'

Wendy smiled with delight, throwing herself into his arms. 'Yes, please, I'd love to.'

He kissed her passionately and for a while they sat entwined until John gently released her. 'I'd best be off, darling. The sooner I get to the London Docks the sooner I'll find out if I can sign on straight away.'

'What will you do if you can't?'

'I don't know, but I'll cross that bridge when I come to it. I know a bloke who signed on and left almost immediately, but I doubt I'll have that sort of luck. There's one more thing. Will you keep an eye on Millie for me?'

'Of course I will, but John – I'm going to miss you so much.'

'It won't be for ever, and when I return we'll have a lifetime together. Come on, I'll take you home, but don't worry, I'll be round to see you again as soon as I get back from the docks.'

Chapter Twelve

Eyes brimming with unhappiness, Millie watched as her brother heaved two suitcases down the stairs before he dumped them with relief in the small hall.

'Please, John, please don't go,' she begged.

'I've got to, Millie. I've told you, if I stay here any longer I'll kill him. He drove Mum into taking her own life and I'll never forgive him for that.'

'I know how you feel, but did Mum really have to kill herself? All right, Dad tried to make her have an abortion, but was it reason enough to do what she did?'

'You know how religious Mum was. She would never have agreed to ending the life of a baby.'

'Then why didn't she just leave him?'

'I don't know.' John's face was etched with pain and blinking rapidly he added, 'I knew she was unhappy about something and since she died I've been eaten up with guilt. I should have made her tell me what was wrong, but instead I let her fob me off with tales about being tired.'

'I still think she could have found another way.'

'Maybe, but her mind must have snapped or something.'

Millie gazed at her brother. Why had it taken them so long to discuss their feelings? Why now, when he was leaving? She too was eaten up with guilt, guilt and anger, but they had never spoken of it before. It was a relief to bring it out into the open, and running to her brother she threw her arms around his waist. 'Please don't go,' she repeated. 'I can't bear to lose you too, and I'm scared of Dad, scared of what he'll do if you're not here.'

'For God's sake, don't do this, don't try to stop me by using emotional blackmail. I've got to go and you can leave too, there's nothing to stop you.'

'How can I leave? I earn less than two pounds a week, and anyway I can't legally leave home until I'm sixteen.'

'Well, until then you'll have to learn to stand up for yourself. You're not a child now, Millie.'

She was shocked by the indifference in her brother's voice. John had always looked after her, stood up for her, but now he was just walking away, leaving her to cope with their father. She reached out to grasp his arm. 'Dad will lose the coal-round if you leave, you know he will.'

'I don't care about the bloody round, and he deserves to lose it. I'm sick of it . . . sick of trying to cover up for him. Christ, lately I've been ashamed to be seen with him and he's getting steadily worse. He's a disgrace, and the talk of the depot.'

'What about Samson? Who'll look after him?'

John laughed derisively, his mouth wide. 'A horse! Now you're trying to keep me here by using the horse! Oh, you're priceless, Millie.'

'Please don't laugh at me. Dad's going to go mad when he finds out you've gone, and you know how unpredictable he is lately. What if he becomes violent?'

Her brother's face softened, and for one heart-stopping moment she thought he was going to stay, but then he leaned forward to gently stroke her cheek. 'Dad only turns nasty when he's had too much to drink, and if he tries to hit you, stand up to him. Throw something at him, because when he's drunk he's so unsteady on his legs that a feather would knock him over.'

'How long will you be away?'

'Probably for a couple of months, but I'm only doing the one trip.'

'Will you come home again then?'

'No, I'm sorry, I couldn't live with Dad. But if it really gets too bad for you, then leave. I don't think Dad will stop you, and before you tell me you can't afford it again, didn't you tell me Pat next door wants to leave home too?'

At Millie's nod he said, 'Get a room together and share the rent. Between the two of you, it shouldn't be hard to manage.'

When Millie realised that nothing she could say would persuade her brother to stay, she flung herself back into his arms. 'All right, you won't live here again, but will you come to see me when you get back?'

His arms enfolded her as he said with a crack in his voice, 'You know I will, and in the meantime I've asked Wendy to keep an eye on you.'

'I still can't believe you're joining the Merchant Navy.'

'I had to do something to get away. I went to the London Docks and luckily got signed up straight away. Now I'm off to Southampton to pick up my ship.' He smiled ruefully. 'Let's face it, I'm used to shovelling coal, so being a stoker won't be so bad.'

John leaned forward now, and after picking up one of his cases he opened the street door. He then grabbed the other one, his voice thick as he said, 'Bye, Millie, and remember what I've told you. Either stand up to Dad, or leave home.'

Millie felt her chest tightening in panic as her brother stepped outside. He turned, saying briefly, 'Take care of yourself, love, and go to Wendy if you have any problems.'

She tried to speak, tried to say goodbye, but her throat was constricted with emotion. *Oh John, John, don't leave me,* she agonised as without a backward glance he walked away. 'No,' she managed to whimper, reaching out both arms beseechingly, but it was too late . . . he had turned the corner.

Millie slowly walked back to the kitchen, and pulling out a chair she sat with her elbows on the table, hands held over her face. John took Wendy out most nights so hadn't been around that much lately, but at least he was there at night and that had helped somewhat to keep her fear of their father in abeyance. What would happen now? Tears threatened and she closed her eyes against them.

Oh Mum, why did you leave us? And now John's gone too, and how will Dad react when he finds out?

For an hour she sat there, but then heard a commotion in the street. She jumped to her feet, rushing outside to see who was causing it, and saw Billy Benson with her father, staggering home from the pub, both drunk and holding each other up as they reeled from pavement to road.

Jessie Hardcastle from number four was standing outside, shouting at them as she indicated the mess on her step. 'Look what yer father's done,' she cried when she saw Millie. 'He's been sick all over me doorstep!'

'I'm sorry, Mrs Hardcastle. I . . . I'll clean it up,' she called, her face bright red with embarrassment.

'I should think so too. He's a bloody disgrace, him and Billy Benson. Three o'clock on a Sunday afternoon and look at the state of them!'

'Shut yer gob, woman,' Billy Benson threatened.

'Don't you dare talk to me like that! I'll get my husband to sort you out,' Jessie cried indignantly.

'Don't make me laugh. Yer old man couldn't knock the skin off a rice pudding,' Alfie shouted derisively. Then, as he neared the front door, his face broke into a sneer. 'Get in, you!' he said, pushing Millie roughly inside.

She stumbled backwards, not only from the effects of his shove, but by the smell of his breath and rank body odour. 'See to my dinner, girl!' he ordered, following her through the door, turning on an afterthought to say to Billy Benson, 'I'll see you later, mate.'

'Yeah, see yer, Alfie,' Billy slurred as he made for his own street door.

Millie crossed to the stove, removing the plate that she'd placed on a saucepan of simmering water, and after lifting the lid that covered it, she was thankful to see that the dinner hadn't completely dried up.

Holding the hot plate with a tea towel she placed it carefully on the table, arranged the cutlery, and then placed the salt and pepper within easy reach.

'Where's the mint sauce?'

There wasn't any mint sauce, she'd forgotten it, and holding her breath she said nervously, 'Er . . . we haven't got any, Dad.'

He threw her a look of disgust, but to Millie's relief he said nothing as he picked up his knife and fork. She made to move away, but his voice stilled her.

'Where's John? Out with his fancy woman, is he?'

He had to know sometime, so should she tell him now and get

it over with? After eating he'd fall asleep as usual, and then wake up in a foul mood. He seemed quite mellow now, so perhaps this was the best time. 'John's gone, Dad.'

'Gone! What do you mean – gone? Where?'

'He . . . he's joined the Merchant Navy.'

'Don't be stupid, girl. He wouldn't do that. My boy wouldn't leave me in the lurch.'

'He . . . he has, Dad.'

For a few moments there was absolute silence as her father stared at her, his mouth gaping with shock. Then, without warning, he sprang to his feet, and placing his hands under the tabletop he upturned it, his plate, cutlery and the cruet set crashing onto the floor. 'I'll bloody kill him!' he yelled, spittle flying out of his mouth.

Millie backed off as her father's eyes narrowed. 'Did you know about it? Did you know he was leaving?'

She stared at him frantically, her brain refusing to function as she edged slowly away.

'Answer me, you ugly thin-faced cow!'

'I . . . I only found out this morning,' she stammered, and as her father lunged towards her, fists raised, she fled the room.

Millie scrambled upstairs and reaching her bedroom, she slammed the door. Swiftly grabbing a chair she jammed it under the handle, praying it would keep her father out, and then stood back, expecting the door to be kicked in at any moment.

After a few heart-stopping seconds, Millie's brow furrowed. There was no sound of pursuit, no shouting. She waited a few more minutes, then biting her lips nervously she removed the chair before cautiously opening the door. He wasn't there and the house was strangely quiet. Tiptoeing downstairs she peeped around the kitchen door, the breath leaving her body in a rush of relief. Her father was asleep, slumped in a fireside chair, his mouth slack as he snored loudly.

Oh thank God, she thought, realising that he'd probably been too drunk to pursue her. With any luck he'd sleep for several hours, and as Millie stared with dismay at the state of the room she saw that his plate had smashed, gravy seeping into the clippy rug she could remember her mother making with scraps of rag.

The salt pot had survived the fall, but the pepper pot was shattered.

She couldn't risk clearing up the mess in case it woke her father, and after a last disconsolate look around the kitchen she returned to her bedroom.

Millie slumped on the side of her bed, dreading the punishment she might receive when her father woke up. John should have told their father himself, instead of leaving her to face the music, and she felt a surge of anger at her brother's selfishness.

She suddenly heard tapping on her bedroom wall, and recognising Pat's signal she threw the window open. Leaning out Millie craned her neck to see her friend, and as expected, Pat was doing the same.

'Millie,' she hissed. 'My dad's so drunk he's passed out. I want to talk to you but I can't leave the kids. Can you come round?'

'My dad's out cold too, but how can I come round? Your father doesn't let you invite people in and he'll go mad if he wakes up.'

'He'll be asleep for ages yet. Please come round, it's important.'

'All right, I'll be with you in a minute,' she called, ducking her head back in and closing the window.

As Millie made her way to Pat's house she struggled to put her own troubles to one side. Her friend had looked so distressed, and as she knocked softly on the street door, she wondered what was wrong.

'We'll have to talk quietly,' Pat said as she ushered Millie into the kitchen.

Pat's two sisters, Bessie and Janet, were sitting in a corner, playing a make-believe game of shops, bits of paper torn into squares for notes and tiddly-winks for coins. Janet was the eldest at ten years old, Bessie eight, and as there was a gap in ages between these two little girls and their big sister, Pat had become like a mother to them. Their voices were little more than whispers as they pretended that one was a customer and the other the shopkeeper.

'Hello, girls,' Millie said.

Both looked up, but just stared at Millie without answering and she was struck by their unnatural behaviour as they went back to their game.

'Sit down,' Pat whispered, indicating a chair.

'What is it? What do you want to talk to me about?' Millie asked, keeping her voice low.

'I saw John leaving with two suitcases earlier. Has he left home?'

'Yes, he's joined the Merchant Navy.'

'Christ, that means you ain't got anyone to protect you now. Your dad came home drunk and I heard him yelling at you, then there was an awful racket. Did he do anything to you? I mean, are you all right?'

'I'm fine, but I had to tell him about John leaving and I must admit it was hairy for a while. He chucked his dinner all over the place, but he was too drunk to do anything else and passed out.'

'I can't believe that John left you to tell him. Your brother used to be so protective of you, and he must've known your dad would go mental.'

'Well, I must admit I was scared for a while. John said I should stand up to him, but I don't think I've got the nerve.'

Pat's smile was more like a grimace. 'Do you know, I've always been envious of you. Your mum was lovely, and you had John to look out for you too, but now . . .' Her voice trailed off.

Surprised, Millie said, 'Envious of *me*! I didn't know you felt like that.'

'Why should you? It ain't something I'd admit to . . . until now.'

Millie shook her head, unable to make sense of this strange conversation, but then Pat spoke again, her face set and hard.

'Men are bastards, and I'm trying to warn you. Your mum's dead, and now that John's gone you'd better get out too. If you don't, your dad will start on you.'

'John suggested that I share a place with you. Are you still going to leave home?'

'There's no chance of that.'

'But before you left school you used to talk about finding your own flat.'

'That was just a silly fantasy, something to dream about to get me through each day. The reality is I can't leave . . . it's impossible.'

'It needn't be. John's right, we could live together and share the rent.'

'You don't understand. I can't leave me sisters.'

'But you talked about taking them with you.'

'I told you, it was just a silly fantasy. How can I take them? I'd need to work full-time and there wouldn't be anyone to look after them when they came home from school – and what about during the holidays? I've always been here for them, Millie, and I can't just abandon them. If I do . . .' She shuddered, her sentence unfinished.

Millie's gaze was sad as she looked at her friend. She had always felt sorry for Pat, thinking how awful it must be to have a father who always came home drunk. Yet she now realised that their lives were similar. Neither had mothers, and her father had turned into a drunk too. 'Well, if you can stick it out, so can I,' she said firmly. 'At least we'll have each other.'

'I can't bear the thought of your father touching you,' Pat said, her tone urgent as she added, 'Get out, Millie. Leave home – 'cos unlike me you don't have to put up with it.'

'Maybe I won't have to. I told you, John said to fight back if my dad tries to give me a clout and perhaps I will.'

'Huh, it ain't clouts that you need to worry about.' Pat's laugh was bitter. 'You're such an innocent, Millie. I can see you don't have a clue what I'm getting at.'

'What is it then?'

'Christ, do I need to spell it out for you?' she exploded, turning swiftly to look at her sisters.

Millie followed her gaze and saw that the two little girls were still absorbed in their game, seemingly oblivious to anything else.

'Listen,' Pat said as she turned her attention back to their conversation. 'You must know something about – well, sex.'

Millie stared at her friend. Sex? No, she didn't know much about it. Her mother had been pregnant and was being forced to have an abortion, but she didn't really understand how the baby got there in the first place. There had been whispered giggles at school, talk about not letting a man touch your bellybutton, but not much else. 'Well, we learned a little about it from Biology lessons, but nothing I really understood.'

'Biology lessons! Millie, you've no idea.' Her face then sobered, and she said abruptly, 'Now that John isn't there to protect you, yer dad will make you have sex with him.'

There was a shocked silence before Millie spoke, her voice high. 'No, don't be silly, he wouldn't do that!'

'Shush,' Pat hissed, her eyes now looking up at the ceiling and her fear obvious, but all was quiet and her shoulders slumped with relief. She then leaned forward, whispering earnestly, 'I'm telling you he will. My dad's been doing it to me for years. He said it's me duty to take me mother's place.'

'Duty? Your duty! No, it can't be, I don't believe you.'

'It's true, Millie, and I'll tell you something else. It's horrible, disgusting, and I hate it.'

Feeling bile rising in her throat, Millie gasped, 'Have you told anyone else about this?'

'No, of course not! My dad would go mad. He told me it's something people never talk about outside of their homes, and I'm only telling you because I can't bear the thought of you putting up with it too. You'll hate it, I know you will. It hurts, Millie, it hurts a lot.'

Millie rose to her feet, her voice indignant. 'What your father's doing to you is wrong, it must be! I'm going to ask Stella Blake, she'll know.'

'No, no, you can't! If my dad finds out I've told you, he'll kill me.'

There was a movement from upstairs and both girls froze. With a horrified expression Pat said, 'Quick, that sounds like me dad getting up. Hurry up. Hurry, you must go, but listen, you mustn't tell anyone. Please, Millie, promise me,' she begged as she hustled her to the door.

'Don't worry, I won't mention you, I promise,' Millie assured her as she ran swiftly outside, and as the door closed behind her she made her way straight to Stella Blake's house, determined to find out if what Pat said was true. And if it was, she thought, still feeling nauseous, she would leave home before her father started on her. Somehow she would get out . . . and as quickly as possible.

Chapter Thirteen

Stella Blake heard someone knocking on the front door and lifted a quizzical brow towards her husband. With a sigh he folded his Sunday newspaper and rose to his feet, saying unnecessarily, 'I'll get it.'

Stella smiled. Cyril tried so hard to make her feel that she wasn't useless, but they both knew that by the time she managed to reach the front door, whoever was knocking would have long since given up and gone away. The stroke had affected her mobility, and now she found it almost impossible to walk, even with two sticks. Not only that, it had affected her memory too, and she hated it – hated her woolly mind. Cyril tried to be patient with her, but she knew he was finding it hard, and there had been many times when she'd seen an exasperated expression on his face.

She strained her ears, surprised to hear Millie Pratchett's voice. She'd hardly seen the girl since Eileen died, but wasn't surprised. It was a wonder how the lass managed it all, working full-time at the coal merchants and running the house. It had been a terrible time for them all, and from what she'd heard from Dora, the family had fallen to pieces.

Dora Saunders helped her as much as Eileen had once done, and Stella was thankful, she really was, but she still missed her friend, finding it hard to come to terms with her loss. Why hadn't she realised that Eileen intended to take her own life? All the clues were there, but she hadn't seen them. Guilt flooded her as it always did when she thought about her lovely young neighbour and the tragedy of her death.

'Millie wants to speak to you.' Cyril said, ushering the girl into the room. 'I'll pop out for a little while so you girls can talk in peace.'

Stella smiled gratefully at her husband, feeling a surge of love for this kind and sensitive man, and as he left the room she beckoned Millie to take a seat. 'What is it, love? You look worried.'

Millie hung her head, hiding her eyes, then gulping she mumbled, 'I . . . I wanted to ask you something.'

'Ask away, sweetheart.'

The girl looked up briefly, showing a face red with embarrassment, but before Stella could offer further reassurance Millie blurted out, 'Is it right that now my mother's dead I'll be expected to take her place?'

'From what I've heard, you already have, pet. You not only work full-time now, but you take care of the home too.'

'Yes, that's true, but it's the other thing I'm worried about.'

'Other thing! What other thing?'

Millie quickly lowered her head again. 'Someone told me that . . . that . . . my father would make me take my mother's place for . . . for . . . sex.'

'*What!* Where on earth did you hear that?'

'I can't tell you, but please, Mrs Blake, is it true?'

'No, of course it ain't, and I can't believe that someone told you such a thing.' Stella shuddered, adding, 'It would be incest, and against the law.'

Millie gave a great sigh of relief and at last she raised her head. For a moment she sat biting her lower lip between her teeth, a habit that echoed her mother's. 'If it's against the law, does . . . does it mean that if someone's father is doing it, they could be stopped?'

Stella felt sick. Although Millie was trying to hide it, she was sure that the youngster was talking about her own father. Hate for Alfie Pratchett surged through her and she wanted to drag Millie into her arms. Oh, to think what the poor girl had been through! How could he? How could he do such a disgusting thing to his own child? 'Listen to me, Millie,' she said urgently. 'You must report this to the police.'

'No, I can't do that.'

'Yes, you can. You aren't to blame and your father must be stopped.'

'But he hasn't done anything yet!'

The answer took Stella by surprise, and she stared at the girl in confusion. If her father hadn't touched her, what on earth was Millie talking about? Perhaps she was frightened; perhaps her father had threatened her. 'Please, love, tell me the truth – has your father been doing things to you?'

'No, I promise, he hasn't done anything.'

Stella shook her head; her brain felt fuddled and she wondered if she had missed something important. 'But if your father hasn't tried to do anything to you, why on earth are you asking me these questions?'

'Because someone told me he'd expect me to take my mother's place and I just wanted to find out if it's true.'

Stella sank back into her chair, utterly bewildered now. She watched as Millie rose to her feet and with a smile said, 'Thanks, Mrs Blake. Thanks for putting me straight. I'd best be off before Dad wakes up.'

And before Stella could put her scrambled thoughts into order, the child had gone, the door closing softly behind her. Exhaustion washed over her, and as so often happened nowadays, she found that her brain refused to function. Unable to think coherently, Stella closed her eyes, soon drifting off to sleep.

'Hello, love, having forty winks, are you?'

Stella awoke to see her husband smiling down at her and moved painfully in her chair. 'It was just a catnap.'

'I'm sorry I've been so long, but I got talking to Gordon Hardcastle. Apparently his wife is on the warpath about Billy Benson and Alfie Pratchett.' Cyril grinned, and scratching the stubble on his chin he added, 'Christ, Jessie Hardcastle is a right old battleaxe and I wouldn't fancy getting on the wrong side of her.'

'Yes, there's no denying that the woman's a bit of a tartar. Anyway, love, there's nothing to be sorry about 'cos I didn't realise how long you'd been out, and I've been fine on my own.'

'What did young Millie want to talk to you about?'

'Millie? Oh yes, she came to see me, didn't she.' Stella struggled to remember, but before she could recall the conversation Cyril patted her gently on the cheek.

'Never mind, it doesn't matter and it's time for your pills.' Then frowning, he added, 'Do you feel all right, love?'

'I've got a bit of a headache, but it's nothing to worry about. I wouldn't mind a cuppa though,' she told him, the talk she'd had with Millie forgotten.

Stella watched Cyril measuring out her tablets. He was singing as usual, the tune familiar, but he was using his own version of the words *'I talk to the trees. That's why they put me away.'*

Normally she would have laughed, but something was niggling at her memory, something that seeing Millie had brought to the surface. What was it? A box, it was to do with a box, but as the thought crossed her mind, Cyril spoke again.

'I'm going down to see the Housing Officer again tomorrow.'

'Are you, love? What for?'

Cyril sighed heavily, his expression sad. 'I told you, don't you remember? I'm pushing for us to be rehoused. You can't manage the stairs and I've asked the council to give us a place that's all on one level.'

'Of course I remember,' she told him, unwilling to admit that this was all news to her.

When Millie returned home she found her father still in a drunken sleep, and her eyes encompassed the mess that she knew would take ages to clean. With his mouth hanging open as usual, dribble running down his chin, she couldn't bear the sight of him and so made her way to the sitting room, where she flopped onto the old sofa.

The room was musty with disuse, the utility furniture plain and ugly, but Millie hardly noticed as she chewed on her bottom lip again, concern for her friend uppermost in her mind.

Mrs Blake said that what Pat's father was doing to her was illegal and that it should be reported to the police. Years, Pat said he'd been doing it to her for years, and Millie shuddered. What would happen to Billy Benson if it were reported? Would he go to prison? Millie was perplexed and unable to answer her own questions, yet determined that somehow she would help her friend. Pat's father had to be stopped, and if the only way was to tell the police, then she would do just that.

Her mind made up, she rose to her feet, deciding to go to the police station straight away, but instead stiffened with fear when she heard her father's shout.

'Millie! Millie, where are you? Get in here and clean up this bloody mess, yer lazy cow!'

Clenching her fists she went warily into the kitchen to see her father's eyes blazing with temper. Quickly averting her eyes from his she bent down to pick up the broken plate, only to gasp when she received a swift kick on her backside that sent her sprawling.

'You little bitch! You knew John was leaving,' Alfie bellowed, returning to the earlier row. 'If you'd warned me I might 'ave been able to talk him out of it!'

'Dad, I told you, I only found out this morning, so how could I warn you?' she snapped back.

To Millie's surprise all the fight seemed to go out of her father; the anger swiftly leaving his eyes to be replaced with despair. With a groan he sat down. 'I need him for the coal-round and we've got to get him back. You said he's joined the Merchant Navy. What port has he gone to?'

Millie stared at her father, wondering if she should tell him. Would he be able to stop John from leaving? Desperate to have her brother back, she said, 'He signed on at the London Docks, but had to join his ship at Southampton.'

'Right, I'm going after him.'

'But it's five o'clock already. How long will it take you to get there?'

'I don't bleedin' know, but if his ship hasn't sailed I've got a chance. If I ain't back in time for work in the morning you'll have to tell Jack Jenkins that I'm ill.'

Millie nodded, watching as her father hurried out, and clasping her hands together she prayed he'd be in time to stop John from joining his ship.

An hour later the mess in the kitchen had been cleared up, and whilst doing it Millie had been constantly thinking about her brother. It was only when she was sponging the clippy rug that her thoughts turned again to Pat.

Her earlier determination to report her friend's father resurfaced, but even as she made that decision, fear gripped her at the thought of Billy Benson finding out. The police would question her and would want her name and address.

For years she'd been frightened of Pat's father, frightened of the way he sometimes looked at her, seeing something evil in his eyes that she didn't understand. Oh God, she couldn't go to the police station, she just couldn't, and hating her cowardice she sank onto a chair.

After agonising for many minutes it suddenly struck Millie that there must be a way to tell the police anonymously. As long as Billy Benson didn't know who had tipped them off, she'd be safe. Standing up abruptly she took the housekeeping tin from the mantelpiece, and fishing inside she withdrew some coins, determination stiffening her shoulders as she made for the telephone box on the corner of the street.

The following few minutes were much harder than Millie could have anticipated. She had given Billy Benson's name and address, told them that he was sexually molesting his daughter, but had finally come to realise that the policeman she was speaking to wasn't taking her seriously. He insisted that she come to the station, saying that they couldn't take any action on the word of an unknown caller. His dismissive, matter-of-fact voice had incensed her, so much so that she eventually lost her temper, screaming down the telephone that Billy Benson was an animal and a brute and that she was too scared of him to give her name. With a final sob she had slammed the receiver down and returned home, knowing the call had been a waste of time.

At seven-thirty Millie glanced at the clock. She had no idea how long it would take her father to get to Southampton and wondered if he'd be back that night.

She was still seething about the telephone call and couldn't settle. Deep down she knew that the only way to stop Mr Benson was to report him in person. Somehow she had to pluck up the courage, but not tonight, she just couldn't face it tonight. The mid-June evening was unusually muggy, and feeling hot and sticky she decided to have a bath, hoping that a good long soak would not only refresh her, but calm her nerves too.

Millie sank back in the water and closed her eyes, trying to push her turbulent thoughts to one side, but just as she started to relax there was a knock on the front door. She quickly stepped out of the bath, hastily wrapping a large towel around her body before padding downstairs.

There was another knock, louder this time, and hurrying, she opened the door, peering around it so that just her head was visible. Her face paled – it was Billy Benson.

'Hello, Millie, is yer dad in? I'm off to the pub and thought he might like to join me.'

'No, he's out,' she said, her voice clipped as she made to close the door.

'Just a minute, girl,' he said, pushing against it with his hand to prevent her from shutting it in his face. 'Has he already gone down the King's Head?'

'No, he's gone to Southampton and I don't know when he'll be back,' Millie snapped, glaring at him with distaste and once again trying to close the door.

'Why are you looking at me like that? I ain't a piece of dirt, you know. Christ, I had enough of that from yer mother!' He then took Millie unawares as he gave the door a mighty shove and it flew open.

Millie jumped back and in her haste the towel unravelled, falling in a heap at her feet. She bent hastily to retrieve it, her heart thudding with fear when she saw that Billy Benson had stepped inside, kicking the door shut with his heel as he stared at her naked body.

'Well, well,' he leered. 'You're nothing like yer mother . . . now she was a right beauty. Still, you'll do, and in the dark I won't have to look at yer face.'

'How dare you! Get out,' Millie cried as she frantically held the towel up in front of her small bust.

'Hark at Miss Snooty Boots. Your mother thought she was a cut above the rest of us too.'

He started to walk towards her, and backing away Millie shouted desperately, 'Don't come near me!'

With a low laugh Billy Benson suddenly lunged forward, and grabbing the towel he whipped it off her. His eyes travelled up and down her body and then he said hoarsely, 'I used to dream about 'aving yer mother and seeing her naked . . . just like you are now. You ain't a patch on her, but you need taking down a peg or two just like she did, and I'll suppose you'll do as a substitute.'

Millie, terrified now, made a grab for the only object within hands' reach, a glass ashtray. Raising it above her head she aimed it at Billy Benson, but with a swift movement he grabbed her arm, forcing it down to her side.

'Good, you've got a bit of spirit,' he said, breathing heavily. Then with a swift movement he dragged her to the floor, saying with a menacing voice, 'You're gonna like this.'

'Get off me! Get off!'

'That's it, Millie. Fight me, go on fight me,' he urged, forcing his hand between her legs.

Millie yelled, but the sound was cut off as his mouth covered hers, the smell of his rancid breath making her gag. She fought, but the more she fought the more brutal he became. She screamed then, screamed in agony as he entered her.

Chapter Fourteen

It was Pat who found her, Pat who held her while she sobbed out her anguish.

'I'm gonna call the police, Millie, and I'd better do it quickly, 'cos I think he's gonna do a runner – the bastard!' she added venomously.

'How did you know?'

'I didn't at first. When I heard you screaming I thought it was yer dad having a go at you, but shortly after that me father came running in, and after one look at his face it sort of clicked. I'll tell you something else – he actually looked scared. Now will you be all right while I pop down to the telephone box?'

'No, don't call the police. I . . . I can't face them. I feel so ashamed, and dirty . . . so dirty.'

'You ain't got nothing to be ashamed of. Look, Millie, I know he's me dad, but he can't get away with this. Doing it to me is one thing, but to touch *you* . . .' She broke off, her eyes dark with anger. 'The bastard,' she spat again. 'I could kill him. No, I've got to tell the cops,' and before Millie could stop her she ran out.

Curling into a tight ball, Millie found herself shaking with fright again. Despite Pat's assurance, shame flooded through her again, shame that she hadn't been able to fight him off. Oh, she'd tried, and finding she was still gripping the ashtray she had lifted it, intending to hit him over the head, but he'd forestalled that action, ripping it from her grip and laughing as he did so. The more she fought, the more aroused and violent he became, until too tired to fight any more she had lain like a stone beneath him, praying for it to be over.

Oh God, what was her father going to say? As she moved

within the blanket that Pat had thrown around her, the smell of her body assailed her nostrils and the stench of Billy Benson made her heave. She had to have another bath, had to get clean and with the need to scrub her body until all traces of the man had been removed, Millie staggered upstairs.

The water was still in the bath, cold now, but she didn't care. Throwing off the blanket she climbed in, shivering as she scrubbed and scrubbed her body until it was red raw.

They never saw Billy Benson again. Obviously terrified of the consequences of his moment of madness, he had scarpered before the police arrived.

Worse was when the police questioned not only Millie, but Pat too. It seemed that a note *had* been made of Millie's telephone call, and when the same name had arisen, Pat was subjected to the humiliation of having to tell them about her years of abuse.

Millie had been seen by a doctor, but refused to go to hospital. Pat, unable to leave her sisters, had insisted that they went to her house, and it was only then that her anger was unleashed. 'How could you, Millie? How could you go behind my back and tell the police about my father?'

'I'm sorry, really I am. Mrs Blake said it was illegal and something called incest. I just couldn't bear the thought of what he was doing to you and wanted him stopped.'

'What! Are you telling me that Stella Blake knows about it?'

'I didn't tell her it was you, honestly I didn't.'

Pat's gaze was hard, but then to Millie's relief the anger seemed to drain from her. With her voice and manner softening she said, 'It's all right, now come on, don't get upset again, you've been through enough tonight. But I still don't know why you won't press charges.'

'I just couldn't face it. If they catch your dad I can't bear the thought of appearing in court. Everyone would know then – everyone would know what he did to me,' she cried, her voice rising hysterically.

'Calm down, please calm down. Look, when is yer dad coming back?'

'I don't know. It's gone midnight and there's no sign of him.'

'You can kip in here tonight if you like,' Pat offered, and at the thought of spending the night alone in her house, Millie agreed.

She slept in Pat's bed, and they snuggled together like two spoons. Millie, who had never shared a bed with anyone before, was glad of the comfort when she felt her friend's arm slipping around her waist.

The next morning Millie awoke just before seven. Without disturbing Pat she slipped out of bed, returning home to find her father asleep in a chair. Her stomach turned a somersault: had he found John? She flew upstairs, taking them two at a time, her heart sinking when she saw that her brother's room was empty. Her father hadn't found him, hadn't brought him back. *No, no,* she cried inwardly. John had always been there for her, but now, when she needed him most, he had gone from her life.

Dispirited, she returned downstairs, her movements sluggish as she filled the kettle and placed it on the stove to boil. She looked at her father, dreading his reaction, because despite her pleading the police insisted they had to interview him.

'Dad, Dad, wake up. It's gone seven and you're late for work.'

'Wha . . . what?' he slurred as his eyes half-opened.

'Wake up, Dad!'

The confusion slowly left his face and straightening in the chair he looked at the clock. 'Christ, I didn't get home until five this morning and anyway it's too late to go to the depot now. When you get to work, tell the boss that I've got a gyppy tummy or something.'

'Dad, I . . . I've got something to tell you.'

'Not now! I need some kip so I'm off to bed.'

'Dad, please listen . . .'

'Are you bleedin' deaf or something? I said not now!' and throwing her a look of disgust he left the room.

Oh, what can I do? Millie thought frantically. She couldn't face going to work, she just couldn't, but with both of them absent she'd have to let Jack Jenkins know. She fished out some pennies and hurried to the telephone box, her face flaming. Had the neighbours found out? They must have seen the police and the doctor arrive, but did they know why? *Please, please don't let me bump into anyone!* she prayed.

There was still soreness between her legs and Millie fought to keep the memories of last night's events at bay. Yet as she pulled open the door of the telephone box and stepped inside, it felt claustrophobic. Unbidden, a picture formed in her mind. She'd been trapped, trapped under Billy Benson's body. *Stop it! Stop thinking about it!* her mind screamed, and gulping she picked up the telephone receiver.

'Jack Jenkins Coal Merchants.'

'Mr Jenkins, it's Millie. Er . . . my . . . my father can't do his deliveries today, and I'm afraid I won't be coming to work either. We . . . We've both got tummy upsets,' she lied.

'What about your brother? Is he ill too?'

Millie's heart thudded in her chest. What could she say? But quickly realising there was no way to hide it, she said, 'John's joined the Merchant Navy and he won't be returning to work.'

'Oh, and was he going to tell me from the deck of a ship?' Mr Jenkins said, sarcasm evident in his voice. 'I'm not blind, Millie, and I know that your brother has been carrying the round for some time. Without John's help your father will need to pull his socks up because I won't tolerate complaints about his deliveries. Now, please tell your father that I will expect to see him in the morning, upset stomach or not.'

'Yes, sir,' Millie murmured.

'I hope to see you back at work too.'

'I'll be in if I can,' she said, and hearing his heavy sigh she quickly said goodbye, thankfully returning the receiver to its cradle.

Millie hurried along Harmond Street again, relieved to be indoors, but at nine o'clock there was a loud knock, and as she opened the street door her heart sank when she saw the police constable on the step.

'My father's in bed,' she gulped, praying he would leave.

'I need to speak to him, miss, so please get him up.'

'Can't it wait until later? He's been up half the night.'

'No, I'm afraid not.'

Millie stood back, allowing him to enter, and once he was seated in the kitchen she went up to her father's bedroom, dreading waking him.

As he listened to the constable, Millie saw her father's face growing dark with anger. He turned then, giving her a ferocious scowl. 'When was you gonna tell me about Billy Benson?'

'I was going to tell you before you went to bed, but you didn't give me a chance,' she said, her words sounding braver than she felt.

The constable intervened, saying, 'It was a serious offence, miss, and I have to ask you if you've changed your mind about pressing charges.'

'No, I haven't changed my mind.'

Her father reared to his feet. 'Why not? Did you enjoy it – is that it? My God, if I get my hands on the bastard I'll kill him.'

'Sit down, sir,' the policeman ordered, and at the tone in his voice her father obeyed.

The constable continued to press her, but Millie wouldn't change her mind; even the fear of her father was nothing compared to the fear of standing in court. She was relieved when the policeman finally rose to his feet, and after seeing him out she returned to the kitchen, dreading the confrontation. To her surprise her father hardly spoke, but he kept muttering to himself as he sat rolling a cigarette.

'I'll bloody throttle Benson with my bare hands.' He struck a match, and as it flared their eyes met. 'Why ain't you at work?'

'I . . . I couldn't face it. I told Mr Jenkins that we've both got upset stomachs.'

'Huh, that's something, I suppose. Did he ask about John?'

'Yes, and I told him that he wouldn't be back. Did . . . did you manage to see him at Southampton?'

'No, it was a waste of bloody time, and I was lucky to hitch a lift home. Them docks are enormous with ships of all sizes, and it was like looking for a flippin' needle in a haystack. Nobody would tell me anything either, the closed-mouthed bastards. Well, sod him. He's no son of mine and I've washed me 'ands of him. If he ever knocks on my door again he'll get it shut in his face.'

'Oh Dad, what about when he's on leave? Surely he can come to see us?'

'No, he can't! He left me in the lurch without so much as a word. I'm finished with him and I don't want to hear his name mentioned again. Now get me something to eat.'

'Millie's heart sank, but too nervous to argue, she just said, 'Will eggs on toast be all right?'

'If that's all we've got it'll have to be, but I ain't finished with you, my girl. I still want to know what happened with Billy Benson.'

'You know what happened. He raped me!'

'So you say.'

'He did! Why would I lie about something like that?'

' 'Cos you're probably a liar and a whore, just like yer mother.'

Something snapped inside Millie and eyes blazing she shouted, 'My mother wasn't a whore, or a liar. How can you say something like that? She was a wonderful woman.'

Turning away from her gaze he mumbled, 'You know nothing . . . nothing about yer mother.'

'What did you say?' she asked in confusion.

'Mind yer own bloody business. One of these days you'll push me too far and I might tell you something that you wouldn't want to hear. Now just shut up and cook those bleedin' eggs.'

To avert his anger Millie scurried to do his bidding, but her thoughts were racing. What wouldn't she want to hear? There was some sort of strange implication in her father's words, something she couldn't put her finger on.

Chapter Fifteen

John had been gone nearly a week, yet to Millie it felt like months. She was still suffering both mentally and physically from the rape. Only a short time ago she'd told Pat that she didn't know anything about sex – well, she did now, and it sickened her.

So far at least, the neighbours hadn't found anything out, though they constantly tried to pump her for information about why the police had been called. After the first few times of answering the door, Millie had ignored their knocks, becoming almost reclusive.

It was now Saturday evening, and as Millie heard a light tapping on the door she again decided not to open it. The letterbox lifted, a voice calling, 'Millie, Millie, it's me, Wendy.'

Oh God, she couldn't ignore John's girlfriend, and rising slowly to her feet she opened the street door.

'My goodness, Millie, you look awful. Are you ill?'

'No,' she said shortly. 'Come in.'

Wendy followed her into the kitchen and as their eyes met she said, 'What's wrong, Millie? Is it that you're missing John? I am too, but it's only one trip then he'll be home for good. Listen, go and put your glad rags on and I'll take you dancing.'

'No . . . no thanks.'

'Come on, it'll do us both good to go out.'

'Sorry, but I'd rather not.'

'All right, we'll stay in then,' and pulling out a chair Wendy sat down, the look in her eyes penetrating. 'Come on, I can see you're upset about something. What's wrong, love?'

'I . . . I can't tell you.'

'Is it your father? I know he can be a nasty sod when he's had a drink. He's not been hitting you, has he, 'cos if that's the case I'll have his bloody guts for garters!'

'No, he hasn't hit me.'

Wendy continued to gaze at her, and obviously concerned, she said, 'Listen, I promised John I'd keep an eye on you and if you've got a problem, maybe I can help.'

How could she tell her about Billy Benson? Once again Millie was filled with shame, shame that she hadn't been able to fight him off. Wendy would be disgusted, and what if she told John? Forcing her head high, she said, 'I don't need any help – everything's fine.'

Still not satisfied, Wendy's eyes narrowed. 'How's your job going? Are you still enjoying it?'

'Yes, it's great,' and anxious to avoid any more questions she blurted out, 'I . . . I promised Pat I'd go round to see her this evening, so if you wouldn't mind . . .'

'I see. All right then, I'll go – but if you need anything, you only have to ask.'

'There's nothing,' Millie said, and as she walked to the front door Wendy followed with obvious reluctance.

'Bye then, Millie. I'll pop round to see you again next week. Hey, I've got a good idea. How about we go to the pictures one night? There's a Gene Kelly film on at the Granada.'

'Er, yes, maybe. I'll let you know. Bye for now,' she said, hurriedly closing the door before slumping with relief.

Returning to the kitchen, Millie sat down again. There was still Monday to face and she dreaded returning to work. She'd been absent for a week, and without a medical certificate to cover her so-called tummy upset, she didn't know how Jack Jenkins was going to react.

Wendy marched down Harmond Street, her back stiff. Christ, Millie had been so anxious to get rid of her that it almost felt like she'd been thrown out. There was obviously something wrong, but if the girl wouldn't talk to her there was nothing she could do. Yet what if it was her father? What if she'd lied and he *was* hitting her? Dare she call on Millie's friend, Pat? If the girl knew what was going on, maybe she could persuade her to talk. Of course, she would have to see Pat when Millie wasn't around and that wouldn't be easy to sort out, yet she'd manage it somehow. Millie looked awful and she had to find out why.

With nothing else planned she made her way home, surprised to see her mother hurrying out of Annie's flat, her face creased with anxiety.

'Thank God you're back. Come and have a look at Annie 'cos I'm worried sick.'

Wendy stood beside her mother looking down on the woman, and blanched. Christ, Annie looked terrible, her breathing ragged. 'Why hasn't she seen the doctor?'

'She wouldn't let me call him, and anyway she wasn't as bad this morning.'

'She'll see him now, like it or not. I'm going to ring the surgery and ask for an emergency house call.'

'Yeah all right, and hurry, love.'

As Wendy ran along Lavender Hill she tried to fight her fears. To her, Annie Oliphant looked to be at death's door and she prayed they weren't too late.

An emergency doctor would be contacted, Wendy was told, and running back home she flew upstairs. 'A doctor should be here soon, Mum.'

'Oh, she looks awful, and I shouldn't 'ave listened to her. I should've insisted that she was seen earlier. What if she dies? It'll be my fault!'

'Leave it out, Mum, of course it won't. It was Annie's decision, and you're not responsible for her.'

'How can you say that? I've been keeping an eye on her for ages.'

'Yes, I know, but even so, if she didn't want to see a doctor you couldn't force her.'

'We're forcing her now, ain't we!'

'Mum, she's unconscious now and can hardly refuse.'

They sat beside the bed, relieved when the doorbell rang, and after a quick examination the doctor said Annie would have to be admitted to hospital.

Everything seemed to happen quickly then. An ambulance was

called, and after hurriedly locking up, both Wendy and her mother went with Annie to hospital.

They sat in the waiting room for what seemed like hours, but at last a doctor came to see them. 'Mrs Oliphant has pneumonia and I'm afraid she's very weak. You can see her, but only for a few minutes.'

'Thank you,' they said, following the doctor into a small side ward, and at the sight of Annie they exchanged worried looks.

'Gawd, Wendy, she looks even worse.'

'Yes, but she's in the right place now.'

'Do you think she's gonna make it?'

'I don't know, but I'm sure they'll do all they can.'

A nurse came to their side then, asking them quietly to leave. 'It's very late, but you can come back to see Mrs Oliphant in the morning.'

'I just hope she's still with us then,' Bertha murmured, reluctantly leaving her friend's side.

On Monday, Millie walked nervously into the office. 'Hello, Mr Jenkins, I'm back.'

'Yes, so I can see, and are you fully recovered?'

'Yes, thank you.'

'Right, let's have your medical certificate and then you'd better get started. There's a stack of typing waiting to be done, and the stuff on top is the most important.'

'I . . . I haven't got a certificate.'

'Why not?'

'I . . . I didn't go to see the doctor.'

'Well, you should have. Without a medical certificate you aren't entitled to sick pay.' He then ran a hand around his chin, looking at her thoughtfully. 'It's strange how your father recovered in a day, yet it took you a week.'

'I had it worse than him,' Millie lied, her face flushing.

'Humph, if you say so. All right, I'll let it go this time, but in future if you're absent for more than two days I want a doctor's certificate. Is that clear?'

'Yes, Mr Jenkins.'

'Right, get on with your work.'

Millie hurriedly removed her jacket, glad to see the pile of papers on her desk. It was just what she needed to take her mind off things, and head bent, she picked up the first letter.

After an hour she took a break, flexing her fingers before leaving her desk to put the kettle onto the small gas ring. It was unusual that Mr Jenkins hadn't demanded tea earlier, and he'd been strangely quiet. The easy banter they'd shared was missing and she guessed it was because he was disappointed in her. Yet as she placed a mug of tea on his desk he looked up, his smile strained as he motioned her to a seat.

'Millie, I'm not happy with your father's behaviour and I've told him to come to the office when he's finished his round.'

'You aren't going to sack him, are you?'

'I haven't made up my mind yet, but something has got to be done. I've had complaint after complaint about not only his deliveries, but his belligerent manner too. On Friday he left three customers short, and when they complained he was rude. This can't go on, Millie. Now I know I shouldn't be telling you this as it's a matter between your father and me, but I felt that you should know. Is there any chance of John returning to the yard?'

'No, I don't think so, and anyway I don't know how long he's going to be away.'

'That's a shame. Your brother was a good worker, as was your father before your mother's death. It's due to your father's loss that I've made allowances, but my patience is running out, Millie.'

There were tears of shame in her eyes, and she couldn't bear to meet his gaze.

'I'm sorry.'

'You don't have to apologise for your father, and don't worry, I'm sure I can talk some sense into him. Get on with your work now, Millie.'

'Yes sir,' she said, finding his dismissal unusually curt. Millie returned to her desk and tried to concentrate on the tasks at hand, but found her attention wandering. Her father's job now hung in the balance and she prayed that if Jack Jenkins gave him a pep talk, it would work.

Jack Jenkins cursed himself. Why on earth had he taken his anger out on Millie? He'd missed the girl while she'd been off sick, but that was no excuse and if he wasn't careful he'd lose another secretary, and this time the best one he'd had. The problem was her father, and he was still annoyed at the man's attitude. Alfie Pratchett had a shiftiness about him, and when spoken to, had refused to look him in the eye. Yes, the man had lost his wife, but it was about time he pulled his socks up. Shaking his head he glanced at Millie again, and seeing the sadness on her face he decided to make amends. 'Millie, how do you feel about helping with the August parade in Battersea Park?'

She looked up from her work, eyes puzzled as she asked, 'But I thought the parade was at Easter.'

'It was, but we didn't win a rosette. There's another one in August and with your help perhaps we can get a first this time.'

Millie's eyes began to lighten with interest as she reminisced. 'I love the Easter Parade, and once my Dad's cart won a first. I was only about twelve years old, but I can remember him spending ages decorating the wagon. Samson looked wonderful too with his plumes and shiny horse brasses.'

'Yes, I remember how proud your Dad was when he won.'

'It was such fun,' Millie said, smiling widely at last. 'Mum and I sat on the back of the wagon in our Easter Bonnets and we had a picnic afterwards by the lake.'

'Perhaps we can persuade your father to enter again, along with some of the other wagons?'

'Oh yes! What can I do to help?'

'I thought we could have some sort of theme. Of course it will be up to the men to choose how they decorate their carts, and as usual I expect competition will be fierce, but as the horses are being gradually phased out I'd like to make this parade a bit special.'

'How about making it historic? We could all wear period costumes, perhaps Victorian.'

'Yes, that's a marvellous idea, but won't it take a lot of organising?' Jack held his breath, hoping Millie would take the bait. Organising the parade might be just what the girl needed to lift her spirits.

'No, not really,' she said, her head cocked to one side in thought. 'Once the men have been told, I'm sure their wives will rally round to sort out the costumes. And if the Easter Parade bonnets are anything to go by, they'll all be vying to wear the best ones.'

'Right then, Millie, I'll leave it to you to get things moving.'

'Yes, and I'd better type out a notice to put on the board,' and as Millie turned back to her desk she was still smiling.

When her father came home that night, he was in a foul mood, and not daring to question him Millie dished up his dinner in silence. At seven o'clock she was holding her breath. Had Jack Jenkins been successful? Would her Dad stay in? For once would he forego his nightly trip to the pub? He looked at the clock, a frown on his face and then stood up. For a moment he hesitated, but then without a word he left, the street door closing firmly behind him.

He had gone to the pub as usual and Millie shook her head in despair. She stood at the window, staring out at the street, and not wanting to be alone with her thoughts, she decided to go next door to see Pat.

'You look a bit rough, Millie. Still not sleeping?' her friend asked, head cocked to one side as she gazed at her across the kitchen table.

'No, not very well, but at least being at work took my mind off it for a while. My boss asked me to organise the parade in Battersea Park.'

'Parade! What parade?'

'It's going to be in August and we're entering four coal wagons. I suggested a Victorian theme and my boss agreed.'

'That sounds like fun. Are you going to wear a costume?'

'Yes, if I can find someone to help me make it. I could ask my Dad if you and the girls could come on the wagon too.'

'No, he'd never agree to that, and after what my Dad did, I don't blame him. I still feel awful about what he did to yer, Millie.'

'It wasn't your fault, and I should've been able to stop him.'

'You couldn't have stopped him, and I should know.'

Millie shuddered. Pat said her father had been doing it to her for years. How had she stood it? It was awful, disgusting, and for as long as she lived she would never let a man touch her again.

'I saw that John's girlfriend called to see you on Saturday night.'

'You don't miss much, do you?' Millie tried to joke.

'No. I spend a lot of time just looking out of the window, but what else have I got to do? Anyway, did you tell her about me dad?'

'No, I couldn't, and anyway the fewer people who know about it the better. Christ, can you imagine what would happen if Dictionary Dora found out? She'd be running round telling the whole street.'

'Yeah, you're right there. Listen, Millie, I've got to get a job.'

'A job, why?'

'With me dad gone there ain't any money coming into the house.'

'Oh Pat, I hadn't thought of that, but what about the children?'

'I'll have to find someone to look after them when they come home from school. Then there's the holidays, so that won't help, but what choice have I got?'

'What about Mrs Norton? She loves kids and might welcome a few extra bob a week.'

'Yes, of course, why didn't I think of that! I won't be able to offer her much, but it's worth a try. Mrs Lewis at number twenty-three is the only woman in the street who knows how to keep her mouth shut, so I asked her if I could get any help financially. She said I might be able to apply for National Assistance. I just hope she's right 'cos I won't earn enough to pay the rent and keep us all. Anyway, I saw that the builder's merchant in Latchmere Road is advertising for staff, so after I've had a word with Mrs Norton in the morning, I'll pop down there.'

'The builder's merchant! Surely they'll want a man.'

'No, you daft cow, they want someone in the office.'

'Oh right, but they'll probably want someone who can type. It isn't easy to learn, Pat, and I should know.'

'I hadn't thought of that. Mind you, I can do a little bit of typing 'cos when I was a nipper me dad found an old typewriter on a dump, and I played with it for ages. Before it conked out I'd got up to a fair old speed with just two fingers. Anyway, I can't face working in a factory, so it's worth a try.'

'What about working in a shop?'

'No, I don't fancy that. I'll have a go at blagging me way into the builder's merchant.'

'All right, good luck, and let me know how you got on when I come home from work tomorrow.'

They chatted for a while longer, but then Pat's sisters grew fractious, vying for her attention. Millie decided it was time for her to leave and after saying goodbye, she made her way home. The silence of the house felt oppressive and she shivered, unable to stop herself from thinking about the rape. Desperate to distract her mind she picked up a book, and curling in a chair she began to read. It was hard to concentrate, and she found herself reading the same sentence over and over again – for once, Dickens was unable to capture her imagination.

The evening dragged on, and when her father finally rolled home she watched him warily. He was drunk, his voice slurred, but the beer had also loosened his tongue.

'Bloody Jack Jenkins! Who does he think he is putting me on a last warning? The Pratchetts have been coalmen for generations – yes generations, and my round was handed down to me from my father, well before Jack Jenkins turned up and bought the place.'

'I know, Dad,' and hoping to calm him down she added, 'Did he tell you about the parade?'

'Sod the bleedin' parade.'

'Wouldn't you like to enter Samson?'

'No, I wouldn't. Now shut yer gob.'

Millie sat quietly, watching as her father's drunken mumblings ceased and his eyes began to droop. She waited until he was asleep then crept out of the room, deciding that bed was the safest place. Yet as she lay there, sleep eluded her and she chewed on her bottom lip worriedly. Her father hadn't stopped drinking, despite the boss's warning, and now it looked like he really could lose the round.

The next morning at work Millie still found the atmosphere strained, and wondered if she and Jack Jenkins would ever get back to their old banter. He didn't mention her father, and after clearing his desk by eleven o'clock he told her he would be out for the rest of the day.

'Take any messages, and lock up when you leave.'

'Yes, all right,' she whispered.

Their eyes met, but it was Mr Jenkins who lowered his first, saying contritely, 'I'm sorry, Millie. I shouldn't be taking my anger out on you, but your father is enough to try the patience of a saint. Did he tell you he's on his final warning?'

'Yes, he told me.'

'He's got to pull himself together because when he's out on the road he's becoming a danger to the public. I told you about the complaints, about his belligerent behaviour, but I didn't tell you that he fell asleep on the cart and it was lucky for him that Samson knew the route back to the yard.'

'No! Oh, I don't know what to say.'

'It isn't your fault Millie, but don't you have anyone in the family who can make him see sense?'

'No, there was only John. My grandparents are dead, and Granddad Pratchett was the only one who could have sorted my father out.'

'Yes, I heard he *was* good at his job, which is more than I can say about your father.'

'But my father was good at his job, and you know he's only changed since my mother died. Please, Mr Jenkins, don't give up on him.'

'All right, Millie, I do understand, but nevertheless the last warning stands. Cheer up, I had a good talk to him and he might just come to his senses. Now tell me, how are you doing with organising the parade?'

'The men have all been told, and five wagons want to enter. They were a bit surprised about the Victorian theme at first, but it seems their wives have got into the spirit of things.'

'Good, and don't forget to send off the entrance forms.'

'I've already done that.'

'Well done, and lets hope your father will join in too. Has he asked to enter?'

'No,' Millie said, unwilling to admit to her boss that her Dad wasn't in any fit state to care about the parade.

When Millie left work that evening and was walking down Harmond Street, Pat came running out to meet her, a wide grin on her face.

'I got the job and I start next week. The pay ain't too bad either at two pounds a week. Mind you, it won't be enough, so I just hope Mrs Lewis was right about National Assistance.'

'That's wonderful, but what about the typing?'

'Blimey, I nearly had a heart-attack when the governor asked me to do a typing test, but thankfully he got called out to the yard. By the time he came back I had managed to make a fair attempt at the short letter he gave me and though it wasn't perfect, he seemed happy enough.'

'What else will you have to do?'

'It's mostly answering the phone, taking orders and messages. There'll be a bit of filing too but I'm sure that'll be a doddle. Oh yes, and Mrs Norton has agreed to have the girls. She said as long as she hasn't got to feed them she'll do it for nothing. Ain't that good of her?'

'The job sounds rather like mine, but the pay's better, and I'm sure the girls will be fine with Mrs Norton.'

'I'll give her a few bob despite what she says, 'cos me sisters are sure to want a sandwich or something until I come home from work. I've left them playing Ludo but it won't keep them quiet for long so I'd best get back indoors. See yer later, Millie.'

She nodded, pleased for her friend, but as she went indoors she found her mood low. So much had changed in such a short time. Her mother's death, John leaving, and then worst of all, the rape. It haunted her, gave her nightmares, and she still felt unclean. Why had Billy Benson raped her? She wasn't pretty, she didn't have much of a figure, so what had she done to cause it?

Stop it – stop thinking about it, she told herself as she began to prepare the dinner. There was only cabbage to wash and chop, and yesterday's cottage pie to heat up. Her father would probably moan, but with money so tight it was the best she could do. Would she get any housekeeping money at the end of the week? God, she hoped so, because if she didn't, the rent wouldn't be paid again. She'd seen the brown envelope addressed to her father — knew it was from the council, but after reading it he'd just stuffed it into his pocket. Surely he knew? Surely he realised that if the rent wasn't paid, they could be evicted.

Chapter Sixteen

'Oh Wendy, I can't believe that Annie's dead,' Bertha sobbed.

Trying to hold back her own tears so as not to upset her mum even more, Wendy said, 'Don't cry, Mum. She had a good innings.'

'I still think I should've called the doctor earlier.'

'It wouldn't have made any difference,' Wendy said gently. 'They said that Annie's heart was failing and it was just a matter of time. Yes, she had pneumonia, but even if you'd called the doctor earlier it wouldn't have saved her.'

'I know what they said, but . . .' Bertha wrung her hands. 'Gawd, Wendy, you could've knocked me down with a feather when the Almoner said they found a letter to a solicitor in Annie's handbag.'

'Perhaps she left instructions for her funeral arrangements.'

'Yeah, that could be it. I never could get Annie to talk about her family, so maybe she told this lawyer bloke to get in touch with them. At least I hope so 'cos I felt terrible that I couldn't tell that Almoner anything.'

'Don't worry, Mum, I'm sure the solicitor will sort it all out.'

It was over a week later when Bertha got the letter, and her eyes widened with shock. She passed it across the table to Wendy, who after reading it said, 'Why would a solicitor want to see *you*, Mum?'

'I dunno, but it's to do with Annie.'

'Yes, I can see that. What it actually says is that it's to do with Mrs Annabelle Oliphant's estate.'

'Mrs! I didn't know she was married, and I don't understand.

What estate? Annie only had the rented flat next door, and she hardly had a penny to her name.'

'There must be more to it than that if a solicitor wants to see you. He'd hardly deal with rented accommodation and a load of worn out furniture. You'd better give him a ring, Mum.'

'Blimey, love, I've never been to a solicitor in my life. Still, you're right, I'd best go to the phone box and make an appointment.'

'What, at eight o'clock? I think you'll find it's a bit early.'

'Of course it is. Christ, love, I dunno what's the matter with me these days.'

'Would you like me to come with you when you go to see him?'

'I'd love you to, but what about work?'

'I don't start my shift until ten o'clock, and if you get an appointment for today I'll ring in sick. This is more important, and I'm intrigued, Mum, I really am.'

'You and me both, love.'

'What! You can't be serious!'

The solicitor smiled. 'The will, and her instructions, are perfectly clear.'

'Look, mate, I think there's been some sort of mistake. The Annie Oliphant I knew lived in a rented flat.'

'From what I understand it took her husband's solicitors a considerable time to track Mrs Oliphant down and so she only recently acquired the property. She also left me a letter, with instructions that I read it to you.'

'A . . . a letter?'

'Yes.' His smile was kind, and taking a sheet of paper out of a folder he started to read . . .

I bet you're sitting there with your jaw dropping, Bertha. It's been fun all these years watching you trying to prise information out of me, but now it's time to tell you a condensed version of my story.

You see, my husband was a hard and brutal man, and when seven years of marriage hadn't produced any children, he blamed me. The affairs started then, one that he conducted openly, and when the woman became pregnant I began to fear for my life. You see, as a Roman Catholic he couldn't divorce me, and knowing what he was capable of, I ran away. I came to London, found work in a bookshop, living in a small room above it, and remained there until I retired.

It became obvious that the bookshop owner wanted me out of the room when he raised the rent to a level that I couldn't afford, so with a limited income I was grateful when the council housed me in the flat above the grocer's. And that was where I met you, Bertha.

Recently my husband died, and as we were never divorced, his solicitor informed me that the property had come to me. I didn't want a house that held so many bad memories, and it has remained empty.

You have been a good friend, Bertha, and I have seen you struggle to bring up a child alone, seen how, despite being short of money, you shared your food with me. Now it is my turn to share what I have with you. Take the house with my love, Bertha. You deserve it.

There was a stunned silence as the solicitor folded the letter, and placing it in an envelope he handed it to Bertha. 'Do you have any questions, Mrs Hall?'

'Yeah, bleedin' hundreds, but I can't get me head around this. The Isle of Wight, you say . . . she's really left me a house on the Isle of Wight?'

'Yes, and I think it is quite a substantial one.'

'And she wants me to arrange her funeral?'

'Yes, and her small insurance policy should cover the costs.'

'But ain't she got any family?'

'No, I'm afraid not.'

'Oh Mum,' Wendy now whispered, 'I can't take this in.'

'I know, love, it's unbelievable, ain't it?' Bertha then turned to the solicitor again. 'Look, me head's spinning and I need time to think. Can we go now?'

'Yes, of course. There are a few papers to sign, but that needn't be done today. How about I make an appointment for ten o'clock tomorrow?'

'Yeah, that'll be all right.' Bertha stood up, her head shaking with bewilderment, and as the solicitor rose from his chair to open the door, she clutched Wendy's arm. She had to admit that despite her reservations, the solicitor had been a good sort, and not stuck-up as she'd expected. If anything, he looked pleased for them and obviously enjoyed reading out the letter. You bugger, Annie, she thought, a small smile on her face as she looked heavenward. I don't know why you couldn't tell me about yer past.

For a while the two women walked home quietly, each with their own thoughts, and then Wendy said, 'A house, Mum. Your own house.'

'I know, but it don't seem real. I keep thinking I'm having a lovely dream and any minute now I'm gonna wake up. I still don't know how Annie managed to make a will. She must have done it recently, but I'm buggered if I know how.'

'Perhaps she wrote to the solicitor and he called round.'

'Hmm, that's a possibility I suppose, but I didn't spot anyone.'

'Mum, you weren't in twenty-four hours a day.'

'I should have thought to ask the solicitor how she managed it. In fact, I will when we go back tomorrow.'

'I doubt he'll tell you, Mum. I think they have to respect their client's confidentiality. Anyway, what does it matter how Annie made her will? She may have written it herself for all we know. She left you her house and I think it's wonderful.'

'Yeah, and I wonder what it's like?'

'There's only one way to find out, and that's by going to see it.'

'What – now?'

'No, Mum, but once all the legal stuff is sorted out there's nothing to stop you.'

'I've got to get Annie's funeral sorted out and that's more important at the moment.'

'Yes, of course it is, but after that there'll be nothing to stop you going.'

'Stop *us*, you mean, 'cos I ain't going on me own.'

Chapter Seventeen

Millie grew more and more worried during the following two weeks. She knew that the council wouldn't stand for the rent arrears, but had no idea how she was going to pay them off, let alone the current week that was due. She'd seen another brown envelope arrive, but after reading it her father had just stuffed it into his pocket. Were they threatening eviction?

Her dad's behaviour was getting steadily worse, and Millie fretted constantly about his job. He hardly spoke, only muttering to himself now and then, but most worrying of all was his smell. His body odour was awful, and when he threw his shoes off, his stinking feet made her stomach heave. Why had he stopped bathing? He still came in through the outhouse, but other than washing his hands and face, he simply threw clean clothes over the dirt on his body.

Millie glanced at the clock, sighing as she realised it was almost time to leave for work, but then heard someone yelling, the sound coming from next door. Her heart began to thump and for a moment she froze in shock. No, surely Billy Benson hadn't come back! Hearing what sounded like the girls screaming she stiffened, and acting purely on instinct, she dashed round to Pat's house.

'Leave them alone – leave them!' Pat was yelling as without pausing to knock, Millie ran inside.

She looked at the scene in confusion, unable at first to take in what she was seeing. A policeman, with a woman at his side, was endeavouring to pull the children outside, while Pat was fighting to hang on to them.

'You can't take them away, you've no right!' she cried.

'What's going on?' Millie asked.

'See what you've done, Millie Pratchett! Because of your big mouth they're taking me sisters into care.'

The distraction loosened Pat's grip on the girls, and seizing the opportunity, the constable was able to urge them into the hall.

'You can't take them away from me, you can't!' she yelled again, rushing forward again to cling onto their arms.

'You've seen the court documents, miss. The children are going into the care of the local authority.'

'But why? Tell me why?'

The constable seemed to grow in stature as he said officiously, 'The accusations you made against your father are serious, and there's a warrant out for his arrest. Also, when you applied to the National Assistance Board for financial aid, your age was brought into question. They liaised with us, and an application was made to the courts. The judiciary ruled that the children must be taken into care for their own protection.'

'But they don't need protecting! Me dad ain't here now and I can look after them.'

'No, I'm afraid not. You're below the legal age to gain custody.'

The fight seemed to go out of Pat and she released her grip, watching with eyes full of anguish as her younger sisters were led outside. Quiet now, she followed behind, but as Bessie and Janet were bundled into the back of the car she heard them screaming with fear, and dashed to the kerb. The woman had got in beside the children and now hastily closed the door to prevent them from scrambling out again.

'I've always looked after them.' Pat sobbed. 'I've always kept them safe.' She leaned forward to peer into the car, hands flat on the window. 'Bessie, Janet, don't cry. I'll come and get you . . . I'll bring you home again, I promise.'

Two small, frightened faces stared back at her as the car pulled away, and as it drove down the street Pat stood gazing after it, tears streaming down her face. Millie, who had rarely seen her friend cry, moved to put an arm around her shoulder.

'Get off me! This is all your fault!' Pat screamed. She then looked around, her eyes wild, and seeing women standing on their doorsteps, arms folded as they watched the scene, she dashed the tears impatiently from her cheeks. 'Had a good look, have yer!' she bawled. 'Call yourself neighbours – you're nothing but a bunch of bloody nosy parkers. Not one of you came to help me, *not one!*'

There was an uncomfortable shuffling of feet, but other than a couple of women lowering their eyes, there was no reaction. With a sob Pat turned on her heels, running indoors and slamming the door behind her.

Millie found Dora Saunders standing beside her, and whispered brokenly, 'I can't believe they've taken the girls away. Oh, it's all my fault.'

'How can it be your fault, duck?' Dora asked, her eyes gleaming with interest.

Millie felt a great need to unburden herself, but knowing what a gossip Dora could be, she held back. 'Forget it, forget I said anything,' she said, clamping her lips together tightly. She then knocked loudly at Pat's door, but when there was no response she bent down, shouting through the letterbox, 'Come on, let me in!'

'No, go away! This is all your fault, and I'll never talk to you again, Millie Pratchett. Never!'

Millie stood up, wondering what to do, but knew that if she hung around any longer she'd be late for work. Perhaps Pat would talk to her later when she'd calmed down. With her mouth still set in a grim line she ran back indoors to get her handbag, and then carried on running nearly all the way to the coal depot.

Dora Saunders pulled out the key she'd been given and let herself into the Blakes' house. 'It's only me, Stella. How are you today, love?'

'Not too bad, but what was all that racket outside? I could only see a bit of what was going on.'

'Well,' Dora said, puffing out her chest with importance, 'from what I could tell, the Benson girls 'ave been taken into care. It was a right old carry-on, and Pat Benson was doing her nut.'

'But why have they taken the girls into care?'

'I dunno, but there's been some funny goings-on lately. If you remember, it was only about a month ago when the police turned up at the Pratchetts', and since then nobody's seen hide nor hair of Billy Benson. I've been asking around, but nobody seems to know what's going on and it's getting on me wick, I can tell yer. It feels like a complicity of silence.'

'A complicity of silence! What does that mean?'

'You know . . . it's when people get together to keep a secret.'

'Oh, I think you mean conspiracy, Dora.'

'Yeah, that's it,' she said offhandedly. 'I was just speaking to Millie Pratchett and she said it's her fault that the girls were taken away. Now, don't you think that's strange? I mean, how can it be Millie's fault? Yet when she tried to get Pat to open the door, she refused, which makes me think there must be something in it.'

Stella frowned, her expression puzzled. 'Millie came to see me recently, I'm sure she did, and the girl was worried about something. Oh, if only I could remember.'

Dora plonked herself on the chair opposite Stella, leaning forward as she urged, 'Think about it. Was it to do with the Bensons?'

Rubbing a hand over her face, brow still furrowed, Stella answered, 'No, at least I can't remember Millie talking about them. I've got a vague idea that it might've been her father she was worried about.'

'Right, now we're getting somewhere. Cast yer mind back. What did she say about her father?' Dora watched as the woman closed her eyes, willing herself to keep quiet and holding her breath in anticipation. This might be a nice bit of juicy gossip and she didn't want to miss it.

The next couple of minutes were agonisingly slow, but suddenly Stella cried, 'Yes, that's it, I remember now!' She shook her head, adding, 'I don't think I can tell you though, it's a bit confidential.'

'You know you can trust me. I won't tell a soul.'

'Well, if you promise to keep it to yourself I don't suppose it would hurt.'

Dora made a sign across her chest, vowing, 'Cross me heart and hope to die.'

'All right then,' and wriggling in her chair as though

embarrassed, it was a few moments before Stella spoke. 'Millie wanted to know if she'd be expected to take her mother's place for . . . well, you know what.'

'You know what! You don't mean *intercourse?*' Dora's mouth was open in shock.

'Yes, and I was horrified, I can tell yer.'

'Never! I can't believe that of Alfie Pratchett.'

'I feel the same. I know he's turned into a drunken lout since he lost Eileen, but to do that to his daughter? Christ, Dora, it doesn't bear thinking about.' Stella frowned again, adding, 'Mind you, if I remember rightly, it was all a bit confusing. At first I thought Millie was talking about her father, but then she spoke as if it was happening to someone else . . . someone she knows, and she wanted assurance that it wouldn't happen to her.'

'If you ask me, that makes more sense. Yeah, it probably was someone else, but who? Who would do that to his own child?'

A silence fell between the two women as they both gazed into the empty hearth. Then, with a sudden start, Dora's back stiffened. 'I reckon she was talking about Billy Benson. He must 'ave been having a go at his kids. Think about it, Stella. Why else would them girls be taken into care?'

'What, little Bessie and Janet? But that's awful. Oh, those poor children.'

'Yeah, it's terrible, but somehow I ain't surprised. I never liked the man and he always gave me the willies. Blimey, no wonder he's disappeared. He must 'ave done a runner when the police found out what he's been up to.'

'I hope they catch the dirty bastard!'

'Yeah, so do I,' Dora said, and then she stood up, her face alight with excitement. 'I must go, Stella, but don't worry – I'll pop back later to get yer shopping.'

'Wait! You promised not to tell any—'

Dora didn't wait for Stella to finish her sentence, she was already on her way out again, anxious to spread the news. She scurried across the road and knocked on Maureen Frost's door.

Maureen had lived in Harmond Street for years and they were firm friends, both loving a good old gossip over a pot of tea. 'I've got something to tell you, so put the kettle on,' Dora urged. 'Mind, you'll 'ave to keep it to yerself.'

'Come in then,' the woman said, her expression eager.

Dora cast an eye around the kitchen, seeing that it was as untidy as ever. Maureen hated housework, and since her husband's death two years earlier she hardly bothered to do any cleaning. She yanked out a chair, finding that she had to remove a pile of old newspapers before sitting down. Then, folding her arms under her bust, and with her head held high with importance, she said, 'You ain't gonna believe what I've found out.'

'Is it about the Bensons? Cor, I knew I could rely on you to find out why them kids 'ave been taken away.'

'Yeah, I've found out, but it's very confidential. Now get the tea made, and I'll tell you.'

After hastily filling an old brown and chipped teapot with boiling water, Maureen placed it on the table before sitting opposite her friend. 'Give it time to brew, and in the meantime, come on, spit it out.'

Dora passed on the gossip, feeling a sense of satisfaction at the shocked expression on her friend's face. Maureen hastily poured the weak tea, and Dora looked at it with distaste as it was pushed towards her across the oilcloth. In a hurry to leave now, she poured some into the saucer, and lips pursed, she blew onto the hot liquid before slurping it from the rim. 'Right, I'm off, but don't forget to keep what I've told you to yerself.'

Maureen watched her friend as she hurried up the street, and after seeing her disappear into Joan Williams's house she scampered back inside. Then, using the back door to run around to her neighbour's, she echoed Dora as she entered, saying, 'You ain't gonna believe what I've got to tell you.'

And so in less than an hour, nearly everyone in Harmond Street knew what had happened to the Benson girls.

Early in the evening, keen for more gossip, Dora Saunders knocked on the Bensons' door, deciding to offer her sympathies to Pat, and hoping that by doing so, the poor girl would confide in her.

''Ello, love, can I come in?'

'What do you want?' Pat's eyes were red and her shoulders

hunched, but in her greed for more information, Dora hardly noticed.

'I just wanted to say how sorry I am about what's happened,' Dora told her as she unceremoniously pushed her way inside number twelve.

'I don't need your sympathy,' Pat said stiffly, 'and I don't remember inviting you in.'

'Now then, love, there's no need to be rude. I've only come to see if you need any help.'

'Help! It's a bit late for that. Where were you when my sisters were being taken away? You didn't help then, did you? No, but you and your cronies enjoyed the spectacle!' And with a scowl she snapped, 'Now please go.'

As Pat tried to push her outside again, Dora reared up with indignation. 'How was I supposed to help you when I didn't know what yer father was up to? You should've gone to the police instead of letting him interfere with yer sisters.'

'What! Who told you that?'

'Er, well . . . I heard it from someone.'

'Who was it?'

'I . . . I . . . can't remember, but it's the talk of the street.'

'It was Millie Pratchett, wasn't it? She told you!'

'No . . . no, it wasn't Millie. I can't remember where I heard it, but everyone is shocked to the core. What yer father was doing to them girls is terrible, and it's no wonder they've been taken into care.'

'He didn't touch Bessie and Janet! I kept them safe and made sure he didn't lay a finger on them!'

There was a shocked silence as her words sunk in, and then Dora placed a sympathetic hand on Pat's arm. 'Oh, I'm so sorry, love. So it was just you he was having a go at.'

Pat shook off the hand, eyes blazing with anger. 'Mind yer own bloody business. *Now just get out and leave me alone!*'

Before Dora could react, she found herself shoved outside, with the door slammed shut in her face. Well, that's nice ain't it, she thought as she scurried off. I was only trying to help the girl.

Pat, trembling with shock, sank onto the bottom of the stairs. The whole street knew, and she felt sick at the thought. Wringing her hands together, she thought about her rudeness towards Dora Saunders, and closed her eyes at the memory. The old woman was a kindly soul really, despite her love of gossip, and didn't deserve to be virtually thrown out of the door.

A sob rose in her chest. It had to be Millie who'd told everyone – she was the only one who knew about her father's abuse. Why had she done it? Why had she lied? He hadn't touched the girls, and Millie knew that, so why had she spread such a terrible rumour?

Pat's emotions were in turmoil; a mixture of anger and pain. Millie had betrayed her – Millie whom she loved above all others. Was it only a month ago when they had slept together in her bed, a time of agony when she had finally recognised her feelings. She had fought to remain calm, fought to stop her hands from straying over Millie's body, whilst revelling in the joy of just holding her. For the first time in her life, the thought of sex hadn't felt repugnant, and she'd marvelled at the discovery.

Yet why was she attracted to Millie? She wasn't even pretty – in fact, only her eyes saved her from being ugly. Doe-like, they always looked dreamy and soft, and looking into them was like seeing into her soul. Pat shuddered then, knowing that her feelings for Millie were abnormal, but since that night spent holding her, she'd been unable to fight them.

Then had come this morning's bombshell. Her sisters had been taken away, and forgetting that her application to the National Assistance Board had played a part, anger surged through her again. The girls were in a children's home, and that was Millie's fault too. She shouldn't have gone behind her back – should never have opened her mouth to the police.

Pat's fists clenched as she thought of the years spent protecting Bessie and Janet – years of making sure her father didn't try it on with them by always offering herself instead. And now it was all for nothing . . . she had failed them.

Jumping to her feet, she ran upstairs to her bedroom, stuffing what few clothes she had into a bag. There was nothing to keep her in Harmond Street now, and dreading facing the gossip, she was determined to leave. Lifting her mattress she fumbled for a purse, a tiny purse that held the little cash she had managed to stash away over the years. It wasn't much, but perhaps enough to rent a small room, and if she could get an evening job to supplement her earnings, she'd manage.

With a last look around her bedroom Pat tightened her lips, deciding to give Millie Pratchett a piece of her mind before leaving.

'Oh Pat, thank God you've come round. I was just trying to pluck up the courage to come to see you,' Millie cried. 'Come in, please come in.'

'Are you on yer own?'

'Yes, my father had his dinner and then went straight out again as usual.'

Pat's smile was more like a grimace, and when they reached the kitchen she stiffened her shoulders, determined to tell her so-called friend what she thought of her. However, the words died in her throat at the concerned expression on Millie's face.

'I can't stop thinking about Bessie and Janet. You're right, Pat, it's all my fault they've been taken into care and I feel sick with shame. If only I'd kept my big mouth shut,' she cried, tears filling her eyes.

Fighting to hold onto her anger Pat spat, 'Why did you tell everyone that my father was interfering with my sisters?'

Millie's eyes widened. 'But I didn't.'

'Don't give me that – it must have been you.'

'How can you think I'd do such a thing?'

'Because Dora Saunders knocked on my door offering her sympathy. You're the only one I spoke to about my father's abuse, but I didn't say he touched my sisters. You must've decided to add that snippet of gossip.'

'I did not! I admit I spoke to Stella Blake, but I didn't mention you, or your sisters.'

Pat stared hard at her friend. 'What exactly did you say to Mrs Blake?'

'I asked her if my father would expect me to take my mother's place for sex.'

'And what did she say?'

'She told me to tell the police, but I said that I didn't need to as my father hadn't touched me.'

Pat began to pace the room, but then turned sharply. 'Mrs Blake must have wondered why you were asking such questions.'

'I expect so, but I told her someone had warned me it might happen, and I just wanted to find out if it was true. I didn't mention you, or the girls, honestly I didn't.'

Pat began to pace again. Stella Blake must have wondered where Millie had got the idea from, and when the children were taken into care was it possible that she'd put two and two together? Yes, it seemed likely, and even more so if she'd discussed it with Dora Saunders. Between the two of them they could have worked it out, and it wouldn't have taken long for the news to spread.

'I'm sorry, Millie. I realise now that it wasn't your fault. You must have made Stella Blake suspicious without meaning to, but I still wish you hadn't gone to see her, or reported my dad to the police. None of this would've happened if you'd kept your mouth shut.'

'I'm sorry, really I am, but I just wanted to protect you!'

Millie's eyes had filled with tears, her distress obvious, and at that moment all the anger Pat was feeling suddenly left her. She rushed forward, pulling Millie into her arms. 'Shush . . . it's all right, I know you were just trying to help. Listen, it'll be hell living here with everyone knowing, so I'm leaving Harmond Street. Come with me. Please come with me.'

'Leaving! You're leaving? Oh Pat, don't go!'

'Didn't you hear what I said? I can't bear to leave you, so I'm asking you to come with me,' and unable to resist she placed her lips over her friend's, kissing her passionately.

Millie wrenched her mouth away, a look of horror on her face. 'Stop it! What on earth do you think you're doing?'

'I love you – I love you!' Pat cried, all her pent-up emotions rising to the surface. 'Listen, we can get a bedsit together. We'll be happy, I know we will. Oh, please say you'll come with me,' she begged, before desperately trying to kiss her again.

To avoid her lips, Millie quickly averted her face, but not before Pat had seen the look of utter revulsion in her eyes. Pain cut through her, and she released her hold, realising that instead of returning her feelings, her friend felt nothing but disgust.

She watched now as Millie suddenly lunged towards the sink, and leaning over it was violently sick. Pat stood for a moment, her heart feeling like a hard lump of lead in her chest, and then in utter desolation she left the house, picking up her bag before leaving Harmond Street forever.

Chapter Eighteen

As the paddle-steamer drew in at the end of a long pier, Wendy hid a smile. Her mother still looked bewildered, and her hat was askew, giving her a comical appearance. It was a glorious July day with hardly any breeze, and her eyes were dazzled by the sun casting a myriad of bright twinkling lights on the smooth surface of the sea.

Before boarding the steamer from Portsmouth to the Isle of Wight it had taken Wendy some time to assure her mother that they weren't going abroad. Bertha Hall had been born and bred in Battersea, and other than a few weeks hop-picking in Kent before the war, she had never left it. Even during the Blitz when bombs rained down, she stayed put, saying that Adolf bleedin' Hitler wasn't going to drive her out of London.

Wendy now took her mother's arm, and after disembarking they boarded the small steam train that would take them down the mile-long pier. They were unusually quiet as the train chuffed along, both taking in the scenery at Ryde, passing wonderful public gardens alive with summer flowers that made Bertha gasp with wonder, before the line took them on to Sandown.

The countryside stretched out – green fields, gently rolling hills – and it was Bertha who turned from the window to break the silence. 'I'm nervous, Wendy.'

'Nervous! Why?'

'It ain't a bit like Battersea, is it? In fact, it's more like them pretty pictures you see on biscuit tins.'

Yes, Wendy thought, it was beautiful, and as the train chugged along she saw a woman tending her garden who lifted her arm to wave as the train passed. 'There's no need to be nervous, Mum.

People are people no matter where they live, some good, some bad.'

When the train pulled into Sandown Station they got off with relief, feeling hot and tired after their journey from London. 'We don't know how far the house is from here, Mum, and I think we'd better splash out on a taxi.'

'A taxi! Blimey, I've never been in one of those.'

'There's always a first time for everything, so come on,' Wendy grinned.

'Are you here on holiday?' the driver asked as they climbed in.

'No, we're only on a day-trip, but we like what we've seen so far.'

'It'll take about fifteen minutes to get to Beech House,' he said, gears crunching as they set off.

The drive took them along the coastal road, and a crowded beach came into view. Away at the water's edge, Wendy could see a child sitting with waves gently lapping over her legs. As the little girl stood up Wendy couldn't help smiling, seeing that the child's knitted swimsuit was so sodden with water that it dragged almost to her knees. A gull flew overhead, its plaintive cry echoing as it soared in the clear blue sky. 'Oh Mum, it's just perfect here,' she whispered.

'Yeah, it's smashing, love.'

They turned inland again and minutes later drove through tall, black wrought-iron double gates and into a sweeping drive. Gravel crunched under the taxi wheels, but then the drive curved to the right, the house coming into view. For Wendy it was love at first sight, and she gasped with delight. Her eyes took in the mellow red bricks, wide steps leading up to the solid front door, and on each side windows glinted in the sun as though in welcome.

As the vehicle drew to a halt Wendy scrambled out, urging her mother to do the same. 'Come on, Mum! Have you got the key?'

'Yeah, but give us a chance, girl.' And leaning forward to speak to the driver, Bertha asked, 'Can you come back to pick us up in a couple of hours?'

He nodded, and after paying the fare, the two women

approached the house. Wendy watched as her mother inserted the key, finding that she was holding her breath in anticipation. Would it be as beautiful inside?

'My Gawd!' Bertha gasped when she saw the hall, which in itself was bigger than their kitchen and living room combined, a carved oak staircase curving up to a galleried landing.

They wandered from room to room, eyes agog at the size of most of them, and running their fingers over antique furniture, they left a trail in the fine layer of dust. White sheets covered furniture in the huge drawing room, and lifting them they saw matching blue satin brocade sofas, wearing thin in parts yet somehow in perfect keeping with the ambience of the room.

'The solicitor said the house has eight bedrooms,' Wendy commented as they finally stepped upstairs.

'We can't keep it,' her mother said abruptly.

'Why not?'

'Think about it, love. It would cost a fortune in upkeep, and we just couldn't afford it. If I sell it we could find a smaller place, and 'ave a few bob over.'

'Oh Mum, it seems such a shame. I just love this house.'

'I must admit it's nice, but what else can we do? Blimey, can you imagine the electric bills?'

They looked around the bedrooms, most nicely decorated and furnished, but one or two needing attention, and then finally went downstairs to wander around the lovely gardens.

At the rear of the house they strolled across the lawn, taking in the perfect flower borders, until at the far end they came to an ancient brick archway, thick with lichen, that led through to a walled kitchen garden. Lettuces and other salad crops grew in neat rows, and they both jumped out of their skin when an ancient man, with skin like a walnut, suddenly popped up from behind some plants.

'Gawd! Who are you?' Bertha gasped.

'I'm Ted, the gardener. I suppose you're the new owners.'

'Yeah, that's right,' Bertha said, and with questions remaining unanswered about Annie Oliphant she added, 'How long 'ave you worked here?'

'I've been here since I was a young whippersnapper and

apprenticed to old Percy Wood, but nobody's paid my wages for the past three months.'

'Oh, I'm sorry, but why have you carried on working?'

''Cos old Percy and me virtually built this garden and I don't want to see it going to rack and ruin. I 'opes you don't mind, but I've been helping myself to ripe fruit and veg, as well as eggs from the chickens. It seemed a shame to waste them, and some compensation for my loss of wages.'

'Of course we don't mind, But tell me, did you know Annie Oliphant?'

'Mrs Annabelle! Course I did, and she were a fine woman. I was sorry when her went off.'

'What was Mr Oliphant like?'

'He were a hard man, but he mellowed with the years.'

'We heard he had a child, is that right?'

'Nah, missus. Many, many years ago I did hear that one of his floozies was carrying, but if I remember rightly it were rumoured that she lost the baby. The governor got rid of her after that, and 'twere a shame Mrs Annabelle didn't come back. Were you related to her?'

'No, but she lived next door to me for over twenty years.'

'Ah,' Ted said as if that explained everything. 'Will you be staying in the house now?'

'No,' Wendy said. 'We've got to go back to London, and I'm afraid we haven't any money to pay your wages. My mother will probably sell the house, so unless the new owners take you on, I don't know what to suggest.'

'I suppose I'll hang around until then,' and bending back to his task it became obvious by his manner that the conversation was over.

They carried on walking the grounds for a while longer, but then the toot of a horn had them hurrying to the front of the house again. The taxi had arrived, and with a last look at the lovely façade, Wendy climbed in beside her mother.

Wendy was quiet on the steamer back to Portsmouth. She stood leaning over the rail, watching the wake of the ship, her mind churning like the paddles. An idea was forming, one that she thought could solve all their problems, but seeing that her mother had dozed off, hat once again askew, she decided to wait until she'd covered all the angles before broaching the subject.

They arrived in Battersea hot and weary, and it wasn't until they were fortified with a cup of tea that Wendy spoke. 'Mum, I've been thinking.'

'So 'ave I, love, and I think it's a shame that we've got to sell that lovely house. It would've been wonderful to live there, but impossible, and I'd better 'ave a word with that solicitor man again. He might be able to tell me how to go about selling it.'

'We may not have to.'

'I told you – we ain't got much choice. We can't afford to keep it, and that's that.'

'Sandown is such a pretty place, and did you see all the holidaymakers?'

'Yeah, I saw them, but what's this leading to?'

'We could turn the place into a guesthouse.'

'A what!'

'Think about it, Mum. There were eight bedrooms, and without counting the kitchen, four rooms downstairs. We could easily take in paying guests, and make a good living during the summer season.'

'Oh yeah, and what about the winter?'

'Maybe we could get a couple of permanent residents, and with what grows in the garden, plus the chickens, we'd almost be self-sufficient.'

'I dunno, love. We know nothing about running a guesthouse, so what makes you think it would work?'

'How hard can it be? All we'd have to do is give them decent food, make sure their rooms are kept nice, and of course make them welcome.'

'It sounds possible when you put it like that, but I'm still not sure. And come to that, what about yer career?'

'Mum, being a telephonist isn't much of a career, and think about it. No more going out early-morning cleaning for you. Instead, we'd be working side by side, running our own business, and if we make a success of it we'd have a decent income too.

Come on, what have we got to lose? If we don't make a go of it we can still sell the house and buy a smaller place.'

Fingers crossed, Wendy watched the range of emotions that played across her mother's face, finding that she was holding her breath until Bertha responded.

''Ave you thought about all the things we'd need to run a guesthouse? For instance, what about bedding and crockery, to name a couple?'

'Of course I have. If you remember, I poked in all the cupboards, and in one I saw loads of linen. The kitchen was full of stuff too – in fact, enough crockery to feed an army.'

Bertha stared at her daughter, but then with a grin said, 'Well, if that's the case, all right, girl. We'll give it a go.'

Wendy smiled at her mother with delight, deciding to keep the rest of her plan to herself for the time being. For now she'd have to give in her notice at the Exchange, and of course, write to John. As the list of things to do began to grow, she prayed that she was right, and in taking on the house they weren't biting off more than they could chew.

On Saturday Wendy stared out of the window, guiltily realising that a whole six weeks had passed since she'd last checked up on Millie, and her intentions to have a word with Millie's friend had fallen by the wayside. Yet was it surprising when so much had happened, so quickly? There'd been Annie's funeral, viewing the house they'd inherited on the Isle of Wight, their decision to live in it, and now all the preparations to move.

It had been her last shift as a telephonist yesterday, and did she regret it? No, not really, but it would be strange to leave the hustle and bustle of London. She wondered whether John had received her letter yet. Oh, she hoped so – it would be awful if he came home to find her gone. Just in case, it might be a good idea to leave their new address with Millie. With this in mind she went into the kitchen.

'Come on, Wendy, give us a hand with this packing.'

'I'll help you later, Mum. I just want pop out for a while to see Millie Pratchett.'

'Well, don't be long. There's all this to sort out and I can't do it on my own. I know we ain't taking any furniture, but we've still got a lot to do by Wednesday.'

'I'll only be gone for about half an hour,' Wendy said, hurriedly leaving and arriving at Millie's house slightly out of breath. She knocked smartly on the door of number ten, and eventually heard the sound of slow footsteps approaching, hoping it wouldn't be Alfie Pratchett who opened the door. No, thank God – it was Millie, but seeing she looked pasty-faced and miserable, Wendy's heart sank.

'I'm sorry I haven't been round for such a long time,' she said sheepishly, 'but a lot has happened.'

'That's all right,' Millie said drearily, standing aside to allow Wendy in.

'I wish you'd tell me what's wrong. You looked awful the last time I saw you, and you don't look any better now.' She was feeling genuinely remorseful now and wished she had kept her promise to John.

Millie's eyes looked veiled, and Wendy wasn't sure whether to believe her when she said, 'I fell out with my friend Pat, that's all.'

'Are you sure that's all there is to it?'

'Yes, and she's left Harmond Street now.'

'Has she? What brought that on?'

'Her sisters were taken into care – we had a row, and then she left.'

'Yes, well, I think that's a bit of a potted version. What did you argue about?'

'Nothing much. Have you heard from John?'

Wendy was annoyed by the dismissive tone in Millie's voice. All right, the girl didn't want to confide in her, but there was no need to be so abrupt. 'No, I haven't heard from John yet, but I've written to him with my news.'

'News?'

Wendy told her about the legacy of a house on the Isle of Wight, finally saying, 'I've given in my notice at the Exchange and we'll be moving out there on Wednesday.'

'It sounds wonderful and you're so lucky,' Millie said, her voice now softer.

'I know, and just in case John doesn't get my letter, would you mind keeping our new address?' she asked, handing out a slip of paper.

'No, of course not, and I . . . I hope he comes home soon.'

'So do I, Millie. Anyway, love, I'd best be off or my mother will have my guts for garters. But are you sure you're all right?'

'Yes, I'm fine.'

Wendy looked at Millie doubtfully, but if the girl wouldn't tell her what the problem was, what could she do? She couldn't even have a word with Pat Benson now, and it was all a bit odd that she'd left Harmond Street so suddenly. With a shrug she followed Millie to the front door, and as they said goodbye, Wendy hoped she was imagining the hint of tears behind the younger girl's smile.

As Wendy hurried down Harmond Street, still worried about John's sister, she was oblivious to the group of children playing knock down ginger, only jumping when a voice shouted, 'Come here, you little buggers! I'll 'ave the skin off yer backs if you knock on me door again!'

The woman stood indignantly on her doorstep, hair in curlers, arms folded in anger, and seeing her, Wendy realised that the Isle of Wight was a world away from all this. Beech House was set at the end of a long lane, and she wondered how her mother would settle in such a different environment . . . but then she berated herself. Of course she would adapt – they both would – and if she could just persuade John to fall in with her plans, life would be heaven.

When Wendy arrived home it was to find Bertha sorting out the kitchen cupboards, with most of the old china going into a bin for disposal. She turned, saying, 'We won't need all this old rubbish now.'

'Mum, why don't you just leave it in the cupboards? Whoever get this flat might welcome it.'

'Yeah, why didn't I think of that? Anyway, how was Millie Pratchett?'

'I'm a bit worried about her. She looks awful, but I can't get her to tell me what's wrong.'

'She ain't your responsibility, love.'

'Is that an echo I hear?'

'What's that supposed to mean?'

'I seem to remember saying the same thing to you about Annie.'

'Yeah, you did, didn't you,' Bertha said with a chuckle. 'Still, if Millie won't talk there ain't much you can do about it. Besides, we'll be living in the Isle of Wight soon and if she's got a problem she'll 'ave to find someone else to confide in.'

'Yes, I suppose you're right, Mum.'

'I am, now let's get our wardrobes sorted out.'

Chapter Nineteen

A week later, early on a Saturday afternoon, Millie was standing at the kitchen table ironing one of her father's shirts.

It seemed ages since Pat had left the street, and Millie missed her badly. At first she'd felt nothing but anger and disgust, but gradually this had been replaced by pity. Was it any wonder that Pat had turned to her for love, a love that, albeit unnatural, must have been brought about by her father's abuse. Where are you, Pat? she wondered again as she finished the shirt and took up a vest to iron it.

The back door opened and Millie stiffened. Her father was home, and he'd probably be drunk as usual.

'Hello, love.'

Hearing the familiar voice she spun round. No, it couldn't be – and with a smile lighting up her whole face, she rushed into her brother's arms. 'Oh John, John! It's wonderful to see you. Where have you been? I thought you'd be away for more than two months. Have you left the Navy? Did you . . .'

'Whoa, slow down,' he urged, leaning back to stare down into her face. 'One question at a time. Now come on, let go of me so I can sit down.'

Still grinning widely with delight, Millie dropped her arms from around her brother's waist, crossing her fingers before asking, 'Are you home to stay?'

'I don't know yet, but even if I leave the Merchant Navy, it won't be to live here. This trip wasn't a long one and I'm off in a few hours to see Wendy on the Isle of Wight, but had to pop in to see how you are.'

Millie's heart sank, but then she tensed, wondering what her father would say when he came home to find John happily sitting in the kitchen. She studied her brother now, noticing how much he'd changed in such a short time. He looked wonderfully fit, ruddy-faced and brimming with self-assurance and maturity. 'So you got Wendy's letter.'

'Yes, and it's amazing news isn't it. Now tell me, what have you been up to while I've been away?'

Millie hung her head, but before she could speak the kitchen door was flung open, her father halting on the threshold when he saw John.

'Huh, so after leaving me in the lurch without a word, you've come crawling back. Well, you ain't welcome, so bugger off.'

'Millie must have told you why I left, and after reading Mum's suicide note, just looking at you makes me sick.'

Alfie's eyes slewed to Millie, dark with anger. 'You little bitch! So, you found the note in my pocket and didn't say a word! All right,' he said, turning to John again, 'the pair of you read your Mother's note, but you still can't blame me. All she had to do was get rid of the baby – she didn't 'ave to bleedin' kill herself. Now get out, John, and take that tart with you for all I care.'

'What are you talking about? What tart?'

'Your sister.'

'Now then, I won't have you calling her that.'

'Oh, so you ain't told yer precious brother what you've been up to. I'll tell him, shall I?'

'No, Dad, no!'

Ignoring her protest, Alfie spat, 'She's a tart all right. She's been shouting rape and naming me best mate Billy Benson. We've been friends for years, but because of that bitch he's had to do a runner.'

'Millie, is this true?' John asked.

'Yes, he raped me,' she answered flatly, adding with a little more spirit, 'I tried to stop him, really I did, but he was too strong.'

John's face darkened as he turned to look at his father. 'What sort of man are you? Our Millie was raped, but all you're worried about is losing a friend. Bloody hell, Dad, you should string him up.'

'I felt like killing him at first, but by the time I found out about it, he'd scarpered. Since then I've had time to think, and I've only got her word for it that she was raped. Who's to know she didn't lead him on? After all, blood will out.'

'Blood will out! What's that supposed to mean?'

'Never you mind,' he said darkly. 'Now do as I say and get out of my house.'

'No, I'm not going anywhere until I get this sorted out. Millie isn't a liar, Dad, and if she said Benson raped her, then he did.'

'This ain't none of yer business! When you left I disowned you, and as far as I'm concerned you're no longer a part of this family.' With a sickly smirk Alfie then repeated, 'No . . . it's none of yer business, and more so than you know. Now, either you walk out on yer own two feet or I'll throw you out.'

'If you think you can manage it, go ahead and give it a try,' John threatened, widening his stance.

Alfie took another step forward, his face now contorted in anger as he grabbed his son's arm, but John just shook him off like a troublesome pest. 'I ain't scared of you any more, Dad, those days have gone. I'm here for a few hours, that's all, and then I'll go – and with any luck, it'll be for good.'

For a moment their eyes locked, but then Alfie Pratchett turned on his heels, shouting as he stormed out, 'You'd better be gone when I get back.'

A silence followed, but then John sat down again. 'Right, come on, Millie. I want to hear what happened with Billy Benson.'

'I . . . I don't want to talk about it,' she said, shaking all over.

'All right, don't get upset, but I'm sorry I wasn't here to protect you. Christ, where was Dad?'

She wanted to tell him – wanted to say that their father was at Southampton Docks trying to stop him from leaving. If John hadn't gone, if he'd still been here at home, it wouldn't have happened. Instead, love for her brother overcame her spite, and she closed her eyes momentarily before saying, 'He was out.'

'Dad said that Benson did a runner. Did the police catch him?'

'No,' she said shortly. 'Now come on, let's talk about something else. What's it like in the Merchant Navy?'

'If you don't want to talk about it, I can't force you. But are you all right?'

'Yes,' she said quietly. 'Now how was your trip?'

'It was terrific, but I've got something to tell you. You see, before leaving I asked Wendy to marry me and she agreed. Now she's come up with the idea that I join her on the Isle of Wight. It seems there's a lot of work involved in running a guesthouse, including decorating and repairs to the house. I haven't made up my mind yet, and I don't know if living in the same house as her mother would work out. Yet even if I decide against it, you know I can't live here, Millie.'

'Oh John,' she whispered. Yet who could blame him? If she had money she'd leave too, despite being under-age. 'If you don't decide to stay on the Isle of Wight, what will you do?'

'Sign up for the Merchant Navy again. I must admit I like the life, and to be honest I fancy a longer trip.'

'Wendy won't like that.'

'I know, but it might not happen. It all depends on what I find when I see her.'

'You will let me know, won't you?'

'Of course. I'll write to you as soon as there's any news, and if I do decide to stay I'm sure you'll be able to come for a holiday.'

For the next two hours they chatted, Millie with one eye on the clock and willing the hands to turn slowly. She studied John's handsome face as he enthused about the Navy, thinking how different they were in looks. In her case it was as if their father's dark colouring, together with the blonde beauty of their mother, hadn't mixed well, and she had turned out neither one thing nor the other. She was just a pale and insipid shadow of both of them – yet not even that, because neither had her thin sharp features.

Finally, with a small strained smile, John stood up, and drawing her into his arms he gave his sister a quick hug. 'I'll be in touch, love. Take care of yourself.'

Millie watched him go, her mind screaming with the need to beg him to stay, but she held back the words, and her tears, until the door closed. Then, with both hands covering her face, she let them flow.

Hours passed and there was no sign of her father. At ten

o'clock Millie scraped his dinner into the waste bin, and not wanting to be around when he staggered in from the pub, she went to bed. She lay first on one side, then the other, tossing and turning as sleep eluded her. It had been wonderful to see John, but much as she loved her brother, she couldn't help feeling resentful. Unlike her, he had the freedom she desperately wanted. He had choices, whereas she had none. Would he stay on the Isle of Wight with Wendy? Or would he sign on for another trip with the Merchant Navy? Either way, it felt like he was lost to her.

Chapter Twenty

Pat Benson stuffed her belongings into a small case, and after closing it she looked around the small bedsit. At last, she thought, at last she was leaving this dump.

Oh, she had been thankful to find it at first, but then in the state she was in after tramping the streets for hours, it had been a welcome refuge. Most of the other lodgings she'd tried had been way beyond her budget, and some landladies had eyed her with suspicion. In her naivety she hadn't at first realised why some asked if she had a job, saying that they only ran respectable boarding-houses.

She had finally ended up in Railway Cottages, having spotted the card in a newsagent's window offering this room to let. The rent was cheap, and only when she'd seen the cottages had she realised why. Cottages, huh that was a laugh! The grim row of terraced houses backed onto the railway, and she still hadn't grown used to the noise of trains thundering past her window.

However, it was the hole she found drilled in the bathroom door that had been the final straw. It was two weeks ago when she'd noticed it, and that was only because she'd caught her slimy little landlord bent almost double with his eye to the door.

When she'd asked him what he was doing, he'd almost jumped out of his skin before scurrying away. Puzzled, she had leaned over to look through the hole, finding to her amazement a view of the other lady tenant, naked in the bath. Pat grimaced now, remembering how she'd lingered longer than necessary, unable to tear her eyes away. Who'd have thought that plain Miss Newbolt could have such a wonderful body?

The landlord had caught her, of course – caught her doing the same thing that he'd been doing, and she would never forget the mockery in his eyes. Pat knew that she should have reported him to the police, or at least warned Miss Newbolt, but how could she? He knew! The nasty, greasy little man knew her secret, and with his insidious remarks he'd almost blackmailed her into remaining silent.

There was a knock on her door and Pat jumped. It would be him, her toad of a landlord, and she braced herself before opening it.

'Right, if you're ready, I'll inspect your room. Of course you know that if anything's damaged, I've got the right to deduct the cost of replacement from your deposit.'

'Nothing's been damaged,' Pat snapped as she stood back to let the man in.

He slowly walked around the small bedsit, his eyes ranging over every measly item of furniture. 'The seat on that chair's torn,' he said, pointing his long spindly finger.

'I know, but it was like that when I moved in.'

'No, I don't think so, and as I'll have to replace it you won't be getting your deposit back.'

Pat drew in a breath, a surge of anger giving her the courage to argue with the man. 'No, I ain't standing for that. The chair was already torn, and you know it, you slimy little bastard!'

'Don't swear at me, young lady. As for the chair, you didn't ask for an inventory when you moved in, so you haven't got a leg to stand on.'

Shaking with rage, Pat stared at the man, her fists clenched. She desperately needed the deposit for the small flat she'd found, and couldn't let him win. Trying one last bluff she spat, 'It ain't too late for me to tell Miss Newbolt about the hole in the bathroom door.'

'Oh, I don't think you'll be doing that. After all, I've filled it in now so you have no proof. Besides, I think you are forgetting I can let it be known that you're an unnatural woman.'

'Do it then!' Pat yelled, her anger overriding her fear of the man. He couldn't prove anything, she suddenly realised, and cursed herself for not thinking of that before. It was her own silly fear – fear of disclosure – that had kept her quiet. For two weeks she'd been terrified he would tell people that she was a lesbian, but this was the final straw and she wasn't going to let him browbeat her. 'You can't prove anything either, and it will be my word against yours. There's nothing to stop me knocking on Miss Newbolt's door this very minute. I'm sure she'd be shocked to hear that you've been spying on her in the bath, and I should warn her that the hole might reappear after I've gone.'

The landlord ground his jaws as he stared at her, and for a moment Pat thought he'd call her bluff, but finally he held out some notes. 'All right, here, you can have your deposit. Now give me your key, and get out.'

Pat took the money, shoving it into her purse, then picking up her case and almost throwing the key at him, she marched from the room. On her way downstairs she surreptitiously took an envelope from her pocket, and checking the man wasn't behind her, she slipped it under Miss Newbolt's door.

Half an hour later, as Pat sat on the top deck of a number 137 bus, a small smile played around her lips as she pictured the scene when the woman read her note. As the bus drove over the bridge, her eyes took in the River Thames and her smile now widened. She had lied about her age to get this new job, and it had been worth it to get a decent wage. Now she was moving to a new area, a new life, and it felt like a fresh start. She'd stood up to that slimy landlord and her head went up with pride. Never again would she let a man, any man, abuse her again. Those days were gone, gone for ever.

As the bus now reached Chelsea Bridge Road she hardly noticed, Millie's face suddenly swimming before her eyes. She still missed her so much and it was the one thing that now marred her happiness. Oh Millie, she wondered, will I ever see you again?

On the Isle of Wight, Wendy ran down the drive, throwing herself into John's arms. 'Oh, John! John!'

He lifted her up effortlessly, swinging her round, and without putting her down, his lips covered hers. 'God, I've missed you.'

'I've missed you too,' she gasped.

John put her down then, his eyes sweeping over the house. 'It's bigger than I expected.'

'Come on, come inside,' Wendy urged. 'We've got so much to talk about.'

'Hello, Mrs Hall,' he said, seeing Bertha hovering in the hall.

'Hello, lad, so you found us then?'

'Yes, and how are you?'

'Fine, fine, but come through to the kitchen.'

With Wendy's hand in his they passed the magnificently carved staircase to the kitchen at the back of the house. It was huge, with a large well-scrubbed table in the centre, around which he saw six chairs. There was a massive range, and as his eyes alighted on it, Bertha grinned.

'It's the bleedin' bane of my life, but I think I've got the measure of it now. Sit down and I'll make you a cup of tea – and what about something to eat?'

'Yes, please,' he said. When Wendy had taken him to meet her mother in their flat above the ironmonger's, he'd immediately sensed her animosity, and it hadn't taken him long to realise that she had ambitions for her daughter, ambitions that didn't include him. Now though, she seemed welcoming, and in no time a sandwich appeared, thick with ham and tomatoes, which he ate with relish.

'Come on, let's go for a walk in the grounds,' Wendy said as he swallowed the last dregs of tea.

John thanked Bertha, and then followed Wendy through the back door, this one leading directly outside to a paved area. The grounds stretched in front of them, and as Wendy hooked her arm through his they began to walk. 'I can't take all this in,' he said as they came to a small copse where Wendy led him towards a bench under a huge oak tree.

'It's amazing, isn't it, but as I said in my letter, we can't manage all this on our own. Ted the gardener's a gem, but it's too much for him now.'

'Wendy, I know nothing about gardening, or doing house repairs.'

'You could learn, and how hard can it be? Mum's happy with my idea too, and for the time being there's a room waiting for you.'

'For the time being?'

'Yes. You see, once we're married we can make a couple of rooms into a small private apartment.'

'You've got it all worked out, haven't you.'

'Darling, surely you can see how wonderful it would be! You're back now, finished with the Merchant Navy, and we can offer you a job.'

'I don't think I fancy working for you. It wouldn't seem right.'

'Oh dear, I didn't intend to make it sound like that. Of course you wouldn't be working for *me*, and in any case we couldn't afford to employ anyone. Ted works for a pittance, supplemented by stuff from the garden, and I'm surprised he has stayed. We haven't any guests yet, but thanks to a double booking at the hotel, we've got our first ones arriving next week. Even that came about thanks to Ted because he knows the hotel manager.'

'So just how do you hope to manage financially?'

'Once we become established it won't be a problem, and next season we expect to be fully booked. This is a very popular area with holidaymakers, and we've heard that rooms are snapped up.'

'And in the meantime?'

'We're coping . . . just. There's a glut of fruit and veg in the kitchen garden, and we have eggs from the chickens.' Her face suddenly fell. 'We're nearly out of money though, and I must admit it's a bit worrying.'

'I can help you out there,' John said, and reaching into his pocket he pulled out an envelope. 'Here, take this. I hardly spent a penny on the trip so managed to save twenty-five pounds.'

'But I can't take that!'

'Why not? We're a partnership aren't we?' he said, pulling her into his arms.

That night, as John lay in bed, his thoughts were twisting and turning. Wendy seemed so sure that he'd stay, but he still had doubts. Yes, he would be living rent free with all his food provided, but didn't fancy the thought of being without a wage. Somehow it made him feel less of a man. They had discussed the situation for hours, Bertha joining in and saying how much he was needed, but even so he hadn't come to a firm decision.

The money he'd given Wendy had brought swift tears to Bertha's eyes, making him realise how tenuous their situation was. Yes, they had guests arriving next week, but what then? If no more were forthcoming they faced the winter without any income. It was then that he came to a decision, the perfect solution, and now with his mind made up he was finally able to drift off to sleep.

When John awoke to the sound of cockerels heralding the dawn, he sleepily rubbed his eyes. The bathroom was just along the landing, and after a quick wash he made his way downstairs, surprised to see Bertha already up.

'John! You're up early.'

'I could say the same for you.'

'It's funny, ain't it. The traffic was loud on Lavender Hill, and when we first moved here I found the silence a miracle. Huh, that was until I realised that the countryside has its own noises. Now it's them chickens that wake me up every morning, and some-times I feel like shooting the pesky things.'

'Yes, the cockerels woke me too.' He turned as the door opened again, Wendy coming in looking deliciously tousled and sleepy. God, she was gorgeous, and he wondered momentarily if he'd made the right decision.

'Morning, darling,' and running lightly to his side she stood on tiptoe to kiss his cheek. 'Oh, I still can't believe you're really here!'

When he saw the joy in her eyes he lowered his head, deciding to put off telling her until later. 'Hello, beautiful, you look good enough to eat.'

An hour later, the three of them were sitting round the table eating breakfast, and it wasn't until they'd finished that John spoke. 'Wendy, I've decided to sign on for another trip.'

'No! You promised you'd only do one!'

'I know, but I've been giving it a lot of thought, and I feel I've made the right decision.'

Wendy's lower lip trembled. 'What, to leave me again? Why, John? I don't understand.'

'Until the guesthouse is established, you have no income. If I go on another trip I can arrange for you to have most of my earnings, and at least that way you'll have money coming in every week.'

'We can't let you do that,' Bertha said.

'Yes, you can. If I'm to be a part of this family, you must let me help.'

'No, John, I can't bear the thought of you going away again,' Wendy cried.

'It won't be for ever, darling, and it's the best solution.'

'But what about the jobs that need doing?'

'There's nothing urgent. Yes, a couple of the bedrooms need decorating, but until next season when you get a lot of guests, they needn't be used. As for the garden – well, Ted will just have to manage for a bit longer, and perhaps you could help him out now and then.'

'Me!' Wendy exclaimed. 'But I know nothing about gardening.'

'Nor do I, darling, but as you pointed out to me when I said the same thing, it can't be that hard to learn.'

'You can't leave me again! You can't!'

John put out a detaining hand as Wendy jumped up, but she shrugged him off, her eyes wild as she fled the room.

'Let her go, lad,' Bertha urged. 'Give her time to come round, and then like me she'll thank you. It's a wonderful thing you're doing and has taken a huge weight off my mind. Wendy thought we'd be filled with guests straight away, but if nobody knows about us, how did she think that was going to happen? I think we both acted too quickly without thinking things through. We saw this house, fell in love with it, and grasped at a way to keep it.'

'It's a lovely place and I'm not surprised you want to hang on to it. It will work, I'm sure of it, but I should think that every business takes time to establish. Next year you'll be inundated with guests.'

'Yeah, I think you're right, but we'll 'ave to do something about advertising.'

'Now there speaks a businesswoman.'

'Me, a businesswoman! No, lad, all I've ever been is an office cleaner.'

'Well, you were wasted then,' John said, finding himself liking

Bertha more and more. Yes, he would do one more trip, with luck a long run to the Middle East, and then he'd be happy to settle down here. All he had to do now was to talk Wendy round.

Chapter Twenty-One

Millie sat on the back of a coal cart, wishing her father had entered the competition, but no amount of persuading had convinced him to join in. Now, as the parade slowly started, she felt a surge of excitement.

'Right, girls, we're off,' Eric Green called as he gripped the reins, and his little daughter laughed with delight.

Millie turned to smile at Mrs Green, resplendent in a costume of dark green. 'Mary looks lovely,' she said.

'Yeah, but how long for?'

The little girl looked so cute in her long white dress, trimmed at the bottom with lace, and in her determination for the child to win best costume, Mrs Green had even covered an old umbrella with matching white lace to make it look like a parasol.

'Thanks for letting me join you on the cart,' Millie now said.

'Leave it out, love. We're pleased to have you, and it was a good idea of yours to wear these costumes.'

In the distance, Millie could hear the brass band that led the parade, followed by the Boys Brigade and Scouts. Next in line were floats advertising various local businesses, and then came the Brewery Wagons, pulled by huge shire horses.

Progress was slow, and Millie strained to see the other carts entered by Jenkins Coal Merchants. They all looked colourful with a variety of decorations. One had paper flowers decked along the sides, another ribbons, a third had made good use of a Union Jack flag. The horses were the most important, and they looked beautifully groomed with ribbons plaited in their tails and plumes on their heads. As the speed picked up a little she could hear the shining horse brasses chinking, and smiled with pleasure.

'Do you think our cart is the best, Millie?' Mrs Green asked.

'Well, it certainly looks wonderful, and I think it's got a good chance. Prancer looks a picture too.'

'Yeah, he's a nice horse and thank the Lord he's gentle.'

Jack Jenkins appeared, his wife on his arm, looking marvellous in a Victorian costume that must have cost the earth. Millie, unable to make her own dress, had been thrilled when her boss had hired one for her, and though not as ornate as the one Mrs Jenkins was wearing, she was secretly pleased with it. It had been so kind of him to hire it for her. He'd dismissed her thanks, saying she deserved it after all the work she had put in to organise the parade.

Gesturing now for her to join them, Millie, careful of her long dress, jumped from the back of the cart, and as she went to their side, Jack Jenkins smiled with delight. 'This is marvellous, Millie, and I feel sure we'll get a first. Well done.'

'Thank you.'

'Yes, you've done well,' Mrs Jenkins said, 'but it's a shame that some of the costumes are a bit tatty.'

Millie bit back the reply that sprung to her lips. What did the woman expect? Yes, the costumes were home made, but with their limited resources the coalmen's wives had worked miracles. Unlike Mrs Jenkins, who had her costume specially made, they had managed to make passable Victorian dresses out of a variety of cotton materials.

'I think they all look lovely,' Jack Jenkins said as they walked along beside the parade. 'Thank you again, Millie.'

They spoke for a while longer, and when the parade stopped momentarily, Millie climbed back onto the cart, sitting with her legs dangling over the back. The sun beat down, the crowds continued to cheer, and as the brass band played a jaunty tune she settled back to enjoy the ride.

It was late in the afternoon before the results were announced, with Jenkins Coal Merchants winning a first for Prancer. Adding to the Green family pleasure, little Mary won best costume.

Millie watched while the coalman went to collect his rosette, and then found Jack Jenkins at her side. 'This is all thanks to you, Millie,' he said, beaming with pleasure.

'No, it isn't. The men did all the work and they must have been in the yard at the crack of dawn to groom their horses. Just look at Prancer,' she added, pointing to a dappled grey horse as Mr Green attached the rosette. 'He actually looks like he's grinning.'

'Yes, he's a fine animal and deserved to win.'

'I'll be sorry to see the horses go,' Millie murmured.

'Yes, but it won't be for a few years yet.' Jack assured her. 'My wife and I are off now as we have a party to go to, but once again, thank you for all your hard work.'

'I enjoyed it,' Millie told him.

'Good. Well, I'll see you at work tomorrow.'

Millie smiled as he walked away. It had been a lovely day – a day of success for the coal yard, one she knew would be talked about for many weeks. Her heart felt lighter as she made her way home – her boss's praise still ringing in her ears, and her problems for the time being, forgotten.

Another week passed and now Millie's stomach rumbled with hunger. To distract her mind she picked up John's letter, but as she read his words yet again, she felt a surge of unhappiness. He'd decided to sign on for another trip, this time a long distance one, and he'd be away for several months.

John then went on to describe the Isle of Wight, and the house, saying that when he returned he would settle there. Millie flung the letter to one side, and instead of feeling pleased for him, she found her thoughts embittered. Not once had he asked how she was coping.

Her eyes now roamed around the kitchen, alighting on the chair that her father had smashed last night, leaving only two tucked under the table. Her mind shied away from the memory of the other broken chair, the one that had been thrown through the window on the day of her mother's death.

Since John's visit her father's drinking seemed to be spiralling out of control and once again he hadn't given her any house-keeping money. Desperate to pay at least a few bob off the rent arrears, there was little of her wages left with which to buy food.

Despite the hot weather she'd made a stew out of scrag end of lamb, but even then it consisted mainly of vegetables.

God, she'd rather be at work – at least it took her mind off things, and she now regretted taking the three days' holiday that Jack Jenkins said she was due.

It was an hour later when Millie heard banging next door, and her lips tightened. At first she'd made friendly overtures to the new family who'd moved into the Bensons' house, but it didn't take her long to find out she didn't like them. The mother thought herself a cut above many people in the street, though what gave her that idea Millie was at a loss to understand. It hadn't taken Dora Saunders long to gather information about the family, telling all those who wanted to listen that Mrs Bradshaw was from Yorkshire and at one time had been a Sunday-school teacher. Mr Bradshaw worked for British Rail, and they had just one child, an obnoxious, snotty-nosed bully of a boy.

Ena Bradshaw had soon found an ally in Jessie Hardcastle, and they spent a lot of time on their doorsteps surveying the goings-on in the street. Both stood with their arms folded and lips pursed at anything they didn't approve of – one such thing being Millie's father when he staggered home drunk from the pub.

Millie jumped as the door flew open, and as if her thoughts had conjured him up, her dad lurched into the room. Her eyes flew to the clock, and seeing that it was only two-thirty, she asked, 'What are you doing home?'

'I've been sacked,' he slurred, his voice fuddled with drink.

'No! What happened?'

'Samson bolted.'

'Bolted! But how?'

'Soddin' kids and cap guns, that's how.' He closed his eyes in despair before adding. 'They're gonna shoot him, Millie.'

'No! Oh no, Dad,' she cried, and not waiting to hear any more she ran from the house.

Millie was panting breathlessly when she reached the coal depot, and perspiration was running down her face as she flung open the office door. Her boss was sitting going through some paperwork and he looked up at her tempestuous entrance.

'Millie,' he said. 'What on earth are you doing here? You should be at home enjoying your time off.'

'Please,' she panted, ignoring his words. 'Please don't shoot Samson!'

The big man sighed. 'There are regulations and I had no choice, Millie. Due to your father's irresponsibility the horse caused havoc and it's lucky that no one was injured.'

'But from what he told me, it wasn't his fault.'

'Your father left the horse and cart unattended outside a public house, and not only that, he was found to be drunk. Yes, there were children playing nearby with cap guns. However, I repeat, the fault lies with your father, and for that reason he has been dismissed.'

Millie stared at Mr Jenkins, her thoughts full of Samson – poor, soft and gentle Samson. The caps going off must have terrified him, and was it any wonder that he'd bolted? 'Can't you do anything to save him?' she begged, not realising by Mr Jenkins' expression how incongruous she sounded, begging to save a horse instead of her father's job.

He shook his head. 'No, and anyway the deed has already been done.'

'No, you haven't shot him!' Eyes wild, she flew at Jack Jenkins, fists clenched as she pounded his chest. 'Oh . . . oh, how could you – how could you!'

'Stop it, Millie, stop this at once!'

All the weeks of worry, all her pent-up fears and emotions erupted like a volcano. 'You're a monster, and I hate you! I'll never work for you again, never – and you can stick your bloody job!' she cried, suddenly turning and dashing out of the office.

Once outside, Millie felt faint, and for a moment she had to pause in the yard, bent forward as she held on to the wall. Someone spoke and she raised her head. 'What did you say?' she whispered.

'I said it's Alfie Pratchett that should be shot, not the horse,' the stableman said bitterly. 'He was a nice animal, but because of your father he's now destined for the glue factory.'

Millie's mouth filled with a bitter taste. Yes, she was devastated about Samson, but now the feelings she had tried to bury resurfaced, the horse's death acting as a catalyst. When she'd found her mother's suicide note, hatred for her father had burned in her chest and now it rose again – hatred so violent that it made her head pound. When John left home she'd repressed her emotions, knowing it was the only way she could cope with living with her father. But now, with anger like a knot in her heart, she staggered across the yard. Her father had caused one death, and now he'd caused another. If it wasn't for him, her beloved mother would still be alive! And so would dear old Samson.

It was only as she neared Harmond Street that another thought hit her. God, she'd told Jack Jenkins to stick his job! Her father had been sacked, and now she was out of work too!

A few days later, Millie sat facing her father across the kitchen table. She just wanted to leave, to get away from him, but with hardly a penny to her name and nowhere to go, it was impossible.

One day, she thought, one day she'd leave and make a life of her own, but for now, like it or not, she would have to speak to him. 'Dad, we can't go on like this. The rent's due again but I haven't got enough to pay it, let alone any off the arrears. I've managed to get another job, but I can't start until Monday, and to make matters worse it's ten bob less a week.'

'It ain't my fault,' he whined, his voice full of self-pity. 'I've had a look round for another job, but there's nothing going. What am I supposed to do anyway? I'm a coalman, from a long line of coalmen, and I don't know how to do anything else. All I'm fit for now is the scrapheap.'

Millie looked at her father's hands and saw they were shaking – his need for alcohol desperate. There was hardly any food in the cupboard, but last night he had managed to drink himself into a stupor. Where on earth had he found the money?

'Give us a few bob, Millie.'

'No, Dad.'

He jumped up, and rifling in her handbag, he pulled out her purse, his eyes darkening with anger when he found it empty. 'You must 'ave some money, so where is it?'

'I spent what little I had on food.'

'Don't give me that! Now you find me a few bob, or else!'

Millie stared at her father, hating him and determined to hang on to the little money she had left. There wasn't much, but she'd had the sense to hide it, and now running from the room she cried, 'You've seen my purse and it's empty!'

Alfie listened to Millie's feet pounding upstairs, and threw her purse across the room in disgust. Christ, he needed a drink. His daughter didn't know it, but he'd received a letter of eviction and unless the rent was paid, plus the arrears, they'd be out.

His insides clenched again, the desire for drink overshadowing the need to pay the rent. Where could he get some money? *Where?* A thought crossed his mind and he grimaced. Joe Nesbitt was a loan shark and was known to be a nasty piece of work, yet the man was his only hope. As kids they had lived in the same street and attended the same school, but that was in the distant past and he'd had nothing to do with the man since.

He pushed aside his doubts, thinking that he wouldn't borrow much. Just enough to pay off the rent arrears and buy a few drinks.

Joe Nesbitt had a room at the back of a sweetshop in Queenstown Road, and it didn't take Alfie long to get there. For a moment he hesitated, but then his craving for alcohol overwhelmed his commonsense, and he strode inside. A woman stood behind the counter, a large jar of humbugs in her hands, tilted as she shook them onto the scales. He skirted an old woman who was staring avidly at the scales, obviously making sure she got her full two-ounce measure, and at his whispered request the shop assistant pointed to a door.

He knocked, and a beefy, pug-nosed man with the look of a boxer opened it. 'Yeah, what do yer want?'

'Can I see Mr Nesbitt, please?'

'What for?'

'A . . . a small loan.'

The man stood back, and as Alfie entered the room he saw Nesbitt sitting behind a desk. 'Hello, Joe,' he said hesitantly. Was it possible? Was this the same Joe Nesbitt he'd been at school with? As a child Joe had been a ragamuffin, with holes in his shoes and knees hanging out of his trousers. Now, with his expensive looking suit and fingers thick with gold rings, he looked prosperous. Obviously the loan-shark business paid well, Alfie thought grimly.

'Well, well, if it ain't Alfie Pratchett,' Joe drawled, his eyes narrowing speculatively. 'What can I do for yer?'

'I need a small loan, and wondered if you can help?'

'I heard on the grapevine that you've lost yer coal-round, Alfie, so how are you gonna pay it back?'

'How did you hear about that?'

'Oh, you'd be surprised how much local gossip reaches my ears. It comes in handy sometimes too, and as I said, if I give you a loan, how are you gonna pay it back?'

'My girl's working now, so it won't be a problem. Anyway, I should be able to get another job soon.'

'How much do yer want?'

Greedily Alfie named a fairly large figure, expecting Joe to refuse, but to his amazement the man nodded. 'Yeah, all right, but you know my rates and I won't tolerate any late payments. If the money ain't paid on time I usually send Dave there to pick it up, and he don't take no arguments.'

Hearing the menace in his voice, Alfie gulped, glancing quickly at the man who had opened the door. Blimey, if he got on the wrong side of him he'd end up like mincemeat. 'I won't be late paying, Joe,' he promised, his hand now reaching out eagerly for the notes being counted onto the desk.

'The first payment, plus interest, will be in a week's time, is that understood?'

'Yeah, Joe, of course it is. Anything you say.' Alfie hurriedly pocketed the money and left the room, a slight sheen of sweat on his brow. Bloody hell, he thought, finally working out the interest rate as he hurried to the nearest pub. It was exorbitant and would take him a year to pay off, but as he stepped into the Railway Arms and ordered a drink, he dismissed the worry, his mouth salivating as the barmaid poured him a pint of bitter.

Several hours later, and Alfie could just about stay on his feet as he stood swaying in front of the bar. Without Billy Benson as a drinking partner he turned fuddled eyes to the man standing beside him. 'Do yer fancy a whisky, mate?'

'I wouldn't say no.'

As Alfie ordered the drinks, fishing money out of his trouser pocket, he didn't notice the wad of notes falling onto the floor, but the man did and his eyes gleamed. He'd seen Alfie Pratchett many times in the local pubs, but usually avoided him like the plague. The man was a sponger, going from customer to customer in his search for someone to buy him a drink, but tonight it was different. Tonight Pratchett had money to spend and he was determined to take advantage of it.

Waiting until Alfie was diverted, he glanced quickly around. No one else had seen the wad of notes and he bent down, quickly scooping up the money and stuffing it into his own pocket. Cor, he thought, smiling inwardly, it looked like a good few quid. He had no idea where Alfie Pratchett had acquired such a hoard, but he wasn't one to look a gift horse in the mouth.

By the time another fifteen minutes had passed, Alfie's legs were caving under him, and solicitously the man said, 'Come on, mate, I think it's time to get you home.'

'Jusht one more drink,' he slurred.

'No more, come on,' and putting his arm around Alfie he held him upright as they left the pub. Christ, the soppy old sod can't handle his drink, he thought, leading Alfie around the corner and into an alley. Once there, it only took one punch and the bloke was out cold. He rifled in his pockets, annoyed when he only found a few coins, and spitting on Alfie Pratchett, he ran off, leaving him lying there.

Chapter Twenty-Two

It took Millie a month to know that she hated her new job, but somehow she had to stick it out. Her manager was nothing like Jack Jenkins, and the work was tedious. Oh, why had she been so impulsive? She'd loved her job at the coal depot, and her boss. Regulations, he'd said, when trying to tell her why Samson had to be shot, but at the time his words hadn't penetrated her fury.

The few days' wages she'd been due had been sent in the post, along with her National Insurance card, and though she had stupidly looked for a note from Mr Jenkins, there was nothing. She should have gone back to see him, to apologise, but shame, not only for her own behaviour, but her father's too, kept her away. The stableman blamed her dad for Samson's death, and no doubt all the other coalmen felt the same. She shook her head sadly, realising that nowadays the name Pratchett was probably hated at the depot.

On Friday, faint with hunger, she took her wages and went straight to the market. Most of the stalls had packed up, but the few left were selling off vegetables at rock-bottom prices. Millie bargained forcibly and managed to get a few more pence knocked off, but not daring to spend money on meat or fish, she hurried home knowing that all she'd be able to make was vegetable soup.

Her father looked up as she went indoors, but he didn't say a word. Millie looked at his face and saw that the bruising on his chin had faded. She still didn't know how he'd been injured, and didn't care. Her own problem was uppermost in her mind, plaguing her day and night. She had gone to the library last week, her face flaming as she sat in the reference section reading the book, finding that her worst suspicions had been confirmed.

'Give us a few bob, Millie.'

God, she was sick of this, sick of hearing the same words over and over again, his continuous demands for money driving her mad. Why didn't he get a job? Any job! 'No, Dad.'

He reared up and she cringed. 'You tight-fisted, ugly, thin-faced cow. I said give me some money!'

'And I said no! Go on then, hit me – but I can't give you what I haven't got.'

Was it something in her tone, she didn't know, but instead of giving her the clout she expected, her father just shoved her out of his way as he stormed out of the kitchen. She heard him go into the outhouse, and moments later the back door slammed.

Alfie crept along the alley, his nerves jumping. Should he risk it? It would have been better to keep out of sight, but with the need for alcohol overriding his fears, he stepped out, scurrying along the street. Someone would buy him a drink, he thought, someone would feel sorry for him, and he licked his lips in anticipation.

It happened just as he reached the corner, and as the car screeched to a halt, Alfie backed against the wall.

'Hello, Alfie. Been avoiding me, have you?'

'No, no, of course not, Joe.'

'Where's me money?'

'I ain't got it on me, but if you'd just give me a day or two . . .'

The car door was flung open. 'Get in!' Joe snapped.

'I . . . I can't, not now. I've got to go somewhere.'

'I said, get in!'

Another door opened and Alfie felt his legs trembling as Joe's minder got out, advancing menacingly towards him. There was no choice, and seeing this he skirted around the man, scrambling hurriedly into the back of the car.

'Good choice, Alfie. You wouldn't want to fall out with Dave. He likes a chance to use his fists or he gets a bit rusty,' and as the huge man got back into the driver's seat, Joe added, 'Take us to the lock-up, Dave.'

'Please, mate,' Alfie appealed. 'Give me another day or two.

Someone nicked the money you loaned me, but I'll pay you back, I swear I will.'

'Don't give me that! The truth is you still ain't working, and I heard your daughter left the coal depot too.'

'But she's got another job. Just give me a bit of time . . . please, mate.'

'Mate – I ain't yer mate! I gave you a bit of leeway for old time's sake, but you've taken the piss and I ain't standing for that. It's been a month and you ain't paid a penny off the loan. You can't say I didn't warn you.'

'But . . .'

'Shut up! Did I tell you to speak? Now not another word – or else!'

There was no ignoring the menace in Joe's voice, and Alfie sank low in the seat, silent now as they drove down Lavender Hill. They turned left at Clapham Junction, and as Dave drove along Northcote Road he veered into a small side street, pulling up outside a row of small lock-ups.

'I'll leave it to you, Dave. You know what to do,' Joe said, reaching into his inside pocket and pulling out a cigar.

The passenger door opened, Dave leaning inside to grab Alfie by the collar. 'Come on, you, get out!'

He felt his bowels turn to water and turning to Joe he pleaded, 'Look, I'll pay you back, honest I will. Just give me forty-eight hours.'

'No, now get out of the car!'

Alfie staggered as he was yanked onto the pavement, his knees barely able to support him as he was dragged across to one of the lock-ups.

Hanging onto Alfie with one hand, Dave lifted his other huge fist and thumped on the door. He then turned, his face dark with menace. 'I'm gonna enjoy this, you little toe-rag,' he growled, and as the door opened, Alfie felt himself being shoved inside.

On Saturday morning, Millie paced the floor. Where was her father? No matter how drunk he got, he always managed to find his way home, so where was he? Maybe I should telephone the police, or the hospitals, she thought, but then the door opened as her dad staggered in. 'My God!' she cried. 'What happened?'

'Mind yer own bleedin' business.'

'But, Dad, you should see a doctor, or go to Casualty.'

'I'm all right,' he said, wincing as he flopped onto a chair. 'Get me a glass of water.'

She rushed to the sink and filled a cup, from which he drank deeply. One eye was shut, a livid purple bruise surrounding it, and his lip was cut and swollen. It was obvious he'd been beaten, and badly. 'Dad, let me call the doctor.'

'No! Now shut up and help me upstairs.'

Millie did as he asked, but it was a struggle as her father was obviously in great pain. Once he was seated on the side of the bed she helped to remove his shirt, gasping when she saw the bruises surrounding his ribs. 'Dad, who did this to you?'

'I said mind yer own bloody business. Now get out and leave me alone. I need to get some sleep.'

With a sigh of exasperation Millie left the bedroom, and on reaching the kitchen she pulled out a chair to sit down, her hands covering her face. What was the matter with her? What did she care if her father had been beaten up? Yet seeing the pain he was in, she couldn't help feeling sorry for him.

You're mad, she told herself, knowing that the beating he'd had was nothing to the one she was likely to get from him when she broke the news. Once again she wished there was someone she could talk to, someone to tell her what to do. Her dreams of leaving home resurfaced, but now more than ever it was impossible. She thought about Pat, once again wondering where she was, and wishing with all her heart that she had left with her.

After being in bed for a few days, her father managed to get up, and when Millie came home from work the following Thursday he was nowhere to be seen. Her brow creased as she wondered how on earth he'd managed to go out when only yesterday he could hardly move. She spotted the letter then, flung in the hearth, and smoothing out the creases, her heart sank. It was an eviction order, and as she read the contents it became obvious that this was the last warning. If the rent wasn't paid, plus the arrears, they were to be evicted. She looked at the date, her eyes widening in horror – there were only three days left.

The door slammed and as her father walked in he immediately said, 'Go and pack yer stuff.'

'Pack! But why?'

'You're holding the letter, so it's obvious, ain't it.'

'But where are we going?'

'I've found somewhere. It ain't much, but it'll do until I sort something else out.'

'How much is the rent?' Millie asked worriedly.

'Mind yer own bleedin' business. Now get yer stuff packed because we're leaving in an hour.'

'An hour! But . . .'

'Shut up! I said we're going in an hour and I meant it. Now you can stay here and wait to be chucked out, or you can come with me. I don't give a sod either way.'

'What about the furniture?'

'I've flogged it to the secondhand shop up the road, not that the tight git gave me much for it. He's on his way now to pick it up.'

'But if you've sold it, what will we use in the place you've found?'

'Stop asking bloody questions! Now if yer coming, go and pack yer stuff!'

In less than an hour Millie was ready, and unable to bear the sight of their furniture being loaded onto the back of a cart, she decided to pop next door to say goodbye to Stella Blake. With a swift look over her shoulder she sneaked out the back and knocked on Stella's door. It was Dora Saunders who opened it.

'What's going on, Millie? Why is yer furniture being loaded onto a cart?'

'W . . . we're moving.'

'Moving! Where to, love?'

'I . . . I don't know, but please, can I come in to say goodbye to Mrs Blake?'

'Blimey, if you ask me it sounds like yer father's doing a flit, and how come you don't know where you're going?'

'He hasn't told me yet. Now please, can I come in?'

'Of course you can,' and as Millie followed Dora into the kitchen she was still being barraged with questions.

'See, I told yer, Stella. Millie and her dad are doing a flit.'

'Is this true, Millie?'

'Yes, the council have served us with an eviction order.'

'See, I told yer,' Dora said again, her chest puffing with importance.

Millie stared at Mrs Blake and seeing how frail the woman looked she was overcome with guilt. 'I'm sorry I haven't been round to see you for a while.'

'That's all right, ducks, but I'm sorry to hear you're leaving.' Her eyes suddenly widened and she slumped forward in her chair, crying, 'Oh, my God.'

Dora rushed forward, her face creasing with concern. 'What's wrong, Stella?'

'Oh, I'm a useless old woman. Useless!'

'Do you feel ill, love?'

'No, no, but for ages I've been trying to remember something. I don't know why, perhaps it's seeing Millie, but I know what it is now.'

'Stella, you ain't making any sense.'

'The box,' she said, before turning to look at Millie again. 'Before she died, your mother gave it to me to look after, and I was supposed to give it to you if anything happened to her. She left it with me 'cos she didn't want yer father to find it. I . . . I think it's her jewellery and she didn't want him flogging it. Oh, how could I forget about it?' she cried, her rheumy eyes filling with tears.

A box, Millie thought, but upset to see Mrs Blake in such distress, she said, 'It's all right. Please don't cry.'

'Oh Millie, when yer mother gave it to me to look after, I should've realised what she intended to do. She was acting a bit odd at the time, but what did I do? Nothing! I did nothing! She was me best friend and I should've known,' she repeated, her voice rising hysterically.

'No, Mrs Blake, you have nothing to feel guilty about. You couldn't have known what my mother was going to do. None of us did.'

Stella wiped a grey and creased handkerchief over her eyes, saying with a sob, 'I . . . I'm sorry, love, you should've had the box ages ago. Listen: go into my sitting room and you'll find it in the dresser.'

Millie left the room, but it was some time before she found the tiny wooden box tucked at the back of the dresser. She fingered the intricate carving, her eyes puzzled. Was this really her mother's? Still unsure, she returned to the kitchen. 'Is this the one?'

'Yeah, that's it.'

The box was light, and as Millie shook it, nothing rattled. She doubted it held jewellery, so why had her mother left it with Stella Blake?

'Ain't you gonna open it?' Dora asked, her eyes gleaming with interest.

'I can't, it's locked.'

'Oh, what a shame, and I suppose you'll 'ave to force it. Hold on a minute and I'll get you a knife.'

'Thanks, Mrs Saunders, but I've got to go and it'll have to wait.'

Dora pursed her lips, obviously disappointed, whilst Millie went over to Stella Blake, kissing her lightly on the cheek. She then did the same to Dora before saying goodbye.

'Will yer promise you'll come back to see me?' Stella asked.

'Yes, if I can.'

'Yeah, come and see us and then you can tell us what you found in that box,' Dora urged.

Millie nodded, but deep down she knew it would be unlikely. She was in trouble, big trouble, and once they found out, they wouldn't want to know her. She'd be ostracised, and probably unwelcome in Harmond Street.

She was ready, and with no time to force open the box, Millie had stashed it inside her bundle. Now, heaving it higher onto her shoulder, she followed behind her father as they stepped outside. Yes, they were being evicted, but why was he in such a hurry to leave?

Several neighbours were standing on their doorsteps, their eyes alight with avid interest. 'Where are you off to?' Ena Bradshaw asked.

'Mind yer own bleedin' business,' Alfie said, a scowl on his face.

'Now then, there's no need for that,' and shaking her head with disgust Ena turned to Jessie Hardcastle, saying in a loud whisper, 'Huh, if you ask me, it's good riddance to bad rubbish.'

Tears of humiliation filled Millie's eyes, yet in a way she was glad they were going. At least now the neighbours would never find out, and she wouldn't suffer an even greater humiliation. Aware of the women's eyes on their backs, she kept her head lowered until they had turned the corner, leaving Harmond Street behind.

Neither spoke as they trudged through street after street, and an hour later the area they reached was unfamiliar to Millie. The surroundings were mostly industrial, but many of the buildings were empty and in a state of disrepair. Her father looked exhausted, his face grey with pain when they finally turned into a gloomy and foreboding alley. She hesitated, but he growled, 'Come on, it's down here.'

She followed him, the smell of overflowing drains rank in her nostrils. There were only a few narrow, derelict houses on one side, opposite an imposing brick wall that looked at least ten feet high. There were spikes on the top to stop intrusion, and the height cut out what little light penetrated this narrow alley. She shuddered. Surely they weren't going to live here!

'This is ours,' her father said, drawing to a halt.

Millie gawked at the battered front door, then at the small window to one side, broken and partly boarded. She aroused herself sufficiently to protest, 'But, Dad . . .'

'It's empty, and it's all I could find, so get that look off of your face. How did you expect me to find anything else with the paltry wage you earn?'

The door wasn't locked, and scraped across the concrete floor as he shoved it open. Millie followed him inside, and as her eyes adjusted to the gloom she saw that the room was mostly empty, except for a battered table and a few old orange boxes stacked in a corner. There was just this one room on the ground floor and she could see a stained and filthy sink in one corner. Oh, the smell, she thought, covering her mouth in horror as the stench of sewage assailed her nostrils.

Rushing to the sink she leaned over it, heaving until what little food there was in her stomach was gone. Then, dashing the back of her hand across her mouth, she reached for the tap. Nothing came out as she turned it on, no water, and she looked with horror-stricken eyes at her father.

'Yeah, I know, it stinks in here. Its probably because the toilet out back is blocked and in a bit of a state. It'll be all right once you've cleaned it up.'

'How am I supposed to do that? There's no water!'

'Yes, there is. There's a tap in the outside yard and it's working. You'll just have to fetch what water we need in a bucket. It ain't that bad and there's another room upstairs. It's got a couple of old mattresses on the floor and I'll bring one down here to sleep on. You can kip up there.'

'Oh Dad, we can't stay here. It's disgusting.'

'It won't be for long, and anyway you might as well know that I had to do a flit. I'm in debt to a loan shark, and if I don't pay back what I owe, he'll kill me. This beating was just a warning and somehow I've got to get his dosh. In the meantime this place is derelict, and with no rent to pay we should be able to manage on what you earn.'

So that was it, Millie thought. That was why they'd left in such a hurry. Christ, a loan shark! She looked around the filthy room again, shaking her head in despair. 'But there's nothing here. No furniture, and we haven't even got blankets.'

'We have. I stashed some upstairs earlier. We'll be all right, so get that bleedin' sour look off yer face.'

Millie crossed the room and sat on one of the orange boxes, her shoulders slumped in dejection. So this was what they had come to. They'd be living in a filthy, damp and derelict house like a couple of tramps. What about when she had to stop work? What would they do for money then? She looked up, her voice barely a whisper as she said, 'Dad, I'm pregnant.'

Chapter Twenty-Three

'Well, that's it, love,' Bertha said as she stood at the window watching the rain lashing down. 'Summer's well and truly over, and in just over a couple of months, it'll be Christmas.'

'Yes, and even though we had another two guests, I don't know how we'd have managed without John's money,' Wendy said, and shivered.

'True, and those extra guests were thanks to Ted again. It was good of him to put the word around. He's turned out a to be godsend, hasn't he, but let's make sure that we advertise ready for next season. Mind you, it was a good idea of yours to offer a Christmas Menu, and we've got a few bookings for that already, with some guests staying on until the New Year. Things are looking up.'

'Yes, and don't forget how that last couple booked in advance for next September. It shows that we made them comfortable, Mum, and they obviously loved your cooking.'

'Yeah, they did, didn't they,' Bertha said, smiling with satisfaction.

'I reckon it was your steak and kidney pie that did it. How many helpings did he have?'

'Now then, only one, and after the first chunk I gave him he had a job to finish it.'

'They were a nice couple.'

'Yeah, and when you think that he's a bank manager, they weren't a bit hoity-toity.'

Wendy joined her mother at the window and saw rain running down the glass like tears, tears she was trying to fight. Oh, she was missing John, missing him badly, and though he'd promised that after this trip he'd definitely settle with them on the Isle of Wight, she had no idea when that would be. How long had he been gone? It felt like years, when in reality it was ten weeks.

Her thoughts drifted to Millie, and she wondered why the girl hadn't replied to her letter. She'd written in September, but there had been no response.

The rain continued to lash down, echoing her mood, and when Ted came to the back door to say there was nothing more he could do that day, Wendy stepped back hastily as a squall of rain soaked the kitchen floor. 'Yes, go home, Ted – and thanks.'

'Don't you want a cup of tea first?' Bertha called.

'No, thanks, missus. I'm soaked to the skin and just want to get home. I'll see you in the morning.'

'Oh Wendy,' Bertha groaned as the door closed, 'we should've thought to send him home earlier. The poor old sod looked like a drowned rat.'

'I know, and I feel awful too. Christ, we aren't turning out to be very good employers, are we?'

'Employers! Blimey, it don't half sound funny when you say that. Hold on, was that a knock on the front door?'

'I expect it's Ted. He probably got round to the front and decided to come in for a cup of tea after all.'

'Yeah, go and let him in, love.'

Wendy ran out of the kitchen and along the hall to the front door, finding it hard to open against the rain and wind, calling to Ted as at last she managed it, 'Thank goodness you changed your mind . . . John! Oh John!'

'Hello, darling.'

Taking a flying leap Wendy jumped outside and into his arms, mindless of the rain as he spun her around, and then their lips met, the kiss lasting for minutes. Effortlessly he then lifted her high, a wide grin on his face, and as she looked down at him, tears of joy spilled over, mingling with the rain on her cheeks.

'I . . . I didn't expect you back yet,' she choked. 'It's only been ten weeks.'

'Well, isn't that enough for you?'

'Yes, oh yes, but how . . .'

'I couldn't stand to be away from you again, and thank goodness I didn't sign on for a longer trip. I realised in less than a month at sea that I'd been a fool to go back, but it seemed the best thing at the time. Now, how about letting me in before we both drown?'

'Put me down then, and I will.'

He lowered her to the ground, and taking his hand she pulled him inside. They were both soaked and seeing this they dissolved into laughter, until Bertha interrupted the scene.

'So, you're back then, John?'

'Yes, and for good this time.'

'Right, lad, well you'd better come into the kitchen and get yourself dried off. You too, Wendy.'

After drying themselves they sat at the kitchen table, unable to tear their eyes from each other, whilst Bertha smiled indulgently. It was good to see Wendy happy again, and though it would be hard to manage without John's money, it was worth it just to see her daughter's joy.

As she looked at the happy couple she didn't think it would be long before they got married – the sooner the better, come to that, because living in the same house was a bit too much temptation.

Bertha bustled about, preparing a meal and silently worrying about their finances. There would be an extra mouth to feed now, but where was the money going to come from? As if sensitive to her thoughts, John rubbed a hand around his chin and then spoke.

'Without my money coming in now, things could be difficult. I'd better see about getting a job.'

'You'll try for one on the Island, won't you? I couldn't bear it if you left again,' Wendy cried.

'Yes, don't worry, I'll find something here. Though goodness knows what.'

'Ted seems to know just about everyone in Sandown and the surrounding areas, so I'll get him to ask around.'

'Good idea. Now listen, love, I'll have to go off again soon, but just for the day. I want to check on Millie to see if she's all right.'

'I wrote to her in September, but she hasn't replied.'

'Really? I wonder why?' John immediately felt guilty, berating himself for not keeping in touch with his sister.

As Bertha listened to the conversation, she began to shred a cabbage, remembering that Wendy had been worried about Millie before they left. 'If the weather's better tomorrow, why don't you go to see your sister then, and why not bring her back for the weekend? Mind you, if it's anything like this, you'll 'ave a rough crossing.'

John laughed, a booming roar that filled the kitchen. It was an infectious sound and soon both women joined in. 'What's so funny?' Bertha finally managed to splutter, wiping her wet eyes on the bottom of her apron.

'I've been at sea for ten weeks, faced gale-force winds with the ship rolling like a bucket, and you're telling me I might have a rough crossing to Portsmouth. Oh, you're priceless, Bertha.'

His laughter roared again, and Bertha felt the first stir of feeling for this young man who she hoped would soon be her son-in-law. He was a nice lad – and to think she hadn't wanted Wendy to get involved with him! Yes, they were young, maybe too young for marriage, but did it matter when they were so obviously in love? Annie's voice seemed to fill her head and she smiled, imagining what she'd say. 'So you're not a snob after all, Bertha.'

The rain had eased, but it was still blustery as John kissed Wendy goodbye. He intended to take Bertha's advice and bring Millie back for a couple of days, but having no idea what his sister's sea legs were like, he hoped the weather improved.

The crossing was rough, but he exulted in it, enjoying the taste of salt on his lips as he stood on deck. In some ways he would miss the sea, but what he'd told Wendy was true – he just couldn't bear to be away from her. They would have to get married soon as he didn't trust himself, and hoped she'd agree to a Christmas wedding.

Hours later, he was walking down Harmond Street, scowling at the thought of seeing his father. With any luck the old sod will be out, he thought as he went round to the back of the house, intending to surprise Millie.

The house was strangely quiet as he entered, and flinging open the kitchen door he shouted, 'Surprise!' only to find the room completely bare. Puzzled, he then ran into the sitting room, finding it empty of furniture too. Bloody hell, where were they? When John returned to the kitchen he saw only two things, a crumpled-up letter in the hearth, and a slip of paper on the mantelpiece.

So, they'd been evicted, and as he threw the letter back into the hearth he was filled with remorse. Millie would have wanted to let him know where they'd gone, but with no idea of what line he'd signed on with, she'd have been unable to write.

Christ, what sort of brother had he been? With his own need to get away uppermost, he'd left without a thought of what would happen to Millie, and now he realised just how selfish he'd been. Was she all right? Was she still with their father?

His hand groped for the slip of paper on the mantelpiece, and seeing Wendy's letter, he wondered why Millie hadn't replied.

Well, he had to find her, had to know that she was all right – otherwise how could he settle down to a new life? If anyone knew where they were it would be Dora Saunders, and closing the door behind him he made his way to her house.

'No, love, I don't know where they've gone – nobody does,' the old lady told him sadly. 'They went about a month ago and we ain't seen them since.'

'Do you know what's been going on, Mrs Saunders?'

'Come in, love, you look frozen.'

John followed Dora into her kitchen, gratified to see a fire burning in the grate. It was unusually cold for October and sitting down he held his hands out to the flames.

'Yer dad's drinking got worse and worse,' Dora told him as she put the kettle onto the gas cooker. 'Then I heard that he lost the coal-round, and his poor horse had to be put down.'

'Samson! Oh no, not Samson!' John went pale. 'What happened?'

'I only got the story secondhand, but from what I was told the horse bolted and had to be shot. Millie left the depot too and found another job, but I don't know where.'

John shook his head, unable to believe what he was hearing, and after gratefully swallowing the cup of tea Dora handed him, he rose to leave. 'Isn't there anyone who might have some idea of where they are?'

'I don't think so. What are you gonna do now?'

'I don't know, but I'll ask around just in case. Bye, Mrs Saunders, and thanks.'

John tried the pubs, but without luck, and then made his way to the coal depot.

'Come in, John,' Jack Jenkins said.

'Thanks. I've just popped in to see if you know where my father and Millie are.'

'What do you mean?'

'They've been evicted and I can't find out where they've gone.'

'Really! I had no idea, but I'm afraid I can't help you either. When you cleared off to sea without letting me know, your father became a complete liability and I had to let him go.'

'Yes, I heard, and I'm sorry that I let you down, Mr Jenkins,' John said, his heart heavy as a picture of Samson swam into his mind. He forced the vision aside; his need to find Millie more urgent. 'I was told that Millie left too. Did she get the sack?'

'No, and I was sorry to lose her. I've had two secretaries already since Millie left and I should have talked her into staying.'

'Why did she leave?'

'When Samson had to be put down, I'm afraid your sister blamed me. Like all the other secretaries I've had, Millie decided I'm a monster.'

'I must say I'm surprised as I know she loved working for you.'

'If you find her, perhaps you could say that I'd welcome her back.'

'Yes, I'll do that, and thanks,' John said, turning to go.

'Hang on, John. There's still a job here if you want it. There have always been Pratchetts attached to this depot and you're welcome to come back.'

'Thanks for the offer, but I won't be living in this area now,' and after telling Jack Jenkins about the Isle of Wight, he shook the man's hand before leaving.

John asked a few men in the yard if they'd seen Millie or his father, without luck, and then tried a few more pubs. As he swallowed a pint he wondered where he could try next, but gradually it dawned on him that there was nothing he could do. Nobody knew where they were, and it was almost as if they'd disappeared off the face of the earth. Yet how could he return to the Isle of Wight without knowing where his sister was?

It was many hours later, hours of trawling the streets, before John finally accepted that his search was likely to remain fruitless. Tired and dispirited, he jumped on a bus to Clapham Junction Station for the start of his journey back to the Isle of Wight, and his new life with Wendy.

Chapter Twenty-Four

Millie sat shivering in front of the meagre fire, her hands blue with cold as she rubbed them together. Though recovered physically from the beating she'd received after telling her father she was pregnant, mentally she was broken.

With her body battered and bruised, she'd been unable to return to work. At first her father, obviously disappointed that his punches hadn't dislodged the baby, had demanded that she get rid of it. Millie had reeled with shock. He had tried to make her mother have an abortion, and look what happened, so how could he demand the same thing of her? Yet suffering from the beating, she lacked the will to argue, and anyway, she didn't want this baby – a baby conceived by rape. It seemed impossible that she was carrying Pat's half-sister or brother, and tears flooded Millie's eyes. Would she ever see her friend again? And if she did – how would Pat react? She shuddered. There would be no abortion now, it was too late, because even a back street abortionist had to be paid, and lack of money had soon knocked that on the head.

Nowadays, with her tummy swollen, Millie knew that they existed on stolen money – knew that her father had taken to petty thieving. Despite her lethargy, there were moments when it occurred to her that she should do something, anything, to get out of this situation, but always the feeling faded before she could act on it. What could she do anyway? She was fifteen, pregnant, with no money and nowhere to go.

John seemed more lost to her than ever, and she sometimes wondered where he was and if he was happy. Once, during one of her more lucid moments, she'd decided to write to Wendy, begging for help, but found that in their hurry to leave Harmond Street, she'd left the girl's address behind.

Now she just existed from day to day, her clothes becoming rumpled and unkempt, and on the rare occasions when her father was in, she hardly spoke.

Millie picked up her mother's box again, the box she kept hidden when ever her father was around, and with icy fingers took out the envelope, simply addressed, *To Millicent*. Why hadn't she been told? All her life she'd wondered why she was different in looks from the rest of her family, and now she knew.

Oh, she wanted to confront her father, to demand the truth, but always fear held her back. He'd beaten her once, and when drunk he would look at both her, and her swelling stomach, with hate in his eyes. No, it would be safer to keep her mouth shut.

At first, when she'd seen the contents of the box she'd been bitter, wondering why she'd been abandoned, but now this bitterness had been replaced by dreams. Dreams that one day she would find her real mother, and be welcomed into her arms.

Maybe one day her father would come home sober, or in a mellow mood, and then she'd ask him – ask him to tell her how to find Joan Marsden.

The door scraped open and she jumped guiltily, but it was too late to hide the scrap of paper she still held.

'What's that?' her father demanded.

'N . . . nothing.'

'Oh yeah?' he scowled, snatching it from her hand. The moment he'd read it his face suffused with colour. 'Where did you get this?'

'Mum left it with Stella Blake.'

'Give that box to me!'

His eyes seemed to burn into hers making him look almost demonic, and shaking with fear, Millie hurriedly passed it over. He rifled inside, his hands trembling as he pulled out the birth certificate. 'Was there anything else?'

'N . . . no.'

He perched on the edge of an orange box, staring fixedly at the certificate, and then snapped, 'Get out of my sight!'

Millie knew better than to argue and climbed the rickety stairs, but after only half an hour the weakness in her bladder forced her downstairs again. She scuttled to the outside toilet, but not before she noticed her father still slumped on an orange box, looking pale and dejected.

It was freezing in the yard and as she hurried back inside Millie hesitated before going back upstairs. Her father was still holding the birth certificate, and desperate to know, she somehow found the courage to ask, 'Dad, where is she?'

'Who?'

'Joan Marsden – my real mother.'

A sneer curled her father's lips. 'So, you've found yer voice again, have you. Well, don't get too brave or I might just knock it out of you. As for Joan Marsden, she's dead, and good riddance to bad rubbish.'

'What do you mean? When did she die? What happened to her?'

'Believe me, you don't want to know.'

'I do, Dad, and . . . and I've got a right.'

'Right? You've got the *right*! Who took you on, eh? Who brought you up? Me – yes me – not yer slut of a mother!'

'Why are you calling her a slut?'

'Because that's what she was. Your mother was a tart – a common prostitute, and she died of the clap.'

'The clap . . . what's that?'

'A disease, and the bitch gave it to me before she died.'

'I . . . I don't understand.'

'What's there to understand, you soppy cow? Your mother was a tart, and she had gonorrhoea. Instead of getting treatment she carried on working, and by the time she finally decided to go to the clinic it was too late. Her insides were rotten . . . just like her! Now get out of me sight 'cos looking at you is a constant reminder!'

As if she'd been given a physical blow, Millie doubled in half, clutching her stomach. It couldn't be true, it couldn't! She stared at her father, sickened by the look of triumph on his face. He was enjoying it – enjoying seeing her distress. God, what sort of man was he?

'I said get out of me sight!'

Millie stumbled up the staircase, hardly reaching the top before her knees gave way. She staggered a few more steps and sank onto the old mattress, closing her eyes in distress. A prostitute . . . her mother had been a prostitute . . . and the words kept going round and round in her mind, drowning out all other thought.

Alfie flopped forward, his breath coming in ragged gasps. He couldn't believe it, couldn't believe that Eileen had left a letter and Millie's birth certificate. Bloody hell, the woman was reaching out to inflict more hurt – and this time from the grave.

He still hadn't forgiven her for leaving him, for taking her own life. All right, he had wanted her to get rid of the baby, but what was so bad about that? Surely a man had a right to his wife's attention, instead of having her time taken up with a squalling brat.

God, he'd hated it when Millie and John were babies, hated seeing her holding them, drooling over them, her face alight with love. Love that should have been given to him!

He'd still been full of resentment too, resentment that he'd been forced to marry her. He hadn't dared to defy his father, but it wasn't right, wasn't fair that at just twenty-four he'd been stuck with a wife, and one with a kid on the way.

Mind you, Eileen was a looker, there was no denying that, and if she hadn't been having a bleedin' baby, things might have been different.

Oh, sod it! he thought, hating the memories and scratching his filthy hair as he tried to push them away. What he needed was a stiff drink. The scrap lead he'd managed to nick from the roof of an empty house had brought in a few bob, and what better place to spend it than the pub.

'Hello, ducks. On yer own are you?'

Alfie turned fuddled eyes on the painted floozy who had taken a seat next to him. She was skinny too, just like Joan Marsden had been. 'Go away,' he growled.

'Now then, don't be like that. I only came to join you 'cos you look so sad. Come on, why don't you buy me a drink and then tell me all about it.'

Through his alcoholic haze Alfie thought he could hear genuine sympathy in her voice, and with a parody of a smile he did as she asked, staggering to the bar to buy her a gin and tonic. He managed to carry it back to the table in one piece, but as he placed it in front of her, the painted face seemed to mock him, just like that other one had. 'Drink it, then bugger off,' he snapped.

She took a sip, then as he sat down she spoke softly. 'There's an old saying: a trouble shared is a trouble halved. Come on, why don't you tell me what's bothering you?'

'Huh, years ago I was made a monkey of by someone just like you. Though in those days I was a mug and had no idea she was a bleedin' tart.'

'Didn't you, love? What happened?'

He stared at her, once again thinking there was something about her that reminded him of Joan. She was a tart too, and uncaring that his words might sound lewd, he said, 'My son was just two months old at the time, and me wife was besotted with him, whilst I was bursting with frustration. Huh, that's shocked you ain't it.'

'No, of course not. A man has his needs, and I should know.'

'I hadn't laid a hand on me wife since she was seven months pregnant – and who could blame me. Christ, she looked disgusting, grotesque, with fat swollen ankles, and it made me feel sick every time I looked at her.'

'Was she a nice looking woman?'

'Yeah, gorgeous, but not when her belly swelled. Anyway, one night when I was in the pub, I met *her*.'

'Met who?'

'A bleedin' tart like you – that's who. I saw her sitting alone at a table and maybe it was the drink, I don't know, but something about her attracted me, despite the thick coat of make up plastered on her face. Why do you wear all that muck?'

'I dunno, but don't you like it?'

'No, I don't, and decent women wouldn't plaster it on like that. Anyway, where was I? Oh yeah, I was attracted to her, though I still don't know why. She was tall and skinny, almost boyish in build, but it was her eyes that got to me. They were huge and seemed to take up most of her face.'

'Are you sure she was a woman?'

'What!' Alfie stared at her, his face purple. 'Of course I'm sure – what do you take me for?'

'Now don't get out yer pram. I was just asking and you never know, there are lots of men who fancy the same sex. Now how about buying me another drink?'

'Yeah, all right,' Alfie said, stumbling to the bar again, this time ordering a double whisky for himself, along with the gin and tonic. What was the matter with him? Why was he unloading onto that tart? Maybe it was all the years of keeping it locked inside, he didn't know, but making his way back to the table, he continued to ramble.

'I had an affair with her, and as I didn't know she was a tart, I fell for her in a big way. Christ, somehow her skinny body became like an addiction, and you wouldn't believe the things we did together.'

'Oh, I think you'd find I would.'

Alfie scowled. 'Yeah, of course, you're probably just like her. No decent woman would do the things we did together.'

'You're very fond of talking about so called *decent* women, ain't yer. Well, perhaps they don't know what they're missing. What about you, dearie? Would you like to see some of the things *I've* learned?'

Alfie hardly heard her comment as he downed his whisky, remembering how the sly innuendoes had begun to reach his ears. Sniggers when he and Joan were seen together, nudges and winks. Then, when the first symptoms of the clap appeared he had gone absolutely mad. He'd never hit a woman before – but he hit Joan Marsden. Hit her until she was black and blue, her face barely recognisable.

'Did you hear what I said, dear? Would you like to see a few tricks of mine?'

'Maybe,' Alfie said, then going to the bar for yet another drink, he propped himself on the counter, thinking back to when he got lumbered with Millie.

The affair with Joan had lasted four months, and after giving her a hiding he never expected to see her again – until one day when she turned up on the doorstep. Alfie scowled at the memory. His son was just sixteen months old at the time, and when Joan arrived clutching a crying brat to her chest, Eileen had stupidly invited her in.

It was his baby, Joan insisted, and he would have to take it in. She was too ill to care for the child and was being admitted to hospital. Oh, he'd ranted and raved, shouting that she had no proof that the child was his – until Eileen intervened. It was the one and only time his wife had stood up to him, and despite insisting that he didn't want anything to do with the kid, she'd been adamant that they take it on. And so he got lumbered – lumbered with another kid that he didn't want.

'You didn't answer my question,' the woman said when he returned with the drinks.

'What question?'

'I asked if you'd like to see some of the tricks I've learned. You won't be sorry,' she urged, her hand squeezing his knee.

'Huh, no thanks, I don't fancy another dose of the clap.'

'I can assure you I'm clean, very clean, and I have regular check-ups to make sure I stay that way. In fact, there's nothing doing unless you wear a johnny. Come on,' she cajoled. 'I'm good – very good.'

His fuddled eyes struggled to focus. 'Yeah, why not,' and throwing back his whisky, he took her to Dobson Alley.

'Blimey, it ain't Buckingham Palace that's for sure,' she said as they stumbled over the threshold. 'I hope you've got money 'cos I don't give out for free.'

'Yeah, I've got plenty,' Alfie slurred.

'Good. Now where's the ladies' room?'

'Ladies' room? Huh, don't make me laugh. It's out the back.'

She went off outside, just as Millie came down the stairs, clothes rumpled, hair greasy, and huge cow eyes wide as she gazed at him. Christ, look at the state of her, he thought. She's a bleedin' beanpole without an ounce of femininity, the pregnancy making her look worse than ever. How could she be his? There wasn't the slightest resemblance to him, or anyone else in the family.

'I've got company, so scarper,' he growled.

'Who is it?'

'A tart, just like yer mother.'

Millie hesitated, her foot on the bottom rung, but then to his unfocussed eyes she seemed to stiffen. 'Why did my mother give me up?'

Oh, so that was it, more questions, he thought. Well, she'd be sorry she asked. ''Cos she was dying, and like a mug I took you in.'

'And . . . Mum, I mean Eileen . . . didn't she mind taking me on?'

Wanting to punish her he spat, 'Of course she minded. Why would she want to take on an ugly cow like you?'

Alfie watched with satisfaction as Millie turned on her heels, face stricken as she scurried back upstairs. Why did she have to look so much like Joan, making him cringe every time he looked at her? Yet despite what Joan had done, he still missed the sex, missed the way she had made him feel. Domination. Bloody hell he'd loved it, loved it when she allowed him to whip her into submission.

He'd never had another affair after that, the dose of clap putting him off for life, and strangely he'd come to love his wife with a passion that surprised him. Only the way she constantly mollycoddled the kids drove him mad, but he'd soon found a way to put a stop to that.

When he demanded that Eileen stopped fussing over the kids, he was secretly thrilled when she protested or argued. Only then could he indulge his sexual fantasies by dominating her into submission. Christ, it was fantastic when he had an excuse to tie her to the bed, having her sobbing beneath him.

A blast of cold air hit him as the tart came back into the room, and partially aroused he advanced towards her. Yes, domination, that's what he loved, and with a smile of anticipation, he grabbed a handful of her hair, enjoying her yelp of pain . . .

'Never mind, love. It seems you've got brewer's droop.'

God, Alfie felt humiliated. He'd tried everything – slapping her, biting her – but without success, and now she lay with a mocking smile on her face. 'Get out!' he said thickly. 'You're bleedin' useless.'

'Now then, duckie, it wasn't my fault and there's no need to be like that. Besides, before I go anywhere, I want me money.'

There was a sound on the stairs, both looking round as Millie came down. She hurried across the room, muttering, 'Sorry, I need to go outside.'

'Who's that?' the woman asked.

'Me daughter, or so the tart I told you about claimed.'

'You don't think she's yours?'

'You saw her, and she looks nothing like me.'

'I saw that she'd got a bun in the oven.'

'Yeah, and I don't want to be lumbered with her or the kid. If I'd known she was bleedin' pregnant before we came here, I'd 'ave left her behind. All I need is a bit of luck, enough dosh to get me outta this dump, then I'm off, and I ain't taking her with me.'

'Hold on, Alfie, I've got a better idea.'

He listened, as the women spoke, a smile crossing his face. Yeah, it was the perfect solution.

Chapter Twenty-Five

Pat Benson trudged home, her feet swollen and aching. After working in the shop for nearly eight hours, with just a break for lunch, she was worn out.

It had been the last customer who'd upset her, a regular who wouldn't take no for an answer, and when she'd turned him down again, he'd said some nasty things. God, she hated her looks, hated the way men were attracted to her, and she was sick of fending them off.

Life was strange, she mused, her thoughts returning as they often did to Harmond Street. How she had envied Millie, envied her for being plain. Yet being unattractive hadn't saved Millie. A man had still abused her. Hate towards her father surged through Pat again like a physical pain. The years of abuse she'd been subjected to were bad enough, but how could he rape Millie?

She squeezed her eyes shut at the memory. It had been the end of June when she left Harmond Street, and she still missed Millie so much. Never before had she known such loneliness. Oh, she'd had plenty of offers to be taken out, as working in a tobacconist's brought her into contact with lots of male customers, but it wasn't them she wanted.

Despite this, Pat knew it wasn't a bad job, and the owner hadn't bothered to check her cards when she'd told him she was over eighteen. He paid her wages, cash in hand, and the arrangement suited them both. The pay wasn't bad either, in fact above average for shopwork.

The owner was an old man who gradually spent more and more time in his upstairs flat, leaving the running of the shop to her. Huh, not that he trusted her with the till. Every day at five-thirty he came down to cash up, checking every sale against stock.

Still, in less than four months, and by being thrifty, she'd managed to get out of that first stinking bedsit, finding the larger room and kitchenette she now rented.

Yet despite making some sort of life for herself, she spent most of her time alone. Why couldn't she be like other women? She was unnatural, and hated it, hated her feelings. There must be others who felt as she did, who had the same preferences, but they were probably hiding it too. After all, there was no other choice.

She now turned into Tedworth Square, heaving a sigh of relief as she approached the entrance to her basement rooms.

'Hello, Pat, you look worn out.'

'Hello, Mrs Lucas,' she said to the woman leaning out of the first-floor window. 'I must admit I'm tired, and I'll be glad to get off my feet.'

'My son will be down later to fix your tap.'

'Thank you,' Pat said, and with a small wave she trod heavily down the stairs. Her landlady was a treasure, and she was lucky to find such a nice place where the rent wasn't exorbitant, but just lately Mrs Lucas's son was becoming a pain. Brian Lucas made no secret of the fact that he fancied her, and she was tired of fending him off. Brian was a nice bloke, and she liked his sense of humour, but that was as far as it went.

An hour later, Pat had just finished eating her supper of sardines on toast and an apple when there was a tap on the front door. She pushed her plate to one side, and went to answer it. 'Hello, Brian, your mum said you'd be popping down. Come on in.'

'I've got a new washer for your tap and it should fix the problem.'

'Thanks, I'll be glad not to hear the constant drip, drip, drip.'

'Not going out tonight?'

'No, I'm going to wash my hair.'

'You've got lovely hair,' he said with a soft smile.

'Thanks,' she said awkwardly, her voice dismissive, but seeing the crushed expression in his eyes she added, more gently, 'I'll leave you to it then.'

'Right, I'll get on with it and it shouldn't take long.'

Half an hour later, Brian was putting his tools back into the bag. 'All done!' he called out. 'Er . . . I'm popping down the pub for a drink. Would you like to join me?'

'No thanks, I told you I'm going to wash my hair.'

'It looks fine to me. Go on – just come out for one drink. I could do with a bit of company and there'd be no strings attached.'

Should she go? Pat wondered. Surely one drink wouldn't hurt, and she didn't think she could stand another night alone in her room.

The friendship between Pat and Brian grew, and by mid-December they were still going out together. Mrs Lucas encouraged the relationship, and had invited Pat to share their Christmas dinner the following week.

It seemed that her son at twenty-eight was very protective of her, and at first this had worried Pat into thinking that he might be a bit of a mummy's boy, but then she found out that Mrs Lucas had a bad heart. Brian made sure that his mother took her medication regularly and didn't exert herself too much, and this endeared him to Pat.

He was such a kind and caring man, and when they went out together he didn't take liberties, until Christmas Eve, when she noticed something different in his manner.

As they walked home she found him quiet, more so than usual, and when they reached her door she shivered worriedly as he smiled down at her. His arms came out, and though Pat stepped back, it didn't stop him. She stiffened, fear mounting as she remembered her father's abuse. But Brian, as if sensing her fear, held her gently without moving until she relaxed.

It was all right; in fact, she felt safe in his arms. There was no threat, no passion and she was surprised to find herself drawing strength from the contact. But then he stepped back, and with his index finger he lifted her chin. Oh God, he was going to kiss her! *No, please don't!* her thoughts screamed. His head came down and Pat closed her eyes, hating the feel of his moist lips. She remained

motionless, finding that if she closed her eyes, shutting out
thoughts that this was a man, she could bear it.

'Goodnight, darling,' he murmured, drawing back from her.
'I'll see you tomorrow.'

She forced a smile, relieved when with a final peck on her
cheek, he left her at the door. What would she have done if he'd
wanted to come in? What if he'd wanted to take things further?
Perhaps she should stop seeing him? Yet at the thought of being
alone again, she wavered.

Despite Pat's reservations, they continued to see each other, and
she grew used to Brian's occasional kisses. They had so much in
common, both enjoying the same things. They played darts in the
local pub, and she surprised Brian by joining him when he went to
watch the local football team. It was freezing on the stands and
he would insist on tucking his own team scarf around her neck,
along with a bobble hat, and somehow she found it nice to be
mollycoddled.

She knew he was going to propose soon, his mother had hinted
as much, and she dreaded having to turn him down. How could
she marry the man? He aroused no passion in her, and she knew it
would be impossible to have a sexual relationship.

Yes, she could bear his kisses, and his soft embrace, Brian
treating her like a piece of fine porcelain. But if she married him it
would change, and he would expect more than just chaste kisses.

When the proposal came just one week later, Pat still found
herself unprepared as he went down on one knee.

'I love you, Pat. Say you'll marry me.'

'Brian, we've only been going out together for just over three
months and we hardly know each other.'

'I know it may seem a bit soon, but I've come to love you so
much. You're different from other women, Pat. You don't mind
freezing on the football terraces, don't mind joining me in a game
of darts at the pub, and not only do I love you, I feel that we're
really good mates. We could just get engaged for now, and then
perhaps in a year or eighteen months . . .'

'I . . . I can't marry you.'

'Why not? We get on so well, and I know I can make you

happy. If you wouldn't mind living in the same house, my mother has said we can have the flat on the top floor. Please, Pat, please think about it.'

'There's no point. The answer will still be no.'

'Don't say that . . . at least give me some hope.'

'There is no hope,' she told him, hating herself for the pain she could see her words were causing.

'I can't accept that. Look, I won't see you for a week or two, and perhaps when you've had time to think about it, you'll change your mind. No, please don't say anything,' he urged, as she was about to speak. He rose to his feet, and with a sad smile he left her.

Oh Brian, you're such a nice man, Pat thought as she sat wringing her hands. You deserve better than me. You deserve a woman who can love you – love you as a woman should.

Why did she have to be unnatural? Why couldn't she have a normal life? Flinging on her coat, Pat felt the urge to get out of her room and walk until she was exhausted. Only then would she be able to sleep that night.

By the time she reached Clapham Junction, Pat was freezing and it wasn't until then that she realised where her tortured thoughts were leading her. She was going to Harmond Street. She was going to see Millie!

She stood shivering on the pavement opposite number ten, wondering if she had the courage to knock on the door. She wanted to plead, to beg that they be friends again. She would ask for nothing more – only that. If they could just see each other occasionally, she'd be happy.

Taking a deep breath, Pat crossed the road. Yes, she'd come this far, and what did she have to lose? Millie might slam the door in her face, but then again she might not, and at least she'd have tried.

The door was opened by a strange woman and Pat's eyes widened, but determined now to see her friend, she asked, 'Can I speak to Millie, please?'

'There ain't no Millie living here.'

'But—'

Pat's words were cut off as the woman abruptly shut the door, and seething with anger at her rudeness she lifted the knocker, banging loudly until the woman appeared again.

'I told you, she doesn't live here. Now clear off.'

Before Pat could react the door slammed shut again, and hearing another voice, she turned to see a woman standing on the doorstep of number twelve. 'The Pratchetts have gone, and good riddance to bad rubbish too.'

It felt strange to see someone else living in her old home, but oddly reassuring too. The house held nothing but bad memories, memories that still haunted her. Her sisters had been dragged away from there, and despite all her efforts, she had failed to trace them. She had tried endlessly with the authorities, but to no avail. The girls were in foster care, she was informed, and that was all they could tell her. She was blocked at every turn, so much so that she'd almost given up hope. But no, Pat thought, her expression determined. One day she would find Bessie and Janet, and when that day came she would never let them be taken away again.

Now, pushing aside her memories, Pat asked, 'Do you know where they've moved to?'

'How should I know? They were evicted and nobody knows where they went. Mind you,' the woman added, her voice low, 'that lot who moved in aren't much better – they're as common as muck.'

'Surely someone knows where Millie is? I'll try Mrs Blake. She knew them well and might have an address.'

'Please yourself,' the woman said, remaining on her doorstep to watch as Pat knocked on Stella Blake's door.

It was Dora Saunders who opened it, looking astonished when she saw who it was. 'Well, stone the crows, it's Pat Benson!' she squeaked. 'Where 'ave you been, girl? Since you went off like that you've been the talk of the street.'

'Thanks, Dora, that's just what I needed to hear.'

'Gawd, sorry, love. My mouth does tend to run away with me at times.' Dora poked her head out of the door, saying with an expression of disgust, 'Ena Bradshaw's 'aving a good look. She moved into your place shortly after you left, and she's a right old busybody. You'd best come in, or she'll be listening to every word we say.'

Pat hid a smile, thinking that Dora was just as bad, but as she followed her into Stella Blake's hall, the woman spoke again.

'How's Millie? We ain't seen hide nor hair of her since she left.'

'I don't know, I haven't seen her either, and I was hoping you could tell me where she's gone.'

'John came looking for her too, but as I told him, we ain't got a clue.'

'John! John was here? He might have found her – did you get his address?'

'No, sorry, love, I never gave it a thought.' And gabbling on she fussed, 'Now, come on, come into the kitchen. Stella will be dead chuffed to see you, and you're just in time 'cos they're moving tomorrow. I'm not usually here at this time of night, but I'm giving Cyril a hand with the packing. They've been given a prefab in Elspeth Road. Them prefabilated things were put up as temporary housing when so many places got bombed during the war, but they're still in use. Mind you, it's a nice place, and better than some of the houses around here that the bombs managed to miss. You should see the kitchen – it's got fitted cupboards and everything.'

Despite her unhappiness, Pat had to grin. Prefabilated! Dora meant prefabricated, but it would be cruel to correct her.

'Look who's come to see you, Stella,' Dora said.

'My goodness, Pat Benson! Is it really you?'

'Yes, and it's nice to see you again. How are you, Mrs Blake?'

'I'm fine, love, and I expect Dora's told you we're moving to Elspeth Road?'

Pat nodded as she glanced around the room. It looked very stark with a couple of cartons in the centre and the rugs rolled up ready to go. 'I won't stop as I can see you're busy. I came to visit Millie, but found she's left Harmond Street.'

'Yes, and I was so sad to see her go. I hoped her father would eventually stop drinking, but instead he went from bad to worse. He lost his coal-round too and shortly after, they were evicted.'

Oh my God, Pat thought, poor Millie. And desperately she asked, 'Isn't there anyone who knows where they've gone?'

'No, I don't think so.'

Stella then yawned widely, and forcing a smile Pat said, 'Well, I'd best be off. It was nice to see you again – you too, Dora.'

She kept the smile fixed on her face as they said their goodbyes, Dora escorting her out, but it dropped as soon as the door closed behind her.

With a last look at Millie's house, Pat's tread was heavy as she left Harmond Street, wondering why everyone she loved seemed to disappear from her life. Oh Millie, my darling, she thought. I have to find you, I just have to!

Pat's loneliness had reached fever pitch by the time Brian Lucas came to see her again. He had left her alone as promised, and two weeks had passed since his proposal.

Her quest to find Millie had proved impossible. A grumpy old man at the coal depot told her that she no longer worked there, and the council offices refused to tell her anything, not even if the Pratchetts had been rehoused. And though she asked at all the local pubs that Millie's father used to frequent, they hadn't seen him either. It felt as though the family had disappeared off the face of the earth, and no matter how many people she asked, nobody knew where the Pratchetts had gone.

Now, as Pat looked at Brian, she saw that his smile was hopeful, his eyes holding an appeal, and she finally made up her mind. Anything would be better than this aching loneliness. Maybe she could make him a good wife. Maybe she could learn to accept a sexual relationship. They had so much in common, and they had become good friends. Surely she could build on that?

Brian's hopeful smile changed into one of delight, as she said, 'Yes, I will marry you.'

Chapter Twenty-Six

Millie had been prepared to hate the child growing within her. When she remembered the horror of how it was conceived, she had tried to ignore the first small fluttering movements in her stomach. But gradually they grew stronger, and when she had first put her hands on her tummy to feel a distinct kick, a deep love had been born. As she tried to imagine what her baby would look like, and whether it would be a boy or girl, she pushed all thoughts of Billy Benson from her mind. It was her child – and hers alone.

Now she was eight months pregnant, and though she herself was thin, her stomach was large. Frightened to face people, afraid of the censure she would see in their eyes, she hardly left the hovel. As an unmarried mother she was aware that her baby would carry the stigma of being a bastard, and at that thought she placed her hands protectively across her abdomen.

Feeling a sudden wave of nausea, Millie gulped. Despite all her efforts, there seemed to be a constant smell of sewage pervading the rooms, and at times her stomach heaved. The street door opened, and as her father came in she looked at him tiredly. It was three in the afternoon, and he didn't usually appear this early.

'Has anyone been nosing around, Millie?'

'No.'

'Good, but just to be on the safe side, keep your head down. We ain't supposed to be here, and if anyone turns up, don't answer the door. Now go and buy some grub,' he ordered, flinging a ten bob note onto her lap.

She grimaced, hating to touch the money she knew came from his petty thieving. Yet what choice was there? 'Dad, I don't feel too good.'

'You look all right to me. Do as you're told and pop down to the grocer's.'

Millie stood up, swaying slightly, and crossing slowly to a nail that had been banged into the wall she removed her father's old overcoat. All her clothes were too small now, and with no money to replace them they stretched tightly across her tummy, the seams bursting. At least the old coat covered her condition a little, and without a backward glance at her father she shoved the money into the pocket, her head down when she emerged from Dobson Alley.

They were now a good few miles from where they used to live, and in a rundown part of Wandsworth, but even so she was terrified of bumping into someone she knew. There were only a few small shops close by, and she made for the grocer's, the bell over the door jangling to announce her entrance.

The grocer stopped stacking a shelf to look at her suspiciously, and she wasn't surprised as he watched her every move, knowing that she looked like a tramp. With only cold water from the tap in the yard, and rarely any soap, she hardly washed, and her hair hung in rat's tails around her face.

'What do you want?'

'Half a pound of streaky bacon, six eggs, a loaf of bread and some margarine, please.'

'Have you got the money to pay for it?'

'Yes,' she said, pulling the note out of her pocket.

The grocer pursed his lips, but at the sight of money he gathered the order, and placing her change on the counter, he pushed the brown paper carrier bag towards her. Millie grabbed them both then scuttled out of the shop, hating the look of disdain she'd seen in his eyes. She hoped her father wouldn't ask how much these few provisions had cost as she wanted to save the change. It could be many days before he gave her any more money, and she had learned to be crafty with what little was left over from the shopping.

The eggs and bacon could be cooked over the fire in the old frying pan her father had managed to bring with him from Harmond Street, and if she shoved some bread in the fat it would make the meal a bit more filling. Licking her lips in anticipation, she hurried home.

'Millie, when's the baby due?' her father asked as she shoved open the door.

'I don't know for sure, but soon, I think,' she said, gasping for breath.

She watched as he pulled on his bottom lip, his eyes narrowed in thought before he said, 'Going by my reckoning you must be eight months gone, and you'll need someone to help you when the time comes.'

Millie reached for the pan, wondering why her father was suddenly showing an interest in her pregnancy. In the last few months he had mellowed a little, and if anything seemed almost happy. Though living as they were, she couldn't understand why.

She knew she should have gone to a doctor, knew that there was help available, but what would happen when they saw the hovel she lived in? The thought of giving birth terrified her and she had no idea what to expect, but the prospect of seeking medical attention made her fear rise to the surface again. If the authorities saw how she lived, they'd take the baby away. She couldn't bear that, couldn't bear the thought of her child going into care. Placing her hands on her stomach again, she felt the familiar surge of protectiveness. 'I . . . I know I'll need help, Dad, but I don't want to go to the doctor's.'

'Of course you don't. The kid's a bastard and we don't want anyone poking their noses into our business. You leave it to me, girl – I'll sort something out.'

There was something in her father's tone, something she couldn't quite put her finger on. He suddenly sounded eager to help, and though pleased, she again wondered why. But, oh God, she was too hungry and tired to work it out.

After eating she rose unsteadily to her feet, gripped by indigestion. 'Dad, I'm going for a lay-down. I don't feel well.'

He didn't argue, and with his eyes sliding away from hers, he said, 'Yeah, all right. You go and have a little rest.'

Alfie watched as Millie slowly climbed the stairs, an avid gleam in his eyes. It was a bit of luck he hadn't abandoned the girl as he'd intended to do when she'd told him she was pregnant. The bitch should've told him before they left Harmond Street, he'd raged, giving her the hiding she deserved. With no money to get rid of the kid, he'd been furious. After all, she couldn't work now, and why should he keep her?

At first he'd hoped the hiding would dislodge the baby, but he was glad now that it hadn't. The brat was his meal ticket out of here. Millie was pliable now too, all the fight gone out of her, and he intended to keep her that way. When the time came he didn't want any protests, so maybe a few more slaps now and then wouldn't hurt.

He rubbed his hands together. Five hundred quid – who'd have thought a baby could be worth that amount? When that old tart had introduced him to Ernie Liddle and his wife, he could hardly believe his ears. Not that Liddle was their real name, they were too fly for that, and in their game he didn't blame them for being careful. Anyway, he rationalised, he was doing Millie a favour really. Once it was over with she'd be able to get back on her feet, earn a living and start a new life. And surely that was better than the alternative!

Alfie looked around the squalid room now, unable to help comparing it to Harmond Street. How had he ended up like this? Once he'd had a nice home, a good job, and a lovely wife. 'Oh Eileen, Eileen, why did you do it?' he whispered. 'Why did you leave me? It's your fault that I took to drink. You must have known that I couldn't cope without you! And what about your son? Yes, he buggered off and left me too, and because of him I lost the coal-round!'

He shook his head in despair. Bloody hell, he was talking to the dead now! He had to get away – had to move away from the area and the memories. If he could start a new life somewhere else, maybe his luck would change.

Not much longer to go, Alfie thought as he scratched his filthy, matted hair, but to be on the safe side he'd leave it as long as possible before bringing the woman to see Millie. If his daughter got any inkling of what was going on, she might just try to put up a fight, and he didn't want that. Yes, he'd be in clover soon – and who'd have thought it would all be thanks to Millie.

*

Another three weeks passed, a period during which Millie often felt weak with hunger and despair. Her stomach was now huge and low, her ankles so swollen that they hung over the sides of her tatty shoes.

When her father came in one evening, she was surprised that he had a woman with him, and Millie stared at her with distrust. There was no denying that she looked clean and respectable, but there was something about the caring attitude she adopted that seemed artificial.

'How are you, dear?' and not waiting for Millie's reply she added, 'Your father tells me that the baby's due soon.'

'Yes, I think it is.'

'Let's go upstairs and I'll have a look at you.'

'I don't need looking at. I'm all right.'

'My dear, you must think about the baby. Please let me check that everything's as it should be.'

Millie hunched lower on the orange box, not wanting a stranger to touch her, but the woman came to her side, placing a hand on her shoulder.

'It's all right, there's no need to be nervous. I'm a midwife and you really should be examined properly. You look a bit run down to me and it might be that you're anaemic.'

Millie shrugged her hand away, but then looked at the woman's face again, thinking that her smile appeared genuine this time. Perhaps I'm just being over-sensitive, she told herself as she agreed to go upstairs.

There was no denying that the woman seemed to know what she was doing as she took Millie's blood pressure, and then gently examined her distended stomach.

'My name is Dulcie Liddle, but you can call me Dulcie. I'm just going to listen to the baby's heart,' she said as she withdrew a funnel-like contraption from her bag. Resting it on Millie's tummy she placed an ear over it, smiling when she raised her head. 'Everything seems fine and there's a good strong heartbeat. Now tell me, my dear, how are you feeling?'

'All right, I suppose, except that I feel constantly tired.'

'Yes, it's as I said, I think you're anaemic, but the baby is low down in your tummy and I believe you'll give birth within the next week. Now stay there while I go down to have a word with your father.'

Millie lay on the mattress. She still wasn't sure about Dulcie Liddle, but her relief at having someone to help her when the time came, overrode her fears. A wave of exhaustion washed over her, and once again she found herself drifting off to sleep, unaware of the conversation below.

'Your daughter looks half-starved, Alfie. You should have made sure that she ate properly. Her blood pressure's a little high too,' Dulcie Liddle complained as she entered the downstairs room.

'Millie's all right. If she ain't been eating, don't blame me,' Alfie blustered as he threw a piece of wood onto the meagre fire.

'If the girl's undernourished there's no way of knowing how the baby will be affected. It's got to be perfect or the deal's off.'

'I dunno why you're so bothered. There ain't much wrong with Millie, and she's always been as thin as a rake. When do you think it's due, Dulcie?'

'Very soon, but this place is disgusting and not fit for pigs, let alone humans. You'll have to clean it up, and make sure there's a fire going when the time comes. I'll bring some clean linen and towels, but be sure you contact me as soon as she goes into labour.'

'Yeah, all right, but I want the money as soon as it's born.'

'You'll get it,' Dulcie snapped. 'Are you sure the girl's agreeable to our little arrangement?'

'She'll do as she's bleedin' well told!'

'What do you mean? Doesn't she know?'

'No, she doesn't, but that won't make any difference.'

'Of course it will, you silly man. What if the girl doesn't want to part with it?'

'She'll part with it all right,' Alfie growled. 'She ain't got a choice.'

'You'd better be right. I've warned you that our transaction must be untraceable, and there can't be any repercussions.'

'Stop worrying. Like me, Millie doesn't know your real name, or where you live, so even if she tried to find you, it would be impossible. Anyway, what about the tart who introduced us? She must know how to find you.'

'Don't be stupid, she's already been taken care of.'

'What's that supposed to mean?'

'Don't be naïve,' Dulcie said with a sickly smile. 'Now I'm warning you, Alfie, my husband won't be happy if this deal falls through. The baby is going to a very influential couple who could cause trouble if we let them down.'

'Oh yeah, who are they?'

'You know better than to ask questions like that. You're being very well paid, and once the transaction is completed, we will never see each other again. Once the deal has gone through we'll be leaving the area, and the phone number I have given you will be disconnected. Is that clear?'

There was a threat in her voice that he couldn't fail to miss, and holding up both hands in a placatory gesture, Alfie said, 'Why would I want to see you again? Anyway, I'll be off too as soon as I've got the money.'

'Good. I'm going now, and don't forget what I said. Telephone me the minute the girl goes into labour. It will take me a while to get here and I don't want anything to go wrong.'

Alfie nodded, and as Dulcie Liddle, as she called herself, left the hovel, he wrung his hands together with glee. Not long to go now – no, not that long at all.

Chapter Twenty-Seven

'I want Millie at our wedding, Wendy, but the trip was another waste of time and I didn't have any luck. Christ, I just don't know what to do next,' John said.

'Oh darling, of course you want Millie there. Look, if you like we'll change the date.'

'No, love. We've put the wedding off once already, and now we aren't getting married until May. Blimey, your mother will have a fit if we delay it again. We'll just have to hope that the advert I placed in the London newspapers will bring some results.'

'What does it say?'

'I couldn't afford a big ad, so I just asked that if anyone knew the whereabouts of Alfred and Millicent Pratchett, would they ring the following number. The wedding is in ten weeks, so fingers crossed.'

'Someone must know where they are. Talking of the wedding, have you told your boss that you'll need time off work?'

'Yes, and old Partridge wasn't too happy about it. The house is behind schedule and the weather hasn't helped. Still, at least the roof's on now.'

'Will the job last out until the summer season starts? We'll be all right then as we've already got plenty of bookings.'

'Yes, don't worry,' John said.

They both went into the kitchen then, and running a hand around his chin John could feel the stubble. 'Bertha, have I got time to pop upstairs for a bath before dinner?' he asked.

'Yes, and anyway, what makes you think I'd let you sit at the table in that state?'

He smiled, knowing by Bertha's tone that she was joking as usual. The delicious smell of roast chicken filled the air as the woman opened the range, and taking out the baking tin she began to baste the golden-brown potatoes. God, he thought, she was a fabulous cook, and though he'd loved his mother's Sunday roasts, he had to admit that Bertha's were even better.

With his mouth watering, he left the room, and lying soaking in the bath his thoughts went back to Millie. It was his sister's sixteenth birthday in March, but where was she? He'd tried every avenue he could think of to find her, but unless the newspaper advert brought success, it seemed unlikely he'd be able to track her down.

'Do you think John will ever find his sister?' Bertha asked her daughter.

'I hope so, but it isn't looking too promising. He's been back to London twice now, and there's still no sign of Millie, or his father.'

'If he finds them, will he invite his dad to the wedding?'

'I dunno, Mum, but I doubt it. As for the wedding, how's my dress coming on?'

'I've still got the sleeves to set in, but other than that it's nearly finished. I just wish the guest-list was longer.'

'Mum, all I care about is that John and I are getting married, and it wouldn't matter if you were the only one there.'

'Well, there's only gonna be sixteen guests, and even if John finds his sister it'll only be one more. None of my old friends are coming, and only two of yours. It's lucky we've met a few people since we moved here, or the church would be empty.'

'I told you, it doesn't matter, and anyway we can't afford a big do. Small as it is, our budget will be stretched to lay on a meal afterwards.'

'I suppose you're right,' Bertha sighed.

When John came back downstairs his nose lifted as he sniffed the air. Bertha smiled; her soon-to-be son-in-law's actions always reminded her of an animal scenting out food. She'd become so fond of him, and there was no denying he was a handsome young man, a hard worker too. When he came home from work he sometimes looked exhausted, but still took on jobs in the house in preparation for the summer season.

Bertha went to the range now, and as she took the chicken out of the oven, she knew that if Wendy found out it was one of their own, she wouldn't eat it. Even she had baulked at wringing its neck, and once again thanked their lucky stars for Ted. And thinking of Ted, where was he? She'd invited him to dinner and it was unusual for him to be late – yet even as the thought crossed her mind, there was a tap on the back door.

'Hello, missus,' he said as he came in, his nose twitching too.

'Sit yourself down, Ted, and you too, John. Wendy, you can help me to dish up.'

As they sat down to their meal, Bertha couldn't miss the fond looks that passed between her daughter and John. She felt a deep sense of contentment, and would be eternally grateful to Annie for leaving them this wonderful house.

Their future looked assured now. The advance bookings were healthy, and if they were anything to go by, the three of them should have a tidy sum in the bank ready to face next winter. Ted had become one of the family now, and once guests started arriving they'd be able to pay him a decent wage. Yet he hadn't complained, and seemed happy to have Wendy helping him outdoors.

Yes, Bertha thought, her eyes roaming around the table, we may be a small family, but judging by the way those two are looking at each other, it won't be long before my first grandchild is on the way.

It was the following Saturday when the telephone shrilled in the hall, and Wendy hurried to answer it. 'Good morning. Beech Guesthouse, can I help you?'

'Er, sorry, I think I must have the wrong number. I'm trying to get in touch with John Pratchett.'

'Yes, he's here. Would you hold on a moment and I'll get him.'

Wendy rushed into the garden, her fingers crossed. The voice had a distinctive London accent and she prayed the call was in answer to the newspaper advert. 'John! John,' she called, her eyes wildly searching the grounds. Oh, where was he? '*John!*' she called again, heaving a sigh of relief as he ran towards her.

'What's up?'

'There's someone asking for you on the telephone, and you'd better hurry because I think it's from a call box.'

With a burst of speed that surprised Wendy, he raced indoors, voice breathless as he said, 'John Pratchett here.'

Wendy hovered behind him, only hearing one end of the conversation, but even that sounded promising.

'Pat! Pat Benson! my God, how are you? Yes, I'm looking for Millie. Have you seen her?'

John's face fell, and Wendy's fingers uncrossed with disappointment.

'No, Pat, I haven't had any luck either. Yes, I've tried everywhere but nobody's seen her, or my father.'

There was a long pause as he stood with the receiver pressed to his ear, and unable to hear what Pat Benson was saying, Wendy's ears pricked up when he said, 'I know, and I could kill your father for what he did to Millie. Tell me, has he been found? No, of course I don't blame you.'

He was quiet again, listening to Pat, and then he said, 'I'm getting married too. Yes, in May, and listen Pat, let's not lose touch again. Is there any chance of you coming to my wedding?'

There was a pause. 'That's great, and please bring your fiancé. Give me your address and I'll send you all the details.'

He listened some more. 'Yes, OK, Pat. If I find Millie I'll let you know immediately, and will you do the same? Oh, you've been to Harmond Street a few times. Yes, I spoke to Dora Saunders too. Well, you never know, if anyone hears anything, it'll be her.'

John paused again and with a smile said, 'Huh, Dictionary Dora – yes, I'd forgotten her nickname. She's a funny old soul, but with a heart of gold, and it's worth checking with her now and then.'

Wendy could tell the conversation was coming to an end.

'Thanks, and we look forward to seeing you in May. Bye Pat, and thanks for ringing.'

John replaced the receiver, and turning he shook his head sadly. 'I thought for a moment that I'd found her, but no luck. That was

Pat Benson, the girl who used to live next door to us in Harmond Street. She doesn't live in Battersea now, but luckily bought the local paper and saw my advert. She'd been looking for Millie too, and hoped I'd found her. Mind you, she sounded a bit odd, almost as if she was talking through clenched teeth.'

'Yes, I gathered it was Pat, but it was probably just a bad line. I'm sorry it wasn't good news, but at least you've had one call in response to the advert, and there may be others.'

'Yes, I suppose so. Anyway, I'd best get back outside to finish that pruning.'

With the feel of his kiss on her cheek, Wendy watched him leave, knowing he still felt guilty for losing touch with his sister. It was the one thing that marred his happiness, and now she lifted her eyes heavenward. *Oh Millie, please get in touch*, she prayed inwardly. *And do it before our wedding . . .*

Chapter Twenty-Eight

Millie awoke with twinges of pain in her tummy that seemed to come and go on a regular basis. With difficulty she crawled off the mattress and then levered herself to her feet. 'Dad! Dad!' she shouted, feeling a wave of panic. It was dark. Was he in? With no idea of the time she listened with bated breath, but there was no answer to her calls.

With both hands clutching her stomach, she carefully made her way downstairs, relief flooding through her when she saw him asleep on the floor, half on and half off his dirty mattress. 'Dad, wake up. I think the baby's coming.'

'Wha . . . what?'

'Please, Dad, wake up!'

His eyes were still thick with sleep as he looked up at her, but seeing her grimace of pain he immediately sat up. 'Is it coming?'

'Yes, and I'm scared. I need Mrs Liddle. Can you get her to come?'

'All right, don't get yerself in a state,' Alfie said as he rose to his feet. 'I'll go down to the phone box, but she won't be here for about an hour. You'd best get yourself back to bed.'

'An hour! Why is it going to take her that long?'

''Cos she don't live around here.'

Millie stared at her father in bewilderment. Why had he booked a midwife who lived outside of the borough? And what if the baby came before she arrived?

'You can wipe that expression off your face,' Alfie snapped. 'You don't look too bad to me and it'll be ages yet before the kid arrives.' He then thrust his hand into his trouser pocket, and counted some pennies. 'I've just got enough for the phone box. Now do as I say and go back to bed. I won't be long.'

Millie made her way back upstairs, pausing halfway as a contraction gripped her abdomen. She lay on the mattress, and despite her fears she was filled with elation. Her baby would be here soon. She would know if it were a boy or a girl. Oh, but she didn't care, as long as it was all right.

How long had she been lying there? Millie didn't know. The pains grew steadily stronger, and though she knew her father had returned ages ago, he didn't come upstairs. Her lips were dry and she longed for a drink of water, but despite calling for him, he didn't appear.

The contractions became unbearable, following one after the other, and though the room was freezing, perspiration was streaming from her body. By the time Dulcie Liddle finally arrived, Millie was screaming in agony as pain ripped through her stomach. 'Help me! Please help me!'

To her relief the woman immediately took charge of the situation, and somehow knowing she was there, Millie was able to relax a little. It was embarrassing to submit to an internal examination, but Dulcie calmed her fears with a matter-of-fact voice.

'My God, it's like ice in here,' she murmured, adding, 'You're nicely dilated and it won't be long now, my dear. I'm just going to give you a little wash before slipping a clean sheet under you.'

Time passed in wave after wave of agony, and Millie was barely aware of the midwife's ministrations. Then, just when she thought she couldn't stand it any more, something changed, and she felt an overwhelming urge to push. Through a haze she was aware that her baby was coming, that she was forcing it into the world, but oh, the pain!

'Hold on!' Dulcie shouted. 'Don't push.'

Don't push! Was the woman mad? How could she not push? The urge was impossible to ignore, and gripping the sides of the mattress she strained with all her might. Millie didn't hear her own screams, she didn't hear anything. All thought was drowned out as the urge to give birth took complete control.

At last it was over, and Millie heard a faint mewling cry. She tried to lift her head, but was so weak that she was barely able to move. 'Is my baby all right? Is it a boy or girl?'

'A girl, and she's fine,' the midwife said as she swiftly wrapped the baby in a thick blanket, before placing her carefully into a long wicker basket.

Millie smiled with joy. He did care! Her father must care to have bought the baby a blanket and crib.

It wasn't long before the woman returned to crouch down at the foot of the mattress again, just as Millie felt something else slipping from her body.

With a small grunt, the midwife said, 'It's just the afterbirth. I'll get you cleaned up and then I'll see to the baby.'

She waited patiently, her eyes never leaving the basket, and as the woman made to leave the room Millie begged, 'Wait, please let me see her.'

Dulcie's lips tightened, but lifting the basket she put it briefly on the floor by Millie's side. 'Just a quick look. She needs to be cleaned up before you hold her.'

Struggling to sit up, Millie only managed to raise herself onto one elbow, her eyes full with emotion as she gazed at her child. She saw fair wispy hair and a small mewing mouth, and with her arms aching to hold her she gasped, 'Oh, you're beautiful.'

As Dulcie picked the basket up again, Millie cried, 'No, don't take her away yet.'

Ignoring her plea the woman left the room, saying, 'I'll just take her downstairs for a bath. Don't worry, I won't be long, and in the meantime get some rest.'

Millie sank back down again, tears of joy flooding her face. Oh, a girl, she had a daughter. A beautiful daughter. In her mind she saw again the baby's pretty mouth, puckered like a rosebud waiting to open. She smiled. *Rose! I'll call her Rose.*

Time passed and Millie began to grow impatient. Where was Dulcie Liddle, and where was her baby? 'Dad!' she called out feebly. 'Dad please come!'

At last she heard footfalls on the stairs and her face broke into a smile. What did her father think of Rose? Oh, she was perfect, how could he not love her! As he came into the room she looked behind him, expecting to see the midwife, but her father was alone.

There was something furtive about the look on his face, and puzzled she asked, 'Where's my baby? And where is Dulcie?'

'She's gone.'

'Gone! But she was supposed to bring Rose back up to me. Yes, I've called her Rose – don't you think it's a lovely name?' Millie babbled with happiness. 'Oh, please go and get her, Dad. I haven't held her yet.'

'The baby's gone too.'

'What do you mean?' Millie asked, feeling a surge of panic. 'How can she be gone?'

'I've given it up for adoption. It's for the best, Millie. You don't want to be lumbered with a kid at your age, and a bastard at that. You need to earn a living, and you can't do that if you're stuck with a baby to look after.'

'*NO!*' Millie screamed. 'No, you can't give her away.' She struggled to get up, feeling a wave of giddiness as she managed to crawl to her knees. 'Please, Dad, you've got to get her back! She's your grandchild!' With her arms held out beseechingly, Millie yelled in agony as a surge of pain shot through her, and looking down, she saw blood forming a pool on the mattress.

'Shut that racket, yer silly cow. I can't get her back. She's gone and you'll just have to get used to the idea. And as for being my grandchild – huh, that's a joke. I don't even know if you're my daughter. Don't forget yer mother was on the streets, so you could be anybody's.'

Millie stared at her father in disbelief. Not his daughter? Her head spun, but one thing was uppermost in her mind and she shrugged off his words. *She had to get out of here; she had to find Rose.*

Ignoring the pain, and the blood, she tried to stand up, but another wave of giddiness made her gasp. Blackness engulfed her, the room became distant, and then she knew no more.

Millie had no idea what the time was when she woke again. Shivering, yet wet with perspiration, she managed to get downstairs. It didn't take her long to realise that her father had gone, since his few belongings were missing. Where was he? Surely he hadn't left her. She had to find him! Only he knew where her baby was.

She drank stale water from the bucket kept by the sink, but was too weak to clean herself up. Her breasts throbbed, and touching them, she winced with pain. Oh God, where was Rose? She had to find her.

Only one thing remained of her father's — his old overcoat still hanging on the nail, and with difficulty she put it on before staggering outside. The pub at the end of the street — he might be in there — and holding the wall for support she made for it.

Hours later she was still staggering through the streets, many people staring at her, and a few asking if she needed help. Fixated on finding her father and Rose, Millie shrugged them off. She lost count of the pubs she checked, and in many she barely got over the threshold before being thrown out. They thought her a tramp, and Millie knew she looked like one, but somehow she kept going.

Her footsteps took her over Wandsworth Bridge, but by this time she hardly knew where she was going. It was dark, and rattling the door of the next pub, she found it locked. It was only then that she realised how late it was. Looking round in desperation, she saw an industrial area with factories and warehouses that looked forbidding in the gloom. Eyes glazed with tiredness, and feeling both hot and shivery at the same time, she carried on walking, anxious to leave the area.

Millie could barely put one foot in front of the other when she eventually turned into the King's Road, and then an arcade loomed. It was dark inside the narrow passageway, but at least undercover, and as she crept inside she saw small, closed and shuttered shops.

There was one, about halfway down, that had a deep doorway, and feeling a wave of dizziness, Millie lurched inside, knees crumbling. She crawled to the furthest recess, and pulling her father's old coat around her, she curled into a ball. Exhausted and ill, Millie slept, and it was eight in the morning before she awoke.

I'm dead, Millie thought, as she looked up to see a woman bending over her. Blonde hair surrounded a beautiful face, and the eyes that looked at her with compassion were vivid green. She thought she was looking at an angel – until the angel spoke.

'Well, what have we here?'

Millie tried to stand up, but was unable to move, and through a haze of pain she was dimly aware of the woman unlocking the shop door. Then, leaning over Millie, she helped her to her feet, saying, 'Come on, my dear. You had better come inside.'

Chapter Twenty-Nine

Vanessa Grey managed to help the filthy, ragged girl into the shop. The interior was dim, and as she flicked a switch that flooded the room with light, she saw with horror how ill this waif and stray looked. 'My God, what happened to you?'

The girl didn't answer as she slumped forward, and it became obvious that without assistance, she would have fallen to the floor. Looking around the small shop frantically, Vanessa was able to drag the girl over to a chair placed near the counter. 'Sit there,' she ordered, her commanding voice filling the small space as she added, 'I'll get you something to drink.'

She then hurriedly switched on the heaters before going into the small back room, and after filling the kettle, placed it onto the tiny gas ring, tapping her foot impatiently as she waited for it to boil. What on earth had she done? What had possessed her to bring a vagrant into her shop, albeit a young girl? Yet seeing the child was freezing – and she looked like a child – how could she have chased her away?

At last, she thought as the water steamed in the kettle, and after making two cups of tea she returned to the shop. The girl was sitting as she had left her, but looked up as Vanessa approached, showing a face etched with pain.

'Here, drink this, and after that I think you should see a doctor.'

'No, please, I'm all right. I'm just tired.'

Vanessa was surprised to hear that the girl spoke well, and as she studied her face she saw huge dark eyes looking anxiously back at her. The poor kid looked like a frightened foal, and how on earth had she ended up in her doorway? Had she been in some sort of accident? Or maybe she'd been attacked. *Take it slowly*, Vanessa told herself, instincts aroused. 'What's your name, dear?' she asked, her voice now gentle.

'Millie . . . Millie Pratchett.'

'Can you tell me what happened to you?'

Huge eyes studied Vanessa as though looking into her soul, and as if seeing something that reassured her, the girl said, 'I had a baby, but I've lost it.' Tears then began to run down her cheeks, making rivulets in the dirt on her face.

Oh, the poor kid. How awful to lose a baby, and she was so young too. But once again Vanessa wondered how she had ended up in the shop doorway. She wanted to ask more questions, but suddenly Millie swayed, almost falling off the chair.

Vanessa sprang forward, and as she held the child she was appalled at her thinness. My God, she was half-starved! 'When did you last eat?'

'I . . . I don't know.'

'Listen, there's a room at the back of the shop with a small couch. I'm going to help you on to it, and then I'm popping out to get you something to eat.'

'No, you've been kind enough already, and . . . and I must go.'

'You can't go anywhere in this state. At least wait until you've got your strength back.'

As the girl tried to stand, her legs gave way, and as though realising that Vanessa's words made sense, she nodded in acquiescence.

Five days passed, five days in which Millie remained in the back room, hardly leaving the couch.

She had been ill, and though Vanessa told her she thought it might be milk fever, Millie refused to be visited by a doctor. She guessed that Vanessa thought she was in some kind of trouble, but despite that the woman had been so kind, insisting that she stay.

Everything Millie needed was left at hand. Food, soap, a toothbrush and towel, shampoo . . . a nightdress and a big warm eiderdown, even sanitary towels for her bleeding. As Millie's strength slowly returned she had managed to have a strip wash at the tiny sink. Washing her matted hair had been difficult, but at last she managed it, relieved to find no sign of head lice when she had tugged at it with a comb.

Vanessa had also left her a clean skirt and sweater from her stock of good quality secondhand clothes, along with some under-wear, and as her senses returned Millie had been surprised to find that her rescuer owned this small shop. Vanessa Grey smacked of quality, and hardly seemed the type to buy and sell used clothes, even though they were of exceptional quality.

'Well, you're looking better,' Vanessa said as she came into the small room.

Millie jumped, surprised to hear her voice so early. Vanessa usually turned up at eight-thirty, and she was sure it was much earlier than that. 'Oh, you startled me! Thank you for the clothes, they're lovely,' she enthused, fingering the soft sweater that felt like silk against her skin.

'You're welcome, my dear, and I've come in early as I think it's about time we had a little talk,' she said before making a cup of tea for them both, with a couple of huge digestive biscuits.

Millie knew she owed Vanessa Grey a proper explanation, but how could she tell her the truth? The woman would be horrified to find out that she was an unmarried mother, and anyway, feeling better now, it was time for her to leave. She had to find her father. He was her only lead to Rose. 'Thank you so much for allowing me to stay,' she said with great sincerity, 'but I'm fine now and I really must go.'

'Wait,' Vanessa commanded as Millie stood up. 'Look, I know something's worrying you and I'd like to help.'

'I don't think you can. You see, I have to find someone and he could be anywhere.'

'Who are you looking for?'

'My father.'

'But don't you know where he lives?'

'No,' she said shortly, and unwilling to answer any more questions, said again, 'Thank you for offering to help, but I have to go now.'

'At least let me give you a tarot reading, Millie. You'd be surprised at what comes up in the cards and they might provide the answers you need.' Vanessa then pulled a small box from her cavernous bag, and opening it took out a pack of cards. 'I'm well known for my accuracy, and I've built up a steady list of clients. Now, tell me, when is your birthday?'

'March the twenty-third,' Millie told her, brows creased. Tarot cards! What on earth were they? She watched in fascination as the woman began to shuffle the pack, and after asking Millie to cut it into three piles, she held her palm over each small stack.

'So, your birthday is only just over two weeks away, and like me you're an Aries, which should give you the strength to survive. Now place your left hand over the stacks as I did, and tell me if you feel heat radiating from one of the piles.'

Still puzzled, Millie did as she was asked, and when her hand hovered over the second stack she was surprised to find that her palm felt hot. 'That one,' she said, pointing in amazement.

'Good,' and picking them up Vanessa began to lay the cards out in rows.

Millie stared in fascination at the strange pictures shown on each card, grimacing at one that depicted a man hanging by his neck, yet strangely with a smile on his face. Vanessa was studying the cards closely and when she spoke, Millie immediately tensed.

'Yes, I can see you've had a baby, but I thought you told me it had died.'

'No, I didn't say that . . . I said I'd lost her,' and somehow once started, Millie was unable to stop. It all came out – her rape, her father letting Dulcie Liddle take her baby away for adoption, and her desperate attempts to find them both.

Vanessa listened patiently, occasionally making sympathetic sounds, and when Millie looked anxiously into her eyes, she saw no censure there – only compassion.

'Oh, my dear, what an awful time you've had.' Vanessa then returned to studying the cards, and after a short pause, spoke again, 'Listen, Millie, I know how desperate you are to find your father, and your baby, but I've a feeling he may have sold your daughter illegally. If that's the case, you really should report it to the police, as without their help it could be almost impossible to find her. If your father had gone through a proper adoption agency, there would have been formalities, such as forms to sign giving permission. Were you asked to put your signature to anything?'

'No, nothing. The midwife said she was taking Rose down for a bath, and that was the last I saw of them both.' Then as Vanessa's words sank in, she cried, 'Sold her! You think my father *sold* her?'

'It's only a feeling, my dear – something I saw in the cards. Many women are desperate for children, and when they can't adopt legally, they'll do anything. I believe that a lot of money can change hands.'

'No, no, you must be wrong! I can't believe my father would do that.' Yet even as Millie said the words, a terrible knowledge gripped her.

'I could be mistaken, and the cards aren't always easy to read, but it seems strange that you weren't consulted before your baby was taken away.'

'What am I going to do?' Millie cried. If her father had sold Rose, what chance did she have of ever getting her back? Somehow she had to find him, make him tell her where Dulcie Liddle was. 'Vanessa, thank you so much for all you've done, but I must go now. I have to find my Dad. It's my only hope.'

'Do you know where to look for him?'

'Only in his old haunts. I tried all the pubs I could find in Wandsworth, but nobody had seen or heard of him. But I'll find him. If it takes me the rest of my life, I'll find him.'

'I understand that you have to go, but you can't cover every district in London. What about at night? Do you know anyone who can put you up?'

'I . . . I'll be all right.'

'I still think you should report this to the police and let them deal with it.'

'All right, I'll tell the police, but I must keep looking myself,' and seeing the concern in Vanessa's eyes, she added, 'Look, please don't worry about me. I'm happy to stay anywhere as long as I find my baby.'

'Oh, my dear girl, of course I'll worry about you. Will you promise me something?' And as Millie nodded she continued, 'If you can't find your father, will you promise that you'll come back here.'

'Back here! But why?'

Vanessa Grey smiled, and then shrugged her shoulders. 'Call it destiny, call it something I've seen in the cards, but I feel you may need me and I want you to come back if you run into any problems.'

'Thank you so much, but I'll find my father – I have to.'

As Millie stood up, Vanessa hurried into the shop, returning with a coat, a comfy pair of low heeled shoes, and a carrier bag. 'Here, take these. I'm afraid there isn't much in the bag, just a few bits to last you for a day or two.'

Millie stroked the fine, brown wool coat with a thick fur collar and stammered, 'No, I c-c-couldn't, you've done enough already.'

'I'm sorry, I threw your awful old one away, along with your other clothes. You can't go out without a coat in this weather, so please, it will make me feel so much happier if you wear it.'

Seeing the earnest appeal on her saviour's face, Millie put the coat on, and after taking the carrier bag she gave Vanessa a quick hug before almost running from the shop, overwhelmed by the woman's kindness.

As Millie left the arcade, a quick glance in the carrier bag showed what looked like a pack of sandwiches, on top of some other essentials, and smiling with gratitude she began her long walk back to Battersea, determined to try her father's old haunts.

By lunchtime, Millie had eaten a cheese sandwich and drunk from the bottle of water she'd also found in the carrier bag. She was determined to conserve the two pound notes discovered in a small purse at the bottom, and thanked her lucky stars that she'd stumbled into Vanessa Grey's shop doorway.

She'd never noticed before how many pubs there were in Battersea; some on the main roads and others tucked in back streets. So far nobody would admit to seeing her father, and on most occasions she'd been given the cold shoulder. Thankfully she now looked respectable, so she hadn't been thrown out, but it was obvious that most of the men propping up the bars considered the pubs to be a masculine domain.

Now she was walking wearily along Lavender Hill, and on

reaching Battersea Town Hall she stopped to sit on the wide steps for a rest, leaning against one of the columns. Despite the warm coat, her hands were blue, and her feet felt like blocks of ice. She shivered and lifted the fur collar to shield her face from the cold wind.

The pubs were now shut until the evening session, and though still looking clean and tidy, she was footsore and weary as she wondered where to look next.

In the distance Millie could hear a horse and cart, and as it drew closer she saw it was a coal-wagon. The horse had the same markings as Samson, and for a moment her heart missed a beat. Her eyes now travelled straight to the young, dark-haired coal-man. Something in the way he sat with the reins held slack in his hands reminded her of John, and as the cart passed she found herself thinking about her brother.

Had he been looking for her? Yes, probably, but she didn't want to be found. In Millie's mind, John had became a scapegoat, a reason for all that had happened. If he hadn't left to join the Merchant Navy, she would not have been raped. Yes, he had come back to see her after his first trip, but he'd gone off again to lead a life of his own, with no thought of how she was going to cope with their drunken father. All he cared about was Wendy now, whilst she'd been left with that hateful man – a man who could order the abortion of his own baby, drive his wife to suicide, and sell his granddaughter. Millie remembered Alfie's words then, remembered how he'd said that he might not be her father.

Her mouth drew into a tight line. *Good – I hope I'm not your daughter*, she decided bitterly. After what he'd done, who would want him as a father anyway!

A burst of laughter drew her attention, and on the other side of the busy road she saw a couple with a small child. Holding a hand each they were swinging the little girl between them, and despite her own unhappiness, the child's delighted giggles made Millie smile. For a while she continued to lean against the column, allowing herself to dream of the day when she had her daughter back, and somewhere nice to live. A pretty house with a garden, and a swing for Rose.

She looked at the back of the cart now as it rolled down the hill, seeing sacks of gleaming black nuggets on the back. Nuggets of coal that turned to ashes, and Millie suddenly saw this as an analogy of her life: sacks full of ashes, symbolic of all that she held dear, now burned to dust. Despair gripped her again, but then she heard a voice.

'Well I never! It's young Millie!'

She looked up to see Dora Saunders gazing down at her, an infectious grin on her face.

'Hello, Dora, how are you?' she asked politely.

'It don't matter about me,' the little woman said, plonking her bag of shopping on the pavement. 'How are you, and where on earth 'ave you been? John's been looking for you, Pat Benson too, but we couldn't tell them where you were. When I saw yer dad recently I asked him about you, but he was too busy flashing all that money about, and didn't answer me. Still, judging by that coat you're wearing, he must 'ave treated you to a few bob. It looks to 'ave cost a pretty penny, and if I'm not mistaken the collar's real fur. Now, get up off that cold step or you'll get piles.'

Oh Dora, Millie thought, her heart flooding with joy on hearing the woman's words. She was as nosy as ever, but so endearing with her motherly concern. 'I'm trying to find my dad, and thanks to you it looks as if I've succeeded. Where did you see him, Dora?'

'I saw him in the Nags Head on Friday night, but he said he was going away.'

'Away! Away where?'

'Bless yer, love, I don't know, and he wasn't saying neither. But he was all togged up and carrying a suitcase. He said he'd just popped back to say goodbye to his old cronies. Mind you, he wouldn't tell them where he was going, just hinting that he had plenty of money and wouldn't be seen again in these parts. Gawd, he was the talk of the pub when he left.'

Millie's heart sank, and all her new-filled joy drained away. Gone – he'd gone, and if he hadn't told anyone where he was going, what chance did she have of finding him? *Oh, Rose, Rose*, her heart cried. 'Dora, please, someone must know where he went,' she said in panic.

'No, I'm telling yer, he wouldn't say. We all thought he must've robbed a bank or something, 'cos where else would he have got all that money?'

Millie's emotions had spiralled up and down again in a matter of minutes, and now, instead of crying she laughed, hysterical laughter that caused tears to spurt from her eyes. 'Robbed a bank?' she gasped. 'No, he didn't rob a bank, Dora,' and she only just managed to stop herself from blurting out the truth. The money must have come from Dulcie Liddle. Vanessa Grey was right – he *had* sold Rose!

'Here, give over, Millie. What on earth's the matter with you? Stop it! Stop them histronicles. Come on, get yerself up and come home with me.'

Histronicles, Millie thought, howling again with laughter. Dora meant histrionics, and as usual she'd muddled up the pronunciation.

'Give over, love,' Dora urged again, and as swiftly as it had started, the laughter died abruptly in Millie's throat.

So, Pat had been looking for her, her brother too. Well, she didn't want to see John. 'Did Pat leave her address with you?'

'No, love, and what with Stella moving away, I didn't think to ask.'

'Mrs Blake's left Harmond Street?'

'Yeah, she was given a prefab in Elspeth Road. I tell you what, once we've been to my place and unloaded me shopping, we could pop round to see her.'

It was tempting to go to Dora's house, tempting to see Harmond Street, and Stella Blake, but she daren't risk it. Dora was a lovely woman, but a terrible gossip and Millie couldn't trust herself not to spill out all her troubles to this kind, homely woman. 'I can't come with you, Dora. I have to go. It was nice to see you again, and give my regards to Mrs Blake,' she blurted as she pushed herself to her feet, hurrying off as fast as her tired legs would carry her.

As soon as she turned a corner and was out of sight, Millie slowed her pace. Where should she go now? There was no point in searching for her father. He could be anywhere – north, south, from Brighton to Blackpool – and with no idea where he'd gone, there was no hope of finding him.

Oh, Dad, how could you do this to me? How could you sell my baby? The questions tumbled in her mind, but there were no answers.

Millie walked aimlessly, and as night fell she still didn't stop, often stumbling with cold and exhaustion. She had no idea where she was heading for, and didn't care. Yet somehow her feet carried her back to Chelsea, and Vanessa Grey's shop.

Chapter Thirty

Vanessa Grey was unaware of the striking figure she cut as she walked briskly along the Kings Road in Chelsea. Tall and slim, with her blonde hair styled in an immaculate French pleat, she was a picture of sophistication. Her black coat, fitted at the waist, emphasised her shapely figure, but she was oblivious to the glances that were cast her way.

Her mind was occupied with thoughts of the young waif and stray she'd found on her doorstep, and she was wondering what had become of the girl. The tarot spread had shown that Millie had suffered much heartache and pain, and Vanessa's heart had gone out to the child. The cards had depicted a difficult future – but how could she tell the poor girl that?

God, she hoped Millie was all right. There was something that drew her to the child, and it wasn't just that her sympathies had been aroused. Vanessa shook her head impatiently. At thirty-six she remained unmarried, so what was it about Millie that brought out these maternal instincts?

The girl had suffered so much, and compared to this Vanessa realised that despite everything, her life had been relatively easy. Her father had died when she was in her mid-twenties, and it had been a shock to find that he'd left the family penniless. Selling their house in Kensington had barely paid off his debts, and soon afterwards her mother had died too, never having recovered from the horror of losing their home and all their possessions.

At the time of Mrs Grey's death, Vanessa's younger brother Mark was away at university. Before the woman died, she had pleaded that no matter what, her son must finish his education. Vanessa had held her mother's hand and given her promise, but without money, it seemed impossible. She remembered how many of their old friends had shunned them, leaving her feeling lost and alone. For a while she had floundered, wondering how on earth she was going to live, let alone find Mark's fees. But then she'd found that they hadn't lost all of their friends, just the shallow ones, and when she made tentative plans, people had rallied round. The shop was an inspired idea, arising from her own need for new clothes. She had lost a lot of weight since losing her parents, but being short of money, the sort of garments she was accustomed to wearing were too expensive now.

Her idea had seemed impossible to implement at first, but then one dear friend had loaned her the cash to rent a small premises, whilst others sifted through their wardrobes for unwanted clothes to supply her with stock. And so *Finesse* was born.

It had been a struggle at first, and there had been times of despair when Vanessa barely made enough money for Mark's university fees. She'd worked all hours, leaving little time for socialising, and in a way the shop had become her baby.

Gradually it became obvious that there was a demand for quality secondhand garments, and the business flourished. Many wealthy people who'd fallen on hard times struggled to keep up appearances, and so her takings steadily rose. The shop didn't make a fortune, but the profits were enough to keep both herself and Mark going.

An image of her brother rose in her mind. When she saw the success he was making of his life, she knew that all the worry and effort had been worthwhile. He was now a psychiatrist, with a private practice in Harley Street. Unknown to his wealthy clients, he also gave some of his time to those less fortunate, working on a voluntary basis in a psychiatric hospital in Tooting. Tall and good-looking, Mark Grey was an exceptional young man, and Vanessa was so proud of him.

Goodness, when had she last seen Mark? It must have been three weeks ago, but with them both being so busy, it was difficult to find time to meet. On the whole they got on well, but Vanessa knew he didn't approve of her tarot readings, and they had had many arguments about it. In the end they had agreed to disagree, and the subject was rarely mentioned these days.

She'd become interested in tarot cards after losing both her parents, when a friend had persuaded her to see a reader. Vanessa remembered how she'd thought it was a mad idea, but she had gone anyway, perhaps hoping against hope that she would find the answers to her problems. The woman's accuracy had been amazing, and not only that, she'd advised Vanessa herself to join a development circle, saying that she had psychic abilities.

And look at me now, Vanessa thought. After taking the woman's advice, and putting a lot of hard work into it, she too had become a tarot reader, with people coming to her on a regular basis. Despite Mark's scepticism, she felt she helped many of them, especially those who came to her looking for proof of a life in the next world after losing a loved one.

Mark hated it, of course, telling her that she had no right to give people false hope, but she always argued her case. He might not believe in an afterlife, but she did, and if it gave people comfort to think their loved ones were in a better place, what harm could it do?

What was her brother up to now? Vanessa wondered. Was he still with the leggy redhead, or was someone new in the picture? So far, none of the women in his life had lasted long, and she suspected that it would take a very special one to put up with the hours he worked.

Vanessa now turned into the Chelsea Arcade, and as she reached the shop her eyes widened. It was like déjà vu to see Millie asleep in the doorway. She took in the girl's appearance, noticing her grubby face and the crumpled coat. She didn't look nearly as bad as the first time, but even so Vanessa's heart went out to her. 'Millie, dear, wake up.'

The girl's eyes opened, and with a bemused expression she looked up. 'H . . . how did I get here?'

'I don't know, my dear, but come on, get yourself inside.'

Millie didn't stay in the shop that night. Vanessa took her home to her small flat in Cheyne Walk. It was situated in a large imposing house, now converted into several apartments. As there was only one bedroom, Millie slept on the couch.

The rooms were large, with high ceilings, and during the nights that followed, Millie lay, unable to sleep, staring up at the cornices and the large ceiling rose. There were cracks in the plaster, and some of these seemed to take on shape and form as she stared at them, one becoming a horse, another a face.

On the day of her sixteenth birthday, Millie was surprised to receive a card and a lovely scarf from Vanessa, and once again was struck by the woman's kindness. Yet even this act of generosity could not distract her from her obsession. She wanted one thing only, and that was her baby daughter, Rose.

Another week passed, and on Monday evening Vanessa's brother Mark called round. Millie saw a tall, good-looking man who frowned when he saw her lying on the couch.

'Who's this?' he asked his sister, rudely ignoring Millie.

'This is Millicent Pratchett, Mark, and she's staying with me for a while.'

Without further ado, Mark took Vanessa's arm and led her into the kitchen, where unaware that Millie could still hear every word of their conversation, he began to question her.

'What's going on, Vanessa? Why is that young girl sleeping on your couch?'

'Because she's ill and had nowhere else to go.'

'How long have you known her?'

'For a short while.'

'What! Don't tell me you've taken a complete stranger into your home! Are you mad?'

'No, I'm not, and I think I'm a good judge of character. The poor girl was in an awful state and I helped her.'

'For goodness' sake, Vanessa, I thought you had more sense! What do you know about her? Where does she come from, and why is she homeless?'

'Millie has been through hell, and though I know about her background, quite honestly it's none of your business. She's a good person, and I can sense that.'

'Oh, not all this psychic mumbo-jumbo again.' Her brother raised his voice. 'It's not good enough, Vanessa, and quite honestly I think you should ask her to leave.'

'Who I have in my home is my business, and I won't be ordered about by my kid brother.'

'Very well, if that's your attitude, then there's no more to be said. I'm off – but don't say I didn't warn you. I just hope you come to your senses before I see you again.'

The front door slammed, and by the time Vanessa came back into the room, Millie was dressed and ready to leave.

'Just where do you think you're going?'

'I heard what your brother said, and I . . . I think it's better that I leave.'

'Oh, don't take any notice of Mark. He's just being protective.'

'I don't want to come between you, and anyway, I can't impose on you any longer.'

'Now listen to me, pet. I'm happy to have you here, and you aren't imposing on me at all. Goodness, you hardly eat enough to keep a bird alive! Do you really think I could let you go without knowing that you've got somewhere else to live, and a job to support yourself?'

'Don't worry. I'll be all right.' Yet even as she spoke, Millie suddenly felt sick.

'Millie, you've gone as white as a sheet! Sit down and I'll fetch you a glass of water.'

As Vanessa hurried into the kitchen again, Millie almost fell onto the couch. She should go, she knew that, but as a wave of dizziness overcame her she also knew that, at the moment, it was impossible.

Another ten days passed, days in which Millie could think of nothing but her daughter. She'd recovered physically, but mentally she was lethargic, still spending hour after hour just lying on the couch. When Vanessa came home in the evenings she made an effort, and they would talk sporadically, the conversation always turning to Rose and Millie's desperation to find her.

'Listen, my dear, I'm glad that you reported your father to the police, and they're now trying to trace him, the midwife too. You must buck up, Millie. I'm sure that given time, they'll be successful. After all, your father can't just disappear into thin air. Meanwhile, I think it's about time we did something to improve your appearance. Once we've sorted out your hair, we'll find you some nice clothes.'

'My hair? But why bother?' Millie said, her voice lacklustre.

'Long hair only emphasises the length of your face. A nice short, feathered cut would suit you and I'll make an appointment for you at my hairdresser's.'

Millie hardly heard her. What did she care about her hair? All she could think of was her baby, wondering where Rose was and if she was happy. Did the people who'd adopted her, love her? Did they give her lots of affection? *Oh please, God, please let them be kind.*

'Millie, are you listening to me?'

'What? Yes, I'm listening.'

'Come on then, get dressed. I'm sure that after you've had your hair cut, we can find some lovely outfits in the shop to fit you.'

'But I don't need any clothes. You've already given me two skirts and sweaters.'

'Now then, my girl, you've lounged about here long enough, and it's time to sort yourself out. I've got something in mind, something that will be good for both of us, but there's a lot to be done first.'

Millie heaved a sigh. She had become very fond of Vanessa, it was impossible not to, but why couldn't she just leave her alone? What did her appearance matter? Deep down she knew that she should pull herself together, but it was hard — so hard to think about anything other than her daughter.

Sitting up, Millie made a huge effort to give herself a mental shake. She couldn't expect Vanessa to support her indefinitely, it wasn't fair, and somehow she had to find a job. What if the police found her father? What if they traced Dulcie Liddle? When she got Rose back, she'd need to find work to support them both.

After forcing herself to leave the couch, Millie had a quick wash in the bathroom, just running a cold flannel around her face. She then threw on her clothes and picking up the hairbrush, flicked it half-heartedly through her hair.

When she returned to the sitting room, she saw that Vanessa was tapping her foot impatiently. 'I'm ready,' Millie said.

'Huh, there's certainly room for improvement,' Vanessa said

dryly, but then picking up her clutch bag and matching gloves, she beckoned Millie to follow her.

Millie had been taken to the hairdresser's where Vanessa gave instructions to a businesslike woman and then went off to open *Finesse*.

Many hours later, when Vanessa locked up for the evening, Millie sat and watched her bustling around, flicking through racks and discarding outfit after outfit. She finally settled on a suit and ordered Millie to try it on.

Despite Millie's protests, Vanessa was determined to give her a complete grooming session and now, as she stared at herself in the full-length mirror, Millie couldn't believe her eyes. Her hair was now short, and beautifully styled, with a long fringe that feathered across her forehead. Blonde streaks had been skilfully applied, and these somehow made her skin appear less sallow.

The effect was startling. Her face didn't look so long, not only due to the haircut, but also by the skilful use of make-up that Vanessa had applied. The woman's choice of clothes was inspired too, and Millie now wore a beautiful chocolate-brown suit with a skirt that finished below her knees. The cut was beautiful, and with the jacket nipped in at the waist, it actually looked like she had a figure.

'Well, what do you think?' Vanessa beamed.

'Oh Vanessa! I can hardly believe it!'

'I know the style is a little old for you, but even so it looks fabulous. I knew there was a lovely woman hiding in there somewhere, and I was right.'

'Lovely! I'm not lovely.'

'Take another look in the mirror, Millie. You look wonderful. Your eyes are magnificent, and with that lovely slim figure you could be a model. All right, you may not be a conventional beauty, but you're striking. In fact, *very* striking. Wait till we go out – the men won't be able to keep their eyes off you. My brother's coming round again this evening, and he's going to see a huge difference.'

Millie stared at herself again, and though amazed at her new appearance, she was suddenly nervous. Yes, Mark Grey *would* see a difference, yet on the second occasion when he'd called round to see Vanessa, his attitude hadn't changed. Finding out he was a psychiatrist, she had quivered in his company, his sophistication making her feel gauche as he continually stared at her, asking her questions that she avoided answering.

No, she didn't want him, or any other man being attracted to her. Even when looking like a mouse, she had been raped and abused, and what would happen now? Suddenly trembling, she unbuttoned the jacket of her suit.

'What's the matter, my dear? You've gone awfully pale.'

'I want to take this suit off, and the make-up. I don't want anyone to see me like this.'

'But why? You look marvellous.'

'I don't want to look marvellous!' Millie cried, taking a handkerchief and scrubbing frantically at the make-up on her face.

'Stop it! Stop it and talk to me. Tell me what's wrong.'

Vanessa listened as Millie sobbed out the rest of her story. She already knew about the rape, but now she listened as Millie told of her mother's suicide. The girl then went on to talk of her brother's desertion, along with losing a friend who had turned out to be unnatural.

The poor kid, Vanessa thought. It seemed that everyone she'd ever loved had gone from her life. She'd been beaten and abused by her father, raped by his friend, and then her child had been stolen. Why had it happened? What was it about this girl that made her one of life's victims? She carried an aura of vulnerability. Was that it – was it because she appeared an easy victim to these awful men?

As Millie continued to sob softly, Vanessa placed an arm around her shoulders, wondering what she could say to bring her comfort. With what she'd suffered, was it any wonder the girl had such low self-esteem? Somehow she had to help Millie to gain her self-respect.

God, Vanessa thought, what a sheltered life she'd had in comparison. Of course, she knew such awful men existed, but had been fortunate in never coming across them. But why was that? Was it because she carried an aura of strength?

Pulling back her shoulders, Vanessa decided that it might help if she could change Millie's demeanour in some way. 'Listen, Millie, you've got a choice now. You can remain a victim – you can let what your father and his friend did ruin the rest of your life – or you can fight back. If you want to, you can choose not to be a victim ever again.'

'How? How can I do that?'

'You must learn to be strong. If you scurry around, always looking like a frightened little mouse, you'll be open to predators. Appearing weak isn't the answer.'

'I . . . I don't understand.'

'You have to appear strong, even if you are quaking inside. Stand tall and walk along the centre of the pavement with your head held high. Say to yourself, "*No one is going to take advantage of me.*" You'll be surprised, Millie. It works, believe me it does.'

'Is that what you do?'

The older woman smiled wryly. For as long as she could remember she'd been strong and, she knew, somewhat dominant. It came naturally to her, being an Arian, and true to her birth sign. Yet with Pisces strong in her chart, she had a soft side, and psychic abilities, but on the whole she knew she projected strength.

Would it hurt if Millie emulated her? Surely not! The girl was an Arian too, but because of what she'd suffered, her fire had been doused. Yes, she decided, it couldn't do any harm to bring out the girl's inner strength.

Smiling, she answered Millie's question. 'Yes, that's what I do, and from now on you're going to practise it too. There's no time like the present, so come on, let's repair your make-up and go for a trial run.'

As they walked along the King's Road, Millie tried to copy the way Vanessa walked. She felt ridiculous at first and wanted to scurry back against the wall, but gradually she gained confidence. Over and over again she inwardly chanted, '*No one is going to take advantage of me,*' and amazingly, it worked. After a short while she found she was holding her head high without realising it, and her strides had lengthened.

'That's it, poppet. Now come on, we're going to have a special dinner.'

They stopped outside a very classy restaurant, and Millie immediately shrank back. 'Do we have to go in there?'

'Another lesson, Millie. Always take care of your appearance. If you know you look good, then you'll feel good. Now come on, there's no need to be intimidated. As we go in, say to yourself, "*I look like a million dollars, and I'm as good as anyone here*".'

Millie drew in a deep breath, her eyes widening at the immaculately laid tables, with their snow-white linen cloths, sparkling glasses, shiny cutlery, and pink linen serviettes in the shape of fans. She had never seen anything like it before, and thought it looked wonderful.

A waiter approached, his action haughty as he ushered them to a table. The man appeared to be looking down at her, his expression disdainful, and once again Millie felt like shrinking. He drew out a chair, and as Millie sat down, shaking with nerves, she knocked over a glass. The waiter affected a pained expression and she stuttered, her face flaming with embarrassment, 'Oh! Oh dear, I'm s-sorry.'

However, at that moment she looked at Vanessa, and was unable to help spluttering. Her friend, with her neck stretched comically, was imitating the waiter and looking down her nose with disgust.

Their giggles eased the tension, and after Vanessa requested the menu, they went on to eat a delicious meal.

Vanessa sighed happily as she picked up a serviette and delicately wiped a touch of Peach Melba dessert from her lips. 'See? It wasn't so bad, was it?'

'No, it was fine,' Millie agreed, realising that she'd enjoyed the experience.

'*Finesse* is doing well and it's nice to have a treat now and then, but tell me, Millie, have you ever worked in a shop?'

'No. I stayed at home for a little while after leaving school, and then I got a job in the offices of a coal depot.'

'What did you do there?'

'Typing, filing, a bit of bookkeeping,' and smiling at the memory, she added, 'as well as being the tea-girl.'

'It sounds as if you enjoyed the job.'

'Oh, I did. It was wonderful.'

Vanessa then abruptly changed the subject. 'Do you know, finding stock for the shop is more and more difficult. I'm inundated with customers, but it's becoming hard to fill their requirements. I need to try further afield, perhaps in some affluent country areas. With this in mind I recently placed an advertisement in *The Lady* magazine, and I've had some positive replies. However, there lies the problem. I can't leave the shop to go traipsing around the country, and that's where you come in, Millie.'

'Me!'

'Yes, you. Listen, I've got a proposition to put to you. I'd like you to run the shop for me while I go out buying.'

'But I couldn't do that!'

'Why not? You're obviously intelligent . . . you need a job, and I need an assistant.'

Millie, recalling some of the very superior ladies who patronised *Finesse*, quaked at the idea of serving them. She wouldn't be able to do it, she just wouldn't.

As if reading her thoughts, Vanessa leaned forward, saying earnestly, 'You can do it, I know you can. I wouldn't have offered you the job if I thought otherwise. The shop is my livelihood, Millie, and I wouldn't risk jeopardising it. You speak well, and now you look wonderful too. Don't worry, I wouldn't just leave you to run the shop without training you first. So, come on, what do you say?'

Oh, Millie thought, it would be so lovely to work for Vanessa. If her benefactor was asking *her* for help, how could she possibly turn her down? What's more, she could start saving for when she got Rose back.

Sitting up in her chair, and drawing back her shoulders, she said positively, 'Yes, please, Vanessa. I'd *love* the job.'

Chapter Thirty-One

The wedding had gone off without a hitch. Wendy was a beautiful bride, and the only thing that marred John's day was the absence of his sister, Millie.

He looked at the spread in the dining room of Beech House, amazed that with money so tight, Bertha had somehow managed to provide a wonderful buffet. The table looked wonderful, and as Pat Benson filled a plate, John frowned. There was something in her attitude that worried him; he had noticed it since she had arrived the previous evening. She appeared stiff, keyed-up, her eyes barely meeting his. Yet when talking to Bertha, Wendy and the other guests, she seemed relaxed. Her fiancé Brian Lucas, was a nice bloke and obviously adored her, but something was wrong, something he couldn't put his finger on. Had she found out something about Millie, but didn't want to tell him? His stomach lurched, and as she now strolled over to the French doors, he followed.

'Are you all right, Pat?'

'Yes, I'm fine, thanks.' Her voice was clipped.

'You're fiancé seems a nice chap.'

She nodded, not bothering to answer him.

'Have I done something to upset you?' John asked, bemused.

'Huh, if you don't know, I'm not going to tell you.'

John looked over his shoulder. Wendy was chatting to her friends from London, and the other guests were all occupied, so taking Pat's arm, he opened the doors and drew her outside, closing it softly behind them. 'Spit it out.'

'Spit it out? But this chicken's lovely,' she said, brandishing a drumstick.

'Don't be facetious, Pat, you know perfectly well what I mean. You're obviously annoyed with me about something, and I'd like to know what.'

'As I said before . . . if you don't know, then I'm not going to tell you.'

'Don't be bloody ridiculous. I haven't seen you for a long time, and other than talking to you on the telephone on a couple of occasions, I can't think of a single thing that I've said or done that might have upset you.'

Pat's eyes blazed as she turned to confront him. 'Christ, you're an insensitive sod. You left Millie to cope with your father, and believe me she went through hell, but worse is that on the day you cleared off, my father raped her.'

'You can hardly blame me for that!'

'Oh, can't I? Didn't Millie tell you that your dad went to Southampton to find you, leaving her alone in the house? No, I don't suppose she did. After all, I know Millie, and she wouldn't want to upset her precious brother. All right, my father still has a lot to answer for, and I know there's no excuse for what he did. But it wouldn't have happened if you'd been there, or even if you'd had the guts to tell your dad yourself that you were going. Instead you left Millie to tell him, and he went off on a fool's errand to look for you.'

John hung his head, unable to look at Pat. *Oh, Millie, Millie*, he agonised, *what a selfish bastard I've been*. They'd lost their mother, reeling with shock when they'd found out their father had caused her death, and in his desperation to get away, he hadn't given a thought to Millie. She had tried to tell him how frightened she was of their dad, but he hadn't listened. All he had cared about was himself, his own pain, and he'd dismissed her fears as simply foolish, telling her to stand up for herself. And yes, he had left her to break the news that he was leaving to their father, with no thought of how he'd react.

When he returned from the first trip, he'd been full of his adventures – full of his future with Wendy, and had chosen to ignore what was right under his nose. He'd questioned Millie about the rape, only to let her fob him off. And not only that, he'd seen his father was still a drunk, and that his sister was obviously scared of him, but all he wanted was to get back to Wendy. Christ, he hadn't even bothered to find out if Millie was coping financially.

'Cat got your tongue?'

John looked up then, saw Pat's scorn, and knew he deserved it. 'I know there's nothing I can say in my defence. Everything you've said is true, and when I went back to Battersea to find they'd been evicted, believe me, some of this hit me.'

'Good, at least you've got a conscience. Now if you don't mind I'd like to go back inside.'

She threw him one last look of disgust before walking off, and John, still full of shock and remorse stood motionless, making no attempt to follow her. The French door swung on its hinges as Pat marched furiously into the room, and a couple of people looked startled. Wendy turned, and seeing her husband silhouetted on the terrace, she left her friends to join him.

'What's going on, darling?'

'I've just had a ticking-off from Pat Benson. No, leave it,' he urged, seeing Wendy's face contort with anger. 'She was angry with me for leaving Millie, and after finding out why, I agree with her: it's no more than I deserve.'

'Your relationship with Millie is none of her bloody business. I know how awful you've been feeling and you've been going frantic trying to find your sister! How dare she? How dare she come here to confront you on our wedding day? Well, I'm not standing for it, and I'm going to tell her to leave – and right now!'

'Wait, Wendy! My sister was raped on the day I left, and if I hadn't run off, it wouldn't have happened.'

'Oh, for God's sake, John. All right, you left, but you've got a right to a life of your own. As for Millie being raped . . . yes it was terrible and when you told me about it my heart went out to her, but you aren't to blame. It could have happened two days later, a week later, or even a year. Were you supposed to stay at home twenty-four hours to protect your sister? No, and after all, Millie is your father's responsibility, not yours.'

'She was only fifteen, Wendy.'

'I realise that, and I know that you're eaten up with guilt, but it happened and you can't change it. Come on, darling, it *is* our wedding day. Don't let Pat Benson spoil it.'

He saw the appeal in her eyes, and forcing a smile, led her back inside. No, he couldn't spoil this day for her, she deserved better than that, but the familiar prayer left his lips. *'Please, God, please let me find my sister.'*

Pat grabbed Brian's arm, hissing, 'Come on, we're going.'

'Going! But why?'

'Because I've fallen out with the groom. Now don't argue, just get your bits and pieces packed.'

Brian, obviously puzzled, left to do as she asked and only moments later Wendy marched to Pat's side. 'Come into the hall, please. I want to talk to you.'

'It's all right, I know what you're going to say, and we're leaving.' Her foot had only touched the bottom stair when Wendy spoke again, and Pat turned, an apologetic look on her face. She knew she shouldn't have come, but all the bottled-up anger she felt towards John made her want to confront him. Yes, she had spoken to him on the telephone, but had wanted to look into his face when giving him a piece of her mind. Yet what good had it done, other than spoiling his wedding day?

'Why did you have to upset John on this of all days?' Wendy asked.

'I'm sorry, really I am.'

'It's a bit late for that. Now please leave as quickly and as quietly as possible,' she demanded, walking away with her head high.

God, she was gorgeous, and John was a lucky man. Though small, Wendy was perfectly proportioned, and no wonder John adored her. Stop it! Stop it! Pat told herself, angry about where her thoughts were leading as she carried on upstairs to pack.

The couple sneaked out of the back door, and only then realised they faced a long walk to the station. Pat refused when Brian offered to go back inside to order a taxi, hoping the long walk would calm her. As usual he fell in with her wishes, and she squeezed his arm in thanks. He hadn't asked again why they were leaving, content just to hold her hand as they started down the drive. Christ, he's such a lovely man, she thought. A man who deserves better than a woman who lusted after her own sex. Would it work? Would marriage to this sweet and kind man work? God, she hoped so. Yet even as the thought crossed her mind she, like John, was praying that one day she'd find out what had happened to Millie.

Chapter Thirty-Two

In July Millie's training was complete. She was a little more self-assured now, but still pined for Rose. Hate for her father ate at her insides, but she had mentally decided to put her old life behind her. She had never met anyone like Vanessa Grey before, and Chelsea, though only over one of London's bridges, felt a million miles away from Harmond Street. Her life in Battersea held nothing but bad memories, and she was determined never to return.

From now on she would try to forget her father and John, and her only desire was to find her daughter. She stiffened her shoulders, determined that this was her new life now. Vanessa had become her mentor, half boss, and half friend.

A customer came in and Millie snapped to attention, a smile fixed on her face. This was her first day alone in the shop and to give herself confidence she'd taken special care of her appearance. 'Can I help you?' she asked.

'No, thank you. I'm just browsing.'

The young woman's smile was warm, and Millie heaved a sigh of relief. Some of the customers were very difficult. It seemed that being forced to buy secondhand clothes made some women imperious, and they treated both her and Vanessa like servants. At first she'd found this difficult to cope with, until Vanessa had explained that they were probably ashamed of having to buy used garments, albeit of excellent quality. Their demeanour covered their feelings, and once Millie understood this, she was able to put up with their demanding attitude.

As the months passed, she came to know other shopkeepers in the arcade. Opposite was a tiny cobbler's, and the kindly old man who ran it never failed to shout out a greeting when he saw her. Next to it was a shop selling mostly antique jewellery. Millie loved to look in the window and once, when she'd been staring at a Victorian pendant, trying to make out what was inside, the owner had come out to explain that it was hair. Ugh, she'd thought, when he went on to say it was probably a memento of someone who had passed away.

There were more premises on that side of the arcade, but most were empty, until the corner, where there was a barber's shop.

On the same side as *Finesse* and to the left was a double-fronted shop selling a mishmash of new and used furniture, and Vanessa was fighting a losing battle with the owner to keep the front tidy. He was fond of putting things outside, the latest an old and battered pram that he was obviously trying to get rid of.

Other than a small stationer's, again there were some empty premises, until the corner café, owned and run by a lovely Italian family. Millie popped in at lunchtimes to buy a sandwich, and the same thing happened every day. As soon as Mamma Baglioni saw her she would hold up her hands in horror. 'Too thin, you are too thin,' she would insist, putting extra fillings into whichever sandwich Millie ordered. The middle-aged Italian woman seemed to ooze warmth, and sometimes made Millie blush when she patted her face, saying, 'You 'as beautiful eyes, *bella mia*, but if you want to find a husband, you must put on weight.'

Another favourite of Millie's was Mrs White, who owned the small haberdashery shop next door and to the right of *Finesse*. When making minor repairs to garments, such as a hem coming down, Millie would often pop in there for matching cotton, and Alice White was fast becoming a friend. Though elderly, she was a kindly soul, and in some ways reminded Millie of Dora Saunders.

Now, as she watched the young customer flicking through a rack of afternoon suits, Millie's thoughts turned to Vanessa. She was so good with the customers, not only with those who came in to buy, but also with those ladies offering garments for sale. She would take them into the back room, and when Millie asked why, Vanessa explained that they wouldn't want to be seen trading in their clothes for money.

When inspecting the various suits, dresses, and ballgowns

offered for sale, Vanessa ignored any minor damage that could easily be repaired, but she frequently had to turn down many of the garments lacking buttons. Again she had patiently explained to Millie that some buttons were impossible to replace, and were an important part of a couturier's creation.

Millie salted away all these facts, astounded at the amount of money an Ascot suit or ballgown could fetch. Even secondhand they cost ten times more than she had ever earned in a week, so goodness knows what they had cost when new.

The customer now fingered a pale-blue, shot-silk suit, a particular favourite of Millie's, but she turned away from it, her eyes roaming around the shop. 'Are you looking for something in particular?' Millie asked as she moved to her side.

'Yes, but I don't think you'll be able to help me. What I really want is a ballgown.'

'We do have some in stock, but they're under covers to protect them. May I take your measurements?'

The covers were labelled with the size and a brief description of the gown, and Millie selected two. The first was satin, in a beautiful shade of deep ruby red, which she thought might suit the young lady's colouring. The top was heart-shaped, and the skirt full, billowing out from a fitted waist. The second gown was long and straight, with an elegant fishtail at the back. It was made of pale-grey beaded silk that shimmered with every movement. More sophisticated than the first, it just might appeal to the young woman's taste.

Millie removed the first cover, and following Vanessa's training, she expertly laid the gown across her arm, fanning the skirt to show it to its best advantage. 'How about this? I think it would suit you.'

The customer gasped, stepping forward to finger the material. 'Oh, it's wonderful. May I try it on?'

'Of course. Come this way and I'll show you the changing room. If you need any assistance I'll be outside.'

Millie found her help was needed for the zip, and as the woman emerged to twirl in front of the mirror she couldn't help but smile at the lovely picture she presented. The dress fitted her to perfection, emphasising her slim waistline, and the deep ruby colour added warmth to her complexion. 'You look wonderful, madam.'

'Yes, it is lovely, isn't it, and I'm so thrilled. I didn't expect to find a gown like this in an old secondhand shop!' Then lifting a hand to her mouth, she added, 'I'm so sorry. I didn't mean to be rude.'

'We only stock the best quality gowns, and most of them have only been worn once. But please, you don't have to apologise. Would you like to try on the other dress?' And moving across to take it out of the cover she once more laid it across her arm.

'Oh, that one is lovely too, but just a little too old for me, I think. No, I've decided on this one.' Her voice became conspiratorial as she said, 'A lovely diplomat has invited me to a ball at the French Embassy. I couldn't possibly afford a really special ballgown, and finding one as wonderful as this seems like a miracle. Oh, I'm so glad I followed my friend Felicity's advice to come here.'

Millie carefully folded the gown in tissue before closing the lid of the large plain box. Having made her first sale whilst alone in the shop, she was elated, and after taking the money and writing out a receipt, she smiled at the young lady. 'Have a wonderful time at the ball.'

'Why, thank you, and thank you for being so helpful. Goodbye.'

Millie found that the rest of the morning passed slowly, and by two o'clock she had done everything that could be done in the shop. She had tidied the rails, checked the stock, and was now dusting the counter.

With nothing else to occupy her, her thoughts once again centred on Rose. Every week she checked with the police, praying they would have some news, but so far they had been unable to trace her father, or Dulcie Liddle.

As time passed she became more and more filled with despair, and though she tried hard to put on a front, it was becoming increasingly difficult. Vanessa told her not to give up hope, insisting that these things took time, but whenever Millie saw a woman with a baby, her heart would leap. So many times she had looked into their prams, hoping to see Rose, only to wilt with disappointment. Some of the young mothers gave her odd looks, probably thinking she was a madwoman, but others smiled happily when she admired their babies.

Sometimes when she saw a baby girl, her arms ached. She had never held Rose to her breast and all she had seen of her was one brief glimpse. Yet even now her daughter's lovely face was imprinted on her mind.

The door opened, and as Alice White poked her head inside, she asked, 'Millie, have you got a drop of milk to spare? I'm dying for a cup of tea but I've run out.'

'Yes, come on in and I'll fetch you some.'

'The shop's been really quiet today – I've only sold a few balls of wool. Have you been busy?'

'No, not really, but then we never are on Mondays.'

The door opened again and a chirpy voice said, 'Hello, Gran, I wondered if I'd find you in here. It's a bit dangerous leaving the shop unattended, isn't it?'

'I've only popped out for a minute,' the old lady said. Turning to Millie again, she added, 'This is Jenny, my granddaughter, and as you can see she's having a baby. By the look of it she hasn't got much longer to go.'

'There's another two weeks before it's due, Gran.'

'Well, you shouldn't be out and about. What if it comes early?'

'Stop being an old worry-guts. Come on now, don't you think we should go back to the shop?'

'Yes, all right. Oh, by the way, this is Millie.'

'Hello,' Jenny said, smiling pleasantly.

'Hello, it's nice to meet you. I'll just get your gran some milk so you can both have a cup of tea.'

As Millie went out to the small back room she couldn't help feeling a pang of envy. Mrs White's granddaughter was having a baby, and she had seen the wedding ring on her finger. Jenny wouldn't have *her* baby snatched away and put up for adoption.

It was only an hour later when Alice White stuck her head around the door again.

'Trade's dead, Millie. I don't fancy leaving Jenny to go home

257

on her own so I'm shutting up early. This is her third baby and you'd think she'd have more sense than to traipse the streets with only two weeks to go. Between you and me, she isn't much use as a mother. She can't stand being indoors for long and likes nothing better than to be out and about with her friends. My poor daughter, Emma, is always getting lumbered with her other two kids, and for hours on end.' Alice smiled wryly adding, 'The trouble is, Jenny's an only child, and my Emma spoils her rotten, I've told her to put her foot down, but she won't listen.'

'How old are the children?'

'Jack's four, and he'll be going to school soon. Maria's two, and she's such a handful that I don't know how my daughter copes with her, let alone the new baby when it arrives. I've told Jenny that her husband should put a knot in it after this one, but she just laughs at me. Oh dear, would you listen to me going on and on. My old man says I must have been vaccinated with a gramophone needle,' and with a rueful smile she added, 'I'll see you in the morning, love.'

Millie said goodbye, waving to Mrs White and her grand-daughter as they passed the window. She tried to stifle the jealous thoughts that crowded her mind, tried not to feel bitter, but it became impossible. She longed for Rose, longed for her daughter. Alice White's granddaughter had two children, with another on the way, and it sounded like none of them were wanted.

When Vanessa returned on Wednesday, Millie was pleased to be able to show her that the shop had done fairly well; so far, takings were up on the previous week. The two women spent several hours checking the new stock Vanessa had managed to buy, and after being dry-cleaned, the garments would make a welcome addition to the depleted racks. It was sometimes hard to find a good selection of sizes, but this, Vanessa's first buying trip outside London, had proved to be very successful.

'Come on, Millie, it's nearly closing time and I'm whacked. I don't feel like cooking, so how about we celebrate our joint success by having a meal in a nice restaurant?'

'That would be lov—' Millie broke off as the door opened, the breath leaving her body in a rush as a policeman entered.

'Miss Millicent Pratchett?' he asked.

'Yes, that's me,' and before the constable could speak she said, 'Have you found my father?'

'Yes, miss, but I'm afraid it isn't good news. Your father's in hospital.'

'In hospital? Where? Is he very ill?' The questions burst from her lips.

'I don't know all the details. The hospital he's been admitted to is in Cornwall,' and flicking open his notepad the officer checked it before adding, 'a place called St Ives.'

Millie turned to look at Vanessa, her expression frantic, 'I must go to see him! Can you manage without me?'

'Of course, but you can't go this evening, Millie. It's a long journey to Cornwall and by the time you arrive it'll be late at night. You won't be able to see your father or find accommodation.'

'It doesn't matter. I'll sleep in the waiting room if I have to, but I must go.'

'My dear, it makes more sense to wait until first thing in the morning, and I'll come to St Ives with you.'

'But what about the shop?'

'This is more important than the shop and it won't hurt to close it for the day, or two if need be. Now, what do you say? Will you wait until the morning?'

Millie wanted nothing more than to rush off and catch the first train to Cornwall, but she could see the sense in Vanessa's words. 'Yes, all right, but can we at least ring to find out how he is?' Turning to the policeman she asked, 'Have you the address and telephone number of the hospital?'

The constable flicked open his notepad again, and scribbling down the details he handed them to Millie. 'We'll need to talk to you on your return, miss.'

Millie nodded, and as the policeman left the premises, she flew to the telephone. It took forever to get through, but finally she was able to talk to the Ward Sister. The conversation was brief, and replacing the receiver, Millie frowned. 'All she'd tell me is that my father's comfortable.'

'Never mind, you'll see him for yourself tomorrow. Now come on, let's go home.'

As they walked side by side to Cheyne Walk, Millie suddenly found herself filled with elation. At last! At last the police had found her father. *Oh Rose, Rose! I'll be able to get you back now.*

Chapter Thirty-Three

'I think he's hallucinating again, Doctor.'

'Yes, poor chap. His liver is in a bad way, probably caused by a long period of drinking and self-neglect. There isn't much we can do, Nurse, except to keep him as comfortable as possible.'

Alfie Pratchett could hear the doctor, but whatever drugs they had given him made it impossible for him to respond. What did they mean, he was hallucinating? Couldn't they see Eileen standing by his bed? The idiots must be blind! '*Did you hear what they said, Eileen? Me number's nearly up. Yes, I know, it's no more than I deserve, but it's too late to change anything now. I don't know where Dulcie Liddle is, let alone the baby. Yes, I know I shouldn't have done it. No, please Eileen, don't go.*' She was fading away, and though he tried lifting his arms, they wouldn't move, and he groaned in despair.

Of course he shouldn't have deserted Millie. But with £500 in cash in his pocket, he had been determined to start a new life, away from London and the memories. But his guilt soon put paid to that. He hadn't expected to feel guilty, but Millie's face haunted him. When the girl found out that Dulcie Liddle had taken her baby, she looked like she wanted to die.

As planned, he'd abandoned her, salving his conscience by assuring himself that Millie would soon get over it. It wouldn't take her long to appreciate the fact that she'd be better off without being lumbered with a brat. Anyway, he'd told himself, Millie was old enough to look after herself now, and she was no longer his responsibility.

He'd arrived in Cornwall, determined to enjoy his new life, but couldn't get her face out of his mind. Why? What did he care about Millie, or her bastard brat. Then it had hit him! Eileen had looked at him in the same way when he'd insisted she have an abortion. Was that why his wife had taken her own life? The truth dawned then – the truth he'd been denying since her suicide.

It was his fault – and it was seeing Millie's reaction to losing her baby that had finally made him realise that. God, he'd been a bastard! He hadn't wanted Eileen to have another kid because he was jealous, and what sort of man was jealous of his own children?

He'd wanted his wife all to himself, but when had the obsession begun? His mind sought around for the answer.

Yes, he'd resented having to marry her, but after she'd given birth to John and got her figure back, he'd seen how her beauty had matured. He also saw her softness and tenderness when she held the baby – and was it then that the jealousy had been born? His mother had never cuddled him, held him, or looked at him in the way that Eileen looked at their son.

When he came home from work it was to find the kid in her arms, as often as not suckling, clamped to the breasts that were his, by right, his alone – and he'd seethed with resentment. Why didn't she ever look at *him* like that?

Then she'd insisted that they take in Millie, and with two children to care for, Eileen had even less time for him. Most nights she was asleep as soon as her head hit the pillow, and he knew she resented his attempts to make love to her.

'It's time for his medication,' Alfie heard someone say, the voice distant but momentarily breaking into his thoughts. Then he was barely aware of the needle pricking his skin as his mind drifted again.

Why had he sold Millie's baby? Oh, he knew the answer to that. It was greed, pure greed, and desperation to get away from London. But what good had it done him? With so much money in his pocket he'd taken to buying bottles of whisky, finding it was the only thing that gave him any peace. The guilt ate at his mind, never leaving him, and drink was the only answer. When he fell onto his bed at night, he was able to sleep, but in the morning the memories returned to plague him.

Eileen was here again, standing beside him, and her face held such sadness. He struggled to speak. '*I drove you to it, didn't I, love, and I'm sorry. What did you say? Yes, I know I've been a terrible man, but I just wanted you all to myself. Instead, I lost yer. Through my own stupidity, I lost yer.'*

'He's mumbling again, Doctor. I think I heard the name Eileen, but I can't be sure.'

'I don't think it will be long now, Nurse. Stay with him. You never know, he might be aware that you're there.'

The voice was still distant, but again Alfie heard it. So this was it – he was going to die now. He saw his life flash by, saw his mistakes, and wished he could put them right – but it was too late.

'I'm sorry, Miss Pratchett. I'm afraid your father died last night.'

Millie stared at the doctor, but her mind refused to accept his words. 'But I have to speak to him. It's very important.'

'I'm so sorry. I'm afraid he had pneumonia aggravated by liver problems and there was nothing we could do. Would you like to see him?'

'Yes, I would. Where is he?'

'Nurse, would you take this young lady to see her father.'

Millie stood up, her expression bewildered as she and Vanessa followed the nurse along the corridors. She'd been so excited at the thought of finding Rose that she'd hardly slept the night before, and her eyes were heavy with tiredness as she rubbed her fingers across her lids.

'If you wait here, I'll prepare your father. I'll come to fetch you when he's ready.'

Millie watched in a daze as the nurse went through a door, and she turned to Vanessa. 'What does she mean? Why has she got to prepare him?'

'She's getting him ready for you to see him. Millie, you do realise that your father is . . .'

Vanessa's voice was cut off as the nurse returned, saying, 'You can come in now, Miss Pratchett.'

Millie saw a tiny room – what looked like a trolley, and as the nurse smiled sympathetically, she stepped forward. No! Oh no! This couldn't be her dad!

The room began to swim as the doctor's words finally sank in. He was dead! Her father was dead!

Questions, they were asking her questions. Her father's medical history, his date of birth, it went on and on. Millie answered as best she could, but the same thoughts kept churning in her mind. How *could* he? How could he die without telling her where her daughter was?

Then they wanted to know what she intended to do with his body, and spoke about a funeral parlour. What did she care about funeral arrangements? As far as she was concerned, her father could rot in hell!

Only last week the police had told her that they had been unsuccessful in tracing Dulcie Liddle, saying that she had probably given a false name. Millie hadn't been able to tell them anything else about the woman, and even though she tried, her description was vague.

Tears spurted from her eyes now, and rolled unchecked down her cheeks. Her father's death had brought all hopes of finding her daughter to an end. Oh, God, I can't bear it, I can't, she thought frantically. How can I live without ever seeing my baby again?

At last they were free to go. With Vanessa's arm supporting her, Millie stumbled out of the hospital.

'It's too late to go back to London tonight so I booked a hotel,' Vanessa told her. 'Millie, did you hear what I said?'

She nodded, hardly aware of what was happening as Vanessa ushered her into a taxi. Everything around her seemed vague, distant . . . and the next thing Millie knew, she was being tucked into bed, Vanessa lightly stroking her forehead as she drifted off to sleep.

Vanessa gazed down at Millie, her heart aching. The tarot spread had been right – they had shown a death. Sometimes when giving a reading, Vanessa intuitively knew what the cards were saying, and Millie's spread had shown that she'd had a long, hard path in life. When she had first found the girl on her doorstep, Vanessa's instincts told her that whatever trouble the child was in was *not* of her own making – and she had been proved right. Millie had been badly used and had suffered terribly.

As she grew closer to Millie, she had became increasingly fond of her, and it hadn't taken Vanessa long to realise that only the thought of finding her baby, held Millie together. So what would happen now? Would she be able to cope with the knowledge that it was unlikely she would ever see little Rose again?

After removing her clothes and make-up, Vanessa climbed into the twin bed, but found sleep elusive. Millie had cried as though her heart would break at first, and though Vanessa could understand her indifference towards her father's funeral, she had surreptitiously taken over the arrangements, writing out a cheque to cover the expenses and leaving it with the hospital almoner.

By the time they were able to leave, Millie seemed to be in a stupor and Vanessa became increasingly worried about the girl's state of mind. What did the future hold for Millie? Would she *ever* find happiness? Without making a sound, Vanessa threw back the bedcovers, deciding that the cards might give her the answers she was seeking.

Wherever she went, her tarot pack went with her, and opening her small overnight case she removed them from the box. Eyes closed, she shuffled the pack, praying that guidance on how to help Millie would be revealed.

Vanessa stared at the cards, unhappy with the spread. Eventually Millie would find happiness, but not for some time — and it was a strange reading. Maybe if she weren't so tired she could make sense of it. She blinked, yawned and studied them again. Without a doubt the cards showed a difficult time for Millie, but there was something else, something Vanessa didn't want to see. Her eyes clouded, and with a shake of her head, she returned the cards to their box.

Yet as she climbed quietly into bed, the thought refused to leave her mind. *Theft*. It was definitely in Millie's spread. No, her instincts couldn't have let her down. No matter what the cards said, Vanessa Grey refused to believe she had befriended a thief!

Chapter Thirty-Four

It was a very quiet and subdued Millie who had returned to London with Vanessa. She still worked in the shop, still served the customers, but it seemed that part of her had died with her father, and only a shell remained.

It was over a month now since Vanessa had been on a buying trip, but worried about Millie's state of mind, she had remained in the shop. However, spring and summer had been busy periods and now, in September, stocks were seriously low. Demand would soon grow for warmer outfits, and with hardly anything to offer her customers, Vanessa had made plans for a trip to the shires, leaving Millie in charge. 'Are you sure you'll be all right on your own for a few days?' she asked worriedly.

Millie forced a smile. She knew how important the shop was to Vanessa, knew it was her livelihood, and somehow had to convince her that she could cope on her own. 'I'll be fine. You won't be gone for long, and I managed well enough last time, didn't I?'

'Yes, you did, but that was before. . .'

'I've told you, I'll be fine,' Millie promised. 'Now you'd better go or you'll miss your train.'

'Well, if you're sure . . .'

'Vanessa – go!' Millie insisted, the smile fixed on her face.

With a small wave of her hand, Vanessa left, and as soon as the door closed, Millie slumped against the counter with relief, glad that she could stop putting on a front. Whilst Vanessa was away, searching out new stock, she no longer needed to hide her unhappiness.

At lunchtime, Millie briefly locked the shop to get a sandwich, and as she entered the café, Mamma Baglioni looked up, her eyes filled with compassion. 'Whatsa matter, bella, you still look so sad.'

'Nothing, I'm fine,' Millie told her. She didn't want to talk about it, didn't want sympathy, knowing it would break her.

'No, I don't think so, You 'as been unhappy for a long time now and I can see it in your pretty eyes.'

'I'm all right,' Millie insisted. 'May I have a cheese sandwich, please.'

The Italian woman sighed, her hands expressive as waving them flamboyantly she said, 'I expect some man 'as broken your heart. You'll get over it, darling, and one day you'll meet a fine gentleman who will give you many children to love. Just wait until you hold your first baby in your arms. There is nothing like it in the whole world, and it will bring you so much joy.'

Millie's face was stricken, her eyes wide as she stared at the woman now busily preparing her sandwich. As Signora Baglioni wrapped it, placing it onto the high glass counter, Millie threw the money down and fled.

Back in the shop, her lunch uneaten, Millie rubbed a hand across her forehead. Her heart felt like lead in her chest. Mamma Baglioni was trying to be kind, she knew that, but her words had only served to remind Millie that she'd never see her daughter again. No, she would never know the joy of holding Rose in her arms.

During the next few days, in an endeavour to stop herself from brooding, Millie cleaned the shop until it sparkled. Every garment on the rails came under her scrutiny too, and her hands were busy as she checked each hem and button.

Several customers looking for autumn garments had been unable to find what they were looking for, and Millie assured them that new stock would be arriving shortly. She was expecting Vanessa to return either that evening, or tomorrow morning, and hoped she'd had a successful trip.

'Hello, Millie.' Alice White came into the shop, clutching a carefully held bundle. 'I've brought my new great-granddaughter to meet you.'

Alice approached the counter and as Millie leaned over, her

heart skipped a beat. The baby, though not newly born, looked just like Rose! The same slick of fair hair, the same little bud of a mouth. Oh, she was beautiful! 'Please,' she appealed, 'can I hold her?'

'Of course you can,' Mrs White said, and as Millie hurried to her side, she placed the baby gently in her arms, saying, 'Now, mind you support her neck.'

Millie wasn't listening; she was staring down at the perfect little face. For a moment she dreamed that it was her own child she was holding. Dipping her head she gently kissed the baby's tiny nose, and as a small fist waved she laughed with delight, whispering in awe, 'Oh, she's gorgeous.'

'Yes, she's a lovely baby and they've called her Susan. Mind you, as usual Jenny isn't showing much interest in the little mite. She's already plonked her with me while she goes shopping. I'd best get back now in case I get a few customers, and I can tell you I could do with some. Perhaps with autumn approaching the demand for wool will pick up, but somehow I doubt it. Business has been slow for some time now. I've still got my regulars, but young people nowadays seem to be losing interest in knitting.'

Millie nodded, her gaze still on the baby, and hardly listening to Alice as she gabbled on.

'So much has changed since the war, and have you seen these coffee bars that are springing up everywhere? When I was a girl you wouldn't find me out night after night like the youngsters are now. My parents would never have allowed it. These kids may have their freedom, but all they do is sit in these coffee bars listening to music on juke boxes and drinking frothy coffee out of glass cups. Music! Did I call it music! Thump, thump, thump, that's all you hear. What's wrong with listening to songs with a nice melody and words you can understand? Give me Marion Ryan or Alma Cogan any day.' Alice paused for breath, and with a wry smile, said, 'There I go again, talking for England. Give Susan to me and I'd best get back.'

Millie didn't want to let the baby go, and said desperately, 'Why don't you leave her with me? I don't mind looking after her.'

'Bless you, love, but I can't do that. She's due for a feed and

I've got the bottles and stuff next door. Jenny won't breast-feed and I think it's a crying shame. Mother's milk is the best thing in the world, but my granddaughter seems to think that breast-feeding will ruin her figure. What a load of nonsense! I don't know what things are coming to these days, I really don't. It'll serve her right if she gets mastitis. Come on now, Millie, give me the baby.'

With a last look at the baby she reluctantly relinquished the warm bundle. Her arms felt strangely empty, and as Alice left the shop, Millie found her mind churning. The baby had been the image of Rose. It could have been Rose! Oh, how she would have loved the child, and cared for her. Unlike Jenny, she thought, her mouth tightening with resentment.

Only a few minutes later the door opened again to admit Vanessa's brother, a redhead clinging to his arm. Millie fixed a smile on her face. She was still wary of Mark, and there were times when she found his manner downright intimidating. He could be charming though, there was no denying that, and she'd lost count of the women she'd seen on his arm.

When he last called to see Vanessa, Millie still felt that he was analysing her, and it made her uneasy. She knew he remained unhappy that Vanessa had taken her in, and in a way understood that he would want to vet her. After all, he was just trying to protect his sister.

'Hello, Millie, is Ness around?'

'No, but I'm expecting her back this evening, or tomorrow at the latest.'

'I must say I'm surprised that she's left you to run the shop again.'

'I don't see why. I've done it before and I'm managing quite well, thank you,' Millie bristled.

'Whoops! Sorry, I wasn't implying that you couldn't cope. It's just that Nessie told me that you recently lost your father and . . .' He broke off then as the redhead pulled impatiently on his arm.

'Can we go now, please, Mark – or have you forgotten that you're supposed to be taking me to lunch.'

'No, Louise, I haven't forgotten,' he said impatiently, before his eyes rested on Millie again. 'A friend gave me a couple of tickets for the Royal Ballet, but as Louise isn't interested in going, I popped in to see if Vanessa would like them.'

'Oh, I'm sure she would.'

'Good. I'll leave them with you if that's all right?'

'Yes, do that.'

Louise had left his side to flick through a rack of garments, but her distaste soon became obvious when she saw they were second hand. With a disdainful toss of her head she said, 'God, how can anyone wear these? Most of them are last season and I wouldn't be seen dead in them.'

Mark grimaced, and then surprised Millie by winking at her before saying to his girlfriend, 'Oh, what a shame, and I was thinking of buying you something.'

'Ugh, you are joking, of course.'

After handing the tickets to Millie they both left, Louise leaving the aroma of expensive perfume in her wake.

Millie smiled inwardly, doubting if this girlfriend would last any longer than the others. It seemed that Mark had no interest in marriage, or settling down, and feeling the same way herself, Millie didn't blame him. She didn't want a relationship with any man, and at the thought of being touched again, she shivered.

Still, she thought, Mark had seemed nicer this time, more relaxed, and she hoped he was beginning to accept the situation. She loved living with Vanessa, and didn't want to leave, but it wouldn't be right to drive a wedge between Vanessa and her brother.

It was five o'clock when Alice White pushed a pram into the shop. 'Millie, I'm at my wit's end. Jenny isn't back yet and I've had the baby since this morning. Would you mind looking after her for a little while, just until I sort the shop out and cash up? She's had a feed and is fast asleep, so she shouldn't be any trouble.'

'Of course. I'd love to look after her.'

'Thanks, love, it's very good of you. Mind you, it isn't right, and I'm furious with my granddaughter. She knows I've got the shop to run, and at my age I shouldn't have to look after a baby.

Anyway, the poor little tyke should be with her mother.' With a harassed expression, Alice wheeled the pram over to the counter. 'I'll be as quick as I can.'

'Take as long as you need,' Millie murmured whilst gazing into the pram, and hardly noticed Alice as she bustled out.

After a few moments the baby stirred, and Millie couldn't resist picking her up. How could Jenny leave her baby all day? It was awful!

Minutes passed, minutes in which she held the baby in her arms, once again thinking that she looked just like Rose. For a while she fantasised that she was holding her own baby, and then a tiny hand reached up. Millie gently touched the palm and little fingers encircled hers as though in ownership, the grip surprisingly strong.

Something happened in that moment; something twisted in Millie's mind, and suddenly she was in another world, the fantasy becoming reality. This *was* Rose! This *was* her daughter, and she was holding her at last. Smiling in wonderment, she whispered, 'Oh, my baby, my baby. Thank God I've found you.'

In a dream-like state, and hardly aware of what she was doing, Millie tenderly returned the baby to the pram. She covered her with the soft, pink blanket, her eyes brimming with tears of joy as she said, 'Come on, my darling. It's time for us to go home.'

Chapter Thirty Five

Alice White had spotted Vanessa striding up the arcade, and hurrying up to her she said, 'Oh, Vanessa, thank goodness you're back. Have you seen Millie?'

'Millie! Isn't she in the shop?'

'No, and I don't know where she is.' The old lady wrung her hands. 'I thought at first that she was probably showing Susan to another shopkeeper in the arcade, but nobody has seen her.'

'Alice, I'm sorry, but who is Susan?'

'She's my granddaughter's baby. I asked Millie to look after her for a little while so I could cash up, but when I came to fetch Susan I found your shop empty. The lights are all on, and the door isn't locked, but there's no sign of Millie, or the baby.'

Vanessa's heart began to thump as she was seized by an awful premonition. *Oh, please, let me be wrong*, she prayed. 'How long ago was this, Alice?'

'It's been over half an hour now. Look, there's Jenny, and it's about time she showed up. Oh Lord, what am I going to tell her?'

'What's the matter, Gran? You look as white as a sheet.'

'Er, nothing, love. I'm just waiting for Millie to come back. She must have taken Susan for a little walk.' Blustering now she barked, 'And where have you been may I ask? You asked me to look after Susan for an hour, not all bloody day.'

'Don't be like that, Gran. I just needed a break, that's all. Mum's got the other two, but Maria was playing up again so the baby would have been too much for her. I didn't think you'd mind having Susan.'

'I wouldn't have minded looking after her for an hour or so, but you take liberties, miss. How am I supposed to run my shop *and* care for a baby all day?'

Obviously feigning tears, Jenny said, 'Don't be cross. I'm sorry, honestly, but it's this post-natal depression. It makes me very forgetful and I didn't realise how late it was.'

'Oh, don't come that one. Post-natal depression my foot! We didn't have that in my day and I had five kids to bring up. The children are your responsibility, and you shouldn't expect your mother, or anyone else to look after them.'

'But Mum loves having them.'

'Oh, yes? Is that what she told you?'

'Well, no, but she's never complained.'

'Huh, and you think that makes it all right, do you?'

'Please, don't let's argue, Gran,' Jenny begged, then changing the subject she asked, 'How much longer is Millie going to be?'

While Vanessa listened to this exchange, her thoughts were distracted. Theft the tarot cards had said, but she hadn't believed them. Now she knew with terrible certainty that the spread had been right after all. There *was* a theft – the theft of a child. *Oh Millie, Millie, what have you done!*

Alice White turned to Vanessa, mute appeal in her eyes. 'You don't think Millie will be much longer, do you?'

Thinking quickly Vanessa said, 'Oh, I shouldn't think so, but she may have taken the baby to the park and it's a long walk there and back.'

'I hope she gets a move on,' Jenny said, looking along the arcade anxiously. 'My husband will be home shortly and will want his dinner. He gets the right hump when it's not ready.'

Vanessa, trying to look and sound composed, jumped on Jenny's words, saying, 'Look, why don't you go home. There's no point in us all hanging around here, and when Millie comes back, your gran can bring Susan home.'

'Would you mind, Gran? It isn't far out of your way.'

'No, I suppose not.'

'Oh, good. Well, I'd better get a move on – see you later.'

Vanessa sighed with relief as Jenny tripped on high heels out of the arcade, but as soon as she was out of sight, Alice said, 'You may have fobbed off Jenny, but I'm really worried. Millie shouldn't have taken Susan for a walk without telling me, and it's a bit odd that she went out without closing and locking the shop.'

Vanessa found her foot tapping nervously as she wondered what to do. How could she placate Alice? Nothing came to mind, nothing to save the situation, and aware that she had no choice she took the woman's arm. 'We need to talk. Would you come into my shop?'

'Why! What's the matter?' Alice cried, alarm now evident in her voice.

Vanessa opened the door to *Finesse* and as they stepped inside she said, 'I'm sure the baby is safe, so please don't be alarmed at what I'm going to tell you.'

'Safe! Oh, God! You're not telling me that Millie might harm her?'

'No, of course not, but it's a long story and I need to start at the beginning.'

Keeping the story as short as possible, Vanessa told Alice a little of Millie's past, finally saying, 'So you see, when Millie's father died, she lost her only chance of finding her baby. I thought she was all right and that she was coming to terms with it, but it's obvious now that she couldn't cope. I should have realised how fragile she was, and wish now that I hadn't left her to go on a buying trip.'

'I still don't understand. What has this got to do with my granddaughter's baby?'

'I may be wrong, and I hope to God I am, but it may be that when Millie saw your granddaughter's child, her poor mind snapped, and she thinks Susan is the daughter she lost.'

'Let me get this straight. You're telling me that Millie has taken the baby because she thinks it's hers. But that means she won't bring Susan back! Christ, what will I tell Jenny! I must go – I must report this to the police!'

'Oh wait, please wait! Don't report it to the police yet. Come to my flat, and if my assumptions are right, I have a feeling that Millie's taken the baby there.'

'That's a bit unlikely. She must know it's the first place we'd look.'

'But don't you see!' Vanessa urged. 'Millie thinks she's found her daughter, so in her mind she hasn't done anything wrong. She'd have no reason to hide and that's why I feel she's taken the baby home.'

'What if she hasn't? What then?'

'Then I'll come with you to the police station.'

'Millie, Millie, are you there!' Vanessa cried as she entered her apartment, almost fainting with relief when she heard her call answered.

'Hello, Vanessa, you're back then,' Millie said, smiling happily as she held the baby in her arms. 'Hello Alice. This is Rose, my daughter, and isn't she lovely?'

Vanessa saw that Millie's face was alight with happiness, and it broke her heart to say, 'No, darling, the baby isn't yours. She belongs to Alice's granddaughter.'

'Don't be silly, of course this is my baby, and now that I've got her back I'm going to make sure that we're never parted again.' She then lowered her head, ignoring both Vanessa and Alice as she crooned a lullaby.

What can I do? Oh, what can I do? Vanessa thought. She had never dealt with a situation like this before, but recognised there was something badly wrong with Millie's mind. Somehow she had to make the girl see sense. If she refused to give the baby back, Alice would go to the police, and what would happen to Millie then? Desperately she asked, 'Can I hold her?'

'No, not at the moment, she's asleep.'

'Look, I've had enough of this. Either she gives Susan to me or I'm getting the law on her,' Alice said, her voice loud with indignation.

'No, please, give me a little more time to talk to her.'

'Talking won't do any good,' and pushing Vanessa aside, Alice tried to prise the baby from Millie's arms.

'No!' she screamed, and jumping up she flew to the other side of the room, the baby clutched tightly to her chest. As Alice advanced towards her again, Millie cried, 'Don't come near me! Dulcie Liddle took Rose away from me, and if you try to do the same, I . . . I kill you!'

'Millie, calm down,' Vanessa begged.

'The girl's off her rocker! I'm getting the police.'

No, oh no! Vanessa thought frantically. Millie wasn't insane, but she must have had some sort of mental breakdown. If the police got involved goodness knows what she'd be charged with, and in her present state of mind she could end up in an institution. Vanessa wrung her hands in agitation, wondering desperately how she could prevent that from happening, and praying for guidance.

At last the answer flew into her mind and she raised her eyes in silent thanks. Mark! Of course! Why hadn't she thought of him before? He would help, and pulling urgently on Alice's sleeve, she said, 'Listen, if the police come there's no way of knowing how Millie will react. You can see the state she's in and we don't want any harm coming to the baby. Let me call my brother, he's a psychiatrist and will know how to deal with this.'

'I dunno about that. What if she hurts Susan? Who'd have thought it? She seemed such a nice, quiet, polite girl, and I wouldn't have left the baby with her if I'd known she was loony.'

'Don't say that. Millie isn't loony, she's just a poor unfortunate girl who's been badly used and abused. Our minds can only deal with so much before we snap, and that doesn't mean she's insane. Now please let me ring my brother. He can be here in under fifteen minutes.'

The old woman drew in a deep breath, her expression thoughtful. 'I certainly don't want to risk anything happening to the baby. Do you really think he can help?'

'Yes, I do. Mark is highly qualified, and I'm sure he must have come across situations like this before.'

There were a few moments of silence during which Alice seemed to be making up her mind, and then she said, 'All right, if you think it's for the best. But if he can't get Millie to give me the baby, then I'm definitely phoning the police.'

Mark Grey listened to his sister, noting the touch of hysteria in her voice. Vanessa was usually calm and in control, so it must be a serious situation for her to ring him.

'Don't try to take the baby from her, and just act normally. I'll be over as soon as I can.'

'All right, but hurry.'

It didn't take him long to prepare what might be needed, and running from his flat he jumped into his car, driving with his foot down hard on the accelerator.

Vanessa opened the door to her flat almost immediately, and putting his fingers to his lips, he followed her inside. He observed Millie as she stood clutching the baby protectively, her back pushed against the wall. Huge dark eyes looked at him fearfully, and for the first time in his life, Mark felt a jolt in his heart. He was used to dealing with psychiatric patients, and found the only way he could cope was to emotionally distance himself. Yet there was something about Millie he hadn't noticed before . . . something so vulnerable that it touched him.

Turning to his sister, he said softly, 'I need to get close enough to give her an injection. Act normally, and suggest a cup of tea or something.'

Vanessa nodded, responding immediately. 'Mark has popped in to see us, Millie – isn't that nice. I know he's dying for a cup of tea and would you like one too?'

To his relief Millie nodded in assent, and moving slowly he sat on the couch, ignoring her presence whilst still chatting to Vanessa. 'How about a biscuit? I'm starving.'

Following his cue, Vanessa forced a laugh. 'You always are and I'll do more than give you a biscuit . . . I'll make you a sandwich. Would you give me a hand, Alice?'

Good girl, he thought, and endeavouring to lift the tension he smiled at Millie, saying lightly, 'As usual my sister is spoiling me, and I suppose that's because I'm her kid brother. I say, is that your baby? Can I have a look at her?'

He noticed that Millie's shoulders had relaxed slightly, but she shook her head vehemently.

'Please yourself,' he said, feigning indifference as he leaned forward to pick up a magazine from the coffee table. *Take it slowly*, he told himself as he opened a page and pretended to read.

Mark could hear the rattle of cups and saucers in the kitchen, and hoped that Vanessa wouldn't return too soon. This girl was badly traumatised and he would have to tread carefully. Out of the corner of his eyes he saw Millie move slightly forward, and holding his breath, he turned another page.

'You can look at her if you like,' she said, perching gingerly on the other end of the couch.

Mark turned his head, giving the baby a quick glance. 'She looks pretty,' he said shortly, immediately returning to the magazine.

'She's beautiful and her name is Rose. Don't you think she's got lovely eyes?' Millie asked, moving a little closer.

'Yes, she has, and the name suits her.'

Millie smiled, her expression dreamy. 'When she was born I saw that her mouth was puckered up like a tiny rosebud. That's why I called her Rose.'

Vanessa returned with Mrs White, and as she placed a tray on the table he saw that Millie was distracted as she watched their every move. He surreptitiously took the hypodermic he'd prepared out of his pocket, hoping for an opportunity, but it didn't come until Vanessa handed Millie a cup of tea.

Without thinking she removed one arm from the baby and held out her hand. In that second Mark leaned over, plunging the needle into her thigh.

'No! No!' she screamed, her eyes wild in horror.

'It's all right, Millie, don't be afraid. Everything's going to be all right.'

'Oh, don't take my baby! Please don't take my baby,' she begged, clutching the child to her chest. Her eyes were still wild, but gradually they dimmed, and as she slumped Mark gently took the baby from her arms.

'Oh Millie! Poor Millie,' Vanessa cried. 'That looked awful, Mark.'

'I know, but from what you told me I didn't think she would have given the baby up easily, and it was kinder to do it this way.'

Vanessa shook her head sorrowfully, but took Susan and handed the still sleeping child to Alice. 'I don't know what to say, except I'm sorry this happened. Thank you so much for keeping the police out of it.'

'Yes, well, I still don't know if I did the right thing. I think the girl should be locked up, but then again, at least this way my granddaughter doesn't need to know anything about it. Mind you,

I'd better get a move on as she must be wondering where I am by now.'

'Let me get you a taxi, it's the least I can do,' Vanessa offered.

'All right. I must admit I'm fair exhausted with all this carry on. I'm not getting any younger you know.'

'There's no need to call a cab,' Mark said. 'I'll run you to wherever you want to go.'

'Mark, your car is only a two-seater, and though the pram folds it still won't fit,' and lifting the telephone, Vanessa added, 'It'll have to be a taxi, I'm afraid.'

The atmosphere was tense as they waited and Vanessa prayed that Alice wouldn't change her mind about involving the police. She closed her eyes with relief when at last the doorbell rang, and lifting the pram, Mark escorted Alice White to the taxi.

When Mark returned he looked down on Millie. 'She'll be out for hours yet, but we'll need to get something sorted out before she wakes up.'

'Like what?'

'Like getting her admitted to a psychiatric unit.'

'No, never! I won't allow it.'

An argument ensued, an argument that went on and on, and Mark closed his eyes in despair. Why did his sister have to be so bloody stubborn? 'Look, Vanessa, I understand how you feel, but you can't run a business *and* look after Millie. Besides, she's going to need specialist help.'

'No! I won't stand for her being locked away. You have no idea how much the child has suffered.'

'Locked away! You make it sound like a prison.'

'Well, isn't it? What about those horrible straitjackets they use? Millie isn't mad, she just needs lots of love and care.'

'Oh Nessie, be realistic. She wouldn't be restrained, there'd be no need.'

'How many times have I got to tell you? Please don't shorten my name. I'm not the Loch Ness Monster.'

'Still touchy about your nickname, I see,' Mark said, trying to bring a bit of lightness to the conversation. Vanessa's boarding school nickname had stuck, and though he knew she hated its use, he reckoned it suited her. When they were children, he'd considered his domineering older sister to be a monster and used to dread school holidays. Only maturity had brought peace to their relationship, and he'd come to recognise her many wonderful qualities. He would be eternally grateful to her for struggling to put him through university, and despite the fact that they were like chalk and cheese, he loved his sister dearly.

'Yes, I am still touchy about it. You have no idea what it was like to be called "The Monster Nessie" at school.'

Mark hid a smile. Vanessa didn't realise it, but she was still dominant now, and he supposed with a business to run she had to be. But it wasn't surprising that she hadn't found a husband. She was so self-sufficient, and how many men would put up with being bossed about by their wife? He knew there was a gentler side to her personality, but she was good at hiding it, and though he'd tried to tell her that men liked their women soft and feminine, she wouldn't listen. 'Then they're not real men,' she always argued.

'*Vanessa*,' he said now, emphasising the correct use of her name, 'when Millie wakes up and finds the baby gone, how will you cope? She might do anything, and may even attempt suicide. Can you watch her for twenty-four hours a day, because believe me, you will have to. When someone is determined to take their own life, it's almost impossible to stop them. They can become very devious, hoarding their medication until they think there's enough to end their lives, or even hiding sharp instruments.'

'Millie won't attempt suicide. She hates it because her mother died that way.'

'Oh Nessie,' Mark said, unconsciously using his sister's nickname again. 'Don't you realise that in some ways it gives her permission? If her mother could do it, then so can she.'

'I'm telling you she won't. Millie has been to hell and back, but she's survived. If she was going to take her own life, and believe me she's had cause, she would have done it by now. No, Mark, I'll look after her.'

'For goodness sake, Millie isn't your responsibility! What is it about this girl that you would risk losing your business for?'

'Oh, I don't know, but from when I first met her I sensed

something. It's as though I'm meant to help her, and that we were destined to meet.'

Mark felt his patience slipping. 'Please, not all that clap-trap again.'

'It isn't clap-trap.'

'Tarot cards, palm reading – it's all nonsense.'

'No, it isn't. I've seen the tarot cards work again and again.'

'It's just coincidence. From what I've seen, there are many ways to interpret the cards, and they can be made to fit any situation.'

'But when I do a spread, I intuitively know what they mean.'

'How is it that nothing has ever been proved then?' Without waiting for an answer, Mark shook his head, sighing heavily. 'Oh, let's stop this, Vanessa. Every time we meet we end up arguing about psychic matters. I'm a man of science, and I will never accept any of your spiritualist mumbo-jumbo. Let's just agree to differ, and anyway, sorting out your young friend is more important at the moment.'

The argument about Millie went on and on, neither giving ground, and then Mark got the shock of his life when his sister began to cry! Never before had he seen Vanessa break down. When their father died she had been the rock they all clung to. Then when they lost their mother, Vanessa had picked herself up, set up a business, and made it very successful too. 'Ness, please don't cry,' he begged, reaching out to pull her into his arms.

'I can't let her be put away . . . . I just can't,' she sobbed.

Mark held Vanessa, his thoughts twisting and turning. She had never asked him for help before, always coping with her own problems. This girl must mean an awful lot to her, but how could he help his sister if she refused to see the sense of admitting Millie to hospital? Why couldn't she understand that constant care, specialist care, was essential? Then there was the shop – Vanessa couldn't run it *and* look after Millie, so she could well lose her only livelihood.

As he continued to hold his sister, Mark's mind drifted. He had worked hard to become successful, and his earnings had risen steadily, so much so that not long ago he'd tried to repay Vanessa for his university fees. Stubborn as always, she had refused to take the money, insisting that he save it for a rainy day.

That's it! he thought. The rainy day had arrived, and he now had the means to help his sister and Millie too at the same time. It would cost him the earth, but Kathleen Blanchard was the best psychiatrist he knew, and her clinic was second to none.

'Listen, Ness, I think I've found the answer.'

'I don't care what you say. I'm not letting you lock Millie into an asylum,' she emphasised again, her sobs finally abating.

'There may be an alternative. I know a woman who runs a small but exclusive private clinic. She only takes six patients maximum, but with any luck I may be able to persuade her to admit Millie.'

'Huh, private clinic! It still means locking her away.'

'Millie isn't criminally insane, or violent. She won't be locked up in that sense, but she will need supervision until she responds to treatment.'

'Then what's to stop her walking out?'

With a sigh, Mark said, 'Look, Vanessa, you'll just have to trust me on this. The clinic is in Richmond, and in a lovely private house. I can assure you Millie will get the best possible treatment there. Now time is short and I'll need to pull a few strings to get her admitted, preferably before she wakes up.'

Vanessa gazed at him for what felt like minutes, then suddenly she sat back, and with her eyes closed she remained silent. He started to speak again, but she held her hand up, indicating in no uncertain terms that she wanted him to be quiet for a little while.

He watched his sister, puzzled at her deep steady breathing, but just when he was about to lose patience, her eyes opened again, and with a small smile she said, 'Very well, Mark. We'll do as you suggest. Something tells me that this clinic is the right place for Millie.'

Mark went to use the telephone, realising it was a long shot. He doubted that Kathleen Blanchard would have a space for Millie, which would mean further arguments with his sister. No matter what, the girl needed psychiatric treatment. His sister didn't seem to realise that when Millie woke up she would blame them both for taking her baby away, and there was no way of knowing how she'd react. It would be an impossible situation for Vanessa to cope with, and one that he was determined to avert.

'Hello, Kathleen Blanchard here.'

At last, Mark breathed. He explained the situation as succinctly as he could, and asking several questions his colleague finally said, 'Well, you're in luck. I discharged a patient today, so I can take her. Do you want me to send a private ambulance?'

'Yes, please, and as soon as possible. I would rather she was moved whilst under sedation.'

'Very well, I'll make the necessary arrangements.'

When Mark replaced the receiver his shoulders slumped with relief. 'Nessie, an ambulance will be here shortly. Will you pack the things you feel Millie may need, while I check that she's still sedated.'

'Will I be able to visit her?'

'I doubt it will be possible until she responds to treatment.'

'Will that take long?'

'It's impossible to say, but when Kathleen Blanchard feels that Millie is ready for visitors, she'll let us know.'

His sister's face was still strained, but she did as he asked, packing a case whilst Mark took Millie's pulse. As he held her wrist he was once again struck by her vulnerability. She looked hardly more than a child, and he still didn't know why she had this effect on him. With all his patients he tried to maintain a professional distance, finding it was the only way he could cope with some of the horrendous stories he heard.

Gently replacing Millie's arm under the blanket Vanessa had tucked around her, Mark felt relieved that he wouldn't be treating her. Somehow he knew that with this girl it would be different, and he'd find it almost impossible to remain objective.

Chapter Thirty-Six

There were voices, but Millie wasn't interested in listening to them. She felt cushioned, as though wrapped in cotton wool. Somewhere in the deep recesses of her mind she knew that something awful had happened, yet somehow she didn't care. Nothing mattered in this warm, soft place.

At one point, vaguely aware of being moved, of being put into a vehicle, she struggled momentarily to arouse herself, but finding it impossible she gave up the fight and drifted off to sleep again.

When she finally awoke, Millie still felt groggy, but seeing the strange room her mind quickly cleared. Where was she? How did she get here? It was then that it all came rushing back. Her baby! They had taken her baby! Oh no, it couldn't be happening again! She could hear terrible screams, an unholy wailing, and it took her some time to realise that the sounds were issuing from her own mouth.

Suddenly the room seemed to fill with strange people, people she had never seen before. When one of them took her arm she reacted violently, and seeing the hypodermic she fought to stop the needle from being used, yelling, 'Get off of me! Get off of me!'

'Hold her still, please!'

Another pair of hands held her, hands that Millie couldn't fight off, and then a voice penetrated her terrified mind.

'It's all right, my dear. I promise, it's all right.'

She responded to the gentle voice and for a moment, gave up struggling. 'Where is my baby? Oh please, let me have my baby.' She felt a prick then, and though she fought against it, Millie once again found herself cocooned in cotton wool.

Millie knew she was in some kind of clinic, and when not under the influence of drugs her thoughts were of Rose. She was full of seething resentment. Vanessa and Mark had conspired to take her baby away, and she hated them. She had no memory of how she'd come to be in this clinic, and again whilst lucid, her mind worked. Vanessa and Mark must have arranged it – but why? She wasn't mad and didn't need to be locked away. Perhaps they wanted Rose? No, that was silly – why would they want a baby? Her tortured thoughts went round and around, but there were no answers.

When the door opened and an orderly carried in a tray of food, Millie pushed it away. She'd told them that she wouldn't eat until they returned Rose, and meant it. If they didn't give her daughter back, she would starve. It had been three days now and surely they'd take notice, but to her dismay the orderly just shrugged his shoulders before walking out again. Right, if refusing to eat didn't work she'd try remaining silent; she wouldn't talk at all. That would show them she meant business.

Millie moved to the wall and sat facing it, her shoulders hunched defensively and her back towards the door.

Night followed day, day followed night, but still Millie refused to speak. She hated them. Hated them all!

It took six weeks for Kathleen Blanchard to break through Millie's defences. At first, all she'd encountered was a wall of silence and open hostility, but gradually she'd been able to gain her trust.

Millie had to understand that the baby she'd taken wasn't her daughter, and when Kathleen finally managed to break this illusion, the girl cried as though her heart would break.

In the days that followed, Kathleen found Millie severely depressed, and though loath to do so, she put her back on medication. In her opinion, Valium wasn't the answer. Albeit useful in the short term, it only served to mask the underlying causes. She was also aware the drug could become addictive, and it was something she strived to avoid.

For the next stage of Millie's treatment to work, she would need the girl to be clear-minded and not partially sedated, but first she had to inform Mark Grey that there had been a breakthrough. The man had been pestering her for reports on the patient's progress, and now finding his number she picked up the receiver.

'Yes, there's been a breakthrough,' she confirmed, 'but I think Miss Pratchett will need further treatment before she's ready to see visitors. It's not that I think there will be any hostility, but I'd like the suggestion that she sees both you and your sister to come from Miss Pratchett herself.' And when Mark replied to this, she said: 'Yes, of course I'll inform you immediately if she makes such a request. Now, if you'll excuse me, I have patients to attend to. Goodbye, Mr Grey.'

Kathleen replaced the receiver with a sigh. Like her, Mark Grey was a psychiatrist, and from what she'd heard he was a good one. Yet the man's impatience regarding this case was becoming a nuisance. Still, as a professional he would know that her first concern was for her patients, and until she thought that Millicent Pratchett was ready for visitors, both he and his sister would have to stay away.

How long had she been in this clinic? Millie didn't know, but now she wanted to get better, and to get out of there. She was less tired now, her thoughts clearer since the medication had been cut down, and she knew that Kathleen Blanchard would arrive soon for another session with her. She wanted to talk to the woman, wanted to unburden herself, and had tried, but the words just stuck in her throat.

So much had happened, so much pain and disillusionment. The woman she'd thought of as her mother, whom she had loved above all others, had taken her own life. Her brother had left home, leaving her with their father, and she would never forgive him for doing that. They'd all abandoned her – mother, father, and brother. But worst of all was the loss of her child, and seething hatred festered in her mind towards the man who had sold her baby. She would no longer give him the title of father; Alfred Prachett wasn't fit to be anyone's father. She was so bitter that it was eating her up inside.

No, she couldn't unburden herself. She was worthless, not fit to love, and how could she let Kathleen Blanchard see what an awful person she was? Oh, she hid it, hid it from everyone, and only Vanessa had managed to get inside her shell. For a short while, with the older woman's help, she'd begun to feel better about herself, but she had now ruined that relationship. Vanessa would never forgive her and now she'd lost her too.

There was a knock on her door, and as the psychiatrist came in she was smiling pleasantly. 'Hello, Millie, and how are you today?'

'I'm all right.' She kept her eyes down, not wanting to look at the woman, immediately tensing at her next words.

'Do you think you could talk to me about your childhood?'

If she wanted to get out of this clinic Millie knew she had to cooperate. Words spun in her mind, but dreading the psychiatrist's reaction, they stuck in her throat. For a long, long time there was only silence, but finally with some patient encouragement from Kathleen Blanchard, Millie began to speak. She faltered at first, but seeing a lack of censure on the woman's face she gained a little confidence, until finally the words came spilling out in a torrent as she told her everything.

During all this Kathleen Blanchard sat quietly listening, just offering the occasional word of sympathy, and as Millie finally stopped speaking the tears came. Tears that somehow acted as a catalyst, until at last, she felt emotionally drained.

'Millie, try to get some rest now,' Kathleen Blanchard advised.

With a tired nod Millie lay down, curling herself into a ball, and almost immediately she fell into a deep sleep, her thoughts, without medication, finally still.

Kathleen quietly left Millie's room. Experience had taught her that most patients waited until they thought the session was nearly over before opening up. It was their safety-valve, a way to avoid talking about the most important issues, and this session had followed the same pattern. However, she was pleased that Millie had finally unburdened herself, and knew this was a positive step.

She now sat in her office, reviewing Millie's treatment before filling out her notes. It was the end of the month and she calculated the current fees, the invoice as usual going to Mark Grey. Millie had hardly mentioned him, and Kathleen wondered briefly why the man was paying for her treatment. Somehow she doubted there was a relationship between them; nevertheless there was some way to go before the young woman made a full recovery and she hoped he would continue to bear the costs.

As she put her notes and the invoice to one side, Kathleen sat back in her chair, fingers steepled under her chin. Yes, there was some way to go with this patient. Millie would need to stop blaming herself for all that had happened. First there had been her mother's death – and guilt always played a substantial role in suicide bereavement, along with anger. Both these issues would need to be taken into consideration. Then there was the rape, and it was obvious that Millie had been ill treated by her father. However, before she could make peace with her past, this patient would need to understand that she was the victim, *not* the instigator.

Of course the main issue was Millie's baby. She would never forget her daughter, but with help, she should be able to come to terms with her loss.

When all these factors had been dealt with, Katheen would then have to concentrate on improving the poor girl's low self-esteem. When that was rebuilt, she was sure that Millie would be fully recovered and able to take up her life again.

It took a lot of sessions, but one by one Kathleen dealt with each of Millie's issues. The real breakthrough came at the beginning of November, when Millie began to stop hating herself. When this happened, the change in the girl was clear to see. Her face became lighter, her eyes clearer, and they glimmered with hope. Millie now spoke of Vanessa Grey with affection, and it became obvious that she was grateful for all Miss Grey had done for her. Then, as they neared the end of one session, Millie said to Kathleen, 'I must see Miss Grey. I need to tell her how sorry I am. Would it be possible?'

'Of course.'

'For a long time, I thought that Vanessa and Mark had taken my baby,' Millie confessed. 'I was so wrapped up in my own misery that I failed to appreciate how much Vanessa has done for me.' Millie's voice was low and sincere. 'She has shown me endless kindness, yet I have been nothing but a burden to her. She took me in, gave me a home and a job, but after stealing the baby I don't think she'll even want to see me again.'

'I doubt that, and I'm sure that she can't wait to see you too,' the psychiatrist said kindly. 'I'll have a word with her brother and try to arrange a visit for tomorrow. Is that all right?'

'Yes, thank you, but I doubt that she'll come.'

'I think you'll be surprised.' Kathleen smiled, and left the room feeling glad to have been able to heal this poor girl's emotional wounds. She felt sure that Millie would shortly be able to leave the clinic, and hoped that Vanessa Grey would still be willing to offer the girl a home. It couldn't be taken for granted. Many people were frightened of anyone with so-called mental problems, confusing emotional breakdown with insanity. She doubted that this would be the case with Miss Grey; after all, her brother was a psychiatrist.

With this in mind she returned to her office to arrange the visit, suggesting that it would be for the best if Mark Grey accompanied his sister.

Will she come, Millie wondered, and as usual when tense, she chewed anxiously on her bottom lip. Vanessa had been a wonderful friend, a true friend, and one she didn't deserve to have. If Vanessa decided that she didn't want to see her again, Millie would accept it – but oh, she'd miss her so much.

Yet somehow she would soon have to leave the sanctuary of this place, to make another life for herself, find a job and somewhere to live. With Kathleen Blanchard's help she felt emotionally stronger now, and more able to cope, but she still couldn't imagine her life without Vanessa Grey in it.

The treatment sessions had enabled her to understand her mental breakdown, and she knew now that she'd taken Alice White's great-granddaughter because her mind had retreated to the past. Then, during further sessions, the psychiatrist had brought her to understand that much of what happened in the past had not been her fault. It felt then as if a great weight had been lifted from her shoulders.

Yet she'd been unable to forgive her father, and though she hoped to cope with the loss of her daughter, hatred for the man who had sold Rose still filled her heart. She didn't want to nurse this hate, knowing that it could destroy her, but every time she thought of Alfie Pratchett it aroused her anger and bitterness. In the end, Millie found the only way to deal with it was to place it in the past. He was dead, and she wouldn't think about him any more. She was going to look towards the future, and this was going to be a new chapter in her life.

As Millie climbed into bed that night, her thoughts were still churning. Yes, she had to move forward, but she prayed that Vanessa would still be part of her life. She tossed and turned, hoping against hope that her dear friend and benefactor would come to see her in the morning.

The next morning Vanessa walked nervously into Millie's room, and smiling she said, 'Hello, my dear.'

Millie's face lit up with joy, her eyes encompassing both Vanessa and her brother. 'Oh Vanessa, Mark – I can't believe you've come to see me!'

'Of course we have. I've been so worried about you, and so relieved that I can visit you at last.'

'I realise now that I've never thanked you for all you've done for me. I . . . I'm sorry for all the trouble I've caused you.'

'There's no need to thank me, and you have nothing to be sorry about. Isn't it wonderful that Miss Blanchard has said you can come home soon. While you've been away I've had an alcove built into one corner of the living room so you can have a sort of room for yourself.'

'Home! An alcove! Do you mean I can come back to Cheyne Walk?'

'Of course you can. It's your home, and I've missed you so much.'

Millie flung herself into Vanessa's arms, and as they clung together Vanessa found her heart full. This child, this girl, had become like a beloved daughter, and one that the cards had shown would come into her life.

Before finding Millie on her doorstep she'd been to another tarot reader, and had laughed at the spread, knowing that at her age it was unlikely that she would ever have a child. But here she was – here was the child who had found a special place in her heart. Vanessa wasn't a demonstrative woman, probably due to an undemonstrative upbringing, but as she held Millie in her arms now she felt a special kind of love. She might not be Millie's real mother, but knew these feelings must be akin to maternal love.

Vanessa looked at her brother over Millie's shoulder and saw a strange expression on his face, one that she hadn't seen before. There was a tender look in his eyes and she suddenly realised that the scene had touched him. Giving Millie a squeeze, she said, 'Mark's been worried about you too.'

'Hello, Mark,' Millie said as she drew back slightly.

'How are you?'

'I'm fine, but I feel such a fool.'

'There's no need.'

'I really did think that the baby was mine.'

'Yes, I'm sure you did,' Mark said, smiling gently.

Millie now moved from her arms, and as Vanessa watched the two of them talking, she marvelled to see Millie so at ease in her brother's presence. In the past she had sometimes sensed her fear, not only of Mark, but also of other men. But now the darkness had gone from her eyes, and she silently thanked Kathleen Blanchard. Somehow the woman had healed Millie, and though she doubted the girl would ever get over the loss of her child, she now had a chance to lead a life without fear.

As Mark continued to talk to Millie, Vanessa went over her plans, and once again felt a surge of excitement. But for these plans to work, she had to persuade Millie to come back to work. Kathleen Blanchard had said she felt that Millie was almost ready, but had advised her not to rush it. There were still wounds, some that would never heal, but with time and patience the psychiatrist said, she was sure Millie would want to get back to a full and active life.

They were bold plans, but Vanessa didn't dare wait too long before putting them into action. Further delay might well mean that she would miss the wonderful opportunity that had presented itself. She had already chewed things over with Mark, and he'd been enthusiastic. Not only that, they both thought this new venture would give Millie something to look forward to.

Why not? She suddenly thought. Why not put the first step in place today? When she and Mark left the clinic, she'd go straight to the agent, and though it would be tight, she'd try to put everything in place for the New Year. Yes, a New Year, and a new start for all of them.

Her eyes were alight with excitement as she looked at Millie, and she found herself bursting out, 'Oh, my darling girl, I can't wait to have you home again. We have so much to look forward to.'

Chapter Thirty-Seven

Pat Benson had come to love Brian Lucas. Oh, not in a sexual way, that would be impossible, but she cared about his happiness and didn't want to cause him any pain. He was so patient and caring, and though she knew he wanted marriage, sooner rather than later, he didn't push her. The courtship was rather passion-less, and she was thankful that Brian was so undemanding. When he kissed her she felt nothing, but nowadays was able to relax in his embrace, drawing comfort from being held in his arms without fear of him taking things any further.

It was because she had grown to love him that she always avoided the subject of their wedding date, not wanting to hurt this wonderful man. What would happen if she couldn't submit to him on their wedding night? Her father's abuse still haunted her, the fear, pain, and disgust she'd suffered all those years never far from her mind.

How could she ever let a man do that to her again? Just as she thought that, Brian smiled at her, and it was then that Pat made up her mind. She *had* to find out if it was possible for her to have sex with Brian before fixing a date for their wedding. And then, if she couldn't do it, she would slip out of his life. Oh, he would still be hurt, but at least he wouldn't be lumbered with a frigid wife. He deserved better than that.

'Shall we have a drink, darling?' she asked, hoping a few shots of spirit would relax her.

'Yes, why not. I'll just pop upstairs to get my wallet.'

'No, let's not go out. I've got a bottle of whisky that I was putting by for Christmas, so let's go mad and break it open.'

293

'All right, if you're sure. It's bitterly cold outside and I must admit it would be nice to stay in the warm.'

Pat forced a smile, and taking the whisky from the sideboard, she poured two generous slugs. Then, with her back to Brian she downed hers in one gulp, before refilling the glass.

An hour later, and through an alcoholic haze, she led Brian to her bed. It would be all right, she kept telling herself. *Just relax – it'll be all right.*

'Are you sure, darling?' he asked, his hands fumbling with her clothes.

'Yesh,' she slurred. 'After all, we're engaged to be married.' She closed her eyes then, and willed herself not to fight.

Was that it? Seconds and it was over! Relief flooded through her. She had done it, and it had been so quick that she'd hardly had time to react, adversely or otherwise.

'I'm sorry, darling,' Brian mumbled, his face red with shame.

'Sorry? But why?'

'I . . . I wasn't very good.'

'Don't be silly, you were wonderful.'

'Really! But I thought you'd be disappointed.'

'No, of course not. It was perfect . . . just perfect.'

'Christ, Pat, this was so unexpected that I didn't use any protection!'

'Never mind, darling, but we had better set a date for the wedding just in case.'

Brian's face broke into a huge grin. 'Just name the day.'

'How about in February? Valentine's Day would be nice.'

On the Isle of Wight there were celebrations too as on Christmas Day, John swung Wendy around and around. 'A baby! We're going to have a baby?'

'Yes darling, but please put me down now.'

'Oh Wendy,' Bertha gasped, her eyes moist with tears. 'This is the best Christmas present I've ever had.'

'Really! So you don't like the dressing-gown?'

'Of course I do, yer silly mare – but a grandchild! Oh, I'm so happy.'

John placed Wendy gently onto a chair. 'You'll have to take it easy now, my love.'

'Don't be silly, I'm not ill.'

'Even so, I want you to cut back. I know Hilda left at the end of the season, but I'm sure she'd be pleased to come back and give us a hand.'

'A hand with what? Yes, we've got Christmas guests, but they'll be leaving soon, and then we'll have a nice break until next season.'

'Blimey, talking of guests, I'd better make a start on the vegetables.'

'I'll give you a hand, Mum.'

'No, you won't. Do as John says and relax.'

'Now listen, you two. If you think you can wrap me in cotton wool for the next six months, you're mistaken. I'm perfectly capable of peeling a few bloomin' sprouts.'

'Yeah, all right, but you can do them sitting at the table.'

Both heard Wendy's huge sigh of exasperation, and with a wink, Bertha smiled at John. 'What do yer fancy, love? A boy or a girl?'

He scratched his head. 'A boy, I think, but then again a girl would be nice too.'

'I'd like a grandson,' Bertha said, a dreamy expression on her face as she absentmindedly began to peel a mound of potatoes. 'Ain't we lucky. We had a marvellous season, our bank balance is healthy, and now . . . Ohhhh.'

'Are you crying, Mum?'

'No, of course not,' Bertha said, dabbing at her eyes, 'Yeah, well a little bit, but they're tears of happiness.'

After a lot of protestations, they finally allowed Wendy to dress the dining-room table, and placing the last serviette on a side plate, she stood back to admire her work. The snow-white tablecloth set off perfectly the centrepiece she'd made of holly, the red berries glinting in the candlelight. For her it was a perfect Christmas, and though she'd been itching to tell John for nearly a month, she'd managed to wait.

It had been worth it to see the joy on his face, her mother's too, and now her happiness was complete. The guesthouse was doing amazingly well, and it seemed the future was assured. She gave the table a last tweak and then left the dining room, pausing to look at the Christmas tree in the hall.

'Come on, you've done enough now. I'll serve the guests.'

Wendy turned to smile at her husband, seeing that he looked immaculate in his dark suit and tie, though he grimaced as he ran a finger around his collar.

'Is Mum still using too much starch?'

'Yes, but for goodness sake don't say anything. She's so emotional at the moment that the least little thing will set her off, and let's face it, we don't want the dinner ruined.'

'Yes, she is rather pleased.'

'Rather pleased! I think that's an understatement – more like over the moon. Ted's just arrived and she's already got the sherry out. Now come on, I think you should put your feet up.'

Wendy grimaced, but had to admit it was nice to be mollycoddled. John was gazing at the tree now, his expression suddenly sombre, and she took his hand, squeezing it gently. 'What's the matter, darling?'

'Millie's going to be an aunt, and I know she'd be thrilled to bits.'

'Don't worry, you'll find her.'

He shook his head sadly. 'It's been so long now, and it's hard to hang on to any hope.'

The guests had been served, the dinner a huge success, Bertha's cooking as usual loudly complimented. Whilst the guests were eating, the family had their own Christmas dinner, sitting round the kitchen table with the sherry in full flow. Bertha's face was getting decidedly flushed, John saw with amusement.

Now there was just the pudding to serve. He watched as his mother-in-law liberally sprinkled it with brandy. 'Go easy, Bertha,' he joked. 'If you put much more on, it'll set fire to the house when I light it.'

There were *oohs*, and *aahs*, as he placed it on the centre of the dining-room table, whilst Wendy, insistent on helping, carried in the jugs of cream and custard.

The guests had just been served when Bertha lurched into the room, and holding her glass high, eyes alight with happiness, she said, 'A toast to my daughter and son-in-law who have made my Christmas perfect.'

The guests were smiling, but bewildered as they too raised their glasses. It was obvious they had no idea what they were toasting until Bertha added, 'She's gonna 'ave a baby. Yeah, my first grandchild.'

There was much laughter then, and more toasts, the guests refusing to let them go back to the kitchen. 'John, go and get Ted,' Bertha ordered. 'We can't leave him on his own.'

He hurried back to the kitchen, feeling decidedly tipsy himself now, only to find Ted slumped across the table, the sherry bottle empty. For a moment he smiled sadly, knowing that the gardener was finally retiring in the New Year, but then he perked up. Yes, the old man might be retiring, but he'd become one of the family and no doubt would spend many hours in Beech House. He thought about the young lad who was replacing Ted, knowing he would feel the lash of the old man's tongue if he didn't keep the garden up to scratch.

John looked around the kitchen, saw the plates stacked high, waiting to be washed, and not wanting Wendy or her mother to tackle the task, he set to himself. Let them enjoy themselves, he thought. They deserve it after all their hard work, and now there were just the New Year celebrations before all the guests left.

Yes, the New Year, he thought, sobering as he washed plate after plate, thinking that he'd never reach the end. And would 1956 be the year that he finally found his sister? God, he hoped so.

Chapter Thirty-Eight

Millie had left the clinic at the end of November 1955, and she was thrilled to be home. Several evenings a week Mark came round to see Vanessa, and Millie was surprised to find herself relaxed in his company. She no longer sensed any disapproval; in fact she enjoyed many lively conversations with him – so much so that she now looked forward to his visits.

During the day, time hung heavily on her hands, and as the festive season had approached she'd thrown herself into preparing what she hoped was the perfect Christmas dinner.

Mark was now sitting opposite her at the dining-room table, talking to Vanessa about his latest girlfriend, and Millie studied his face, loving the way his eyes crinkled in the corners when he laughed. When his latest girl's attributes were exhausted the conversation came to a halt and she now saw Mark's eyebrows rise. As though an unspoken signal had passed between brother and sister, Vanessa suddenly turned, her expression eager as she said, 'Millie, do you think you'll be ready to come back to work in the New Year?'

'Oh, no! I don't think I could ever face Alice White again.'

'You won't have to. Her shop was losing money, so rather than renew the lease Alice decided to retire.'

'I still don't know if I'm ready,' Millie said timidly, knowing that even though Alice White had retired, she would still have to face all the other shopkeepers – and what must they think of her? Vanessa's face fell and Millie could see she was trying to hide her disappointment. 'I can't expect you to hold my job open indefinitely,' she now said quietly. 'It might be better if you find another assistant.'

'No, it's all right, I'll manage. I'd rather wait until you feel ready to come back.' There were a few seconds of silence before Vanessa spoke again and now her voice was alight with excitement. 'Millie, I've been given a wonderful opportunity for expansion and want to tell you all about it. However, I'm rather nervous about these plans and would like to hear what you think.'

'You, nervous! No, I can't believe that. Just what are these plans?'

'I think it's time to expand the business, and with this in mind I've bought the lease to Alice White's shop.'

'But why? You have enough trouble finding new stock as it is.'

'I won't be using it to sell second-hand garments.'

'You won't? Then what will you be selling?'

'Wedding dresses, bridesmaid dresses and all the accessories.'

Millie's brow creased. How on earth was Vanessa going to fund this new venture? 'But surely it will cost a fortune to stock, and is there enough demand?'

Vanessa's laugh was one of delight. 'There speaks a born businesswoman. Perhaps I'd better start at the beginning. Abigail Bellinger, an old friend of mine, came to see me recently. Her daughter Lucinda studied Fashion Design at college and it seems she has a wonderful flair for creating wedding gowns. However, it's very hard to get attached to an existing fashion-house so Abby came up with the idea of supplying her creations to just one shop, on an exclusive basis.'

'But how can she make enough dresses to stock a shop?'

'She won't have to make them, Millie. You see, as far as my friend is concerned, money is no object, and she'll do anything to ensure her daughter's success. Lucinda designs the gowns, but women will be employed to create them. One, or maybe two of each design will be held in stock, and when we get an order the dress will be made to measure. We'll also sell a range of bridesmaid dresses, along with gloves, shoes, tiaras and veils, but I'll have to find a supplier for those.'

'Oh, I see. So if money is no object, why doesn't this friend of yours open her own shop?'

'Because she doesn't want to. She has no need to work, Millie, and even if she did, she has no experience in the retail trade.

We've been friends for years, and in fact it was she who loaned me the money to start up *Finesse*.'

Vanessa took Millie's hand, gripping it hard. 'I can still start to get things moving until you're ready to come back to work. There'll be loads to do – the fitting out of the shop, choosing the colour scheme, not to mention finding suppliers for the accessories, and then we'll have to look at advertising.'

Millie couldn't help but be infected by Vanessa's enthusiasm. What was the point of sitting in the flat every day? All she did was brood about Rose and that didn't solve anything. Working might be just what she needed to take her mind off it, and Vanessa's plans sounded wonderful. She smiled, her mind made up. 'All right, Nessie. Yes, I'll come back to work.'

Vanessa squealed with delight, 'Yippee! Oh, it's going to be so much fun, and wait till you see some of Lucinda's creations – they're out of this world! Hang on, what did you call me? Nessie! Oh no, not you, too. See what you've done, Mark?' she complained, her smile belying the cross expression she affected on her face.

Mark had kept silent during the whole conversation, his eyes never leaving Millicent's face. She drew him, drew him around to his sister's flat several times a week. Millicent, yes, she had matured so much that the given name suited her and from now on he would no longer shorten it to Millie.

There was a serenity about her, and stature that had been lacking before her treatment. He compared her now to some of his girlfriends, thinking that beside Millicent they appeared shallow. All they seemed to care about was having a good time, their thoughts filled with fripperies and their conversation dull. They talked about the latest fashions, gossiped about other friends, and whatever event was in season – Ascot, Wimbledon, or the Henley-on-Thames regatta to name a few, with hats under constant scrutiny. Whereas when he spoke to Millicent, the conversations had depth and meaning.

He knew she wasn't completely recovered, because her eyes sometimes gave her away, yet why did he find her so fascinating? She wasn't his usual type. There was a waif-like quality about her, and many times when he noticed her absorbed in thought, the expression on her face was heartbreaking in its sadness. In fact, Millicent rarely smiled, yet when she did it lit her whole face and he saw a fleeting beauty. With her long slender neck, she looked a little like Audrey Hepburn, with that same aura of fragility. Maybe that was it! She brought out his protective instincts, and perhaps he just felt sorry for her.

'What do you think, Mark?'

'Sorry, what did you say?'

'Oh, for goodness sake, you're in a world of your own sometimes. I asked you what you think about Millie coming back to work.'

'If she feels ready, then I'm all for it.'

'I think I'll be all right,' Millie said.

Yes, Mark thought. She might be able to return to work, but he doubted that she was ready for a relationship. He shook his head, annoyed about where his thoughts were taking him. Millicent, though more mature now, was still just a child of sixteen, whereas he was thirty and far too old for her. Smiling now he said, 'Yes, I think you should go back to work, and I can see by Nessie's face that she's absolutely delighted.'

By the end of January 1956, preparations for the new shop were well under way. Vanessa had decided to call it simply *Brides*, and already shopfitters had transformed the somewhat old-fashioned interior.

The décor was now typically Vanessa, and smacked of elegance with its pale peach and cream colour scheme. She was hoping to be open by the end of February, and today she was off hunting for suitable accessories to complement Lucinda's creations.

'Millie,' she called, her head barely in the door of *Finesse*, 'I'm going to see a supplier in Brick Lane, one that specialises in bridal accessories. Are you sure you can manage on your own?'

'Yes, of course. Remember – I coped well enough before when you went off on buying trips for days at a time.'

'Yes, sorry, silly me.'

Millie forced a smile. Since her breakdown Vanessa was overprotective, and somehow she had to convince her that she was now fine and fully recovered. This new venture was tenuous,

Vanessa throwing a lot of money into it, and the last thing Millie wanted was to be any sort of burden. She had grown to love this wonderful woman and desperately wanted the new shop to succeed.

Goodness knows how much her treatment at the clinic had cost. Once, when she had tried to raise the subject, Vanessa had quickly dismissed her enquiry, just saying something about Mark checking the bill. Yes, Millie thought, Mark might have checked the bill was in order, but it was Vanessa who had borne the cost, and now she'd do everything she could to pay her back. She had already suggested a drop in wages, but Vanessa had refused, saying that if anything, with Millie running *Finesse*, she must have a raise in salary. Despite protests, her wage-packet was larger, but now the extra money was going towards saving up to pay Vanessa back.

'I just hope this supplier has a better range than the last,' Vanessa said, her expression harassed. 'I'd best get a move on, but I'll ring you later to see how you are.'

'There's no need to do that. For goodness sake, I'm fine!'

'All right, if you're sure?'

'I am, now go!'

With a small wave of her hand Vanessa closed the door, and Millie sighed with relief. She began to check the stock, pleased to see there was sufficient for the rest of the winter season, and hoped the advertisement they'd placed in several glossy magazines would bring in good secondhand garments suitable for the spring. Would she be able to handle the women who wanted to sell their outfits? Would she be able to deal with them as efficiently as Vanessa?

Millie pushed back her shoulders in a determined manner. Yes, she would have to. Vanessa had enough to do with running *Brides*, and trusted her to see that this shop still ran efficiently. Well, she wouldn't let her down, and despite her trepidation, she'd make sure that she only bought garments of the finest quality.

Millie closed the shop at five-thirty that evening and made her way next door, but as she entered *Brides*, her eyes widened. Vanessa was holding up a wedding gown, and smiling with delight at the lovely young lady standing by her side. But not only that, Mark was there too, his gaze equally warm and his eyes riveted on her blonde beauty.

All three turned as she entered, but it was Vanessa who cried, 'Hello, Millie, come and meet Lucinda, and look at this gown. Isn't it wonderful?'

'Hello, Lucinda, it's nice to meet you, and yes, the gown is fabulous.'

Lucinda's large blue eyes were warm. 'Hello, Millie. Isn't this exciting?'

'It certainly is, and if that creation is anything to go by, I'm sure Vanessa will be inundated with orders.'

'Oh, I hope so,' Lucinda said.

'Now then, let's not have any doubts,' Mark cajoled, and seeing the way he was still looking at Lucinda, Millie was surprised to feel a surge of jealousy. Her face reddened, her mind spinning with confusion. It was true that since her treatment at the clinic she'd lost a lot of her fear of men, but the thought of being touched still made her stiffen with fear. Yes, she looked forward to seeing Mark when he came round to visit Vanessa, but only because she was beginning to feel he was a friend. Yes, just a friend, and she could never let a man get closer than that. Anyway, she told herself, Mark would never be interested in *her*. Lucinda with her perfect features and beautiful clothes was more his type, and that was obvious by the attention he was giving her.

'Are you all right, Millie?' he asked suddenly. 'You look rather flushed.'

'I . . . I'm fine,' she said, her eyes refusing to look at him and focusing on Vanessa. 'I can see you're busy, so I'll go on home and leave you to it.'

'No, don't do that. In fact, how about we all go out to dinner? Oh, and how did the shop do today?' Vanessa asked.

'Not as well as last week,' Millie had to confess, 'but we're only down a little.'

'That's to be expected. With spring on the way we won't sell many winter garments now. Don't look so worried, my dear. Once the new season arrives, takings will go up again.'

Lucinda spoke then, her tone conciliatory as she said, 'I'm

sorry, Vanessa, but I'm afraid I have a previous engagement and can't join you for dinner, though many thanks for the offer. In fact, I must go home to change and had better get a move on or I'll be late.'

'I'll run you home if you like,' Mark offered.

'Oh, would you? That would be wonderful,' Lucinda told him, her lovely face lighting up with delight.

'Right,' Vanessa said, her voice again businesslike, 'as you can see by the quality of the work, the team of seamstresses I managed to find are superb. I can't find a single fault in this gown and they've worked miracles to get most of the range ready. The rest of your designs will be finished by the end of this month, and with this in mind I've decided to schedule our opening day for the first of March.'

'That's marvellous, darling, and I'm already hard at it designing another collection for next year.' Lucinda looked anxiously at her watch. 'Sorry, but I really have to go.'

Both Lucinda and Mark said their goodbyes, but Millie found Mark's rather brusque. He went off, still smiling at Lucinda, and as the door closed behind them, Vanessa said, 'My brother seems rather smitten with Lucinda.'

'Yes, he does,' Millie murmured, once again feeling a surge of jealousy. *Stop it – stop it*, she berated herself. She didn't want a man – any man.

Chapter Thirty-Nine

Pat Benson's feet were sore and tired and she sighed with exasperation. The wedding was only two weeks away but she still hadn't found anything to wear. All the dresses she'd seen so far were fluffy and feminine, and the thought of wearing one made her cringe. God, if she didn't find something soon she'd be walking down the aisle in her birthday suit.

There had been one gown that was less fussy, with straight lines and a high neck, but it was way beyond her price range, despite Brian giving her what he thought was sufficient. She'd tried Oxford Street without success, and today she was looking in the King's Road, but with aching feet she stopped at a small Italian café, deciding to rest for a while.

It was as she sat down with an espresso coffee, that her eyes alighted on a girl who had joined the queue. Her face stretched with delight. No, it couldn't be – could it? 'Millie! Millie, is that really you?'

The tall, elegant girl spun round, her large, immaculately made-up eyes lighting up. 'Pat? Oh Pat, how wonderful to see you!'

Pat stood up hastily, knocking the table, and mindless of the coffee spilling into her saucer as Millie flew into her arms. The girls clung together, both sobbing with happiness, whilst Mamma Baglioni, a broad smile on her face, surveyed the scene.

'Millie, where have you been? I've been trying to find you for ages, and your brother has too. Are you all right? Oh, what a daft question, you look marvellous!'

'I'm fine, but listen, I've got to get back to work. I'm alone in the shop and only locked up for a few minutes to snatch a sandwich. Can you come back with me?'

'Wild horses wouldn't stop me,' and as Pat walked by Millie's side she was still unable to believe that she'd found her.

They came to a small shop, Millie unlocking the door before they stepped inside. With so many questions crowding her mind, Pat didn't know where to start, but it was Millie who spoke first.

'I've never stopped thinking about you, and wondering where you were.'

'I live in Chelsea, in Tedworth Square, and I work in a small tobacconist's shop. My God, Millie, I can't believe you work here, and have only been a stone's throw away. But enough about me. What about you?'

Millie's head went down, but then she swiftly turned the door sign to Closed. 'I don't think Vanessa will mind if just for once I shut the shop for lunch. Come on, let's go through to the back room and we can talk.'

At first their conversation was stilted, but gradually they relaxed in each other's company, their old camaraderie returning.

The years of friendship they'd shared resurfaced, and when Millie began to open up, Pat listened with growing horror to her story, her eyes moist when Millie came to the part about stealing a baby, thinking it was Rose. She was glad that Alfie Pratchett was dead, because if he were still alive she would have strangled him with her bare hands.

She fought to bring herself under control, and as Millie finally stopped speaking, she said, 'Oh Millie, your baby is my half-sister.'

'I know,' Millie murmured.

'It's been impossible to find Bessie and Janet, and now I've lost another sister too.'

'I'm so sorry,' Millie said, beautiful eyes full of compassion.

God, she's wonderful, Pat thought. Here she was, offering sympathy, when she had been through so much herself. 'Listen, Millie, John's been trying to find you for ages, and you must ring him. I went to his wedding, but I'm afraid I lost my temper and told him what I thought of him. Since then we haven't been in touch.'

'No, I don't want any contact with him.'

'Look, I know you want to put your past behind you, but when you and John were kids he fought all your battles, and you know how close you were. Since having a go at your brother I've had time to think. I know he went off and left you, but if you'd been in his position, wouldn't you have done the same thing?'

'No, I don't think so – well, maybe. I was advised by a wonderful woman, Kathleen Blanchard to face the past. She said I had to find forgiveness, and though I can never forgive my father, or yours, maybe I can forgive John. Look, if you have his phone number, maybe I'll ring him later, but not at the moment. I can't face it at the moment.

Pat rifled in her bag, handing out a slip of paper which Millie looked at briefly before stuffing it into her pocket. It then became obvious that she wanted to change the subject as she said, 'I've noticed your diction has improved, so what have you been up to?'

'Yes, well, it's due to someone I've met. He and his mother speak well and I decided to emulate them. Not only that, would you believe I'm marrying him in two weeks?'

'You're getting married! Oh, I'm so pleased, and I . . I sort of guessed that what happened between us was just a result of what you'd been through.'

'Yes, well . . .' Pat said, her voice trailing off in embarrassment. She hadn't expected Millie to bring that up.

'What is your wedding dress like?'

'Don't talk to me about wedding dresses. I've looked everywhere, but the only ones I like, I can't afford.'

'We've got a few for sale. They're not new, but are couture models. Come into the shop and I'll show them to you.'

'Second hand? Oh, I don't know about that, Millie.'

'Reserve judgement until you see them, and I think you'll be pleasantly surprised. The dresses must have cost a king's ransom when new, and after all, they have only been worn once.'

'All right, I'll take a look since I must admit I'm getting pretty desperate.'

Millie was right, Pat thought as she looked at one lovely satin gown. It was completely plain, without a single bead or sequin, but the cut was exquisite. With a smile of delight she eagerly tried it on, and as she came out of the dressing-room Millie said, 'Oh,

Pat, it's perfect – just perfect – and doesn't even need altering. It could have been made for you.'

Pat gazed at herself in the mirror, and in the reflection she could see Millie standing behind her. A thought crossed her mind and she blurted out, 'I know it's short notice, but will you be my bridesmaid?'

'Me! But surely you want some cute little girls.'

Pat was momentarily stricken. God, if only she had found her sisters. They would have made lovely bridesmaids. For a moment she was silent, but then the joy of finding Millie lifted her spirits again. 'It would make my wedding day perfect if you were there, walking behind me down the aisle. Please say you'll be my bridesmaid.'

Millie hesitated, and Pat widened her eyes in appeal. She then squealed with delight when Millie said, 'Yes, all right, but I just hope we can find a suitable dress.'

They looked at the small selection of second hand bridesmaid dresses on offer, disregarding most as being too fussy. Then, thankfully, they found one in a shade of cerise that suited Millie's colouring. It was fitted at the top, the skirt tulip-shaped and ending just below her knees.

'Perfect,' Pat said as Millie emerged from the changing room. 'How about coming round to my place tonight to meet my husband-to-be?'

During the following two weeks, when Pat wasn't seeing Brian, the two girls spent as much time as they could together. Their friendship grew stronger, both as happy in each other's company as they had been in Harmond Street.

Occasionally Pat still nagged her to ring John, and Millie had finally decided to contact him, but not until after Pat's marriage.

The last revelation came on Pat's wedding day when Millie was helping her to dress. She was just adding the finishing touch, pinning a veil to Pat's newly set hair, when her friend spoke in a strangled voice.

'I . . . can't do it, Millie.'

Through lips clamped around hairpins, Millie mumbled, 'Can't do what?'

'I can't marry him.'

Millie spat the pins onto her palm before saying, 'You're just having last minute nerves. Brian's lovely, and anyone can see how much he loves you.'

'Yeah, but I don't love him. Well, not in that way.'

'What do you mean?'

'Oh Millie, you have no idea how lonely I was when I met Brian. I'd given up all hope of finding you, but even if I had, I knew we could never have *that* sort of relationship. I . . . I just wanted us to be friends again. Then I met Brian, and we get on really well. He's nice, Millie, gentle, kind and undemanding. I agreed to marry him because I want a normal life, to have a family, and I thought I could make him happy.'

'Pat, you're not making sense.'

'I . . . I'm a lesbian, Millie,' she said, trembling with the effort of confessing.

'Don't be daft, of course you're not,' Millie said cheerfully. 'If you're thinking about that time when you kissed me, it didn't mean anything. And it certainly doesn't mean you're a . . . a lesbian.'

'Millie, I'd like to believe I'm normal, but I'm not, and it wasn't just kissing you that made me realise that. I'm attracted to women, not men, and as much as I've tried to fight it, I can't.'

Millie slumped down on the side of Pat's bed, her mind reeling, but before she could find anything to say, her friend spoke again.

'Do you remember when your brother left Harmond Street and you suggested we find a flat together?' And at Millie's nod she continued, 'Can't we still do that?'

'What! Oh, but as you said earlier, it couldn't be that sort of relationship.'

'I know, but finding you again has been wonderful. I just want us to be friends, Millie, and that's all I'm asking for – your friendship.'

Oh Pat, Millie thought. If only they had found each other earlier, things might have been different. With a small shake of her head she said sadly, 'I'm sorry, but I love the life I have now.

I'm so happy with Vanessa in Cheyne Walk, and she's so special to me, like a mother as well as a friend.'

'But I'm your friend too. Please, at least think about it!'

Millie did think. She thought about all that Vanessa had done for her, compared herself now to the wretched broken child who had ended up in her shop doorway, and realised that the old Millie had gone. She had a new life now, and felt like a new person. 'I'm sorry, Pat, but the answer must be no.'

There was a moment of silence, the atmosphere strained, but then flicking her veil forward to cover her face, Pat said huskily, 'All right, Millie, I understand. Now come on, let's just forget it and get this wedding over and done with.'

'What! You're going to marry Brian after what you've told me?'

'Yeah, and don't look so worried. We had a trial run and the sex wasn't so bad.'

'But you just said you aren't attracted to men.'

'I'm not, and never will be, but I can't face the rest of my life alone. It's as I said, Millie; I want to be normal, and to have children. And anyway, even though I'll be a married woman, we can still be friends, can't we?'

'Of course we can.'

'Right then, come on, hand me my flowers because the car's here.'

Millie walked down the aisle behind Pat, praying that her friend was making the right decision, and that it wasn't just her refusal to share a flat that had forced Pat's hand. Yet as she saw Brian turn to see his bride, his face alight with love, she couldn't help feeling a twinge of envy. Would a man ever look at her like that? Would she ever walk down the aisle? Her brother was married now, and did he look at Wendy with that special expression of love? It was then that Millie made another decision. She would telephone John – and she would do it tonight.

Unbidden, her thoughts turned to Mark, and she had to admit that she missed his company. Since dating Lucinda he rarely came round to Vanessa's flat, and she wondered just how serious the relationship was becoming. Distantly she heard Pat and Brian making their wedding vows, only snapping back to attention when the Vicar pronounced them man and wife.

The rest of the day went off without a hitch and as the couple departed for a few days' honeymoon, Millie, along with other guests, threw handfuls of confetti over the happy pair. And they did look happy, she thought.

Pat turned just before the car sped off, giving her a little wink, and seeing this Millie heaved a sigh of relief.

Shortly afterwards, she too left the reception, and on reaching Cheyne Walk she again decided to ring John. The flat was empty as Vanessa was out having dinner with Lucinda and her mother, so taking the number out of her bag, she picked up the telephone.

'Hello, Beech Guesthouse.'

It was her brother, his voice unmistakable. 'Hello, John. It's me, Millie.'

'Millie? Millie! Oh my God, it that really you?' he shouted, the joy in his voice ringing down the line.

Chapter Forty

Millie had to admit it had been wonderful to find her brother again. When she saw his smiling face waiting for her at Ryde, she'd flown into his arms, all the past anger dissipating.

At first, seeing Wendy's stomach swollen in pregnancy, she felt again the intense pain of losing Rose. However, not wanting to spoil their reunion, she did her best to hide her feelings.

During one conversation, John described his efforts to find her, and then told her about his visit to the coal depot. She smiled when he talked about Jack Jenkins, and felt guilty all over again for the way she'd walked out on the man. She owed him an apology, and before the conversation turned to other matters, Millie decided that one day soon she would ring him.

The time flew by, with Wendy and Bertha drawing her into the family, until finally, on the last day of her holiday on the Isle of Wight, she felt able to tell John what had happened to her.

They were alone in the drawing room, and as her story came to an end she was surprised to see her big, strapping brother with tears in his eyes. Yet somehow these tears brought healing, and she realised then how much he loved her.

'I wish I could do something,' he said in a choked voice. 'Find your daughter – my niece.'

'It's impossible, John. The police have done everything they can. Dad was the last link to Dulcie Liddle, and if he hadn't died before they could question him, there might have been some hope.'

'I should be sad that Dad's dead, but at the moment all I can feel is anger,' he muttered.

Millie was unsure about showing John the letter and papers, yet hadn't there been enough deceit? She'd been lied to all her life, and now she didn't want these lies to remain between them. 'Listen, I've got something else to tell you. You see, you may not be my brother.'

'What! Don't be daft, of course I am.'

'You'd better look at this,' she told him, reaching into her bag to hand him the letter and her birth certificate.

After reading them John was quiet, his head lowered, but then as they sat side by side on the sofa, he reached out to put an arm around her shoulder. 'Millie, I don't care what these bits of paper say. You're my sister, and you'll always be my sister. I want you to stay here, love. Wendy, Bertha and I have been talking, and we can offer you a home and a job.'

It was amazing, Millie thought. At one time she'd been homeless, trawling the streets looking for her father, but now, in the space of just one week, she'd been offered two homes. For a moment she was tempted, but then she shook her head, giving John the same answer as Pat. 'Thanks, but I'm afraid my answer must be no. You see Vanessa Grey has come to mean so much to me. She rescued me, and then she and her brother saved my sanity. I . . . I like the life I have now, and my job.'

'But we're your family, Millie.'

'I know you are, but we can still see each other regularly, can't we? You can come to London, and I'll come to stay with you as often as possible.'

John sighed, but finally gave her shoulder a further squeeze. 'All right, Millie, it's your life and I won't interfere. Do you know, I can't believe how much you've changed. Not only do you look great, but you seem so mature for a sixteen year old.'

'I'm seventeen next month, and sometimes with all that's happened I feel more like a seventy year old.'

'Yes, you've been through the wars and back, and I still wish I could think of a way to find your baby.'

'Thanks, John, but I've accepted now that it will never happen. Anyway, I'd better pack my case or I'll miss the boat.'

John followed her into the hall, and as Wendy came out of the kitchen he said, 'Hello, Miss Piggywig, Millie's off to pack.'

'Will you stop calling me that! Miss Piggywig indeed! Just because I can't chase you, you're taking liberties.'

'You'd be able to if you stopped stuffing your face.'

'Huh, you can talk, and anyway I'm eating for two. Isn't that right, Millie?' and without waiting for an answer her eyes travelled back to John, the love reflected in them plain to see. It was obvious how happy these two were, and as she had at Pat's wedding, Millie once again felt a twinge of envy. Would she ever know love like theirs? No, she doubted it, and anyway, at the thought of a man touching her, she still cringed.

'I'm going upstairs before swords are drawn,' she said, pushing these thoughts to one side.

'Do you need a hand, Millie?' Wendy asked.

'No thanks, and anyway John would kill me if I said yes.'

'He is a bit much, isn't he? I keep telling him that I'm perfectly capable of working, but he won't let me. Can't you have a word with him?'

'No, I wouldn't dare. He always was a bully.'

'Me, a bully! Since when?' John protested.

'Only joking, brother dear,' Millie told him as she ran lightly up to her room.

Two hours later the goodbyes were emotional, but as Millie stood on the deck of the steamer she was happy. She and John wouldn't lose touch again, and the Isle of Wight wasn't that far away. There would be holidays, times of celebration when his child was born, and did it matter what her birth certificate said? Whether John was her brother, or not, she was just glad that she'd found him, and that he was happy.

When Millie returned to London, she arrived at Cheyne Walk to find Mark having lunch with his sister. He looked up to smile at her as she entered the room and she suddenly felt that her stomach was full of butterflies.

'Hello, my dear,' Vanessa said. 'There's some chicken casserole left if you're hungry, and how did your trip go?'

'It was wonderful to see my brother again, and his wife is having a baby so I'll be an auntie in June.'

Mark and Vanessa exchanged glances, and then with a strained smile Vanessa said, 'If you're not too tired, can we talk?'

'Of course. You look worried, what is it?'

There was a moment's silence, and then Vanessa blurted out, 'Will you be going to live on the Isle of Wight now?'

'No. As I told my brother, I love my life here too much. And it's even better now that I've found my friend Pat again.' She hesitated, an awful thought striking her. 'Why are you asking? Do you want me to leave?'

'No, no, my dear, and I can't tell you how thrilled I am that you're going to stay with me. You see, I had thought that with finding your family again, you would want to live with them.'

Millie's eyes flicked to Mark, and she was surprised to see him smiling happily too as he said, 'You have come to mean a great deal to my sister, and I think the time has come for me to apologise for my earlier behaviour. When she first took you into her home, quite honestly, I thought her mad. Now, of course, I realise how wrong I was. I'm glad you found your brother again, and feel you've made a full recovery from your earlier breakdown. Kathleen Blanchard has certainly lived up to her reputation.'

'Yes, she was marvellous, but I still feel awful about how much her fees must have cost Vanessa.' Turning to look at her friend she added, 'I know you have tried to dismiss this in the past, but I'll pay you back, I promise.'

'Pay me back! But it was Mark who paid the fees.'

'What? *You* paid for it all?' Millie cried, her eyes now on Mark again and her cheeks pink.

'Think nothing of it. I was glad to help,' Mark said offhandedly, his smile warm, but Millie, still red with embarrassment, was only able to thank him before fleeing the room.

When reaching the bathroom she closed the door, leaning against it as her heart thumped against her ribs. Why hadn't she realised it before? She had fled the room, but not with embarrassment that Mark had paid her fees at the clinic. No, when she had seen the softness in his eyes, the knowledge had hit her like a sledgehammer. She loved him! She was in love with Mark!

Millie slumped, her eyes filling with tears. It was hopeless, and she knew it. She couldn't compete with the beautiful girls like Lucinda who Mark favoured, and somehow she had to accept that.

'Oh dear, I think I've put my foot in it,' Vanessa said as the door slammed shut behind Millie.

'I did ask you not to tell her,' Mark said reproachfully.

'I know, but I could hardly pretend it was me that stood the fees when she was insisting on paying me back. Now what?'

'Just tell her that I owed you money, and it was your suggestion as a way to pay you back. That should do the trick.'

'Yes, all right. Oh Mark, I'm so relieved that she isn't going to leave. I really did think that she'd want to live with her family.'

'We obviously misjudged how happy she is to be living here with you.'

'Yes, and isn't it wonderful?'

'As long as you're happy, Ness, that's all I care about, and it's obvious that Millicent means a great deal to you.'

'Millicent? Yes, I've noticed that you use her full name now. Would you mind telling me why?'

'Because it suits her.'

'I see,' Vanessa said, her eyebrows raised. 'And how are things between you and Lucinda?'

'Not too good. In fact, I think Lucinda has her eye on someone else.'

'Really! And there was I, worried that you wouldn't treat her right. My goodness, how do you feel about being given the heave-ho for a change?'

'Oh, you know me, Ness – easy come, and easy go. Now, what's for pudding?'

'Oh, you . . .' she said, rising abruptly to her feet, but as she made her way to the kitchen, Vanessa couldn't help wondering about Mark's feelings towards Millie. On many occasions she'd thought he had looked at the girl with fondness, but then he'd seemed so smitten with Lucinda that she'd dismissed her suspicions.

Millie seemed fond of Mark too, and was always so pleased to see him. Was it possible? Was it possible that the two people she loved most in the world would get together?

Chapter Forty-One

Within three months the new shop was buzzing, business was booming, and in June Vanessa declared that the venture was going to be an undoubted success.

Millie was waiting in the bridal shop whilst a young lady was being fitted, thinking that the head seamstress Vanessa employed had turned out to be a godsend. A team of women made up the gowns, with Mrs Salter in charge of taking the complicated measurements to ensure a perfect fit.

It wasn't practical to have more than a token fitting carried out in the shop during the day, so appointments were made for between six and eight, two evenings a week, and the arrangement worked well.

On rare occasions there was the added bonus of being able to re-purchase a gown, or the bridesmaids' dresses, to sell in *Finesse*. They still cost a great deal of money, but the quality of the dresses spoke for themselves and they had no trouble in shifting them.

Vanessa had handed over the total running of *Finesse* to her, but Millie had to admit she was secretly disappointed not to be working in the bridal shop. Yet she could understand the impracticalities of trying to train up a new girl to take her place. Instead, Vanessa had taken on a junior assistant to help her in *Brides*.

However, as Vanessa closed the door on the customer, and Mrs Salter, she clicked her tongue impatiently as she tidied the shop. 'Honestly, Millie, I made a real mistake in employing Linda. The girl's slapdash and hopeless. She's been late three times this week, and I'll have to let her go.'

'Will you advertise again?'

'Yes, but I hope we get a decent applicant this time. I know it will take a bit of time, but if I do find someone suitable I'd like you to train her up to run *Finesse* and you can join me in here.'

'Oh, I'd love that!'

'Good, I'm glad that's settled. Now let's get a move on. Thank goodness I only had one fitting this evening because Mark's coming to dinner. Mamma Baglioni has made me a lasagne to take home and it's his favourite.'

Since breaking up with Lucinda, Mark had started to join them for dinner again, and sometimes Millie found herself longing to see him. Yet on other occasions she was filled with dread as she prayed her feelings didn't show. Only last week she'd caught him gazing at her with a strange expression on his face and her heart had skipped a beat. Was it fondness she saw? But then, only two days later, her hopes were dashed when he turned up with yet another beautiful girl on his arm.

'You've gone very quiet. What are you daydreaming about?' Vanessa asked as she locked the shop.

'Oh, nothing much,' Millie said quickly before her thoughts flew back to Mark. She had to stop this hopeless dreaming, and anyway she didn't know if she could bear a man touching her. Yes, Kathleen Blanchard had removed her fear of men, and she sometimes longed for love, dreaming of how it would feel to be in Mark's arms. Yet at the thought of sex, she still shuddered.

'Blast! I forgot to order those special Italian bread rolls,' Vanessa now said as they walked through the arcade.

'I'm sure Mamma Baglioni will have some left. It's funny really, I'd never tasted Italian food before I came to the arcade, but now I can't get enough of it.'

'Yes, me too, and when more people get the taste I think there will be loads of Italian restaurants opening up in London.'

Millie laughed at the thought. 'No, surely not. Meat and two veg, that's our standard diet, and I can't see the average working-class man eating spaghetti bolognaise, or pizza. Fish and chips will remain a special treat.'

'Perhaps you're right, but they don't know what they're missing. Now come on, let's get a move on.'

'That was smashing,' Mark said as he wiped his lips with a napkin. 'What's for pudding?'

'Honestly, you're like a bottomless pit,' his sister sighed. 'I didn't get a pudding so will a piece of fruit do?'

'I suppose it'll have to, Ness.'

'Stop calling me Ness!'

'Yes, sorry, but I'm afraid it's hard to break the habit.'

'Well, try harder. What about you, Millie, would you like some fruit?'

'No thanks, but I think I'll make some coffee. Would you both like some?'

'Please,' Mark said, and as Millie left the room he turned to Vanessa, saying quietly, 'It's wonderful to see how Millicent has blossomed, though I think there will always be a trace of sadness in her eyes. She will always carry the wounds of losing her child, but she seems to be coping with it now.'

'Yes, I agree – and, by the way, when will you tell the girl how you feel about her?'

'Feel about her!' He went crimson. 'What on earth do you mean?'

'Oh Mark, you must think I'm blind. It's as plain as the nose on your face that you care for her.'

'No, you're wrong. I admit I like the girl, but that's all she is – a girl. I'm far too old for her.'

'Don't be silly. In my opinion men shouldn't settle down until they're over thirty. A woman needs a mature man, one who has sowed his wild oats and has achieved some success in his life.'

'Listen, Ness, you know me. I have no wish to settle down, and I like the way it is, with no strings attached. I've seen too many unhappy people in my office who've been torn apart by failed marriages. Not only that, you know full well that none of my relationships last, and knowing how vulnerable Millicent is, do you really want me to hurt her?'

'You've never been in love before, so it would be different this time.'

'*Love?* How on earth can you say it's love? I have no idea what my feelings are, and anyway I think they're more akin to pity.'

'Pity! You have no need to pity Millie. She's been through hell, but has come out the other side. She's survived, Mark, and is so much stronger now – stronger than I think you realise.'

'Maybe, but you must admit she still looks fragile.'

'She will always be unhappy about the loss of her daughter, but in all other ways she's a different person since she came out of Kathleen Blanchard's clinic. I must say I was against the idea of her being admitted in the first place, but I'm glad you talked me round. And since returning to work Millie is more self-assured, more mature, and I think you're mistaken about her vulnerability.'

'Maybe, but I won't risk it. If I took her out and it didn't work, I don't know if she could cope with the rejection.'

'Huh, that cuts both ways. Have you thought that Millie might reject *you*? Go on – ask her out, my dear. If you don't take the risk you might miss out on the chance of happiness.'

'For God's sake, will you shut up about it! I've said no, I mean it, and I don't want to have this conversation again.'

Vanessa's lips tightened. Honestly, she could shake her brother, but before she had time to argue her case any further, Millie came into the room, a tray of coffee in her hands. As she gave a cup to Mark, Vanessa saw the look that passed between them. It was obvious that these two were in love, but remembering her brother's words, Vanessa's heart sank. He was judging all marriages by the things he'd heard in his consulting rooms, and once his mind was made up, Mark rarely changed it. She remembered his stubbornness as a boy and shook her head, deciding that no matter what he said, she would somehow try to bring these two beloved people together.

Later on that evening, the telephone rang. Millie answered it, and her face lit up with happiness. 'Oh John, a boy – how wonderful! And how's Wendy? . . . Yes, I'll come out as soon as I can, and in the meantime give your son, and Wendy, a huge kiss from me. . . . Oh, Anthony, what a lovely name, and eight pounds in weight too. All right, I know you want to get back to them. Thanks for ringing, and I'll see you soon.'

Millie replaced the receiver, her eyes sparkling. 'That was my brother to tell me that half an hour ago, his wife gave birth to a baby boy. Oh, he sounds over the moon.'

'Wonderful,' Vanessa said, clapping her hands with delight. 'You can go to see them tomorrow.'

'But we can't just close the shop.'

'I'll put Linda in there for a day or two, and run *Brides* on my own.'

'Oh, I don't know about that. I don't think I trust Linda to run *Finesse*.'

Mark listened in amazement to this conversation. To think he'd worried about his sister taking in Millicent, and here she was talking as if the shop was as important to her as it was to Vanessa.

When she'd taken the telephone call her eyes had been shining with happiness, but they were now shadowed with concern, her head cocked to one side in thought before she said, 'No, I think I'll wait until Saturday evening and then shoot across to see the baby before coming back on Sunday.'

'Are you sure?'

'Yes, definitely, and anyway it'll be nice to give John and Wendy some time on their own.'

Gosh, she's marvellous, Mark thought. He caught his sister looking at him, saw her eyebrows go up, and frowned with annoyance. Vanessa would have to realise that he meant what he said. Yes, he thought Millicent was a lovely young woman, but that didn't mean he was going to risk starting anything. He stood up, determined now to leave before his sister started nagging him again. God, Nessie could be impossible sometimes.

Chapter Forty-Two

Millie sat opposite Pat in the coffee-bar, suddenly realising that her friend had been married for over a year. And what a year it had been! She had not only found Pat again, but her brother too, and little Anthony, her nephew, was now ten months old. He was so cute, and already trying to toddle on sturdy little legs. She smiled, remembering a wonderful Christmas spent on the Isle of Wight, but then Pat spoke, snapping her out of her reveries.

'Millie, I've got something to tell you.'

'Well, spit it out because my lunch-break is nearly over and I've got to get back to the shop.'

'I . . . I'm having a baby.'

'Are you? That's wonderful!'

'You don't mind?'

'Mind! Why should I mind?'

'I thought, with losing your daughter – my half sister,' Pat whispered, 'that it might upset you.'

'Oh Pat, of course not. I'm thrilled to bits for you and I bet Brian and his mother are over the moon.'

'Huh, that's an understatement. I think his mother thought that it would never happen.'

Millie looked into Pat's strange cat-shaped amber eyes and saw they were brimming with happiness. She thought back to the conversation they'd had on Pat's wedding day, and couldn't resist saying, 'Your dad interfered with you as a child and it isn't surprising that it turned you off men, but surely you realise now that you're not a lesbian.'

'But I am, Millie. Yes, I went through hell with my father, and I think it's a miracle that I didn't get pregnant by him, but even so

it didn't turn me into a lesbian. I . . . I think I was born this way.'
She shrugged, adding, 'Still, I'm happy with Brian and we have a
good marriage, but if anything we are more like best mates.
Thankfully he isn't very demanding sexually, and when we do
make love it's over in a flash. If it wasn't, I don't think I could
stand it.'

'B . . . but you're pregnant.'

'Just 'cos it's quick, it doesn't mean it's ineffectual.'

'I still think you're mistaken about . . . you know, preferring
women to men.'

'Millie, when I see a beautiful woman I can't keep my eyes off
her.'

'That doesn't mean anything. When I see beautiful women I
admire them too.'

'Yeah, but you don't imagine them naked in your arms.'

Millie burst out laughing, causing heads to turn, but unable to
stop she found her eyes filling with tears of mirth. As though it
was infectious, Pat joined in, finally managing to splutter, 'What's
so funny?'

'It's just the things you come out with. Naked indeed, and my
mind boggles at the thought of you in bed with another woman.'

'Cor, just give me the chance.'

Millie chuckled again, thinking that Pat was incorrigible, but
then she glanced at her watch. 'Goodness – look at the time. I
really must go.'

'Yeah, all right, and I'll see you tomorrow. Leave the bill, I'll
pay it.'

Millie stood up, smiling at her friend, 'Thanks, mum-to-be.'

'Yes – it really is great, isn't it?'

'It certainly is,' Millie said, before hurrying out of the coffee-
bar and along the King's Road. She was thrilled for her friend, but
unable to help feeling a twinge of sadness. She'd had a baby, lost
her, and it seemed unlikely that she'd ever have another. She still
dreamed about Mark, but was mostly able to hide her feelings as a
string of lovely girls came in and out of his life. Instead she had
thrown herself into her work, determined to help Vanessa in
making *Brides* a huge success.

As Millie reached the shop her thoughts were still on Vanessa, and she thanked her lucky stars that she had such a wonderful boss. Out of the three jobs she'd had, two of her employers had been marvellous, and on that thought her eyes widened. Jack Jenkins! God, she'd been so busy that she'd forgotten her determination to telephone the man. She still owed him an apology, and no matter what, when she arrived home that evening she'd do something about it.

Vanessa checked the sales figures, and grinned with delight. It was over twelve months since *Brides* had opened and the shop was still doing amazingly well.

She smiled at Millie as she hurried in from lunch, knowing that there wasn't a hope in hell of getting another assistant like her, and blessing the day she'd found the girl in her shop doorway.

Yet how could she class Millie as an assistant? She was more than that, yet it was impossible to describe their relationship. At times she felt like a mother and Millie her beloved daughter, yet they were also best friends. She supposed it was a result of living and working together, and Millie's enthusiasm for the shop equalled her own. The girl worked tirelessly to make sure everything looked perfect, not only tackling the cleaning, but she was a wonderful sales assistant too. She seemed to have a natural eye for which style of wedding gown would suit each customer, and those who were short in stature or tubby would be shown long narrow flowing gowns, whilst those who were tall and slender looked wonderful in the full-skirted styles. Of course, some refused to follow her advice and would choose a gown that was totally inappropriate for their shape, but as with all the customers, Millie remained patient and attentive, so much so that she hardly ever failed to make a sale.

Last month had been Millie's eighteenth birthday, but she looked older, and even after all this time there were still occasions when her eyes clouded with sorrow. When this happened Vanessa knew she was thinking about Rose. Sometimes they spoke about her, and she hoped it helped. Millie had accepted that it was unlikely she would ever find her daughter, yet she had wistfully said that it was impossible not to hold on to a spark of hope.

On the regular trips she took to the Isle of Wight, Millie took delight in her nephew, talking about him non-stop when returned.

'Did you have a nice lunch?' Vanessa asked her now.

'Yes, thanks. We went to that new coffee-bar, and Pat had some good news.'

'Oh, what was that?'

'She's having a baby.'

'Really! I must congratulate her next time she comes in.'

'I wonder if it'll be a boy or a girl.'

Vanessa saw the wistful look that crossed Millie's face and sighed, knowing that what she needed was a husband and another child to love. And oh, how she would love that child to be her own niece or nephew.

Now stop this — stop dreaming, she told herself briskly, *and get back to your sales figures*. Yes, they were very good, but unless she carried out her plans they would be unlikely to improve. The problem at the moment was space, and sometimes with two or three brides coming in for fittings at the same time, the shop felt as if it was bursting at the seams. She'd made tentative enquiries with the landlord, and now, seeing the healthy sales figures, she decided to go ahead with her plans.

Her eyes roamed around the shop as she assessed new display cabinets and changing rooms. The existing glass case carried a small selection of tiaras in a variety of styles, some tall, decorated with drop pearls, others small and encrusted with tiny jewels. But the case was far too small and many lines had to be kept in the stock room. If a bride couldn't see one she liked, it took many trips back and forward, so larger cabinets would make all the difference. Veils too were difficult to display, but a nice wooden drawer unit would make storing them so much simpler. And what about the new colour scheme?

There was so much to think about, and her mind was twisting and turning with ideas, until finally coming to a decision she called, 'Millie, have you got a moment?'

'Yes, what is it?'

'I've been thinking about the problem we have with space, and I've come up with a solution.'

'Oh, good.'

'I'm going to close *Finesse* and knock both shops into one. As long as I take out a ten-year lease on both premises, the landlord has agreed.'

'Are you sure you're doing the right thing? I thought the other shop was showing a good return.'

'The figures aren't bad, but profits are down on last year and I think it's due to the times. So much has changed recently. The King's Road has become the centre of young fashion, and Mary Quant's boutique *Bazaar* is always buzzing with life. I don't think the young girls who frequent the area are interested in the type of classic clothes on offer in *Finesse*.' She looked at the skirt Millie had bought recently at *Bazaar*; it was far too short. There was no denying that her legs were shapely, but you could see at least an inch of thigh above her knees. 'Yes, well, to get back to what I was saying. Despite our combined efforts we're finding it almost impossible to get enough of the latest fashion to stock the shop, and it's youngsters who are spending all the money nowadays. It also takes up too much of our time – time that we really can't spare.'

'Yes, I must admit it's growing more and more difficult, and expanding this shop sounds like a good idea. Mind you, with so many appointments booked for fittings I don't see how we can close up whilst the alterations are carried out. Yet how are we going to run the business with builders on the premises?'

'The changes won't be drastic. I'd like an archway through to the second shop, and in there we can have the fitting rooms, plus extra display cabinets for accessories. That leaves our existing space clear for showing gowns to their best advantage. We could have them hanging outwards instead of crammed on rails as they are now.'

'Sounds good so far,' Millie murmured.

'Yes, and I quite fancy adding a range of pretty lingerie to our stock, and perhaps some fancy garters. This peach and cream décor is looking a bit jaded so we need a new colour scheme. How do you feel about a soft shade of green?'

'Yes, or Wedgwood blue and white with a pale grey carpet . . . and I like the idea of lingerie. I often get asked for fancy garters and it sounds as if you've thought of everything . . . except for the dirt and dust when the work's carried out, of course. And what about Mrs Lewis? She's done really well since she took over the running of *Finesse*.'

'We'll need extra help in here, so if she wants the job, it's hers. As for the building work – it's only one wall really, and a shop-fitting company has assured me they can do it in a day,' Vanessa told her. 'If I pay extra I'm sure they'll agree to do it on a Sunday. But tell me, Millie, do you really think it's a good idea?'

'Yes I do, and we certainly need more room. I mean, look at this gown for instance.'

Vanessa watched as Millie held the beautiful wedding dress against her slim figure. It was Lucinda's latest creation and she thought it was her best yet. The dress was magnificent, with yards and yards of material giving a crinoline effect to the skirt.

If only Mark could see Millie wearing it, Vanessa mused. He'd be unable to resist her. God, her brother was so pig-headed and even though she had told him that Millie obviously returned his feelings, he still said that he wasn't the right man for her. Vanessa sighed, realising that she would have to give up. She had tried every trick in the book to get them together, but nothing had worked.

Since breaking up with Lucinda there had been many girls on his arm, but none that lasted, and she knew the one he was seeing now would also fall by the wayside. It was heartbreaking to see the look on Millie's face when she saw Mark with his latest girlfriend, but she hid her feelings well, with only her large expressive eyes revealing her pain.

Millie pivoted in front of the mirror now, saying, 'Oh, this dress is an absolute picture. Shall we remove the other gown and display this one in the window? I'm sure we'll get loads of orders.'

'No, put it in the stock room for the time being. Mrs Windlesham's daughter is getting married in June and I've promised she can be the first to view it.'

'Right, but I can't say I'm looking forward to seeing the woman. She was absolute murder to serve when I worked next door, and her daughter seems such a timid mouse of a girl. She looks so browbeaten that you can't help feeling sorry for her.'

'Yes, Mrs Windlesham is very difficult, and rules her daughter with a rod of iron. I think she's only agreed to the marriage because the husband-to-be is wealthy. She has also decided to choose the wedding gown, and won't be bringing Priscilla with her.'

'But that's awful! Surely the girl has some say in the matter! After all, young women have more freedom nowadays.'

'Maybe, but when I think about my father I realise that he ruled our home. I've always considered myself strong, but I wouldn't have dared to disobey him.'

'Yes, and who am I to talk? My mother was a soft and gentle woman, but I was terrified of my father and jumped to his command. I wonder now why I didn't fight back, and I guess us women haven't as much freedom as we'd like to think.'

'You're a different person now, Millie, and somehow I can't see a man ever ruling you again.'

'You're right, and I have a lot to thank both you, and Kathleen Blanchard for. Yet after my experiences with men I can't see myself getting married. It would take someone very special – someone who would let me carry on being me, not just a chattel. When I think about my mother's marriage I realise that she had no life of her own. Her days were spent cooking, cleaning, washing, and waiting hand and foot on my father and brother. She had no money of her own and hardly went out, except to sneak off to church when my father was out. I don't think I could live like that. I'd need to work, to have my own income and independence.'

'If you find the right man, one who sees marriage as a partnership, you can have all that.'

Millie fingered the lovely wedding gown. Yes, there was a man, a very special man, but it was hopeless to dream. Time spent on the Isle of Wight with her brother had shown her how wonderful marriage could be. He and Wendy seemed happier every time she saw them, and little Anthony gave them so much joy. Bertha too strutted about, the proud gran, insisting that each and every guest saw her grandchild.

Pat too, despite what she'd revealed about her preferences, seemed happy, and was obviously thrilled to be having a baby.

They were such happy couples, and seeing this had made Millie believe that, with the right man, she could now face a sexual relationship. Yes, she thought sadly, but the right man wasn't interested in her.

Chapter Forty-Three

Two days had passed since Millie had rung Jack Jenkins and now, ready to leave, she hurried to answer a ring on the doorbell. 'Oh hello, Mark. You're early and I don't think Ness has dinner ready yet.'

'You look nice, Millie. Off out, are you?'

'Yes, I'm going to see Jack. He's a lovely man who I haven't seen for a long time, and I owe him an apology.'

'Oh,' Mark said, a small frown appearing on his forehead, but before he could say anything else, Vanessa appeared in the hall.

'Mark, I've got wonderful plans for the shop. Come through to the sitting room and I'll tell you all about it.'

Millie grabbed her coat from the stand, and throwing it on she called, 'I'm off, see you later.'

'All right, and have a lovely date,' Vanessa called.

Puzzled, Millie turned, but with a small wink Vanessa took Mark's arm and dragged him away. What was all that about? she wondered. Vanessa knew she was finally going to see her old boss Jack Jenkins, not on a date. Her telephone call to Jack had gone well. He'd been delighted to hear from her, insisting that she come to see him, even going so far as to say he'd wait at the depot until she arrived.

Dismissing Vanessa's strange behaviour, Millie hurried to catch a bus, a smile on her face when she arrived at the depot. Flinging open the office door she cried, 'Hello, Jack.'

'Millie! My God, is that really you? You look wonderful and not at all like the girl I remember. You look so pretty.'

'Was I ugly before then?' Millie asked, hiding a smile.

'Oh, bugger it, I've put my foot in it again. What I'm trying to say is . . .'

'Never mind, Jack. You'll only dig a deeper hole for yourself.'

He roared with laughter, his hand raking his hair in a familiar gesture that made Millie grin when it stood up on end. Oh, she had forgotten how much she liked this man – a man she would have loved as a father.

'Millie, I can't tell you how glad I am to see you, and is there any chance of you coming back?'

Oh, Jack, Millie thought. Yes, there was a time when she would have loved to return to the coal depot, but not now. Her life had moved on, and she felt a different person from the girl who had once worked for Jack Jenkins. Sadly she shook her head. 'I'm sorry, but I have a wonderful job and I don't want to leave it.'

'Shit! Oh sorry, there I go again. Is it any wonder I can't keep a secretary for more than five minutes.'

'Why don't you try a school-leaver again? You never know, if you're her first boss, she might just put up with your language.'

'It isn't just my language. It's my temperament that seems to upset them. To be honest, you're the only one who knew how to handle me.'

'Jack, if you remember, we got off to a tricky start, yet I have never forgotten your kindness. Yes, you can be difficult, but I soon realised that under your harsh exterior you're an old softie really. Perhaps you should show that side of yourself to your next secretary.'

'What, and have her taking advantage of me! You must be joking – and if I give the men an inch they take a yard.'

'Did I take advantage of you?'

'Well, no, I suppose not.'

'We're not talking about the men, Jack, we're talking about a secretary, and you can't treat a young woman in the same way you treat the coalmen.'

'Humph, maybe you're right, but listening to you I can't believe it's the same Millie Pratchett I'm talking to. You seem so mature now, and not at all like the frightened little girl who applied for the job in my office.'

'I'm still the same girl, but I've had some hard knocks and I guess I had to grow up pretty quickly. But to get back to your next secretary, why don't you give a school-leaver a chance? I know you won't be able to moderate your language, and as the old saying goes, a leopard can't change his spots, but you can at least stop treating her like one of the men. Go on, give it a try. After all, what have you got to lose?'

'I suppose I'll have to, but when you rang me I was hoping you wanted your job back.'

'I phoned to apologise for the way I left and for my awful behaviour. My goodness, I still can't believe that I attacked you.'

'Yes,' he said with a grin, 'you were rather like a little she-cat, but forget it, Millie. You were upset about Samson and it's understandable. Now tell me, how is your father?'

She paled, but managed to stammer, 'He . . . he's dead.'

Jack's face stretched with shock. 'I had no idea! I'm so sorry, Millie. Your brother came to see me some time ago. He was looking for you both, but I couldn't help him.'

'Yes, John told me, but at the time he didn't know about our father's death.' Millie frowned, still finding that she hated putting the word *Father* to the man. Would she ever come to forgive him? No, she doubted it.

'So, you've seen your brother?'

'Yes, he's living on the Isle of Wight with a wife, a lovely son, and a thriving business.'

'I'm glad. I liked that young man and was sorry to lose him. Now come on, perhaps if I ply you with drink you'll change your mind about coming back. I'll take you over the road to the local pub. Mind, with you looking like that, we'd better go in the saloon bar.'

Millie smiled as they walked across the road, finding it incongruous that she was actually going to a pub with her old boss. They sat in the bar, chatting for over an hour, and she found she was getting tipsy as Jack ordered her yet another sherry. He kept pressing her to work for him again, but she was finally able to persuade him that she didn't want her old job back. Then, when they parted, it was with the promise to stay in touch, and giving the bear of a man a quick hug, Millie left the pub, hoping against hope that Mark would still be at Vanessa's when she arrived home.

'Who's this Jack that Millie has a date with?' Mark asked Vanessa, his face still dark with annoyance.

'I'm not exactly sure, but I think it's someone she knew some time ago.' It was naughty to lie, but Vanessa didn't care. Mark was jealous and she played on that, deciding that this might be just what he needed to bring him to his senses.

He glanced yet again at his watch, his foot swinging with impatience. 'It's getting late and she isn't home yet. I hope she's all right.'

'Oh, for goodness sake! Millie is a grown woman and perfectly capable of taking care of herself.'

Both looked up then as they heard the sound of a key in the door, and pink-faced but smiling happily, Millie lurched into the room. 'Hello, Mark, you're still here then?' she said, before flopping onto a chair.

'Have you been drinking?' he demanded, his expression tense.

'Yes, Jack took me to a pub and I had a few glasses of sherry. Oh, he's wonderful and it was so lovely to see him again. I treated him badly but he still wants me back . . .' Her face suddenly paled, and rising quickly she rushed from the room, her hand over her mouth as she gasped, 'Sorry, I feel sick.'

Mark made to follow her, but Vanessa put a detaining hand on his arm. 'Leave her to me and I'll get her to bed. Silly girl, she obviously isn't used to booze.'

'What does she mean – he wants her back?'

'I should have thought that was obvious,' Vanessa said, secretly enjoying herself. Mark actually looked stricken at the thought of Millie having a boyfriend, but now it might be better if she got him out of the flat. Millie might come back and give the game away, and she didn't want that. 'Look, I really must get Millie to bed or she'll be fit for nothing in the morning. Be a good chap and go home.'

With a face like thunder Mark stormed from the room, the front door slamming behind him, and with a smile of amusement Vanessa made her way to the bathroom.

She tapped gently on the door, and went in to find Millie sitting on the closed lavatory seat, looking decidedly green.

'I take it you had a nice time,' she said.

'Yes, and did I tell you that Jack offered me my old job back?'

'Yes, you did, and what did you tell him?'

'No, of course. I could never go back to the depot, Vanessa. Other than Jack, there are too many bad memories associated with the place – things I would rather forget.' Millie went to the sink, slashed cold water on her face and patted it dry.

'Well, as I would hate to lose you, I can't say I'm sorry. Now come on, my dear, I think you should go to bed or you'll feel terrible in the morning.'

'But I wanted to see Mark.'

'Didn't you hear the front door slam? Mark's gone.'

'No, I'm afraid I was being very sick. Remind me never to drink sherry again.'

'Don't worry, I will,' and as she watched Millie dragging herself to bed, Vanessa wondered how long it would take Mark to find out that this so-called boyfriend of Millie's was fictitious. And what would be his reaction when he realised she had lied to him?

Chapter Forty-Four

A week passed with no sign of Mark, and now Vanessa fretted in case she had over-played her hand. Instead of bringing Mark and Millie together, had she dragged them further apart? The door to the shop opened, and as often happened when Vanessa was thinking about someone, Mark walked in.

His eyes flicked around the shop, his expression grim when he saw Millie, and as though wanting to inflict hurt he said loudly, 'Hello, Ness, I've come to tell you about this wonderful girl I've just met.'

'Really! And what happened to the last one?'

'Oh, you know me. Anyway, if you've got nothing planned I thought I'd bring Sylvia to meet you this evening.'

Vanessa bristled, unable to resist saying, 'Yes, do that. I'm afraid Millie won't be in though, as she's going out with Jack.'

Her brother's lips tightened, and moving across to Millie he said, 'I hear you're seeing Jack this evening. Well, I don't think much of a man who takes a young girl to a pub and plies her with drink. You should have more sense, Millicent, and now if you'll excuse me, I have things to do. What a shame you won't be in to meet my latest girlfriend. She's quite a dish.'

Before Millie could respond, he turned abruptly, leaving the shop with a curt goodbye.

Vanessa saw that Millie's eyes were stricken, and cursed herself. Instead of helping, she had caused the girl more hurt. Yet for Mark to behave like that, he really must care for Millie and perhaps it was time for her to tell him the truth.

Millie, meanwhile, had fled to the stock room, dashing tears from her eyes. Why had Mark spoken to her like that? Yes, she shouldn't have drunk so much sherry, and was determined not to do it again, but there had been such cruelty in his eyes. He had also thrown his latest girlfriend in her face almost as if he wanted to hurt her, but why? To distract her mind she slipped the cover off Lucinda's latest creation. It really was a fabulous gown, and any girl wearing it would look like a fairy princess.

Vanessa came into the room, helping Millie to put Mark out of her mind as she said, 'I wonder if Priscilla Windlesham will end up wearing that dress? I'd love to do a tarot reading for her. The poor girl has never had a say in anything and I'd like to see what her future holds. She's been so sheltered, taught by a private tutor, and has hardly mixed with anyone of her own age. The household is like a relic to Victorian times, with Mrs Windlesham the ruling dowager. Maybe Priscilla's astrological chart is all water signs and she needs a bit of fire to fight her mother's dominance.'

'To be honest, Vanessa, I don't think I'd be able to go up against Mrs Windlesham either. She frightens the life out of me too, and thank goodness I don't have to live with her. But how is she going to afford a dress like this for her daughter? We have a few secondhand gowns next door and I'd have thought she'd be better off looking in there.'

'Not this time. Apparently the groom has decided to buy the gown and money is no object.'

'Lucky Priscilla Windlesham.'

'You wouldn't think that if you saw her fiancé. He's old enough to be her father. Honestly, Millie, it's as if the girl has been sold, and all to swell the family coffers again.'

'Oh, how awful.'

'These things happen, my dear. It's the way of the world, and who knows, maybe Priscilla is using this marriage as a means of escape.'

'Huh, some escape!'

As Millie re-covered the beautiful dress, she pictured Priscilla Windlesham in her mind's eye and knew that the gown would be perfect for her shape, despite the young woman having no say in the matter. She also prayed that her groom would be kind and loving. There might be a huge age difference, but if he was a good husband the poor girl might find some happiness in life – once she had escaped from her ghastly mother.

Millie loved working in the bridal shop and looked forward to the expansion. It was such a pleasure to handle all the wonderful materials, and there was nothing like seeing the happiness on a young woman's face when she found the perfect wedding dress. Millie had yet to see a bride-to-be who didn't look beautiful when she wore the whole outfit – dress, veil and tiara – finding that when they saw themselves in the mirror it brought a special kind of glow to their faces.

Though eternally grateful to Vanessa for giving her the job, Millie hadn't enjoyed working in *Finesse* half as much. Most customers were easy to deal with, but there were others, like Mrs Windlesham, whom she dreaded serving. It was different in *Brides* and not once had she had a difficult customer.

Just then, the shop door opened, and as a young woman came in, Millie hastily hung up the dress. Then fixing a professional smile on her face, she stepped forward. 'Can I help you?'

Many selections later, Millie still hadn't found the perfect bridal gown for this client. The young lady had bright red hair, and her face, arms and chest, were sprinkled with freckles. Every gown she had tried on so far had emphasised her pale colouring, making the freckles stand out vividly.

Millie studied the girl again and then her eyes lit up. 'I think I have it,' she cried, and searching the racks, found just she was looking for. This dress was one that had been among the first range they'd stocked. The gown hadn't sold well because it wasn't a popular shade, most brides preferring white, but Millie felt it would be just right for this young woman's colouring.

She now unzipped the cover to reveal a satin dress in a very pale shade of biscuit. It was overlaid with lace in a slightly darker tone which allowed the gleam of the paler satin to shine through. The top was boned and strapless, but with the overlay of lace Lucinda had cleverly fashioned a high neckline and narrow fitted sleeves. 'What about this one?' she asked, laying it across her arm.

'Oh, I don't know. I wanted to wear white . . . but the dress is lovely, isn't it?'

'Why don't you try it on?'

'All right. I suppose it won't hurt to see what it looks like.'

When the customer emerged from the changing-room, both she and Millie knew the dress was perfect. The colour added tone to her skin, and with the lace overlay and sleeves, few freckles could be seen.

'It's wonderful,' the girl gasped as she gazed at herself in a full-length mirror.

'Yes, it's definitely the dress for you. Now – what about accessories?' Millie asked, ever the perfect saleswoman. She found a veil, the only one in stock that toned with the dress, and after several attempts, a lovely tiara, set with cream pearls.

Millie was now on her knees, pinning the hem ready for alterations, pleased that she had finally found the perfect ensemble for this lovely young lady's big day.

The alteration finished, Millie rose to her feet, unable to help wondering if she herself would ever wear a bridal gown. *Stop it, stop being stupid*, she told herself. It was hopeless and somehow she had to put Mark out of her mind. She still didn't understand why he had spoken to her so harshly, nor why he had felt the need to brag about his latest beautiful girlfriend.

Millie tried to accept that Mark would never want her, and that it was an impossible dream, but even now, as she held the gown against her and imagined walking down the aisle, Mark was the groom.

Chapter Forty-Five

Business was brisk during the following week. There was a whole series of minor fittings to be carried out, along with evening appointments for Mrs Salter to handle the more difficult measurements. Veils were flung across mirrors, tiaras needed replacing in display cabinets, and satin shoes littered the floor when the women were finally able to close the shop.

Both Millie and Vanessa were exhausted, but couldn't go home yet as Mrs Windlesham had at last been in touch about Lucinda's latest design. She insisted on a private viewing, saying that she didn't want anyone else to see it, and her appointment was booked for five-thirty.

The woman arrived an hour late and by this time Millie could see that Vanessa was seething. Mrs Windlesham thumped impatiently on the door, and when Millie unlocked it, she swept imperiously into the shop without so much as an apology.

Vanessa, obviously struggling to contain her temper, hissed, 'Blast the woman. Mark rang to say that he's footloose and fancy free again and is coming for dinner tonight. Now it looks as if we'll be late home.'

Mrs Windlesham sat on one of the gilt chairs provided for customers, her neck stiff and a disdainful expression on her face as she flicked open her old, fox fur stole.

Both Vanessa and Millie stared at the woman, unable to believe her attitude; however, she herself seemed unaware of the charged atmosphere as she said, 'Well, come on then, I haven't got all day. Let me see this dress.'

Millie heard Vanessa's sigh, but she managed to contain her

impatience, removing the cover and placing the gown expertly over her arm.

'Humph, not bad. Bring it closer, woman.'

With tight lips Vanessa did as she was asked, and stood holding the gown patiently while it was inspected.

'It's difficult to know if it would suit my daughter without seeing it on.'

'Why don't you bring her in for a fitting? She could look at some of our other gowns too,' Vanessa suggested.

'Until I've made up my mind which gown she will wear, that won't be necessary. My daughter has absolutely no taste, and as I told her, the wedding dress will be one of my choice.' She paused for a moment, fingering the material, and then looked at Millie appraisingly. 'You, girl. You're about the same size as my daughter. Model it for me.'

'M . . . me?'

'Yes. Who else do you think I mean? What on earth's the matter with you? Come on, girl, get a move on!'

'Please, model it, Millie,' Vanessa appealed.

As Millie took the gown and went into the changing-room, Vanessa said, 'Excuse me, madam, but she may need assistance. I'll be back shortly,' and as soon as the curtains were drawn, she whispered, 'Sorry, Millie, but if she doesn't make her mind up soon we'll never get away.'

'B . . . but I've never modelled before. What do I do?'

'Just hold your head up high when you come out, and walk slowly across the room. Now hang on while I go and get a veil.'

When Millie was dressed, she stared at herself in amazement. Oh, the dress looked wonderful, billowing out around her in a cloud of chiffon.

Vanessa returned to hurriedly pin a veil to her head, adding a high jewel-encrusted tiara for the finishing touch. 'My dear, you look absolutely stunning!'

'Me? I'm not stunning.'

'Yes, you are, and in that dress even more so. Look in the mirror again, and see for yourself. I'll go out now, and then in a second or two I'll sweep back the curtain. Now don't forget, walk tall.'

After one final look in the mirror, Millie turned, her eyes on the curtain, and waiting for Vanessa to fling it back. Suddenly, she heard the shop door open, her heart thumping when she heard Mark's voice. 'Hello, Ness. I've been to the flat but you weren't in.'

Vanessa's voice sounded excited as she answered, 'Oh Mark, just wait until you see Millie.'

The curtain then opened with a theatrical flourish, and as Millie emerged she found her eyes going straight to Mark. He stared, whilst she stood frozen to the spot, but then his feet seemed to move him unconsciously forward. 'Millicent, tell me you're not getting married!'

Married! What on earth did he mean? The look on his face made her stomach flutter, but the moment passed as Mrs Windlesham called, 'Turn around, girl! Let me see the back.'

Mark stepped away, and nervously Millie spun around in two full circles, yards of silk chiffon billowing like a cloud around her. The effect was mesmerising, but obviously lost on Mrs Windlesham.

'Slowly, you silly girl! Turn slowly!'

Mark made to step forward again, but Vanessa hissed, 'Stay back. Millie is modelling the gown and I don't want to lose the sale. That dress costs a king's ransom.'

'Modelling it! Oh, thank God. For one dreadful moment I thought . . .'

'Don't just stand there, girl. Come closer and show me the back,' Mrs Windlesham demanded.

Millie saw the dark look that Mark cast the woman, and then he was moving towards her again. She waited, her breasts heaving with emotion as his arms came out, and then she found herself enfolded, his lips to her ear as he murmured, 'God, I thought I'd lost you. I must have been mad to deny my feelings for so long.'

'Will you get out of the way, young man! I can't see a thing,' Mrs Windlesham cried, her voice imperious with indignation.

Ignoring her, Mark whispered, 'Millicent, I know you've been seeing Jack, but you can't love him, you just can't. Tell me that I'm not too late. I love you, Millie, and please say you'll marry me.'

Puzzled, Millie said, 'Jack! But he's just my old boss.'

'Your boss!' Mark cried, for a moment looking nonplussed, but then he laughed with delight. 'Oh, I see, another of Vanessa's games, but one I'm glad she played because it brought me to my senses.'

'You . . . you really love me?'

'I most certainly do,' he said softly, 'but you haven't answered my question yet. Will you marry me?'

'Yes please,' Millie choked, feeling as though she would burst with happiness. Was she dreaming? This couldn't be real – could it?

'Young man, I said would you please move out of the way!'

As though he hadn't heard the woman, Mark dipped his head to kiss her, and feeling the warmth of his lips, Millie knew without a doubt that this *was* real. He drew back, smiling gently, and then with her hand in his, they both turned to look at Vanessa, the delight on her face plain to see.

Mrs Windlesham's voice boomed again. 'What is the meaning of this? I want that dress for my daughter!'

Mark drew himself up, and turning to face the irate woman, he said firmly, 'I'm sorry, madam, this dress is sold.'